THE BUILDING

THE BVILDING

A NOVEL BY

THOMAS GLYNN

ALFRED A. KNOPF

NEW YORK

1 9 8 6

THIS IS A BORZOI BOOK
PUBLISHED BY ALFRED A. KNOPF, INC.

Copyright © 1985 by Thomas Glynn

Library of Congress Cataloging-in-Publication Data

Glynn, Thomas, [date]
The building.

I. Title.
PS3557.L93B84   1986   813'.54   85-40226
ISBN 0-394-54582-6

Manufactured in the United States of America

FIRST EDITION

May it be delightful my house,
From my head may it be delightful,
To my feet may it be delightful,
Where I lie may it be delightful,
All above me may it be delightful,
All around me may it be delightful.

NAVAJO HOUSE BLESSING

DIRECTORY

THE BUILDING

1

THE Building is huge, a grotesque magnificence. At times large holes appear in walls, which are quickly boarded up, covered over with tin, or stuffed with cinder blocks and cemented. The apartments are vast, with parqueted floors and oak doors. There is a gargantuan lobby with a marble floor, a gold-leaf ceiling, and vacant urns. In the courtyard, filled to the height of the first floor with garbage, is a marble fountain with the statue of a child, his head and finger upraised, and over him is an upturned grocery cart.

In the lobby, dank, where water drips and the only light is what has been hot-wired from a street lamp, where the marble has been broken with a sledgehammer, where the blood from muggings is brown, where torn and shredded parts of wallets and pocketbooks lie, where broken glass is etched into the cement, there are two elevators. Neither of them works. When one did, it flew to the top, six floors, and fell down. Still, they have been inspected year after year.

On the walls, on the doors that are not battered down, on the windows, and on the frames that are still intact are the scrawls of the city's refugees. The doors that still stand bear the rivets of dozens of Fox police locks that barricade the inhabitants in at night. Rivers run through the apartments, following the course of pipes, veering off to follow the plaster lathing and rush with a suddenness that quickens the heart along the riverbed of parqueted floors, pumping torrents of upstate water that falls through apartment after apartment until it sinks to the basement. Electrical storms, violent in intensity, arc quickly across the waterlogged wires, sometimes pausing briefly at a wall outlet to discharge excess power when a lamp is plugged in or a TV turned on. These surges of power, generated miles away, flash through the

Building like unrepentant sins, causing instant fires, screaming mothers, children dropped from windows, smoke billowing through apartments, and old gas pipes buried in plaster and long forgotten, to explode.

On the roof, where the pregnant Scandinavian whore flew to her death like a crippled bird, are many fireman-chopped holes where the rain comes in and sneakered armies of sodomizers lower themselves to the apartments below. On the roof, where the crumbling chimney bricks lie, where jagged kitchen knives are left, where the handguns with exploded barrels are tossed, where screaming children are dragged, the tar, cold from the evening, waits for the sun.

In the morning the Building is frozen, even when it is hot, and the stillness that creeps up to hold the bricks in its dry grasp, the prevalence of sleep, the quiet embers of burned-out apartments (with their charred ashes that lie Egyptian-like in their beatitude), the sudden silence of testy babies, the doors that are not knocked off hinges, the sweet green of the walls still wet with morning soot, the holes in pencil-gouged-out plaster, the caterpillars of tied-together Keds thrown over street lamps, the rubber tires stacked against apartment doors still smoldering from fires set the night before, all these manifestations seem to freeze, while the lights that still work flicker, momentarily, as Steckler, having hot-wired his electric arc welding apparatus to the box in the basement (putting on rubber boots to walk through the underwater stream in the basement, the same fishing boots that used to belong to Grandmaster Eschopf who fished these very waters back in the twenties before the chemicals hit the aquifers and would pull seal-sized sturgeon which swam underneath the city and haul them up to the drier zones of the basement), begins his transformation of the Chevy Nova he is supercharging in his apartment (whose other refinements include five-foot tires and railroad springs so that the car can survive the fall from its launching), and the purple lady, name unknown though variously called Matilda, Matty, Sausage, Violet, or Runny, lays out her clothes for the morning, which include white shoes, white socks, white undergarments (yellowing), and a dress of the same shade, and sets alongside these the cream, a rich white cosmetic cream which she slathers over her black face in layer after layer until her face is purple, coating then her hands and finally her hair, the entire ritual taking the better part of two hours (panties, blouse, bra, worn for a week and then washed, dress washed every two weeks, shoes whitened each weekend, and stockings washed every night and hung up to dry over the sink on twine). In the morning, the sudden stillness of the Building comes as a shock, even to the owner, strolling the streets, wondering if the liens against his Building (Better Burner Service, $4,897; Top Flight Plumbing, $3,987; Northwind Fuel Oil Company, $5,896) will fall due before the foreclosure of the first mortgage (Queens County Savings Bank, $123,498) or the disclosure of the second mortgage (Imperial Investment, $43,945), or if the purchase-money mortgage he made to Golden Realty ($66,744) will come due at the same time as the deed he signed over to Farnsworth Realty ($22,335), or if any of them will sue before the city takes over for back taxes ($54,887), which he hopes he can forestall long enough to continue collecting his Section 8 rents (totaling $4,780 per month) and the welfare payments from the city for rents he just raised (totaling $3,778 per month).

In the evening, the music of the night begins to play. Cuzz (part-time mugger, Puma devotee, dropout from a government public-works program to train security forces) rolls over in bed and switches on some rap music from one of the blood stations and finesses the dregs of an exquisite powder sequestered in a bullet hole in the wall, one of many, and placing it in an opening in his body, reminisces over the shrubs that used to grow in front of the Building and which, one night, were secretly dug up for the owner by a raving lunatic who had just been freed from a large state mental institution, and transported in seven large bundles by subway from three A.M. to seven A.M. by the lunatic and planted for the owner around his house in Brooklyn (the lunatic carefully prepared the ground, using perlite for proper drainage, manure from the elephants in Prospect Park, peat moss from Canada, and leaf-composted soil, planting all thirty-seven shrubs so that from the time they had been taken out of the ground until the time they had been put back in no more than four hours elapsed, and after finishing the job went into the owner's garage and shot himself several times with a pearl-handled twenty-two, finally dropping the pistol after the fourth shot, none of which killed him). In the early evening the roof-sequestered walls begin to vibrate to music, to chatter, to the hum of voices, groans, extended vowels, splattered bits of sentences, shouts, moans, snatches of syllables, hints, sputters, and the smells, soft as silt, holier than water, produce a diaphanous cooking haze that settles over the entire borough, a fine layer of grease, pink at the edges, rancid in smell.

It was a strange odor to the Mormon missionary from Utah, who was used to smelling white bread and mayonnaise. He wore long underwear, even in summer, and tried to convert everyone in the Building, getting into a fistfight with a Sikh who left the Building and his apartment to a woman on a bad LSD trip who spent her days tearing her clothing into shreds while her son ate Wing Dings and drank Yoohoo and they lived over the apartment that was used by the muggers who rode up and down on the top of the elevator when it worked and peed on the rabbi and his wife through a trapdoor and the urine-soaked rabbi refused to ride all the way up to the sixth floor to visit the last Jew in the Building, the last Orthodox Jew, who was bedridden and couldn't go to temple (so the rabbi was bringing temple to him) and while he lay in bed the Mormon missionary barged in and started to harangue him about Joseph Smith and the Prophets and would probably be doing it now if the rabbi, still urine-soaked, hadn't changed his mind when he heard about the Mormon's attack on the bedridden Orthodox Jew, charged up the stairs, no more elevator for him, and threw the offending Mormon out on his ear, took off his coat, and sat with the old man for several hours, and then leaving the Building, holding his coat at arm's length because of the smell, was mugged by those who before had peed on him and left him his coat but little else while he cursed them in several exquisite languages. As he lay on the sidewalk in front of the Building the Mormon missionary shouted his vision of prophecy at him, arousing the muggers who came back and stripped the offending missionary of everything but his long underwear, and the Mormon, upended on the sidewalk near the rabbi, shouted the worst curse he knew at the fleeing muggers, "Seventh-Day Adventists!" It was a phrase pregnant with meaning whose fullness only the Mormon could comprehend, certainly not Mother Ozmoz, whose doubledigit pregnancies extended to every color of the rainbow and who, some claimed, was living proof of parthenogenesis. Even the Mormon, a stout believer in the multiplicity of souls, indeed a promoter of same, was shocked at the hue and variety that gushed forth from Mother Ozmoz; hers was a fecundity that rivaled hothouse tomatoes. Her gestation period was eight months, back to back, with no pause, so that every two years she had three children, six children in four years, twelve in eight, twenty-four in sixteen. Biologists were excited by her periodicity. She popped her gestations out with little effort, on staircases, in hallways, wherever she happened to be, and their entrance into the world was eased by the fact that Mother Ozmoz had a vagina whose opening was hand long and hand wide; she was in a permanent state of dilation. She was on welfare, though welfare had strict guidelines that allowed her children only three pairs of shoes, so the shoes—small, medium, and large—served all twenty-four children, which meant that on any given day only three out of the twenty-four were in school; each child was in school one out of eight days. Twenty-four kids in four rooms, one of the rooms a kitchen, the other three nominally living room, dining room, and bedroom, but all three, no all four, were bedrooms, the younger ones sleeping in the kitchen cabinets under the sink, awakened in the night by the perpetual drip, a leak, that came with every kitchen in the Building. But parthenogenesis was not a stranger to the African Dictator who lived in the Building with his wives, cows, his most exalted pillow bearer, and a small ferret-faced man who crowed the hour every hour. He had temporarily vacated his throne ("Oh you should have seen it," he said, "such a splendid thing, leopard skin and rhinoceros horn, ebony and silver, gold and diamonds, the private parts of large animals . . .") after a power struggle in which he lost rule of his landlocked country to a group of junior officers, former Eagle Scouts and certified Methodists turned Marxists, the only people in the country who could fly the nation's single aircraft, a C–47 that had been previously owned by Howard Hughes and Arthur Godfrey, and then was converted to crop dusting. The pilots pried open the rigid windows, using spears and a machine gun, and flew around the capital dropping explosives. The king, his most exalted pillow bearer, the cockcrower, four of his ten sow-shaped wives, and the king's food taster escaped in a 1947 Chrysler Town & Country convertible whose trunk was filled with chickens. Unfortunately, the huge car overturned on the banks of the Zambesi River, drowning the chickens, the food taster, two of his four elephantine wives, and causing the king to vow that he would bar scouting forever from his country and eat the remaining Methodists. As a political dissenter he was welcomed by the United States, where he was treated no longer as a king but merely as a dictator. He sold wood-frame bungalows in Jamaica, Queens, to Vietnamese boat people and Pakistani newsdealers. "In my country we had miles and miles of everything," he said, "and what we didn't have you could always order out . . . Coca-Cola, pizza, we even had the Burger King and the Wendy's. And they would always deliver, I made sure of that. If they didn't, I would eat the owners. Ha-ha (smile). But here, they won't even deliver. It is abominable, this not delivering." He said that he was collecting his forces for a final assault on those "small-penis pig scouts." It would, he promised, be a glorious invasion. The United States government, the world's wealthiest, was giving him guns, parachutes, planes, and tanks, even an atomic bomb, a small one, about the size of one of the attaché cases he carried money to Switzerland in. The invasion, he said, would be a grand spectacle. Hundreds of brightly colored parachutes opening in the sky, soldiers dropping from planes in their new military boots with the high laces. "We will cut off their small penises and do their women in," he promised. "After, we will celebrate. It will be a big affair. I want the whole world, and especially the McDonald's and the Wendy's, to come. We will drink banana wine and eat crocodile eggs." There are other celebrants in the Building. The professor returns from the University and is let in through the five-locked door by his companion, the African dwarf, who, unable to speak any recognizable human language, has spent the day in the apartment cleaning the sheets and brushing the dirt from his bed into one corner for the gecko lizard, and looking up at the professor, speaking the sounds that only the professor can understand, reminds him of their weekly Sunday perambulation, when the dwarf, dressed in the clothes of a child from the Ming Dynasty and placed in a baby carriage, will be wheeled to the Brooklyn Botanic Garden where he can swing from the limbs of the Chinese pines and swim, oblivious, with a straw in his mouth to breathe, underwater, in the pond of the Japanese Garden. During the evening, when the Building settles on its foundations because of the eternally flooded cellar (which waters a dandelion that pushes its way through a crack in the cement courtyard, uncrushed in the garbage because it is cuddled in the urine-soaked arms of a charred and blackened panda from the Key Supermarket), when plumbers come from New Jersey in the spring to finish stripping the copper risers from the Building's heating system so the loss will only be discovered in the fall, assuming there is heat then, which may depend upon how high the water rises in the cellar and whether the pilot light from the furnace can stay lit, when the warmth or chill of the day has so gripped the Building that once again the sign that says "This building adequately wired by Sal Hepatica Electrical Contracting Corporation" begins to loosen, threatening to fall, Stern pulls the fading light onto his canvas and quickly scrapes up the spaghetti-squished tubes of oil on the floor with a spoon, the rounded edge of which he uses to spread the paint on the canvas, and only briefly sympathizes with the naked girl in his room (sagging, numbed by the cold, even in spring and by the inadequate amount of money Stern is paying her, when he pays her) and then asks her to assume some new pose, one in which the arms and legs, splayed out at awkward angles, can only be held for a few minutes but which Stern insists she hold for hours, and while painting Stern begins to speculate on the fact of his being the last Jew in the Building which was once filled with many Jews, most of them Orthodox, and thinking about this Stern shouts to the woman to stop complaining about the absurd pose he has asked her to assume, asks her to hold it longer, tells her that he must now turn on the light, they will work through the night, locks the door so she can't get out, barks at her, and paints with the light coming in through the hole in the ceiling and the light from his own bank of floods, shorted intermittently by Steckler's arc welder, and by the Doberman pinscher upstairs who once again was not let out by its owner and so is forced to relieve itself next to a wall outlet, the acidic urine finding its way behind the outlet plate and shorting the wires, blowing a fuse that puts out all the outlets along a common wall, and Stern, tapping on the ceiling with a canvas frame, hopes to frighten the dog and stop it from peeing, or at least get it to hold its pee until its owner, who works two shifts for a meat wholesaler on Atlantic Avenue, can come home and let the meat-starved creature out.

The Building sits solidly in the middle of the evening now, and the deaf-mute's wife has put him out in the hallway because their daughter has come home and he has yet to overcome a fondness for stroking her. He roams the halls near his apartment, his hand soiled from rubbing the walls and the shaky wood and iron banister, while the paraplegic in the apartment next to his, with three door locks, a double set of braces (one for each leg and a single one for a shortened arm), boarded there by parents who also maintain a house in Bensonhurst for themselves and their walking children and come in three times a week to bring groceries and replace the light bulbs, listens to the all-news station, hoping she can tune in on the disaster of the day, a burning of tenements, a plane dropping out of the sky, a mass epidemic in some faraway city, a hurricane in a crowded Asian ghetto, and clicks her braces with glee when she spots a disaster, bending the apparatus (risking the wrath of her parents who resent its high cost and believe that those responsible are the international metal cartels in Switzerland), and above her sits a man in his rocking chair who is thoroughly undistinguished except for the desire to place a large-caliber bullet in the head of whoever happens to be the president of the country and who has been labeled "psychotic and dangerous" but certainly not by the Vietnam veteran who lives above him who learned the skill of strangling dogs in Asia from a Muslim, nor by the original super, a man of immense talents whom no one has ever seen, including his wife, who left him three years after they were married and lives in another wing of the Building with a T'ai Chi master who paints floral designs for a living and is able to press himself off the floor with one hand. In the night, the Building sighs, the great hum of evening settles in, a shrill cicada of music, rifle fire, car door locks sprung, children's shouts, and the snarls of wild dogs. The energies of the night expand, to laughter and broken glass, and the Building celebrates the memory of Tubbo Rivera, Harvard M.B.A., Bach devotee, who had his own Lear jet, which he flew down to Colombia to buy the dope he meticulously weighed in glassine envelopes with a jeweler's scale and kept in a safe placed near an exterior wall so it wouldn't fall through the floor, and who, one night in the dead of winter when the owner hadn't paid the fuel oil company and there was no heat for a week, was broken into by dope thieves who bypassed the Fox police lock on his iron door and flew in through the window on clotheslines and before the glass had finished shattering and before they untangled themselves from the ropes began firing at Tubbo who jumped behind a sofa where he kept an M–16, which jammed immediately, while the soft sound of twenty-two-caliber bullets kept plopping through the sofa and Tubbo, rising, bleeding in a fit of entrepreneurial anger, began to fling five-pointed Ninja daggers at the intruders, one of whom was stabbed in the neck, falling out the same window he had entered moments before, while the others, having exhausted their ammunition, began to slash at Tubbo, who was now swinging a broken bottle of Jack Daniel's but was finally subdued, carted to the basement where he was tied, still alive, to a kitchen chair, half submerged in fast freezing water (this time they had no trouble getting the rope around his waist which they couldn't do before when he weighed four hundred pounds, but he was now down to a svelte two-ninety thanks to a $40,000 city-paid-for operation that stapled part of his small intestine to reduce his weight); they left him there, after failing to saw off his leg, their efforts bloodying the water, and Tubbo was found during the next thaw, below the navel encased in a massive block of ice and above that a foot of water, while in his apartment the dope was gone but his Luxman hi-fi still played Bach's Toccata and Fugue in D Minor, even though his serigraph collection was shredded by a starved and maddened cat. To the memory of Truth, whose skin was so black it was almost purple and who used to spend evenings studying the Koran and lived on sardines and saltines for three months while he wrestled with certain tenets of Islam, bending his North Carolina Baptist faith to incorporate the wisdom of the Koran until he burst like an overly stoked steam boiler and spread himself about the apartment, projecting parts of his body on the ceiling, walls, and floor and so lived in that dismembered state for a month until he collapsed and was shocked back into one body by a telephone caller selling subscriptions to *Turkey World* and went back to North Carolina where he enlisted in the marines. To the memory of the time when the owner hired a new German doorman who stood six and a half feet tall and dressed in a blue-and-gold replica of a Balaban and Katz usher, solemnly opening and closing the lobby door for the new tenants who had just arrived from the Lower East Side and who always kept a fresh carnation in his buttonhole and shaved his head so that his cap and visor left a ring of red around his head, a groove in his pink skin that children loved to run their fingers along and who was inexplicably called back to Germany before the Second World War. Honor the Shabbis Goy, Mr. Tontine, from Norway, who replaced Mr. Gustafsen who replaced someone else, and kept in his apartment a piece of ancient Norwegian wood which he and his wife and children worship (*"Erdmutter,* Thou Blessed Sapling!"*) and who fully understands the mysteries of electricity and can follow any line that holds current, whether buried in plaster, wood, or concrete, and can tell what state it is in and where it is leaking. Pay homage to soft walls and the Wilson Sisters, acrobatic dancers of the thirties and forties who, scantily dressed in thinly knotted scarves, turned their bodies into sailor's knots for the edification of multicolored audiences, and who, now, in their apartment, boarded cats and plants, using the waste from one to fertilize the soil of the other, and who, while picking up champagne glasses in creases in their stomachs and other parts of their body on the eighty-sixth floor of the Empire State Building on December 31, 1936, both came to the conclusion that in a matter of years there would be a craze for hula hoops. And Abdul Karim, who, while misinterpreting the directions on "Sunrise Semester," managed to push two Eberhard Faber Mongol 482 #2 lead pencils up his nostrils and, held thusly, wrote the first two chapters of Aristotle's *Poetics* on a Pathmark shopping bag which the day before he used to carry twelve cans of tahini, which he smeared over the walls of his bedroom to seal out the evil waves coming from the paraplegic who, he was convinced, had the power to cross men's eyes and shrivel their penises if she so desired, and that was precisely her intention ever since he had met her in the hallway and accidentally bumped her braces, soiling his clothes with the essence of paraplegism; and Tonton Tute, Haitian computer designer, who floated candles in water at precise times of the month using Tupperware bowls that the Wilson Sisters sold to supplement their acrobatic pension and who disemboweled live chickens on the Formica table in his kitchen with an army-surplus machete using the intestines to make a chicken hot dog spiced with Haitian herbs which he bought on the street corner from a man who trucked up watermelons from South Carolina; and Cool Cal and the gang who one summer occupied an apartment where they slept in between gold-chain snatchings in the subway, all of whom were tossed out of their homes by parents who no longer would or could care for them and who were finally tossed out of their apartment by a family who lived downstairs and got tired of the whooping noise they made when they came in from their subway excursions; and Heavy Hannah, who lived not so much on welfare as in it, and managed to blossom up to a weight that defied the sanctity of scales, who looked like a collection of feed sacks tied together, wore bed sheets dyed blue and orange, could not get out the door of her apartment and had to be removed by crane through the window, which curtailed her trips to the point that she soon became immobile, her legs unable to support the bulk wrapped in layers around her body and developed bedsores sitting on the sofa and had to be treated in her apartment by a young doctor who gagged on her smell and threw up in the bathroom right into the specially braced toilet each time he came to tend the purple mushrooms that exploded over her body, some of which he could only reach by standing on a chair while she lay down, placing an elbow in the sponge-rubber mountain of her buttocks so he could slice open the festering sores and let out the pus; and Puff the Magic Dragon, a large unapproachable German shepherd who requisitioned the electrical supply room in the Building for himself and lived off the contents of garbage cans and small homeless dogs, cats, rats, and other creatures not adept at defending themselves against the predations of a one-hundred-fifty-pound dog. Pray for Glasho, a Japanese mystic, who believed the secret of the universe was to be found in fecal matter, and collected it whenever he could, mercifully keeping it in airtight mason jars with rubber lids and compressed wire holders, sometimes painted with gold flecks, or soaked in plaster, or sealed in plastic, or when it was a consistency that he deemed proper, would draw and write with it in a book he had specifically prepared for the purpose. Marvel at Hobson, who one day decided to organize the human species into twelve groups and twenty-four subgroupings and taught the entire system to a group of cockroaches that were dining off some rice pudding he had left in his sink, after which he went on cable TV to announce that a tribe of anthropologically superior insects was roaming the city and then rented a tuxedo to crawl up a cable to the top of the Brooklyn Bridge, where he was picked up by a helicopter and arrested for loitering, thus giving him an opportunity to make the evening news and expound briefly on his theory, where it was heard by Cuzz, who went searching his kitchen and bathroom for one of these erudite insects, resolving to learn all he could, but found none of them who could, or would, talk to him and so, exasperated, plunged a pair of kitchen shears into the palm of his hand and made bloody handprints on the wall which later served as the focal point for a documentary film on the decline of housing in the city. Further into the evening, late at night, while the Building settles on its brick and mortar haunches, when rat-gnawed wires sputter and the mysterious rivers that flow through the Building carve canyons into the mortar, tiny spiderweb networks of plaster cracks appear, spawned by the vibrating bodies of the Wilson Sisters, who are convinced that the walls of their apartment are alive and need to be tended to in much the same manner as their plants, and so they have stripped the plaster and exposed the brick and mortar, which they proceed to rub with their naked and wrinkled eighty-year-old breasts, giving a sheen of oil and human dirt to the masonry so that it emits a gray glow, and it is this sound of their work, this soft rustling of sandstone and crumbling cement that arouses the thin ears of Abdul Karim, who, convinced that the paraplegic has unleashed one hundred thousand moths to eat through brick and mortar and attack him, is now opening jars of peanut and other nut butters in a frantic effort to add their greasy coat to his walls, reciting pertinent passages from the Koran, facing east (though in this cursed country, this wretched city, this abominable borough, one can never be sure which way is east or indeed if there is an east), while in the apartment below, the deaf-mute, almost hearing the bare feet of the Wilson Sisters overhead, is reminded of the peninsula near his hometown of Aguadilla and can hear the silent sound of the tiny waves, silvery blue, as they lap against the white sand of the bay, and farther out in the bay, which one can walk in for miles before the water reaches waist level, hears the cries of the sea birds as they wheel and dive for the fat round blue-green iridescent fish that cruise in the waters, and he can hear the slap of the oars as the fishermen set out, their excited shouts as they spot the fish, the splash of the nets and sinkers hitting the water, the popping of the bubbles that rise to the surface, the soft thud of the waves hitting the wooden boats, the slap of the fish against the bottom of the boat, and later, the scraping sound of the wooden boats being dragged up on the beach, followed by shouting and laughter or sometimes by silence, and all this, and more, the deaf-mute can hear by placing his hands on the ceiling and hearing the Wilson Sisters walking can dream sounds that flood back to him before he lost his hearing so that the Wilson Sisters walking becomes a mnemonic device that he uses to force out of his mind the impulses that control his hands, and every morning his wife finds a kitchen chair placed in the middle of their living room and handprints on the ceiling, and she has to drag the chair back to the kitchen, tilting the chair back and dragging it by its rear legs, a sound that convinced Hobson that the cockroaches were returning to his kitchen sink so that he could complete his lecture, or else they had recruited new legions of cockroaches who could hear about his marvelous categories and subcategories, causing him to prepare a cockroach feast for the slippery insects by removing all the food from his refrigerator and leaving it open in the sink, awaiting his guests, preparing his lecture, feeling that the time for opulence, long passed, like some tattered party guest, could now be revived, propped up, dressed in tails and presented, and it is this sense of urgency that causes Hobson to imagine that the walls of his apartment are expanding, that fleurs-de-lis have sprouted on his ceiling, soon to be followed by a condensed version of the Sistine Chapel, that moldings, bows, and the frippery of sculptured plaster, the embossed and flocked wallpaper, the brass gaslights, the oak wainscoting, the velvet rugs and tassels, the ceramic madonnas artfully posed to hold flowers and other accouterments of refinement, the ebony table with its carved Chinese dragon legs, the cherry breakfront with carved crystal trim and marble front, the china crescent bone dishes, sterling flatware, fine Irish linen tablecloth, that all these have flooded into his apartment, magically, by midnight movers whose only intent is grandeur, and that while other apartments must suffer under the indignity of Formica and linoleum, his has need of more spectacular furnishings, all of which causes him to affect a certain dignity in his carriage, stepping gingerly over the broken glass he grinds underfoot in the dank and darkened lobby, ignoring the floor-high pile of garbage in the courtyard and the railings torn off the walls and the gouges in the brick caused when someone drove a Buick Roadmaster through the front doors, removing them neatly at the hinges and taking part of the frame and then proceeding onward tried to ram the statue of the boy nymph in the courtyard, done by a grandson of the Brooklyn Bridge Roebling, failing to do so only because the garbage slowed the car to a halt, where it remained for three months until it was stripped down to its chassis which was then jammed underneath a descending elevator, the one that worked, until it was crushed, jamming the elevator and causing the pissed-on rabbi to shout for help, which came when someone pried open the doors and set up a stepladder so the rabbi and his wife could step out, vowing never to enter the Building again or even to come into the neighborhood, and that was just a week before the sniper appeared on the roof and bathtubs were wrenched from apartments and dragged to the roof to be pushed over the edge onto social workers and housing administrators who began to visit the Building, searching for people to talk to about violations; it is this dignity that Hobson secures in the lenses of his glasses, ignoring the menacing glares of Cuzz, that convinces him that the Building is about to undergo some new metamorphosis, some startling resurrection.

Should the Building shake itself, flicking out occupants like so many stray drops of water, then Hobson will view this as a vindication of his lectures, confirmation of his power of communication, further proof that he is destined to speak for all insects on TV, and the deaf-mute, perhaps dumped into the street by his desperate wife, unable to hear the sounds of the city and unable to keep his wandering hands off the bodies of young girls, will roam the streets, palms up, perhaps joined by Glasho with his suitcases full of balls of waste. In fact, there was a premonition that something was about to happen, and it spread through the Building, gradually choking and infuriating the residents. Various social agencies in the city began receiving calls, setting up tremors in layers of city government, and the word, some vague, ominous word, still unspecified, spread out into the community of social activists and a meeting was held in the apartment of Mary Smith. During this meeting it was suggested to the tenants that they go on rent strike. Tonton Tute thought they were advocating higher rents since the services were so bad, and while he failed to see the logic in that, he was willing to go along. Abdul Karim thought it was a call to begin a Holy War. Stern was unmoved (he with his wood stove, street-lamp-plugged-into wiring, and bottled water) and he was prepared to settle in for a long siege, a thought also shared by the professor and the dwarf, though from different viewpoints. The paraplegic was struck by how calm everyone was, and she began to furiously pick her nose and fiddle with her braces, believing this might be something the radio would want to talk about, that she would find herself in the eye of disaster, the very center of catastrophe, and the prospect so excited her she wet her braces, the pee trickling down her leg, and Steckler, only half finished with his supercharged Nova, feeling nauseated by the lack of mechanical ability in the room, longed to go back to his apartment and turn on his welding equipment and feel the crackle of energy surge through his torches. The dwarf, who sat on the professor's shoulders, stared at Tonton Tute, thinking either that Tonton represented a breakthrough in genetics or that parts of him had yet to be called up, that they were still stashed away in some depot, and the dwarf wondered if in some way, perhaps with fire, he could rectify that. Fire, he knew, was in the bowels of every living thing, and only had to be let loose to achieve its consummation, a fact of such common knowledge among his people that he was shocked to discover that these people, white and black, had no idea of the thing, and he wondered about the wisdom of the professor who had purchased him in the marketplace in Nairobi, and about the wisdom of whites in general. Fire, as the dwarf knew, was the equalizer of men, the ultimate element, the only signature that remained permanent in the universe, while fire, as the owner knew, was that instant flash of fortune, the giddy gift that could turn theoretical money into real, and he alone shared with the dwarf the belief in the purging and curative effects of fire, applauded its redemption, wanted to seek out its solace.

2

Cuzz wakes up in the early morning, on sheets that are barely damp from the ocean mists, and rubs his skin to see if it is still black, rubs his arms and then his thighs and then the tops of his feet, rubbing with a vigorous back and forth motion using the two front knuckles of his fingers, wondering if he can rub the black off and underneath find white, but finding instead his own skin, as black, as soft, as richly smooth as ever. "Shit," he says to himself under his breath.

He stands naked before the mirror, dividing the mirror in two, the light half, almost silver, shimmering around his blackness. There is a glow, a yellow series of waves that follows the shape of his body. He takes his penis in his hand, pulls on it as if to reassure himself that it won't come off. He wonders what it would be like to have a removable penis, one he could take off and wear around his neck, and then put back on when the occasion demanded. He wonders what he would look like with no penis, just balls hanging down. Then he wonders what it would be like to have no balls, just a hanging-down penis. That makes him think about the screaming babies.

Lately he has been thinking about screaming babies, set afire, flying out of windows, fluttering their little hands like wings, yelling with fire in their lungs, dropping to earth. He thinks about screaming babies because the owner has once again asked him if he would burn the Building down. He would pay one hundred dollars. He would pay two hundred dollars. One or the other, he wasn't sure which. The owner is a short man in baggy pants who can't decide where to start shaving; he has an erratic hairline beside his ears.

The owner meets him in the hallway.

"Burn it down," he says. "I'll give you three hundred. Four hundred."

"Which is it?"

"One or the other. Why do you want to live in a shithole like this?"

"What about the screaming babies?" Cuzz asks.

The owner is ignorant of screaming babies. When he bought the Building from Eschopf, the Turkish chess master and arm wrestler, there was never any mention of screaming babies, only parquet floors and twelve-foot-high ceilings and lobbies with painted murals show-ing Turkish vineyards. Eschopf made him promise that he wouldn't take his name off the side of the Building and the owner had prom-ised him that, and had also promised that the line of chess figures —pawn, rook, bishop, knight, queen, and king—chiseled in stone un-derneath the roof would remain intact for all eternity, and probably beyond.

There was a rumor that Eschopf was buried in the cellar, under rocks, next to the river that flowed through the cellar, and those who visited the cellar claimed they saw him walking on the water, his velvet bag on his head and on top of that his chessboard with the pieces set for play, and Eschopf would beckon anyone who came down to the cellar to play chess with him. If you played chess with him and lost you could never leave the cellar.

The owner, Cuzz thinks, is a diviner of money, a man who simply by stretching out his hands could sense where the profit was, could feel the tingle of gold in his fingertips, could quiver and quake whenever economics was at stake. It was some innate sense, Cuzz thought, some animal instinct, a survival mechanism. He could walk through a build-ing and his feet could feel the profit in the floors. Such a man was to be watched.

Cuzz counted how many babies were in the Building. The figure he came to was seventeen. Not all of them would be screaming, but some would. How many screaming babies was the Building worth?

He feels he should ask someone. He feels that the economics of the Building would be simple if some sort of equation were set up, so and so many hundreds of dollars equals such and such number of screaming babies. He doesn't know who to ask, and then thinks he should ask the one man who can't give him an answer.

The deaf-mute was walking the halls when Cuzz found him. He was a small man, almost white but not quite brown, as if the color of his skin was in the process of deciding its hue. He walked with his head cocked to one side, thinking that was the position his head should be to hear the one sound he was bound to hear, the one sound that no one else could hear. He wore a Hawaiian shirt and loose gabardine pants with many folds, gathered in by a thin belt at the waist. He rocked back and forth, as if moaning, hearing something that Cuzz could not hear. His arm was extended, like a blind man's, to reach the walls, and though his eyes glazed and were fixed on the horizon, also like a blind man's,

Cuzz knew that his vision was excellent, that he could see Cuzz long before Cuzz could see him. He went up to greet him. The deaf-mute greeted him with a high-pitched whine. His head kept bouncing back and forth long after the whine.

Cuzz spoke slowly. The deaf-mute could probably lip-read, so he exaggerated the consonants, twisting his face so that it seemed his mouth was writing the words. He told him how the owner wanted to make money off the Building, how it was a liability and he couldn't sell it, and how he was willing to hire Cuzz to burn it, and now, he, Cuzz, wanted to know if that would cause any great inconvenience, if the deaf-mute would prefer that he didn't. He talked slowly, cautiously, unconvinced of the deaf-mute's response, afraid that he might sputter some strange gibberish, that he would think he was being threatened, that he might attack him. He had heard stories about how strong deaf-mutes were, how they were quick to hit, loved to kick, bite, twist off ears (he also heard they could talk while they were having an orgasm). But the deaf-mute only nodded his head, seemed to understand what he was saying, and Cuzz was comforted by this man who could not hear what he was saying, as if what he had to say was too awful for anyone with ears to hear.

The deaf-mute grabbed him by the arm and started to whine. He opened his mouth, almost forming words. He kept rocking back and forth on his heels, whining. Then he pulled him up the stairs. They continued to climb until they reached the roof. The deaf-mute threw open the door with a bang. He walked out on the roof and motioned Cuzz to follow him. He walked over to one corner of the roof and picked up some rags, showing them to Cuzz. Again he whined, and leaned his head back, tilting his eyes back and letting them roam around inside his head. He stamped his foot on the roof and pounded his fist into his palm. He looked up at Cuzz, smiling. The rags, which he still held in his hand, were ripped and faded and had taken on the pale color of the roof. He shook them in his hand, as if they were dancing rattles, or pompoms that he was waving. He expected Cuzz to understand something, and Cuzz knew, not so much by looking at him but by looking across to the rest of the city, seeing the flat roofs with their tar strips, the wooden water tanks propped up on stilts, the glittering array of chimneys and vent pipes that seemed to sprawl about each roof, and seeing these, he knew that he did not understand him, and he also knew that somehow the deaf-mute had misinterpreted what he had said.

In a fit of anger he grabbed the deaf-mute by the shirt and shouted "Fire!" into his face, shouted it again and again, until the force of his voice rang hoarse, hoping that his shout would carry through the deaf-mute's ears, breaking through bone and whatever it was that kept the man from hearing, and emerge heard, understood. But his shouting only seemed to excite the deaf-mute, who started to jump up and down, as if he had a great secret. He wanted to pick the deaf-mute up and throw him off the roof, but instead let himself be led by him, down the stairs, through the hall, until they reached his apartment. He knocked on the door. Cuzz wondered how he could hear the voice inside.

He waited, then opened the door and motioned Cuzz to come in. He led him into a bedroom, and roughly pushed him down on the bed. The deaf-mute went over to a dresser and opened a drawer. From the drawer he took out a red velvet dress and laid it on the bed alongside Cuzz. He looked at him, smiling. He took his hand and stroked the dress with it, still smiling. Then he took Cuzz's hand in his and drew it the length of the dress so that he could feel the whole fabric. The deaf-mute turned to him, smiling, and waited for him to say what he could not hear.

3

IT is Abdul Karim who notices Cuzz boring holes in the plaster ceiling, and it is obvious to him that Cuzz is an agent for the paraplegic and that she has sent him to test the permeability of the walls and so learn what will easily pass through them. Abdul runs a newsstand in the subway, and he is sensitive to these people, knows that if Plexiglas partitions are not put up and heavy lead weights placed over the newspapers the entire contents of his newsstand would disappear. The city breeds these people, these "disappearers," and he has watched them. They are not, as most people assume, isolated cases, misappropriated personalities looking to their own physical survival, but part of a master plan, a raving band of agents directed by a control who lives in one of the tunnels below Grand Central Station. He suspects that this control may be the paraplegic, but he is not sure. Perhaps the control, along with the paraplegic, is part of some ring of controls, themselves controlled by another control. Of this he is not sure. What he is sure of is that nothing happens by chance, and that everything that happens is part of a plot, a plot that has been unfolding for centuries.

He is not sure where the Building fits into this scheme, though he knows it does. The plot, however, is being revealed chapter by chapter on "Sunrise Semester." It is in code, of course, and he is busy translating Aristotle's *Poetics* into Arabic and then into Greek (though he could read the original in Greek he feels that the substance of the thing would be lost if he did) so that the first step in the plot, the takeover of all subway newsstands by Pakistanis, can be deciphered in detail. Cuzz's boring holes in the ceiling will affect the material composition of the Building and, more importantly, the code of the Building. Agents come by to read the Building, to decipher the graffiti, and the borings in the ceilings (seemingly an inconsequential act) provide instructions for those who mark up the walls. Agents who read the walls report back to "Sunrise Semester," where instructions are then sent out, in code, to agents throughout the city. Common to everyone who aroused Abdul's suspicions was their addiction to "Sunrise Semester." The paraplegic, he decides, is a Pakistani agent, and Cuzz is her subaltern, her slave, and with the sexual equipment these Moors are noted for, is also satisfying her in that way. And yet Cuzz may be an unwilling corporal. There is something about him that does not suggest the eager obeyer, some slow sullen resentment, and Abdul thinks he may be recruited. He notices the size of the holes that Cuzz drills. They are moth holes. He knows for a fact that the paraplegic breeds moths in her apartment because how else can he account for the strange rustlings and chortles and static that come to him through her walls, and he also knows that people of this type breed moths as a form of defense, as a willing army to achieve their designs. He has noticed the garbage at night, seen the dead moth bodies being packed into plastic bags, seen the exterminator come to kill the cockroaches that compete with the moths for food, seen the holes in clothing that signify moths.

It had taken Abdul Karim years to sort out the city. When he first arrived he was struck by the magnificence and decay. Why should the richest city on earth, the richest city history had ever seen, allow itself to crumble? The reason, he now knew, was because of a plot. Certain patterns were beginning to take shape. The directions for the plot were found in the graffiti on walls and in the subway, and further instructions were broadcast on television and every third day in the *New York Post.* (How else to explain, in a city of such culture and sophistication, such bizarre headlines and concerns?) The broad outlines of the plan escaped him, but certain details were becoming clear. He felt that messages were being transmitted through electrical lines, and so he had taken a course in electrical repair. That explained how an ordinary plug in the wall could make fires appear inside glass and tiny people dance inside boxes, make steel rods turn, make heat appear. Something strange and wonderful was happening inside those tiny lines that appeared in one's apartment, and he wanted to understand that. But all the course taught him was how to attach one line to another, turn a line off or on. The question he wanted to ask was *how,* and more important, *why* such a marvel could move through a piece of steel. The instructor could not answer that, and told him he was in the wrong class. So he took a class in physics. Again, he wanted to know the why of it. The instructor talked about something called electrons. They did some little dance along the lines and carried things as they moved. But when he asked the instructor to show him these things, show him what they were carrying, and why these tiny things could move so fast, there was no answer. He knew no more than when he had started out, except for some fantastic stories of the imagination (what did they take him for?), Ohm's law and the Bohr model of the atom, pretty fictions themselves and he marveled at their imagination, but they did nothing to explain anything, and he told the instructors so. He then thought that Westerners were mystics, that they lived in their imagination, and that explanation would never suit their needs, that understanding was beyond their comprehension, that knowing the *why* of a thing was something they could not grasp, but the *how* of a thing was quite accessible to them. As soon as he comprehended this, life in New York City made sense. New Yorkers, he knew, might know the details of the plot that was shaping their city, but the overall design, the why of it, they would never comprehend. It was simply beyond their capacity. It was a flaw in the makeup of the Western mind. He, being a Kurd, was exempt from that flaw.

When he first came to the city he learned to drive. One day he was driving across the Fifty-ninth Street Bridge and came to a stop at the foot of the bridge in Queens. A woman, in a knee-length coat, wearing high-heeled shoes, approached him. There were other women standing with her. There were no other cars or trucks with him. She walked over, and without saying a word threw open her coat. Underneath the coat she was naked. The power of her naked body, her breasts, her pubic hair, seemed to assault him. He felt as if he had been punched in the face, as if tires had bounced off the back of his head. The woman behind her laughed. He said nothing. He was unable to move the car. He could only stare. It was as if the woman held him in a tight grip with her legs. His breath, forced, pumped, wheezed out of him in little spurts. Quickly she closed the coat, laughed, looking once more fully clothed. Cars appeared behind him, honking their horns. He drove on, then stopped. Since then, the borough of Queens appeared to him as a great couch covered with fur, holding many women. He got a job delivering phone books in Queens, was fired for trying to force the books, signature by signature, through the letter slots in doors. He got a job selling Feenamint chewing gum to drugstores. He quit after three months, despite a raise, because he began to feel uncomfortable with the name. He repaired tires, rode around in a Pepperidge Farm truck and stocked display cases, wholesaled checkerboard shoelaces, sold Snap-on Tools from the back of a van, operated a pet franchise, which he had to give up, fleeing for his life, when one day he decided to let all the animals loose in the neighborhood of his store, sold replacement cartridges for ballpoint pens, franchised frozen curry to Indian restaurants, labeled envelopes, and sold subscriptions by phone for *Popular Mechanics*. Each job left him with the feeling that there was some grand pattern he had been missing. He felt there were small stores throughout the city that assigned numbers to people, and that somehow he hadn't yet heard about these stores, that they hadn't picked out a number for him, that his place in the city hadn't yet been assigned. He wrote to the mayor asking what his number was, and got a reply back notifying him of civil service jobs for sanitation men. He decided not to take the exam because he did not feel it was proper for men to go around cleaning other men. He himself washed every night, in olive oil, and assumed it was everyone's responsibility to do likewise.

Then an uncle in Kurdistan was caught between two camels making love, and Abdul inherited several thousand dollars, which he used to buy a subway newsstand. He had picked a subway newsstand because the night before he had dreamed about crows and owls, the former circling the latter, and upon waking the next day bought a newspaper that showed an ad for Crow and Owl Whiskey. He decided then to buy a subway newsstand. Thereafter, he searched through every newspaper to find Crow and Owl Whiskey, but couldn't. The Advertising Bureau had never heard of the brand, nor had the National Retail Liquor Association.

Crow and Owl Whiskey was the first hint that a plot was unfolding in the city. Once he suspected this, other elements, graffiti, "Sunrise Semester," nude women wearing coats, fell into place. He began to predict the next day's weather by how the subways stopped at his station. There was also, he noticed, a group of businessmen who wore suits and sneakers.

It is like drilling holes in the sky, Abdul thinks as he watches Cuzz methodically gouge out the neat tubular holes in the ceiling that will hold the gasoline-soaked rags. Abdul begins to devise pentagrams from the placement of the holes, and in their pattern he can discern a code that corresponds to the graffiti on the walls. Abdul wonders if the Moor likes chocolate, if he likes trinkets and other bright objects. He still cannot understand why the Moors in the city buy newspapers from his newsstand. He thinks they use the newspapers for purposes other than reading, that reading is a skill they have not been taught, that they can mimic certain signs, like macaws, but that the functional level of words remains a mystery to them, as the deeper level of words remains a mystery to all Westerners, the idolaters of the practical.

As Cuzz drills, Abdul begins to sing. He sings in two languages, neither comprehensible in the West. The music comes out through his nose, and he sings as if his lungs are in his mouth. He punctuates the notes by alternately sniffing his nostrils, sometimes sniffing in the notes as if he were not yet ready to release them. It is a wail, a moan, and yet a melody, and Abdul can feel the notes reverberate in his ears and in the top of his head. The notes revolve around his head, and he begins to revolve around the floor, singing faster and faster but not turning faster, keeping to the same speed, forcing a disjuncture between the power that sings and the power that turns. He incorporates into his song the sounds of the transistors on the street, the shouts, the cries, the shots, the crashes, the moans of love, the arguments, baby wails, curses, whispers, the sound of sneakered feet making their way into apartments. His voice becomes higher, pushing against the upper parts of his nostrils, fleeing his throat.

The drill drowns out the music, and yet doesn't, the two combin-

ing to form a third melody that climbs above the Building and floats
up to the roof where Tonton Tute is busy cracking coconuts with his
machete, having cleared a corner of the roof by sweeping to one side
the rusty syringes and the bloodstained panties that accumulate there
nightly.

When Cuzz stops drilling he still hears the sound of the drill. He
punches the button with his finger; the sound continues. He yanks the
cord out of the wall, and the drill, now a soldier marching to its own
tune, keeps humming, and Cuzz throws it against the wall, cracking the
drill, plaster, and frightening the roaches. He then turns to the hallway
and notices Abdul spinning, making the sound of the drill, and feeling
spied upon, no, mocked, insulted, almost maligned, he prepares to
throw the drill at Abdul and begin some other form of business upon
his person.

But Abdul stops, sensing his consternation, and looks his way. He
bows very deeply from the waist, returning the upper half of his body
with a ghostly smile on his face, a smile that Cuzz recognizes is not a
grin but an apparition.

"Motherfucker."

Abdul bows again, smiles again, and this time produces a carnation
from his lapel. The word evoked in him a certain memory, a newspaper
of the mind. He could imagine once, perhaps, his father, and wondered
where in the hills of Persia he had been gutted and what his mother had
felt when she had discovered the body or had been told about it and
was forced to climb into the hills and bring the body back and wash it
and prepare it for the funeral. He was young when he died, about fifty,
having fathered only twenty or so children to three wives, but half of
the children were girls and Abdul did not know if they were still alive.
But in death his mother had adorned his father with carnations, a
flower virtually unknown to their land.

"Kissass."

Abdul bows, and imagines the extravagant possibilities of the
anatomically difficult act, imagines that it is a particular form of Pakistani perversion, that the Pakistanis, who were probably the original
settlers of this country, this land of New York City, had adorned their
structures with excrement-shaded colors and signs to signify this
abominable perversion they could not overcome and so wished to
inflict it on civilizations that followed. The city, he thinks, is under the
Pakistani curse, and that explains the betrayal of brother to brother,

knives and guns hidden instead of displayed openly, the broken buildings, the fires.

Abdul looks up and sees the arm, long, gigantic, a girder over his head with something hooked at the end of it, and it reminds him of a bird he once had as a child, a hawk that had been crippled by a brutal falconer and left to die and he had taken the hawk and nursed it back to health, the only problem being that the hawk, far from being grateful, tried to kill him, tried to scratch his eyes out and tear at his entrails every chance it got, until he could no longer approach the hawk untethered but had to tie the beast with long cotton cords so as not to damage its feathers.

Abdul smiles, considers the possibility of being hurt, wonders if the hurt would coalesce for him the meaning of the graffiti, if suddenly "Sunrise Semester" would make sense, if the city, now a paradigm for confusion, a maze for mystics, would shift, like a long crystal in a complex molecule that suddenly realigned itself so that its structure would show clear, if that hurt would suddenly reveal the crack in heaven his father talked about, the moment of eternal truth when gut-bled camels rise up on their forelegs with a look on their faces that suggests wisdom, when women, giving birth, at the peak of pain, with the infant's head threatening to rip them in two, suddenly know, and he wonders if that hurt, that sudden cleavage would bring with it a rush of understanding, an instant burning knowledge.

He decides not, and steps aside, as Cuzz's spike plunges to the floor. He lifts up his leg, giving Cuzz a tap that sends him sprawling. Rushing to his apartment, he locks the door.

4

BEFORE Cuzz can set his fire, before Hobson's cockroaches can speak, and before Stern can finish his painting (the big painting that covers the side of his wall and features his blue-veined waitress, undergoing electroshock therapy while depicting the Stations of the Cross), Glasho, the excrement artist, has set himself on fire. He is a small man, almost round, and when asked his religion states, "Dime-store Buddhist." His skin, almost yellow, crinkles up like dried leaves after the fire and falls noiselessly like leaves to the ground. Glasho dehydrates, forcing his heart to pump furiously to make up for the lack of liquid in the cells, and it is during this extreme sense of exertion that he receives the instructions that propel him on for the next year. He lies in the hospital bed remembering these instructions, and after the bandages come off and he can use his arms again, he writes the instructions in a small violet notebook he carries with him. He loses the notebook, forgets the instructions, and spends the next months trying to remember where he put the notebook and what the instructions were, and then spends the months after that trying to remember what he was trying to remember. It is this sense of remorse, this sense of forgotten nostalgia that propels the excrement artist, that makes him scan the neighborhood for further examples of his art and for suitable containers to hold his art.

Glasho, displaying no known human emotion except that of amazement, for some reason attracts the enmity of a Puerto Rican lady known as Sister Torres, who has on several occasions tried to cut off his kneecaps with a meat cleaver, which Glasho neatly parries with a bowling pin, and this enrages Sister Torres's husband, who then tries to do in the excrement artist with a baseball bat, which Glasho parries with the same bowling pin, dancing in his straw sandals, and the T'ai Chi master observes the moves that Glasho makes, incorporating them into his five animal forms, but Glasho, totally ignorant of any form of martial art or other acrobatic training, simply moves with what to him are natural moves of avoidance according to precepts laid down by the *I Ching:* waiting, collecting, open, broken, redeeming.

Glasho has no known source of income, and no known source of outgo. He lives as a weed lives, sprouting wherever he is placed, placing his hands on the cracked plaster walls to feel the energy of the Building and allows that to surge through his veins. Cuzz broke into his apartment, but found nothing to rob, nothing he wanted to rob, and immediately afterward Glasho went to Cuzz and invited him to use his apartment anytime he wanted to, doing it in such a way that Cuzz knew he knew who had entered his apartment. Cuzz declined, and avoided him in the halls. Glasho gave him a present. Not an example of his art, but a book of poems written by an eighteenth-century pantheist.

Glasho's self-immolation confined itself to his apartment, necessitating that the fire department break down several other apartment doors due to the amount of equipment that was available at the moment. Glasho helped the firemen put out the fire that was consuming his body, and then went meekly to the hospital. Once in the hospital he became interested in the contents of bedpans, a curiosity that sparked interest among the hospital personnel. Glasho offered to do duty for his floor, and this was declined by the head nurse, not because she couldn't use the help but because the impropriety of it bothered her even more.

Glasho was the soul of propriety. Meek, mild, given to deceptive condescending, this dime-store Buddhist could hardly wait to find something to apologize for, and often took to apologizing for other people, a habit that got him in trouble with Sister Torres. And the Glasho smile seemed to be, in some way, a pained smile, a thing not put on so much as ingrained, as if it were an extension of his mouth. Sometimes, at night, he would hook up lights in the entranceway of the Building so that muggers wouldn't hang around. Not that he minded muggers. Once, he allowed himself to be mugged simply to give the boy confidence. Then, smiling, he broke the boy's hand, ending his career. He did it without malice, simply as a lesson.

He sees no plots. Nothing is a plot. Plots, he believes, do not exist. He believes in tofu, in brown rice. He believes in this because he cannot remember his parents, cannot remember if he had any, cannot remember where he came from. He appeared in the city one day, years ago, perhaps from another part of the country, perhaps from overseas. Everything, suddenly, was clear to him. He thinks perhaps that he had been breathing quietly for several years, and that between exhalations, he suddenly knew. What he knew, of course, could not be told.

Glasho's apartment is a mausoleum to his mind. He refuses to repair anything. Cracks appear, pipes leak, wires sputter, and Glasho builds a shrine to each of these imperfections, seeing his apartment as an aging parent, something that must be gently nurtured. When the hundreds of thousands of cockroaches in the Building migrated from apartment to apartment, when Steckler shorted the lines and burned out several feeder lines, when the voice of God spoke through the Doberman pinscher, when the Catskill Water Reservoir was diverted through his apartment, Glasho remained a piece of sea grass, simply bending . . . but not breaking. When the army of muggers descended on the Building one night and broke into apartments, raping and looting, Glasho smiled, opening the door before they broke it down, and invited them to take the contents of his apartment. When the sniper appeared, Glasho smiled again and quickly administered to the victims (mainly dogs).

He folds paper, half and half over again. He has no opinion about anything. Which means that he hesitates to say, "It is not up to us to have an opinion." Things are. He acts on both sides. He redeems mistakes, and watches clouds. "Someone must watch them," he says. "They expect to be watched." He looks around the city and takes it for what it is. What that is, what he sees most, is excrement.

Shit. From dogs, cats, horses, humans, other creatures, some not yet named or guessed at. The city is organized around it, created from it, covered in it. Glasho recognizes this. He sees it everywhere he goes, and he accepts it, not just as an artifact but as something real, not as a symbol but as a thing unsymbolized, not as a harbinger or a metaphor but as something sticky, something that smells, something that needs not explanation but recognition.

Glasho, like his Japanese namealike of several centuries ago, Bashō, is an artist. He walks the city at night in black pajamas and straw sandals and is untouched. He is quick, elusive, good in shadows, full of wit and glee. What he takes as a joke others don't; so he stands at a special distance, a thing apart. He feels that time moves around him, and if he is still he can watch its motion, can see the eddies that it makes in the air.

In his apartment he removes his sandals and sighs at the noises of the night. He walks slowly around his apartment, listening at the walls. Sometimes he retreats to the roof, and squats on the tiny building that houses the stairway to the roof. He was there the night the Scandinavian whore flew off the roof.

When Glasho set himself on fire, he did it in a giant stone urn. It had been a fountain, but Glasho carried it upstairs to his apartment and planted moss at the base. The night he set himself on fire he sat cross-legged in the urn and started the fire with his toes. Soon the flames moved up: foot, ankle, leg. Glasho's skin screamed, but his mouth did not scream.

It was Abdul Karim who smelled burning flesh. It was he who called the fire department, and it was the fire department together with Tonton Tute who chopped down the door and rushed in to find Glasho on fire, a merry funeral pyre was the way Glasho put it, the flames crackling about his body and turning his robes to ashes. All this happened quickly, and it was thought that someone had entered Glasho's apartment and robbed him, tied him up, and set fire to him. The ropes disappeared in the fire. But nothing like that happened. It was Glasho himself who had set the fire, though it was not Glasho who put it out. The fire, Glasho believed, was already burning in his veins, and he merely let it out, let it dance on the surface of his skin.

All this happened while Cuzz had been preparing his fire. He had come to a financial settlement with the owner, and the preview of his fire in Glasho's fire disturbed him.

When Glasho came back months later, skin still tender, eyes widened, heart seared, Cuzz wanted to talk to Glasho, wanted to explain the lay of the land.

One evening he knocked on Glasho's door.

Glasho, who was throwing the *I Ching,* invited him in.

The room had a sandalwood smell to it, like something kept damp for a long time and recently dug up. Glasho was tending his miniature trees, which he kept in milk cartons. Cuzz walked around the room, examining the paintings on the walls and the jars, filled with an unrecognizable substance, which seemed to be everywhere.

Cuzz meant to talk to Glasho, but he kept staring around the room. Before he could say anything he had to take in the contents of the room, had to figure out why anyone would want to be surrounded by such objects.

Glasho closed his book, and turned to him.

The words that Cuzz expected to use on Glasho, those carefully prepared phrases, now deserted him. What came out were separate pieces, phrases that had little connection with each other. But this jumble, this garbage of sentences, did not seem to confuse Glasho.

He apologized for setting himself on fire.

He promised Cuzz that it would not happen again or, if it did, he would promptly apologize to him soon after it happened. He was sorry that it had taken him this long to apologize.

Cuzz felt comforted, and yet uneasy.

He reached out to put his hand on Glasho's shoulder, and the shoulder was not there. Glasho, though, was still there.

He tried again, and again it was as if his hand were moving through an apparition, as if fog and lights had congealed to form the specter of a man.

He reached out for the neck, with both hands, and grabbed nothing. Still, Glasho was there, talking to him, apologizing, and smiling. The room seemed to hum, to vibrate. Perhaps Steckler was doing something with the electricity.

He felt a need to explain to Glasho how it was. How the Building was already a relic, a corpse waiting for someone to come and tell it that it was dead. Nothing worked. The wires shorted, all the pipes leaked, the mortar was crumbling. The economics of the thing simply demanded that the Building be burned. He explained all this to Glasho and knew that Glasho didn't comprehend what he was saying but then again did, simply by the tone of his voice that accompanied his apology, by the insistent way he spoke. Glasho listened to people not by what they said but by how they said it.

Glasho explained to Cuzz that he could move, he could live anywhere, that where he lived made little difference. But, he added, I can't speak for the other people.

Why was he explaining all this to Glasho?

He had come here to do something quite different, something violent. Cuzz lit a cigarette. Glasho breathed in the smoke.

He looked around for a place to put it out.

Glasho offered his palm.

The cigarette, lit, was pushed into his palm.

Cuzz winced. He could feel the pain in his own palm, feel it shoot up his arm and rattle his head. He was annoyed with himself for feeling the pain, and yet he felt as if he had no choice.

Glasho put the butt in the garbage.

A dull hum came up from the streets.

Cuzz wanted to push Glasho out the window. When he stepped forward to do that, he stumbled, got dizzy. He spun around, but couldn't fall; the room wouldn't let him fall any more than it would let him stay on his feet. He seemed to be created with a perpetual tilt, as if gravity and his own center were on different planets.

There was nothing more he could say to Glasho, and yet there was a lot more that he had to say to him. He couldn't speak. The deal he had with the landlord, the business of his setting fire to the Building, was off. He knew that. Glasho stood in the center of the room, and Cuzz spun around him. He kept spinning, and noticed that the sun, which had set, had risen again, and was following him around the room. And Glasho, though at the center, always faced him, as if he were turning as fast as Cuzz did. The room started to fly apart, in small sections; bits of furniture flew up and clung to the walls, and Cuzz noticed small flames clinging to Glasho's robes. The wind, he knew, was absolutely ferocious.

Glasho noticed his discomfort, noticed his spinning and his stumbling and did nothing, could do nothing. In the face of this maelstrom, he merely observed. He had done the same thing the night the Scandinavian whore had flown to her death. He had been up on the roof, squatting on the tiny building that housed the stairway, his sandals hanging from a TV antenna, watching the paintings in the sky. He heard the noise on the floor below, thinking that someone might be strangling someone else on the stairs. But it was not a strangling noise he heard. It was shouting, and screams, and he could smell the death of the woman coming up the stairs, preceding her, not a tiny thing at all but a huge cloud, a hippo of fear, the blimp angel of death, clanking up the stairs before the two men who were dragging the screaming and kicking whore, who tried to dig her nails in the plaster, in the steel balustrades of the stairway, tried to grip the treads, which she did, and which she was forced to let go of when one of the men stomped on her hand. The three, a hurricane of violence and shouting, which no one in the Building seemed to hear, proceeded slowly up the stairs like a huge cargo ship battling unfriendly currents. Finally they reached the roof, and the woman wrestled with the doorway, planting her arms and legs in the frame of the door, like Leonardo da Vinci's ideal figure, while the two men battered and kicked at her arms and legs, loosening one only to have another find a new hold, until one of the men simply backed down the steps and rushed forward, bowling her out the door and onto the roof, and she lay there, too stunned to yell, and the men came over and took her by the arms, lifting her under the arms, and as they did they turned and looked at Glasho, but in looking at him did not see him, thinking perhaps that he was a fixture of the roof, and they began to drag her across the roof to the edge, her shoes, the tips of her shoes acting like plows, dug furrows in the tar, but she remained on her feet, and the woman, now in the fist of fear, lost control of her bladder and the urine ran down her leg and onto the roof, and she kept losing control of it even after the men had launched her into the air so that as she flew off the edge of the roof she kept urinating, trailing a thin stream through the air.

5

THE woman who would be Ingrid had been propositioned on the corner but hadn't realized it until she got in the elevator in the Building and noticed the missing lights and the smell of urine from the time a gang of kids peed on the rabbi and his wife the week before while he was visiting the old Jew on the fourth floor. The elevator took her up to the fourth floor where she had to get out and walk one more flight to the fifth.

Mama Jujubee had told her she shouldn't go flying tonight. She had no intention of doing that. Mama told her there were devils in the air and that she should stay out of the night air. The numbers are bad, she said, the numbers add up to bad and the moon is bad and the time is very bad for you to be out flying. Mama lived in a storefront and burned incense and kept snakes and wore fudge-colored clothing. She was big and brown and chocolate thick, and she wore yards and yards of heavy brown-and-gold velvet all wrapped around her brown sugar fat. Mama smelled like fried bananas, and her skin looked like freshly licked milk chocolate. Every time she saw Mama she wanted to take off her clothes and crawl inside with Mama, deep inside those yards and yards of velvet wrapping and run her hands over Mama's milk fat and put her head next to Mama's big teat.

She mumbled something to Lisa and went inside her room and paced off the circle and lit the candle and got undressed and took out the book and put it between her legs, way up between her legs, and then sat down on her legs with the book still up there and started to chant. The curtains fluttered against the broken window, and she kept chanting but thought about the jimmied window lock and the time those kids swung down from the roof and jimmied the lock and swung themselves in when she was in bed. She woke up that night to find seven of them in her bedroom. One of them had started to masturbate in her dresser drawer. She didn't like to think about that night.

The devil is out tonight. That's what Mama had said. He's all big and thick and gummy and you got to play him, coax him, praise him, otherwise you be in big trouble. She kept chanting and then remembered the man on the corner and hoped that Solly wouldn't show up tonight and then she could feel something happening and she reached out with her hands to claw the floor and could feel the waves coming to her hips and she looked up and could see Mama's lips talking to her on the wall, lips inside lips, dozens of lips talking, jabbering, chattering on the wall until the walls started to shake and purple tongues curled along the wallpaper and slithered along the floor and started licking her legs and hips and breasts. She shuddered, rolled over on the candle, dipping her shoulder in hot wax. The wind tore through the hole in the window. She was covered with sweat, and cold. She walked naked over to the window and watched some kids jumping on a car roof. They were framed through a piece of broken glass in the window, and when one of them jumped his head appeared in her line of sight first through the glass and then through the hole. She wondered what it would be like to cut a child's throat on broken glass, her own two daughters, her own unborn baby. Solly was going to be mad when he heard she was pregnant again. She didn't want to tell him. Mama had given her something to abort but it was too early to tell if it had worked. She had to wait a week. Anything could happen in a week.

The kids were still jumping on the car roof when she pulled on a faded cotton robe with lumpy little balls that hung from straggly strings at the edges of the robe. There were a dozen imaginable and a half-dozen unimaginable stains on the robe.

Everything was moving too fast. She had the feeling that things were cranked up half again as fast as they should be and that part of her was always being left behind in the older, slower time. She was always just missing out on a job, or a bus, or getting the ends of her clothes ripped. She told Mama Jujubee about that and got some pentagrams for it but wasn't sure how well they worked. She thought that a mile below the surface of the earth time ran slower and that there was a world that fit her rhythms. Everything there would be dark and lumpy and a brown ooze would slow everything up; even orgasms would last longer. The men down there would be three feet tall, with bandy legs and big bellies and penises that looked like tiny bowling pins.

Chains. Look for chains. Chain herself to the bed and chain the bed to the floor and chain the door shut and chain the windows but how the hell could she do that if she was chained in bed? There were five points to the pentagram and she had to chain herself to five points on the bed and five points on herself and the chain had to pass through the slit in her ass and over her vulva and then hook up with another chain around her waist and loop around her neck so that if she tried to move any part of her body, if she did anything else than lie perfectly still, she would choke.

She got up and looked at the pictures on the wall. Lisa was cleaning her fingernails with a razor blade. She wanted to take that blade and slit her throat and then cry because she had killed the thing she loved the most. That was how she knew she loved someone. When she wanted to kill them. Knives were to be avoided around people she loved.

She collected old skin. She had patches of it in a small black box with a gold lid and the inside lined with mirrors. The skin was gray, transparent, and almost looked like bundles of hair held together by old gelatinous glop. She had pieces of skin from old boyfriends and not so old, from men she knew for one or two nights and from men she hardly knew, knew just long enough to fuck or be fucked by them. She had skin from her daughters and her own mother, and each time she asked for it she had invented a different reason, each reason being as plausible as the next. Patches came from the heel or the elbow or, if the donor was sleeping, from somewhere else. She pressed them all together, like old butterflies, and wrapped them in gauze. It made no difference if the skin was black or white or yellow, or some other color; they all turned into one vague gray inside her box, pressed tightly together with gauze strips. So that when she got lonely or crocked, when a crack in the afternoon threatened to swallow her whole, or else lay over her shoulders like a downed hippo full of warts and waterbags, then she went to her box and played with her skin. She had the name of each person written on the skin.

Solly would be mad when he came. When he heard that she was pregnant again, he would start picking his nose because that's what he always did when he was mad. He would probably bring Mobutu with him, that big black bastard. Solly sold paintings and jewelry in the Village and borrowed money from women. Nobody knew what Mobutu did. His job was wearing a leather jacket and scowling at whites. He had a silver ring through his nose and tribal scars on his cheeks. There was a rumor that he had loved several women to their death.

Solly would come in smelling of hay and want to go downstairs to the painter who lived below who was always trying to get her to pose. Whenever they met in the hallways he would bend forward at the waist, as if trying to clutch a hernia, and ask when he could expect the pleasure of her company. She kept putting him off, somehow not being able to refuse him outright. His wife was pregnant; she had been pregnant for the last two years. He had paintings of her all over his apartment with her huge belly button sticking out of the paintings. They had one child whom no one had ever seen. The child was only heard late at night, moaning.

Lisa lay like a leopard on the sofa. God, how that child did nothing. Whereas she, Lisa's mother, was always busy, always moving, always erupting. Mama Jujubee told her that. "You always connecting with someone," Mama said. "Only person you got to watch out for is Professor Death. He around you all the time."

She went into the bedroom and put on a tasseled G-string and a purple-and-red velvet Turkish robe and nine bracelets on the right hand, seven necklaces, four bracelets on the left hand, and five rings. That was five pentagrams. Silver, gold, glass, copper, wood, marble, onyx, steel, and ebony. She put on a pair of huge cotton muff slippers that made her feet look like mushrooms and padded about the apartment like an aardvark. Then she put on shoes with hard toes and heels.

That painter, what was his name? Stein, Steig, Sternberg, something Jewish, like the landlord Haber, who was not only Jewish but Orthodox. She was Scandinavian, couldn't even remember her own name . . . it would come to her later on. Maybe it would help if she had fucked more Jews; she had let it out for Catholics, Protestants, Arabs, blacks, just about anybody from Turkey. Jung said it was better if the races mingled. That was the problem with the Scandinavians, not enough mingling. She was trying to make up for that. Genius, she decided, only came through bastards. She had married several times, but her two children had never been fathered by her husbands. It had been a problem because two of her husbands had been black, and she had gotten pregnant when she was with them and both times delivered white babies.

Look at those walls. The roof leaked and her walls were water-stained, long brown python stains that wrapped about the room crushing the plaster and rotting the wood and warping the floors until the whole room sat cockeyed. She took a crayon from the sofa—she remembered Lisa had left it there ten years ago when she was four—and traced the lines along the walls. Following the cracks, the crayon chipping off bits of plaster and paint, which fell to the floor in a soft flutter, she wore the brown crayon down and had to keep peeling the paper from around it like an orange. She worked around the edges of the cracks, deepening them and widening them until she had accentuated the original split, using the crayon like mascara, so that the whole room was surrounded by this haunting, brooding line, this eye, this face, this graph of terror.

She sat back on the sofa and looked at it and remembered the several previous minutes of terror that had invaded her body and now it had been removed from her body and put on the wall where she could look at it and study it and feel this thing that moments before undulated like some huge sea snake inside her. Now it lay coiled and still, a dead remembrance, crushing the room. She took lipstick and drew a circle around one end. It looked like a giant sperm. Or the trail of an egg. A red egg. Growing inside her. Then it looked like waves rolling across the wall and the waves spelled out a message she couldn't read and the message turned into a picture of hay and a farmhouse and people running up the hill and a fruit tree with a swing and something in the tree and something else hanging down from the tree, a child falling, falling in the air—no, an apple, or leaves falling, or a bracelet. She blinked her eyes and it was gone.

She shivered, drawing the robe around her.

It's going to be a cold night, she said to herself; then she asked herself why she said that and didn't know the answer, as if the statement came through her from somewhere else.

It was hot in the apartment. She opened her robe and looked at her body. At one time it excited her to look at herself, to smell herself and taste the different things that came from different openings in her body and feel with her fingers the way her hair grew under her arms and elsewhere. Now it just sat there, or lay there, this body, a rag doll of white with openings and closings and secretions and inhalations. She looked at her darkening nipples and heavy patch of pubic hair and it seemed she was looking at herself from somewhere up in the ceiling, spying on herself the way she had spied on so many others, and that she was part of some big circle of secretion and inhalation, a dot of flesh through which waves passed, pressed tightly together with other dots of flesh.

She wondered about abortions, about her abortions, about children who never were, where they went. Who fed them, clothed them? Who imagined them?

Lisa came in, smiling. Why was she smiling? Why did she have any right to smile? She had no idea how Lisa was doing in school, had long ago stopped talking to her teachers, didn't even know if she was going to school anymore, was afraid to ask, afraid to imagine what she was doing if she wasn't going to school.

Then she remembered that Lisa took a subway and a bus to school and that once, no, several times, there had been trouble on the subway with a man who did something to himself underneath his overcoat standing next to Lisa on the crowded subway. She seemed to attract these people. There was something too gentle and unresisting in her face, some smile in her mouth, resignation—like an animal put to slaughter—in her eyes, and her skin was too white, too perfect, it was an affront to the blotched skin of most city people. Her own face was hard, and even now was splotchy red with pimples. She was always in the process of just becoming a woman, as if each night she became a neuter and then went through puberty in the early hours of the morning, awakening to find new swellings, new hair, and new desires in her body.

Why hadn't Haber fixed anything? The damn toilet was stopped up. Tampax floated around in the toilet bowl. Now even the plunger wouldn't get it down. They needed a plumber; she would have to call one and take it off the rent and fight it out with Haber when he came around. That rat fuck pig.

Once she had caught a rat swimming in the toilet and flushed it down only to find that it had surfaced in the bathtub a few minutes later, a leer on its rodent lips. She threw a bottle of perfume at it but the rat scampered up the sides of the bathtub and disappeared in a clothes hamper. For weeks afterward she found rat turds on all her towels.

She looked up to find Solly and Mobutu standing in the doorway. They looked like they had been standing there for minutes. Solly was cleaning his fingernails with an ice pick.

"Your lock is busted," he said. "You should get it fixed—you never know who's going to walk in."

He spoke as if he was taunting her to fix it, as if he, Solly, had just broken it, which he might have, and now it was her responsibility to fix.

"This whole Building is crummy, busted. Someday the sanitation men will cart it away."

He said "sanitation" the same way the police say "perpetrator," with some unease, despite long years of use.

He laughed, poking Mobutu in the ribs, who only glared at him. Solly turned to her.

"What did you find out?"

"Nothing that I didn't know before."

"What the fuck kind of answer is that?"

"The only kind you're going to get."

He jumped at her and swung. She leaned back.

"Naw, that's too easy," he said.

"I'm pregnant. Is that what you want to hear?"

"That I know."

"I didn't abort."

"That I didn't. I don't want no crummy pregnant woman working for me."

"I'm not working for you."

"Did you ask me!! Did you sonofabitchin' ask me!!!"

"I don't want her to hear this. Please, Solly."

He went into the next room, dragging her into the living room by the arm. She seemed to flow after him, like a banner or a streamer attached to his arm.

"Beat it."

She looked at him.

"Beat it, get laid, get the fuck out of here."

Mobutu grabbed her by the arm and propelled her out into the hallway. She bounced off the wall, as if she were in sections and parts of her were whirling beyond her control. Lisa got up from the sofa, and Solly pushed her down. Mobutu slammed the door.

"God, Solly . . ."

"Don't give me that shit about her just being a kid. She's old enough to fuck, she ain't no kid."

"For Chrissake . . ."

"Aw, shit."

He went into the kitchen and brought back a bottle of bourbon. He took some, gargled, screwed up his tiny rat mouth, and spit it out.

"No one likes doing it to a woman that's pregnant. What a dumbass thing to do to yourself."

She looked at the wall. There was Solly, on the wall, spread out in cracks and covered with crayon.

"I'm not working no more."

"The hell you're not. When I met you you were dishing it out for free. I just showed you how to make some money off it. You should look upon me as a high-priced financial adviser. That's what this whole thing is about."

That was the last thing she heard Solly, or anybody, say, because Solly and Mobutu grabbed her and dragged her to the stairs before Lisa even knew she was out of the apartment, and when she realized what they wanted to do she was halfway up the landing, starting to scream and kick, scratch, bite, but the two men, having decided beforehand what they were going to do, only listened to her as one listens to a nuisance, and they dragged her up to the roof, still screaming, starting to pee, the fear stiffening her face and curling her hands and feet into claws. The last person she saw was neither Solly nor Mobutu but a strange Oriental figure perched over the doorway to the roof, and as she flew off the roof her final memory was the look on Glasho's face.

THE voice of God came to the meat dealer after a night of fitful sleeping in damp bedclothes and twisted sheets. He had been dreaming about his ears falling off and women squashed by steamrollers on damp blotters when the voice roared through the first-floor apartment of Tonton Tute, knocking over the silk voodoo doll, climbed the flaking plaster and dripping water lines in the next apartment, empty after the fire, and still not finding him climbed farther, up through the charred walls and into Brown's apartment, frightening his pet fox who peed on the floor every night so the wiring shorted out in the apartment below and flames leapt through the ceiling, jumped the drain pipe two more floors, past Steckler and the supercharged Nova, past Abdul Karim, the Kurdish hemp smoker who was stoned on gage, busy trying to stuff a pencil up his nostril because he misunderstood the instructions on "Sunrise Semester," and now angry it shook the apartment looking for him, dropping chunks of plaster and paint with a vengeance and exposing the gray, dry lath underneath and the subfloor of the apartment above, and rushed into that apartment with a roar, whirling around the room with a crackle of energy, causing a red-orange glow to grow over the fringes on the curtains and a dull light to creep into the bulbs as it looked for a mouth to speak for it, threatening fire if it could not find that mouth, which could not be His mouth, not yet, so this voice threatened objects in the room, charged them with a glow that promised fire if it could not find that mouth, threatened to suck objects out of the apartment if it didn't find a mouth to speak, until, on the edge of flame, it found the dog and entered the Doberman pinscher and began to speak, and he woke to hear the dog speaking, certainly not expecting it, but not surprised.

The dog spoke softly, in a voice that was clear and yet devoid of all tone, all pitch, all timbre. The meat dealer thought he was dreaming the sound but knew he was hearing it more clearly than if he were awake, an idea destroyed by the fact that he was awake and not dreaming and that no one could ever dream this voice. He shuddered when he heard it because the voice demanded an end to dreams and dreaming, an end to speculation, exhortation, an end to venality. It was an angry voice, angry and demanding, and yet full of sorrow. It spoke in sentences he could barely understand, and what mattered was not so much the description as the sense, as if the words that were pictured in his mind were not put there by words but by something else. The voice did not speak through the dog's mouth. The voice spoke through the dog's asshole.

"Shoot," the dog said.

He set himself up on the roof, on the other side of the roof from the José chimney and away from the chicken man—the Yellowman, he called him. It was dusk. A musty, greasy fog hung in the air, and the lights of the evening looked blunted and strangely hairy. He brought up pillows and a thermos of lemonade and a portable radio, his box, and waited. He watched people through the scope of the rifle. He traced the progress of heavy women with rolled-down stockings and battered shoes that barely contained the fat of their feet. He followed small children as they hopped over stoops and banged on garbage cans. He zeroed in on the eyeballs of men coming home from work. He knew someone across the street had seen him on the roof with the rifle, probably saw him now, aiming it, checking the lever action, and adjusting the crosshairs on the scope. He didn't care. Apparently they didn't either.

People were meat. He dealt with meat all day long. What you did with meat was hack, cut, slice, chop, pound. Meat was gray, blue, red, white; meat was meant to be pierced. He saw pork chops, lamb chops, steaks, and hot dogs walking down the street. They needed to be sliced, gutted, burned, prepared, so they could be eaten.

The meat dealer weighs people by the pound, adds and subtracts people on his scale, decides where the most expensive cuts of meat will be and who will carry them. Veal burns in his brain. He sees sides of veal walking down the street, in convenient strips, light meat, portable.

He shoots the neck off a stray dog in the gutter.

The animal is picked up, as if by a kick, and thrown backward, banging against a car, with a fist-size scoop out of its throat. The animal doesn't seem to bleed at first. It gurgles, drowning in its own blood. No one seems to have noticed the dog dying, or the dog dead. Another dog comes over to sniff at it. The sound of the rifle has been covered over by a huge speaker set in an open window, pumping out a loud crescendo of noise. He adjusts the windage on the rifle, and raises the elevation.

7

NEWS of the sniper reached the owner, Haber, through the lunatic who came back to the Building to dig up several bushes in the back that he had missed and lug them to the owner's opulent house. While carrying the burlap-bagged bushes across the street, the lunatic had seen the dog shot, saw him bounce against the car, a fist-size hole in his neck, and watched the animal bleed to death, the tiny rivers of blood that ran in the gutter mixing with water from the open hydrant.

He knew where the shovel was in Haber's garage and began digging holes for the bushes, thoughtfully filling in the roots with elephant dung from the zoo and dead leaves, watering them, and then carefully tamping the earth around the bushes with the flat side of the spade. He left depressions in the earth with each tree the focus of a cavity so that rainwater would be collected and directed to where it was most needed. Haber noticed him from the window, watched him for several minutes, and then walked quickly to the rear windows of his study, marveling at the competence of the madman. He walked out to congratulate him, and the lunatic looked up, tightening his grip on the shovel. Haber stepped back, suddenly alarmed.

It was the way the lunatic looked at him, so sure of himself, so confident in his digging and planting, that Haber felt the lunatic sensed in him some slight uncertainty, a moment's hesitation.

Then the lunatic told him the story of the sniper, in bits and pieces, as if he was vomiting up things that could barely be connected. Haber paid him five dollars, as much for the story as for the bushes.

Haber ignored the sniper. If God willed that he would be shot, he would be shot. He saw himself stretched out on the sidewalk, prayer book in hand, face up, a neat hole drilled above his nose, an absence of blood (all the damage had been done inside the braincase).

But God had willed that he buy the Building and, in buying, collect the rents, though He was strangely silent on the repairs Haber should make, and Haber took that to mean that God didn't occupy himself with such small matters as fixing leaky faucets or repairing broken concrete. Still, you never knew about God. Haber's brother claimed that God was a little old black lady who begged for money in front of Zabar's on the Upper West Side, and he insisted that Haber come up with him and speak to Him, to Her, which Haber did with great reluctance. The conversation almost convinced him that his brother was telling the truth, and he was almost going to tell his wife about his brother's "find" when his wife reminded him not to believe anything his brother said or did because he had been off his medicine for a week. "He refuses to take it, claims the pills are made of turtle vomit. His wife wants to put him away, again." Haber would probably sign the commitment papers.

He owned buildings all over the borough. Some he repaired, some he didn't. It was all on whim. Some people said he was crazy to own so many buildings. He said he wasn't crazy. His brother was crazy; that was his job, to be crazy. Not mad, not insane, not a lunatic like the lunatic, but crazy. His job was to buy buildings, sometimes to sell them; to collect money when he owned them from the people who lived in them, and sometimes to collect money when he didn't own them from the people who lived in them. No one who owned a building was crazy. No one who owned a substantial amount of property could be called crazy; crazy was the province of the landless, the empire of the renter.

Haber loved his house. It was the only piece of property he owned that he didn't collect rent on. It looked like an old turtle with warts, or a large toad with several smaller toads clinging to it. The house had many levels, and many turrets, dormer windows, foot-wide roofs that careened down the side of the house like ski runs, a backyard porch with a wooden railing (covered in concertina wire), French doors (Medeco locks and a taped burglar alarm), a killer Doberman pinscher who lived in the basement and could be brought up by dumbwaiter when the occasion demanded, and several guns locked in strategic places around the house. Haber had placed sensing devices in the bushes, on the driveway, in the grass, at the front door, and he spent much of his time in his command center, watching several oscilloscopes to see if anyone had intruded on his space. Before he went to the window he knew what he would see, so that when he went it was anticlimactic, like a premature orgasm.

Haber repaired very little in the Building. He couldn't remember why he had bought a roof for the Building from gypsies, though he remembered that they had told him it was a used roof and that was why they could offer it so cheap. They let the gypsy woman do most of the talking, and Haber was fascinated and repelled by her in some odd sexual way, and bothered by her because she reminded him of his brother and made him think of having sexual relations with his brother through her, which was an impossibility, since he had just that week signed the papers committing his brother to an institution. The woman had a hole in her tooth, his brother didn't; she had a mustache, his brother didn't; and there were other dissimilarities, including the usual female ones. Still, his brother abided in her. He wanted to pay the woman to look up her dress. Instead, he bought a used roof from her, which turned out to be stolen, indeed stolen from one of his own buildings in another borough. The next time he saw the gypsies he told them about the roof having been stolen from one of his own buildings, and they offered to replace it with another used roof.

After that he vowed to do no more repairs on the Building. He felt that it had double-crossed him, though he couldn't say how, and certainly couldn't say why. It sat taunting him, a huge mortar presence, a brick pillbox.

Haber tried to get Cuzz to burn it down, but Cuzz couldn't seem to get the rag torches lit, or didn't want to, and Haber despaired of ever getting his money out of the Building. It was a sponge. It tied up his cash.

The Building sat on him, sat in him, and when he went to visit his brother who was in one of those institutions where the buildings are made of gray stucco cement and the wood trim is a finely polished and oiled oak, he spent most of the time talking to his brother about it, and his brother listened sympathetically, nodding once in a while to reinforce a point that Haber made, and Haber thought that he had never seen his brother so sane, as if the institution were charged with some special sort of rationality, some current of logic they filled the air with and pumped into the rooms while the patients slept. He had brought his brother flowers and chocolate, as if his brother were his date, and the flowers sat on the wooden table between them, looking bruised and vulnerable, while the chocolates melted in their plastic pockets because the heat had been turned up. It was an unseasonably warm fall day.

His brother was in the institution for six months. During that time Haber hardly noticed the change in the tenants, which was strange, since he noticed everything else. But the names of the tenants changed. There were names with unfamiliar consonants, people from countries that hadn't existed years or even months ago. Skin color changed; not just black and brown but yellow and red and, he swore, a family with near-green skin. Strange objects appeared in the garbage, objects he could neither describe nor explain the function of. Mezuzahs were pulled off doorposts, and on some doors there were geometric designs that looked like the kinds of things you would see when you put a kaleidoscope to your eye. He smelled odors he had never smelled before, spices he never knew existed, and the children of these tenants seemed to be small and ferret-eyed with little apparent connection to their parents. Brothers, sisters, cousins, uncles moved into apartments at will . . . who were these tenants? He did not remember renting to any of them, but they all seemed to be tenants in his Building by some sort of divine right, as if God Himself had moved them in. Haber had trouble keeping track of them, but he knew he must. He had to squeegee out the freeloaders, otherwise the Building would sink under the weight of squatters.

He saw armies of them on the subways: a strange race of small multicolored people whose adults looked like children and whose children looked like dolls. The men seemed to wear short-sleeved white cotton shirts which they wore outside their pants. The pants were always too baggy in the seat—American pants, Asian ass—and the bottom of the pants ended at the top of the ankle. They all read newspapers written by people who couldn't even speak or write English. Haber thought the country had been invaded by Asians and that the president, for whatever reason (possibly he had been bribed), had deliberately kept the information from Americans. Haber wanted to write a letter to the editor but didn't because they wouldn't print it since the editors had also been bribed. Indeed everyone in the country had been bribed to keep quiet about the invasion—everyone except him. It was a gigantic conspiracy to keep him in the dark. Undoubtedly the Rockefellers were behind it; they were the only people rich enough to bribe an entire nation. What had he done to the Rockefellers that they hated him so?

He had to teach these new tenants what not to flush down the toilet, had to tell them to take the garbage down and put it in the can, had to plead with them not to kick the lobby door in when they forgot their keys, not to steal the light bulbs from the lobby, to report to the police anyone prying open the mailboxes. These were people from the hills; this was their first contact with civilization. Why did he have to play social worker?

When inflation drove up the price of number 6 heating oil, he told the tenants to put weatherstripping around the windows and wear warm sweaters; he was turning down the heat. But the furnace room was broken into, the thermostat turned up, and on bitterly cold days he would find tenants with their windows wide open, radiators whistling a merry tune, and the cellar thermostat cranked up to eighty. That winter he had to choose between the oil bills and the taxes; the Building wouldn't support both.

He had other properties, more promising properties, that needed infusions of capital. He raised the rents, fired the doorman, hired a part-time super as a replacement for the full-time super.

His mother died, leaving him some money, and he hired a lawyer to dispossess those in low-rent apartments and put in welfare, which paid more. What was happening to the city? Where did the Jews go? The Irish? The Italians? What were the languages these new tenants were speaking? Some of them claimed to be speaking English, but it was a claim he doubted.

Now the Building looked dirty. He suggested to some tenants that they wash it. "You can hang from ropes, I'll buy the ropes," he said. "I'll buy the Ajax, people will hand you cleaning water out the windows, the Building will sparkle, the bricks will look crisp, like maple candy." The tenants laughed at him.

Let them laugh, Haber thought. There are people around who will hang from ropes, who will wash the sides of buildings, tenants, and I will find them.

He had in his mind the ideal tenant, Jewish or German; Irish or Italian wouldn't do. These Jewish and German tenants were polite creatures, clean and pious to a fault. If they had children, the children were minuscule, and something was wrong with their vocal cords so they could never speak above a whisper. They were grateful beyond reason, paid the rent before it was due, polished the halls and walls outside their apartment, went around picking up garbage in their spare time; the men wore neckties and looked industrious, and the women were obedient and kept out of the way.

He mentioned the ideal tenant to his brother, and his brother thought that such a creature could be constructed, fashioned out of mechanical and biological parts, built like an erector set with screws and cells. "As a matter of fact," his brother told him, "I'm glad you gave me the idea. Bioengineering and biogenetics are two emerging growth fields, and I aim to capitalize on both of them." Haber was sorry he mentioned it. He felt let down, like a small boy who has one of his ideas taken seriously. He had meant it more in the abstract, thinking that there was some agency that only dealt in ideal tenants, and that during the night, when no one was looking, he could exchange the less-than-ideal for the ideal.

One day when he was on the roof he found several chicken bodies with their twisted heads lying several feet away. The chickens were not plucked; the heads had been twisted off when they were alive. Haber tried to discover who was killing chickens on his roof, climbing up the stairs at odd hours and finding for his trouble more heads and bodies. Sometimes the heads had objects inserted into the beaks, sometimes the chicken bodies had small slim objects pushed up their anuses. Once he found a chicken impaled on a spike, which was stuck in the roof. White feathers blew about the roof, a snowstorm of chicken down.

He questioned the tenants about it, but they refused to talk to him. He mentioned it to his brother who told him it was part of a voodoo ceremony that took place during a full moon. A menstruating woman, after the appropriate ritual ceremony, would wring the chicken's neck and then offer it to the priest, who would raise the recently decapitated chicken to his lips and let the blood pour into his mouth. Haber felt like the Building was being soiled, as if some sort of sacrilege was being carried out against a building that was by rights Judeo-Christian. He climbed to the roof during a full moon, but found no ceremony, only chicken bodies. Chicken blood and chicken feathers provided a sort of slimy rug over the roof, a slippery stained thing that weathered badly and eventually turned to hollow shafts sticking in the tar, the feathery part having disintegrated and the blood having turned to a deep brown, which began to dry in cracks, flaking, turning to dust and being blown away. He wondered if dogs brought chickens up to the roof to kill them, but he could find no teeth marks on the chickens. It was, he felt, some sort of private ritual.

Haber's brother, out of the institution, a smile on his face and money in his pocket because of the death of his mother, listened attentively to Haber tell about the chickens, and nodded his head appreciatively when Haber explained how the chicken blood coated the roof and how the feathers were mixed up in the blood.

"Let's go talk to God," his brother said.

And suddenly Haber realized why his brother was out of the institution, and would remain out for a long time, and if he had to go back in, would only remain for a few months before they let him go. His brother was simply too exasperating to be around for any length of time.

"She's not in front of Zabar's anymore. They made her move. She took her shopping bags over to the Shopwell. She's got a camp stool."

How reasonable he is, Haber thought. So reasonable that Haber found himself believing him, because if God didn't sit in front of the Shopwell with Her shopping bags, where else would She be? Where was there a more appropriate place for Her to exhibit her splendor, to ply Her trade?

"We'll drive up," his brother said. "I got my license back. I went down and reasoned with them and got my license back."

His brother had his license taken away for driving his Chevrolet Caprice on the subway tracks in Bensonhurst.

"I simply explained to them how long I had been waiting for a train," he said.

The ride up was placid, his brother obeying all known traffic laws and observing a politeness to other drivers that frightened Haber. He parked in front of a fire hydrant, opened the trunk, took out a Civil Defense can that was colored a deep brown and had raised yellow letters that said it held water and crackers (Haber wondered why anyone would want to mix water and crackers), placed it over the fire hydrant, and then took out a small avocado plant and placed it on the upended Civil Defense can.

"You see the reasoning behind this," he said to Haber.

Haber shifted his head, sort of up and down but sort of back and forth.

"No one will move a can that has a plant sitting on it. They've done studies about cans and plants. A can without a plant gets moved. A plant solidifies a can, anchors it."

Haber nodded.

"Say, there's something I've been meaning to ask you," his brother said.

He looked around the street to see if anyone was near.

"Does your penis fit inside your wife? I'm doing a survey."

Haber wasn't sure. At times he felt as if he rattled around inside her, and then there were other times when no amount of pushing would get it in.

"There she is," his brother said.

He pointed toward a small black lady who was seated on a camp stool in front of a toy electric organ. She wore a purple sweater and a white skirt that came to her knees and had on sneakers and tube socks. She had a prayer written in pencil on a piece of white cardboard covered with cellophane that was Scotch taped in the rear, the whole affair pinned to the side of the toy organ with paper clips. She was singing a hymn and accompanying herself on the organ, and though Haber didn't know what a hymn should sound like he knew it shouldn't sound the way she was singing it.

"We'll ask her about the chickens," his brother said.

"No," Haber said.

"She knows about chickens."

As they walked closer, Haber noticed that her face and hands were covered with a thick white cream which made her look purple. Haber felt nausea, his stomach suddenly pitching and twisting, as if a hand were inside twirling it around.

"I'd like to leave," Haber said.

"Don't be silly."

"I . . . don't want to . . ."

Now they were right in front of her. His brother held him by the hand, having to drag him the last several steps. Haber wanted to run. His body was making preparations for it, and he felt that parts of him had already left, were halfway up the next block. She kept on playing, ignoring them.

"The chickens," his brother said.

She kept on playing, smiling, and pointed to a tin cup that sat on top of the organ. Haber's nausea increased. His stomach was revolving, and he felt that his knees had lost some cartilage and that if he stepped one way or the other he would tip over. He found it difficult to balance. His stomach was being thrown violently from one side of his abdominal cavity to the other.

"The chickens," his brother repeated in a way that suggested it was the password to further conversation. But the suggestion was lost on the purple lady, who continued to play her organ and sing off-key, or in a key that simply didn't exist. Haber felt that he was going to tip over.

"The chickens on the roof," his brother said, "the dead chickens . . ."

Haber threw up in the tin cup—that is, some of it landed in the tin cup, the rest splashed against the side of the toy organ and ran down the purple lady's tube socks. He turned his head quickly and ran for the gutter, falling forward as he did so that he lay on the sidewalk, his face in the gutter, still vomiting, gurgling, the sputum coming up through his mouth and nose. The purple lady kept playing. Haber noticed that some of the vomit had sprayed against the prayer card, making it illegible. There is a purpose, he thought, to cellophane.

While he lay in the gutter his brother went into the Shopwell to buy him some aspirin. A circle of people gathered around him, merely to look, and the purple lady mistook this circle for appreciation, and proceeded to play even worse, even louder. Haber wished he was home.

Which he was, soon, having been driven there at high speed by his brother, who parked the car on Haber's lawn, causing the sensing devices to go wild.

Later that evening, his nausea replaced by a dull throb in his leg, Haber went back to the Building and climbed the stairs to the roof.

There was no longer a full moon, hardly a moon at all. But the sky looked pink or red, as if a slag furnace were just over the horizon, and Haber felt there was a fire somewhere, the reflection caught in the clouds. He could smell no smoke; the air felt scrubbed, as if it had been passed over small round white rocks and then bubbled through clear water. He could smell the ocean, but he couldn't remember the last time he had seen the ocean, and he knew that if he did remember, he would not be able to remember what he had done there or whether he had actually stepped in the water, rode on it, or merely looked at it. He associated the ocean with high-rise apartments and people afraid to come out at night.

The Building was strangely quiet. Haber wondered if everyone had the flu. He opened the door to the roof, listening to the squeal of the rusty springs that kept the door shut. He stepped out on the roof, thinking he heard something. It was silent. He could smell the odors coming up from the apartments below: rice, onions, black pepper. The moon came out from behind a cloud. It was misshapen, as if someone had imperfectly shaped a thick paste made from fireflies. Haber looked at the roof, his roof, the one he had bought from the gypsies that replaced the one that Eschopf had also bought from the gypsies, so that the Building had two gypsy-bought roofs, both of which leaked.

He thought he heard something behind the José chimney, thought it was leaves rustling or a rat. He couldn't imagine what a rat would be doing up here. The rats in the Building were so large and fat he couldn't see how they could climb the steps to the roof.

He heard the noise again, a sort of low squawking or clucking. There was another rustle behind the chimney, and Haber peered around to look. He saw a man, a small man, with a farmer's cap, holding a chicken up to his waist. He heard sounds and thought the man was talking to the chicken, but there were no words that accompanied the sounds, or no words that he could recognize as such. The man had not noticed him, and Haber felt a strange tenderness for the way the man treated the chicken, as if some sort of special communion existed between the man and the chicken. The man held the chicken with both hands, looked up at the sky, and moaned. Then Haber realized what the bond was between man and chicken. He stepped closer, and the man, between groans, the chicken embracing his groin, half turned in his direction. He smiled at Haber, showing gaps in his teeth, and a long scar that ran from one ear to his throat. But it was the eyes that startled

Haber. They stared off in different directions and darted around in his head as if they were independent of each other.

Haber shouted at him.

"You're fucking chickens, on *my* roof!"

Startled, the man dropped his hands and stared at Haber, the chicken hanging from his penis. He seemed to become very agitated, and started to jump up and down, and the chicken, still connected to his body as if by an umbilical cord, flapped around with his jumps. Haber heard a loud squawk, then several, and thought it was the chicken until he looked at the man's mouth. The man raised and lowered his arms and started to hop away, squawking and flapping his arms. Haber noticed a pile of decapitated chickens where he had been standing.

"Fucking pervert, get the hell off my roof."

The man ran around the roof, squawking, the chicken flapping at his waist. He ran in little hops, almost a two-step, as if there were something he wanted to tow behind him. "You slime," Haber shouted. From the way he squawked and flapped his arms, Haber thought he might try and jump off the roof. Then he realized he was standing between the chicken-fucker and the door to the stairs. He stepped aside so the little man could hop down the stairs. Shortly afterward Haber noticed him in the street, staring up at the roof. Haber gathered up the chicken bodies and chicken heads and started to throw them at him.

"No," the man shouted.

In a frenzy, Haber gathered all the chickens he could find and threw them over the edge of the roof. People came out of their apartments to watch. No one seemed to notice the man with the chicken attached to him. After he had pitched all the chickens from the roof, he went to get a lock for the roof door.

The chicken man, removing the chicken from his body, walked back into the Building and went into one of the apartments. Haber felt betrayed, a feeling that was reinforced when the elevators finally collapsed in a heap and the Buick Roadmaster was wedged through a small opening in the lobby wall. He exploded. It felt as if the top of his head had been lifted off. The Building was having its revenge: this aged, arthritic, crippled structure was self-destructing. Haber felt that he had been insulted, that the glowing engineer's reports on the Building and the ease with which the Queens County Savings Bank had lent him the money to buy the Building were all part of a plot to humble him, to humiliate him.

His wife told him he was crazy and he decided that she was also part of the plot, Rockefeller financed, Mafia controlled, led by Smiley Burnette, and that when his back was turned, as it had to be quite often, his wife rushed off to Smiley's apartment and sucked his dick. Haber had a sense of these things. He knew events, knew how they could conspire, how they could twist facts until the earth itself could no longer stand the abominations and performed some violent cleansing action. The earth cleansed itself with fire, and he could put wrong to right by giving the earth this burnt offering, his Building.

8

THE lunatic thought Eschopf was still alive, but if he were alive, Eschopf would be eighty, maybe ninety, probably still playing chess with the worn-out pieces he always carried with him and arm wrestling with his great thighlike arms. Eschopf's mustache would still be waxed, would still point up, like a pair of bullhorns, only now it would be white, or maybe a dirty blond since his hair had been brown, though at one time red, and when it started to turn white it went through blond, a color whose yellowy traces could still be seen in the white that made his hair look dirty, stained, discolored.

Who was left to remember Eschopf?

Not the Balaban and Katz doorman, who was called to Germany in the thirties, or the dozens of old Jews, Irish, and Germans, who were now merely dreams in their children's heads. The youngsters remembered Eschopf, and the lunatic was one of them. As a young boy riding his scooter he remembered Eschopf, and could still picture him now, fixed forever in his mind, like an oil painting that becomes thicker and darker with age, leaning back in a chair with his arms folded over a tremendous stomach, and he thought that Eschopf was some transplanted Mideastern prince who was more than the owner of the Building, more like a lord of the area, director of this fiefdom in Brooklyn. The lunatic, when he was a boy and before the whole idea of being a lunatic came to him, noticed dozens of people who approached Eschopf with caution, soliciting his opinion, asking advice or favors, counsel or aid, and Eschopf would deal with each one of them separately, usually with a few words or a wave of the hand, and the power of those words or the motion of that hand was noticed, physically, in the faces of those who approached him, some acting as if they had been slapped, others caressed, still others made more thoughtful or perplexed. There was a ring of power that extended around Eschopf, and those who crossed that circumference felt that power, and the lunatic, still a little boy, sought to test that power one day by approaching the Grandmaster while he was sleeping in his chair, tilted back against the brick wall of his Building, the late afternoon sun etching the edges of the bricks, and he approached cautiously, on tiptoe, coming closer, until he could reach out and touch him, and standing before the sleeping Eschopf, he could feel no force or power and went away, saddened, until that night, when lying in bed, he had a strange burning sensation in the palm of his hand, the same hand and palm that he had reached out to touch the sleeping Grandmaster.

Eschopf lived in the basement, the lunatic knew, on the banks of the river that ran through the Building and from which he pulled the huge sturgeon and bass that he ate, and when the lunatic saw Eschopf in the basement, he was without his head—that is, it was not in its customary place on his shoulders but rather under his arm, and he spoke to the lunatic through his navel in a voice that was very deep and yet somehow constrained, almost nasal. He wanted to know why the Building was falling down. The lunatic ran, over or through or on the water which always flooded the basement, but he didn't seem to be able to find an exit. Eschopf made him sit down, and he put his head back on his shoulders in such a way that it never seemed to have been removed, and he told the lunatic about the Building, how it had been built in the thirties with a special facing brick that came from Indiana and that the cherry and oak in the parquet floors came from the Adirondacks and the marble fireplace in the lobby came from Vermont along with the stone quarry floor, and the cut glass in the chandelier at the front of the lobby was hand-blown in West Virginia and hand-forged in Red Hook. Three men were killed putting up the Building, he said, two falling from the roof and the third buried somewhere in the cellar, no one knew just where, or why, for that matter. Just before the Building was completed, before the ceilings were plastered, one of the workmen hung himself in a closet over the weekend, with the door shut, and wasn't noticed until a week later when the smell got bad. There were bushes imported from China planted around the Building, bushes with thin, feathery leaves that when boiled in water cured arthritis and gout and improved sexual performance and in the spring added a sweet nostalgic fragrance to the air that made men think of the women they had loved and wronged or the women they hadn't loved who had wronged them. There was one week in spring when this smell was so intense and the feelings it produced so strong that to linger near them was to invite disaster. The archway over the front door was taken from a church cupola in New England, the stone busts were carved in Venice and represented Turkish Grandmasters—Fethi Bey, Ismet Inonv, and the most famous of all, Mustafa Kemal, generally credited with inventing the Ramazan defense. The leaded glass in the small oval windows near the front door, which was beveled and cut so precisely that when the sun hit it right a tiny rainbow of the visible spectrum would be projected inside the lobby, was from Vienna, personally purchased by Eschopf on one of his many trips to the Austro-Hungarian empire. The brass door handle and brass door knocker (never used) also came from Vienna though they could have just as easily come from Bremen since they were made there (the iron ore came from the Ruhr and the coal from Scotland). The sidewalk was gray slate that buckled and had to be reset several times until the land under and around had settled into its accommodation with the Building. Years later the gray slate was pickaxed apart and carted away, and a cement sidewalk laid. Indians lived on the banks of the river in the basement, and Eschopf claimed he was the only one who understood their language, which was, in fact, a Turkish-Ubic dialect from a region near where he had grown up.

Very little was known about Eschopf. He had no friends, though everyone knew him. He addressed people rather than talked to them, and while he was included in many gatherings he seemed uncomfortable if only one person was around him; he preferred many or none, usually the latter. For a popular man he was remarkably aloof, though that was probably the key to his popularity. When he first appeared on the docks of New York, it was rumored he was a bashibazouk, a member of the notoriously brutal nineteenth-century Turkish irregulars. He had a burro for several years and sold it for a large sheepdog, traded the dog in for an arm-thick snake coiled in a basket and a parrot that rode on his shoulder, sold them both for an Abyssinian cat, traded the cat in for a fox, and then one day the fox disappeared. Eschopf didn't seem to mind. By then he had acquired the Building. He seemed to have given up on animals, even chasing pigeons off the roof. He rented to people with few-syllable names, no matter their nationality, had a set of rules printed up for his tenants that stressed general moral tone and behavior, and acted as doorman after eleven, chiding those who came in late. Then he stopped acting as doorman but still handed out the printed rules. He had copies posted in the lobby and hallways, and from time to time would query a tenant about rule number six, or number three, or any other number that took his fancy. Tenants either avoided him or memorized the rules. And then in his late fifties or early sixties he decided to sell the Building. He disappeared soon after. Some believed he went back to Turkey, others said he was roaming the deserts of the Southwest. Only the lunatic knew for sure where he was. As soon as he sold the Building, Haber had the lobby door taken out and put in his home, removed the glass chandelier and had that put in his dining room (with the result that it filled up the room, allowing no space to put food on the dining room table, a fact that proved to be inconsequential when the chandelier tore loose from its moorings and crashed through the table, bringing half the ceiling and the floor above with it), had the small oval windows removed and placed in his sun parlor (the empty space was bricked over), and probably would have removed the elevators and had them installed in his three-story mansion if he had known of any way to do it cheaply, and also if he hadn't somehow gotten it into his head that elevators were one thing the tenants deserved (with fifty units and six stories). The bushes were removed by the lunatic who complained that Eschopf was angry at him for digging them up.

The only reminder of Eschopf were the granite faces set under the roof, staring placidly down, and those remained intact, except for the one the sniper managed to pry loose during a garbage riot years later in the Building and sent crashing down, narrowly missing several sanitation men and a fire marshal. The granite bust landed in a pile of garbage, its fall cushioned, still intact, and because it weighed close to five hundred pounds no one stole it and consequently it ended up in the backyard of the Brooklyn Museum. The marble fountain in the courtyard was another Eschopf device, a delicacy stolen from the Uffizi in Italy before the war and shipped to Istanbul, where it was put aboard a Turkish freighter and placed in the hold disguised as a crate of figs.

Haber would have taken this had he discovered that only two small bolts held it to the cement, but by the time he had investigated, the marble boy nymph, with upraised finger and nonrunning water (a piss green before it dried up), was cracked by flying beer bottles and wedged in by garbage and the Buick Roadmaster whose bumper sat just inches from the statue's tiny penis, miraculously not yet broken, though shiny from fondling.

And the roof, Haber would almost have taken that too, sold to Eschopf by roof gypsies who told him it was the first prefabricated roof, and therefore inexpensive, though quite serviceable. Eschopf believed them, though in fact the roof was stripped from several adjoining buildings by the Romanies and put on his.

SHE couldn't remember the last time she had walked up the stairs. Maybe it was never. She did remember when she was five years old and her father carried her up the steps with her leg braces clicking together like cockroach antennae, and she remembered then looking down at them and wondering why she had these two growths hanging from her hips that had a life of their own and obeyed nothing she would tell them. They clicked together in time to her father's measured puffs up the stairs and she thought, Well, now I know more about my legs than most people will ever know about themselves. And that is nothing, absolutely nothing.

But that was ten years ago. Now they lay propped up on the wheelchair like pieces of a suspension bridge whose machinery was jammed. She could never understand why she needed braces if her legs didn't work. What was it all the wires and bars and straps were supposed to straighten out? None of the wires and bars and straps inside her leg worked. It was all a dream of her father's. If he could put enough nuts and bolts outside her leg maybe it would get those inside her leg working.

He couldn't carry her up the steps anymore. She weighed two

hundred pounds and at the age of fifteen was completely a woman. The strange thing about her was that she was very shapely. It was just that everything was exaggerated. She had large breasts and wide hips and heavy swelling legs with huge rolling calves. That was also strange. Most cripples had stick legs, no flesh, just extensions of bone and tendon with traces of muscle. But she had all this heft, this flesh, enough to support two people.

She thought of herself as some sea creature, a sort of floating cow, and when someone had jammed the elevator mechanism so she couldn't go outside she used to sit by the window and dream of opening it and then just floating gently to the ground. It was always on an overcast day when the sky and the ground looked the same and the wind scattered the paper in the street until all the scraps looked like vast schools of fish flitting back and forth.

From her window on the third floor she looked down on the abandoned cars on her block, and they reminded her of pictures in the *National Geographic* of tiny vicious creatures who lived in stone shells and darted out eating the small and curious. The garbage looked like seashells to her, and if there was enough of it, which there usually was, a vast multicolored coral reef. Rats played in the garbage the way brightly colored fish swam in and out of the countless coral openings in the Great Barrier Reef off Australia.

Kids raced up and down the block on broken grocery carts shouting unbelievable curses whose anatomical possibilities she couldn't begin to fathom.

The lights in the apartment had flickered twice this morning and three times this afternoon, and when she wheeled herself into the kitchen and checked the clock with her watch there was a total of four missing minutes. They had just flown out the window, like everything else. But she knew what had happened. The meat dealer upstairs hadn't walked his Doberman again, and the dog had used the corner of the kitchen to shit and pee. She could see the stain on the ceiling deepen in color. She could hear the dog whining and pacing the apartment, the click clack of his nails beating a staccato on the peeling parquet. Several times she heard the dog bark as someone tried the door. She wondered what she would do if they tried her door.

She wheeled herself back to the window and watched some Puerto Rican kids jumping up and down on the roof of an abandoned car. Except for the trampoline-shaped roof, the car looked new—maybe an

Eldorado. The sound of their feet hitting the roof was delayed a second after she saw them hit the roof, so that when she heard the sound they had already started on the next jump. It was like watching a movie whose sound track was out of sync. Another kid was trying to push a street sign through the front windshield. The license plates on the car said New Jersey. Why did all the abandoned cars seem to come from New Jersey?

She heard the sound, and saw the windshield splinter, as if a highly intricate web of lines was instantaneously drawn on the glass. The boy kept battering the glass with a steel pole, spraying bits of glass until a small hole appeared. She could feel the car sigh, as if mechanical life were being given up.

She knew that sound. Every morning when her parents got up she could hear them sighing. When they put water on to boil that sighed, and so did the alarm clock that woke her up in the morning. If the elevator in the Building wasn't working and Mr. Curtis had to come up and wheel her down three flights of stairs and then wheel her in the van that took her to school, she heard Mr. Curtis sigh when he knocked at her door in the morning. And then at school she heard sighs all day long. She heard them from teachers who tried to make some sense out of the spastic's sentences or propped up an arm or leg that had fallen into the aisle and couldn't be retrieved, and she heard it from her guidance counselor whenever she brought up the subject of college. The world was full of sighs, and days would go by when that was all she could hear, as if the very earth itself was moaning in sympathy with humans.

She heard someone turning her doorknob. It was done slowly, and when the knob came to the end of its turn, the door was rattled softly in its frame. She prayed the Doberman upstairs would bark. She didn't know whether it was better to shout out or keep quiet. She was afraid of her own voice if she shouted out—it might seem too soft, or squeaky, it might seem as if the person attached to it could be easily overpowered.

She rolled herself into the kitchen. Opening the drawer she took out a carving knife. She hardly knew how to hold it. Her father carved the meat and shooed her away whenever she wanted to use it. He thought she was always on the verge of cutting herself, of falling out of her wheelchair, or dropping something.

The rattling sound at the door had stopped. But she hadn't heard anyone walk away. She thought she could hear breathing, or muffled voices. Something scratched against the door. Then she heard something put in the lock. She listened intently for the sound. She listened so hard she could almost feel a sensation in her legs.

The lock turned, and then stopped. She wondered if the other locks would hold, and then wondered who or what was on the other side of the door. Then she peed in her pants.

She heard nothing. Outside, the kids had stopped battering the windshield, and the only thing she could hear were the sex screams of Mrs. Foley in the apartment across the way. When she had first heard the screams she had asked her parents to go over and help the lady who was being beaten, but they had acted strangely, first as if they hadn't heard, and then as if nothing were happening, as if a woman screaming were the most normal thing in the world. She had talked to a friend of hers, a precocious deaf-mute at school who was sexually promiscuous, who had explained to her, with a snigger, what the screams were all about. Ever since then she had been frightened of sex, and mysteriously attracted to it. All sizes and shapes and hues of men made their way into Mrs. Foley's apartment. Her parents seemed to ignore what went on across the hall. Mrs. Foley had two daughters, thirteen and sixteen. Frequently they were in the apartment when she was screaming.

Mrs. Foley had stopped.

So had the scratching at her lock. She thought she heard voices, and then silence, or just breathing.

She wheeled herself into the living room and sat with the kitchen knife across her lap. She was afraid to turn on "Lucy" or "The Love Connection." She took the knife and put it against her cheek and then lay the edge alongside her throat and then, bringing it up to her mouth, carefully licked it.

She placed the knife alongside her legs and then put it between her legs, shivering at the steel. When she took it out the knife was warm, and there was blood on it. She didn't know where she had cut herself.

The door handle was turned again, then softly rattled.

Nothing.

She heard the sound of Latin music coming from the hall. It came from one of those big radios Puerto Ricans always carried on their shoulders, the kind that only seemed to get in bongos and congas, the kind where the men sang like women.

The hammering at the door started with the music. It seemed to keep time with the drums, getting louder as the drums got louder. The door shook in the frame, then the frame shook in the wall. She could feel the door groaning as the battering continued. She thought someone had a car on the other side and was ramming the bumper into her door.

She grabbed the kitchen knife and made chopping motions in the air. She looked like a child trying to wave a baton, or a spastic trying to paint the wall. Her motions were too short and choppy, not long and gliding like the men who knew how to use knives, men who made the knife dance in the air like a hawk killing a snake.

The knife fell to the floor. It lay on the floor like a piece of fish. It reminded her of the time she had tried to invite a boy over for dinner and how her mother was upset because he wasn't Orthodox but he came over anyway and spilled their fish on the floor. He had a harelip and spoke with great difficulty. She never could understand him, but he had the most beautiful fingernails she had ever seen, like oysters.

The hinge was giving. It was being torn loose from the door frame. It was crying in pain. She was terrified. The wood in the door screamed at her.

You had to be a virgin and then on your wedding night you had to bleed on the sheets so your mother-in-law could come over the next day and wave the sheets out the window and show all the neighbors the blood, and she wondered where you had to cut yourself to bleed on the sheets and why you had to bleed anyway and was it like shaving your head and washing the soles of your feet in vinegar and why didn't the men have to shave their heads too but they never even shaved their faces and left all that underbrush on their face.

A corner of the door leaned into the apartment.

She could hear Latin music and someone yelling and the smell of garbage in the hall. When they first moved into the Building ten years ago you would put your garbage into a neat little bundle and put it on the dumbwaiter and give a little ring and Mr. Gustafsen in the basement would take it off and put it out in the street for the garbage truck. The garbage seemed to be neater then. It was packed tighter in boxes and bags and there wasn't so much paper. Then there were the fires in the dumbwaiter and the dead dogs thrown in the basement that clogged the mechanism, and one night Mr. Gustafsen was knifed to death and his TV taken. They could never find a replacement for Mr. Gustafsen, not for a man who swept the stoop every day and painted the cellar once a year and kept stacks of books in Swedish in an old sea chest in his room next to the boiler. They had to pay more money and give more room, above ground, to a man and his family, who didn't seem to know how to do anything, didn't want to do anything. That was all Haber's fault. He was the owner, Orthodox, who came around in baggy pants and collected the rent and had a heart attack every time someone tried to take him to court. Haber was filling up with welfare and didn't care about the rest of the Orthodox living in the Building, was getting more money from welfare tenants who burned their apartments every few months so they could get relocation money.

There was a hand over the door. Why didn't she call the police?

What did they want with her? She was too fat, had braces, made men turn their faces.

The door fell down and they came in. They weren't big like she expected. She thought they'd be big and black, with sweat on their lips, smelling like dogs, ebony skin glistening. They were small. Thin and small, with small mustaches. They must have been twins. They both wore white T-shirts and had packs of cigarettes rolled up at the shoulders, and when they came at her she couldn't yell or scream or make a sound. They just smiled. She noticed that one of them was wearing tan pants and had brown-and-white perforated shoes. The other wore black pants and sneakers. They didn't say a word. They brought the radio in with them and wheeled her into the other room.

10

WHEN the roaches left, Hobson knew the Building was doomed. He had never seen roaches leave anything. They moved from meal to meal like broken field runners, sliding under a pile of dishes or climbing over the lip of a glass, but they always came back.

This was different. They marched in straight lines, crawling down the drain pipes and alongside the waste pipes, ass to antenna, oblivious to the light. At night when he lay in bed, they dropped from the ceiling on him, confused, struggling for a foothold on his slippery skin. He would pick them up and throw them against the wall, trying to crack their shells, but all they did was bounce, sometimes back on him, more often on the floor, where they righted themselves and scurried away.

He turned on the light, smashed squads of them with the wide end of a Pepsi bottle; they hardly noticed. They were like water, a river flowing toward a lower gravity. He held a lit match along the outside column, burning legs and antennae, but they hardly noticed.

They headed toward the professor's apartment. He wondered if the roaches were piling up in the professor's apartment, or if they were leaking into the one below. Hobson wondered what the professor's dwarf would do about the roaches. Probably eat them. He ate anything that moved, and many things that didn't. The professor was away, and while he was gone the dwarf kept house: a fastidious cleaner, a polisher of ferocious magnitude, a spit-shiner of tables, and a good buffer of glassware. The dwarf never answered the door because he couldn't reach the handle. He slept in a dresser drawer. All these things the professor, whose speciality in the philosophy department was structural philology and metalanguage, told him one day in the hallway when Hobson happened to catch sight of the dwarf. The dwarf spoke a language only the professor could understand, and it consisted mostly of tongue clickings and raised eyebrows, as far as Hobson was able to tell. Hobson imagined the dwarf collecting the roaches in a shoe box and ladling them into his mouth with a spoon. He would enjoy the crunch they made, and the sound of his eating would remind him of his own language.

Hobson knew he would have to follow the cockroaches. They had divined something, knew something about the course of events that he didn't. They were some sort of early warning system. Since the dwarf couldn't reach the doorknob and the professor wasn't home, he didn't bother knocking on his door, but went down one flight, where he could picture legions of roaches crawling over Steckler's supercharged Nova. But if the roaches were piling up in Steckler's apartment he would never know, or if he noticed them he would assume it was oil or blood leaking from the apartment above, and go back to his arc welding, most of which he did early in the morning because it tended to short out the wiring in the building.

Steckler ignored his knocking, perhaps had welding rods stuck in his ears, or wasn't home (not true, Steckler was always home because he feared someone would steal his supercharged Nova from his apartment, but the car was probably the most unstealable car in the city since

Steckler had been assembling it piece by piece in his apartment). Hobson tapped lightly on Steckler's steel door and then tapped harder, receiving no answer, though he could hear the buzz and crackle of Steckler's equipment behind the door; and when he pounded, the words "go away" came back to him through the door. Hobson shouted through the door, asked him if he had seen any cockroaches streaming down the waste pipes and, if he had, to tell him where they were going. Hobson had never seen the inside of Steckler's apartment, had no need to, but if duty called he was determined to enter the welder's home. He pounded again, and again heard only the buzz and crackle of the equipment, the lights in the hallway flickering each time the welder made contact.

Hobson walked downstairs. The door to the paraplegic's apartment was thrown open. He walked in without knocking. Noises that sounded like metal clicking together were coming from another room. He thought he heard grunting, and the sound of a rocking chair going back and forth. Hobson walked back outside the door, knocked, and reentered. The floor was shiny, almost icy, and there were streaks of rubber on the parquet. A wind chime was tinkling in the doorway. Now Hobson could hear heavy breathing, as if someone was out of breath but trying to muffle his presence. He wanted to say "hello" to announce his presence, but something stopped him, and he waited, standing in the middle of the floor, listening for whoever was listening for him. The sound of the silence became heavy, and Hobson thought he heard the tiny shelled feet of millions of roaches scurrying across the floor, excited, antennae clicking and fringed mouths rubbing one another, and he kept quiet, feeling the presence in the next room. Silence obliterated silence, and before he stepped into the next room Hobson could imagine the paraplegic lying on the floor, her limbs trapped in steel girders, roaches crawling over her like Lilliputians over Gulliver while she remained on her back, turtle fashion, waving what legs and arms worked in a useless dance to free herself of the insects, which by now would have blackened most of her body with their presence. So that when he stepped into the room, she was as he had imagined, and yet not. The window by the fire escape was open, and someone, the flash of a heel, was going up. A lamp in the room was on the floor, and the paraplegic was lying on the floor, her wheelchair overturned, a bedsheet wrapped around her neck, the bedcovers pulled down on the floor, and a great noisy stillness filled the room, the silence after violence, and the room seemed to recede and advance in Hobson's mind, tilting, bellowing a great silent shout. The paraplegic was nude from the waist down, the clothes on the lower half of her body having been ripped, a pair of panties, in shreds, dangling from one of the braces on her leg. Seeing her lying helpless, Hobson was enticed and horrified. Lust and fear boiled in his breast, as well as in other parts of his body, and her nakedness, her pubic area both frightened and attracted him, and yet all this flesh, surrounded by braces, these fat thighs pinned in by steel wires and plates, reminded him not so much of a woman, but of some animal, held in a trap, an object of fur or food. She lay on her back, legs raised. Hobson stood over her for a few minutes, trying to decide if she were dead, hurt, passed out. Then he noticed that she was watching him, had been watching him in silence, waiting to see what he would do. And what would he do? He looked at her, as one might look at a beached fish, stunned by his embarrassment and yet unable to move, hoping that the desire for motion would overcome the fear of her helplessness. She looked up at him, not in fear, or anger, or even in puzzlement, but in a way that suggested his looking at her, as if her eyes were mirrors to him.

"Would you," he said, "like a cup of tea?"

She nodded, or would have.

Hobson didn't know whether to help her dress or help her get in the wheelchair, half nude, and then turn his back while she dressed. And yet, could she dress? Who pulled her clothes on for her? Did someone come in every day and dress and undress her, and should he find out who that was and call them, even before he helped her into the wheelchair? And if he helped her into the wheelchair first, wouldn't she think he was attempting something else? Was lifting her into the wheelchair, nude, the first priority?

"I don't know what to do," he said.

She said nothing, determined not to help him, bothered not so much by her situation as his indecision.

He righted the wheelchair and helped her into it, surprised at how weak and wobbly her thick legs were. She wheeled herself over to a dresser and got out a pair of pants. Hobson watched her.

"Please go into the next room," she said.

He made tea in the kitchen, and while he waited for the water to boil, he noticed the way the plaster was flaking around the water pipes as they emerged from the wall, and how the rectangular molding on the·

wall was peeling away from it, and on the ceiling some mysterious stains, and the layers of paint over cracked and peeling paint until the surface buckled and heaved, swelling and bubbling, and the squares of linoleum that had lifted up at one corner, and the white porcelain sink that was worn down to metal in spots, and far from depressing him, the signs of wear lifted his spirits. All things, he rejoiced, will crumble, and I too.

She wheeled into the kitchen. Hobson had set out two cups of tea, with sugar, lemon, and two small spoons. This almost exhausted her stock of china and silverware. She looked at the tea, then wheeled over to the radio and turned it on.

"Today," she said, "is the day."

"For what?"

"Bombs. They're bombing today. I don't want to miss it."

The radio talked of no bombs, but it was full of "news," what Hobson called "olds," the same things he could hear any day on the radio. He gave himself two spoonfuls of sugar and stirred until he could feel the heat of the tea in the spoon.

"Do you want a doctor?"

"No. What those men did, is that called love?"

She said it in a way that suggested neither anger nor fear, but curiosity. Hobson felt unable to answer. He felt prone to grandiose schemes, wanted to run from her apartment and imagine mantels made of cherry and hard maple, marble wainscoting, brass lamps, and gaslights. He knew that she was like teachers he had in school; he would never be able to answer their questions. What they asked, and what she asked, went deeper than what he knew about anything, and ultimately that—his not knowing—was the most profound thing one could say about him.

The small animals know, he thought, but I don't.

"I didn't think it was. Not that I know what it is, but I know it's not that."

She wheeled to the table and drank the tea Hobson had poured, drank it straight, no sugar, only lemon. Hobson puckered his lips. When she lifted her arm to drink the tea he noticed a huge patch of hair under her arm. It seemed to run up her arm, and down her side. He shuddered. He was afraid of that hair, could imagine himself getting lost in it.

"Did you notice any roaches?"

"Not then. I tried to stab one of them with my knife."

That was why he couldn't find a knife to cut the lemon. And why when he had opened the drawer to take out the spoons and closed it, there was nothing left inside to rattle.

Hobson's choice: to be in this room at this moment, talking to the paraplegic, when at this very moment his beloved insects, the guardians of the natural order, the givers of laws, cleaners up of waste, those scaly beetles that fled from light and slipped so easily from underneath the back (or front) of a hand, had fled.

"They got out through the window," she said.

"The window?"

"Fire escape. I think they went up."

He had seen them going down, following the pipes, a falling water of insects that seeped through holes in floors and followed the openings made for pipes, slipped between ill-joined boards. Had they done a U-turn? Were they privy to some new bit of information about the Building, did they sense a resurgence, some new rehabilitation that was about to take place? Hobson pondered this for a moment, thinking that the matter was not as clear as it appeared. He smoothed the wrinkles on his black suit and looked down at his shoes.

The paraplegic was heavy and ponderous inside her cage. She had steel braces and wires and pulleys that could be pushed and pulled to make her legs move, and her heavy arms could propel the rubber-tired wheelchair anyplace in the apartment. He wondered what she thought of cockroaches.

"They are not outdoor creatures," he said.

"They're slime."

"They're quite dry really."

They made a crunch when you stepped on them. They tasted bitter. If cornered on the ceiling they could half fly, half glide, to a lower space. They laid their eggs, ignored their young, left tiny specks of shit, had a distinctive smell, could be driven out of a room by ants, avoided spiders.

"I never knew it was like that," she said, sipping her tea. "Not that anyone told me. They never told me anything. No one did, not my parents. I suppose I could have found out through books, but I never did."

She was talking more than Hobson wanted to talk. He wanted silence, he wanted to be out of here, he wanted to follow the wanderings of his little creatures, but the paraplegic was jittery and if he left her now she would get upset. Why would that bother him? He didn't know. He wanted to stay and leave. The sight of her heavy arms and breasts, her smell, her hair made him think she was several women compressed into one. She would talk, and by talking get inside him. He could smell the way she talked, could smell a sort of damp-woolness about her voice. She would tell him more things than he wanted to know, explain, apologize, try to get him to understand.

"I don't know why I am so heavy. I don't eat that much."

He almost said, you need exercise.

"When the elevators worked I could get outside. I could get all the way to the corner and always find someone to push me over the curb, and it never took me long to get to the park. Is the park still there? I hope so. I love to watch people run on the grass. Is the grass still there? Do children run in the park?"

"I think so. I mean, sure."

"In a way, it doesn't bother me. It doesn't upset me. Does that upset you?"

It didn't.

"I mean, it wasn't as bad as I thought. Though in some ways it was worse. But it was funny too. Do you know what I mean?"

He didn't.

"I think they were scared. I know they could have killed me. But then, I'm just a cripple."

You can smash half a cockroach and the other half will live for hours, days, trying to pull its smashed half across the floor.

"Half of me is already dead. So if they killed me, they wouldn't be killing a whole person. It's not the same. I think about that sometimes."

He had no particular reverence for cockroaches. He would on occasion smash them, fling the brown puddles of their bodies into the garbage when they became too numerous. Their one shortcoming was that they couldn't control their own numbers.

"I don't know if I could have a baby. I don't know if the dead part of me includes the baby-making part. I don't know if I could take care of a baby."

Baby cockroaches didn't move as fast as adults, weren't as cautious, could be smashed easily with the tip of a finger.

"What do you think of babies?"

"I never had one."

"I can't imagine a crippled baby, can you?"

"No."

"I've never seen any tiny braces, or tiny crutches."

As a child he had trapped insects and pulled off their legs. The insects didn't seem to mind; they struggled around as best they could with a reduced number of legs, showing no animosity toward him (not that he could have known how they could show animosity). He did it out of curiosity. No matter how many legs he pulled off, the insects always continued going about their business, and if he left them with one leg, or none, they did whatever could be done with one or none. He stopped as quickly as he had started. When it rained, he went around protecting ants' nests by building small leaf umbrellas.

He heard fire engines. One block away a building was burning. No one screamed. It was a calm fire, and he could see that the men who were putting it out seemed to move slowly, as if they were moving underwater, or had elastic binding their limbs. The people on the block were waiting on stoops until the fire was out. When the ashes were still warm they would go in and strip what was left.

"I wonder why there are so many fires," she said. "Fires, rapes, and robberies. There's an r in each of them. Also one in *murder*—two there, *burglary*—two again, *arson, riot, revolution, disaster, revolt, war, rebellion, hurricane, tornado* . . . several more."

"That doesn't explain all this," Hobson said.

"Also *rigor mortis.*"

Hobson was seized by an inexplicable urge to explain everything, to tie in decrepit buildings, arson, selfish landlords, rotten tenants, decay, abandonment, devastation, and greed into some tidy little bundle. It was, he knew, not a vain hope, though the size of the bundle and the shape of the explaining it did would perhaps not be so neat, nor so small; he knew such an object could be constructed.

"They take us for fools," Hobson said. "They think because we're suffering through it, we don't know what's happening. We not only know what is happening, we know why."

She started to shiver. The cup rattled in the saucer, spilling tea on her immobile legs, and she put the teacup on the table as her arms and trunk and then head shook violently. Even her legs started to thump up and down, as if they were beating time to some unheard melody. She shook rigidly, captured mouse to a cat of uncontrollable muscle spasms.

"It's just a fit," she chattered. "I'll need my medicine."

But before she could tell him where it was, her eyes widened and a toothy smile froze on her face. Hobson went to the bathroom and looked in the medicine cabinet. He could hear the thumping noise she made with her legs on the floor. There was a small glass bottle that looked like a prescription, and since there was no other, he assumed it was the correct one. He brought a glass of water with the medicine vial. There was no mention on the medicine vial as to the number of pills one should take. He extracted one and carefully placed it on her tongue. Then he lifted a glass of water to her lips. She swallowed with great difficulty, never closing her lips, some of the water dribbling down her front. Hobson sat opposite her in the chair and watched her thump and shake for another ten minutes. When she stopped, her jaw relaxed, and the sides of her mouth dropped toward her chin.

She looked as if she had just woken from a deep sleep.

"Hold me," she said, "please hold me."

11

DEATH and destruction, MasterCharge and Visa. They threw MasterCharge out of school when he was six for peeing on the teacher's desk and Visa for scuzzing up the coatroom. At ten they carved each other's name on their shoulders, and at eleven they were kicked out of school again for putting a dent in a kid's head with a pipe, but first MasterCharge and then Visa kept coming back to school, when they felt like it, because there was no other place to go. The special schools were jammed and MasterCharge's mother kept all the dates with the social worker and he kept his mouth shut, only opening it when they wanted a response. Visa had no parents, no known address. At twelve they raped a teacher in the teachers' lounge, Visa first, with MasterCharge holding, and then the other way. They made her do some other things and when they were finished she was too frightened to say anything, so no one knew except the three of them, and they held it among themselves as if they were members of some very exclusive social club.

At fourteen school was, at best, a memory for both of them. MasterCharge was smart, had a high IQ, but couldn't keep his attention on anything. Visa was beyond dumb and did whatever MasterCharge told him to do, which included jumping from three-story buildings, slicing through the tip of his finger to see if he could find the bone, and swallowing a pound of stones. MasterCharge woke up each morning expecting to die, in some way, during the day. He had never killed anyone, but that was only by accident. Death was as easy to come by as the fur-covered rabbi's hats he swiped from the Hasidim. Visa didn't know what to think, had to be reminded to wake up, mugged people when he needed money, or thought he needed money, raped for pleasure or when told to by MasterCharge. MasterCharge dealt weed, and picked up pocket change by writing essays for some of his friends who still went to school. He based his fee on the grade they got, and changed styles to fit the person he wrote the essay for. But it was low-paying, sporadic work. He had been in court and had always gotten out, placed in the custody of psychiatrists who talked about latent sexual urges and repressed hostility focused at a father figure, and he had the jargon down so well that once when the psychiatrist was out of his office, MasterCharge held a session with one of his patients, explaining that "The doctor was called away very quickly to a conference on 'Anal-Compulsive Psychotics in the Prenatal Stage.'"

Kicked out of his mother's apartment, MasterCharge moved with Visa into a vacant burned-out apartment on the top floor of the Building. A redheaded Marxist moved in next door. MasterCharge knew he was a Marxist because after he had gotten Visa to rob his place and steal the TV and the stereo he tried to sell the books but the bookseller told him there wasn't much call for all "this Marxist crap." He had the redhead explain the theory to him and in a week learned more than he had in seven sporadic years of school. Class struggle and worker exploitation kept bouncing around in his head. At night he dreamed of animals and barber poles, one lecturing the other, but he didn't know which was doing which. The next time he robbed Red's apartment he wrote him a long note, rephrasing the theory of exploitation, and the following week Red moved out.

At seventeen, Visa was waiting, but he had no idea what he was waiting for. It wasn't that he enjoyed mugging that much, but it was something he could do, and do fairly well. He knew who he would have trouble with and who he wouldn't, and he rarely made mistakes. Mugging was a career, a profession, and the only thing he remembered from school was the counselor saying that you needed to go to school to have a profession. He liked the idea of having a profession. It conferred on him, in some mysterious way (of which he wasn't clear), status, social acceptance. The TV was always saying how important it was to have a profession. Visa was always writing away to those drive-a-tractor-trailer ads on TV, but usually slept through any appointments he made. He didn't want to go to New Jersey, which was where all those schools were. New Jersey frightened him. Going over water frightened him. Going outside of Brooklyn frightened him. He told MasterCharge that the "motherfuckin' TV comes flying through the air, sheeet" and MasterCharge knew what he meant: the TV signal came through the air. Visa had thought that the TV signal had come in through the place where you plugged in the TV, and when he learned that it didn't, that it flew through the air, was invisible, he became very frightened. MasterCharge could do nothing to calm him. Visa groaned at the thought of all those TV signals flying through the air, going through him.

The landlord came around to collect the rent, a little man in baggy pants and a white shirt with an outsize collar. He carried the money in a leather bag which he put inside a paper bag, and Visa thought about mugging him, knocking him to the ground and taking his money. It would have been so easy. The landlord knocks at their door. Master-Charge answers the door.

"You live here?" the landlord asked.

"Sure."

"How come you don't pay me rent? This is my Building."

"I don't like to pay rent. I don't like to pay nothing."

"You got to pay rent, otherwise I throw you out."

"Like motherfuckin' hell."

"You got a big apartment here, maybe you don't need something so big, I got a smaller apartment you could rent."

"I don't pay no motherfuckin' rent."

"You could pay a little."

"Why pay rent with no fuckin' services in the Building?"

"I come around again Monday. You could pay a little then."

He walked down the hall to knock on the next door. MasterCharge heard him knocking, yelling "rent," and the scurry of feet. The motherfucker didn't even have enough sense to yell something else, something that wouldn't frighten them from answering the door. Now if Master-

Charge and Visa walked around with him, he'd get his damn rent. Make sure of that. Hell.

He heard a knock on his door.

"Ain't got no rent," he yelled.

"Talk. You got time for talk?"

The landlord was standing at the door again, looking like a clown with his lunch. The look on his face had changed. He looked almost girlish, like a fag.

The landlord stepped, uninvited, into his apartment.

"Hey," MasterCharge said.

The landlord didn't seem to hear him. He walked around, looking at the rooms. He rubbed his finger along a door and watched the paint flake off.

"It's not so bad," he said. "I seen worse, believe me, much worse."

"What you want?"

"Just a talk."

"I told you, I ain't got no rent."

"How would you like to work off your rent?"

"A job?"

"It's so easy. Hardly any work."

"What."

"Can you set a fire?"

"I never set one before."

"There's not much to it."

"Where you want the fire set?"

"Here."

The crazy asshole.

"Burn my own apartment?"

"The whole Building. I'll show you. Just I can't be here when you do it."

"You crazy asshole. You want to burn your own Building?"

"I got to be away."

"You want to burn this Building?"

"Just the top floor. I need to fix the roof."

"What about all the people in the Building?"

"No one gets hurt."

"Motherfuckin' asshole."

"We'll talk about it next Monday."

But it was Visa, oddly enough, who convinced MasterCharge to do it. Except that before they set the fire, they decided to rape the paraplegic. And it was Hobson, diviner of insects, who caught them, in progress, causing them to climb out the window and clamber up the fire escape. MasterCharge made it up to the roof. Visa decided to take a shortcut and climbed into Steckler's apartment through the window Steckler kept open because of the heat of his equipment. The noise of his welding and the mask he wore hid Visa's entrance into Steckler's workroom and might have hid his exit if at that moment another fuse hadn't shorted in the basement, causing Steckler to put the mask down, and looking up, he found Visa by the front bumper of his Chevy Nova.

12

THE Building was convenient for Steckler because of the elevators. When they worked he was able to move his equipment: Lincoln arc welder, Chevy Nova frame, 454-cubic-inch V–Eight, various tires, chains, ports, headers, exhaust manifolds. When they didn't work he was able to keep his equipment in the apartment, bolting, welding, chaining, or otherwise locking the parts together. There was talk that Steckler lived in the Building but did not sleep there. Where he slept no one knew, any more than they knew if he slept.

No one had heard Steckler say anything other than "go away." (Perhaps the only words he knew.) He was about six feet tall, but looked smaller. He was wiry, his shoulders drooped, and he walked with a rolling gait, as if he had bricks in one of his pockets. He had flat hair, which fell forward, a small sharp nose, and eyes that looked like lug nuts on a car wheel.

Steckler had been kicked out of a karate school for breaking a student's nose. The master, an Okinawan, back-kicked Steckler through a plate-glass window, from a height of two stories, which gave him enough time to land on his hands and feet. He was subsequently kicked out of a kung fu school (Pak Mei) for pushing a student's two front teeth into the upper part of his mouth, out of a Japanese karate school (Gojo Ryu) for breaking an arm, out of a Tae Kwon Do school for a demonstration of rib breaking with a side kick, not a side-thrust kick (which some claimed), and shoved out of an aikido school for breaking three wrists, all of which were on the same person, one having been broken before and reset.

His black belts hung in a closet, looped, to hold welding rods. The Lincoln arc welder he kept in the kitchen, away from the refrigerator, and the cable for it ran down the hole for the steam riser into the basement near the boiler and then took a right turn for the junction box. The Nova was worked on in the living room, tires kept in one bedroom, transmission and suspension parts in another bedroom, and engine parts in the dining room.

Not particularly aggressive, except when angry, Steckler, though, could hardly be called mild mannered. He had a total lack of remorse, a feature he shared with Glasho, along with complete indifference, a feature not shared with Glasho though probably shared with Visa and MasterCharge. His dominant trait was impatience, a trait often con-fused with aggression but quite distinct, and indeed, if Steckler had taken the time to look at himself, which of course he would never do (since introspection, self-analysis, or any similar traits were as foreign to him as was remorse), he would probably view himself in a benign light, and see himself as almost passive. He could not understand any other view of himself, though he was completely indifferent to any view of himself, or of anything else.

The Chevy Nova was unpainted, that is, it had what was left of the original paint, and the spots where it had worn or chipped off Steckler had painted on Rustoleum. There were three bolts secured to the beams in the ceiling; a set of chains with a pulley was attached to the bolts and used to pull the engine from the Nova and then swing it over to where he could work on it, an old dining room table reinforced with angle irons. The car was up on blocks while he worked on the suspen-sion (rechromed, with added leaf springs, heavy-duty shocks, overload springs, and rubber mounts to prevent bottoming), one of the most crucial features of the car since he was intent on launching the vehicle through the window.

When Steckler worked with the arc welder on the Nova's frame, he removed his shirt so that the ultraviolet rays from the electric arc would give him a tan. However it gave him not so much a tan as a series of burns that ran in bands across his stomach and chest, like fading rivers

or sunsets. Once he had forgotten to use the mask while welding—
impatience again—and that night his eyes felt as if they were being
attacked by pins. He stood in the shower, the water streaming on his
face, screaming, the water masking the screams. After that he always
remembered the mask, flipping it forward over his eyes before he made
the connection with the arc.

Breaking bones and welding were his pastimes, and recently the
latter had supplanted the former. Heating metal, watching it slowly
change color from dull brown to dark red to glowing red and then to
orange and yellow, the latter a yellow-white, sparks flying from the
liquid like a penny sparkler, Steckler could feel some immense energy
being unloosened in the steel, could feel it flowing through the little
puddle of molten metal he was making, could feel one metal flowing
into the next, as if a transmigration of souls had taken place, and in
seeing this and feeling the mysterious dance of energy, felt that steel
was a river, frozen, and that he held in his hands an instrument to
unfreeze that river and make it flow.

The welding torch performed for him; it sang and danced and cut
arabesques and fused into one things that were separate. It was a baton
he tapped the metal with, flicking it gently up and down to maintain
the arc, almost crying when he had laid down a neat welding bead, one
in which the little puddles overlay one another perfectly. He could
control his fire, and focus its energy on one tiny spot that traveled the
length of the metal. The energy traveled not just through the metal but
through him, rushing into the earth to be picked up again by the
kitchen table and once again sent through the frame and then through
Steckler and beyond.

When the lights flickered, as they did frequently, Steckler waited
a moment, to see if the stunned electric lines could bear up under the
sudden demand for current.

People were a nuisance to Steckler. He put up with them because
he had no choice, but he kept his human contacts to a minimum and
put his trust in machinery: welding rigs, engines, transmissions, chain
and pulley hoists. When the landlord came to collect the rent, Steckler
slipped it under the door. Once, inadvertently, Steckler had left the
door open and the landlord came in, demanding his rent. Steckler
threw him against the wall, and was about to repeat the process when
he remembered that he had left his torch on. Momentarily distracted,

the landlord scurried out the door, rentless. Steckler, now with his torches, had already forgotten the incident.

What Steckler did that allowed him the time and the money to weld a Chevrolet Nova was unknown to anyone in the Building.

For Steckler, the machine displayed those attributes one might want in a human relationship. It did not talk back, as humans were wont to do. It was much more predictable, certainly more reliable, capable of progressive perfection, improved with age as various improvements were focused on it, had few requirements, was replaceable in whole or in parts according to one's dictates, and did exactly what you told it to do, provided you knew what to tell it. Steckler enjoyed the control he had over machines, and appreciated the fact that he didn't have to throw them against the wall. A machine when thrown against the wall would probably damage either the wall or the machine. A man, thrown against the wall, certainly would not damage the wall.

It would not be correct to say that Steckler loved company. Or tolerated it.

Visa, on the other hand, did not exist without someone close at hand. He felt the need for other rhythms to match and mix with his own. He wanted other ears to hear what he had to say, to convince him that he had something to say, and he wanted to hear the blather of other tongues, even if he didn't or couldn't understand what they said. Visa was a replica, a clone, a mirror image of some unknown force. When he mugged he could feel that person's presence through his arm, or fist, or the back of his hand.

Visa was happy to see the apartment occupied. But he was ignorant of Steckler. A welder, that's what he knew. Steckler glued pieces of metal together. Sometimes there was the sound of an engine running in his apartment.

Visa came in through the open window. He was startled to find a car in the living room. Other surprises awaited him. When Steckler noticed him, Visa was running his finger along the chrome bumper. The smoothness, and the grotesque shape of his finger due to the mirrored curvature of the bumper, fascinated him. By looking at himself in the bumper, and then feeling the bumper, Visa could feel the extension of himself in the car; he was a tiny figure painted in the landscape of the Chevy. Steckler caught him there, welded, in a manner of speaking, to the Nova. He would remove him as one removes rust;

he would scour the decay. Visa looked up, noticing Steckler. He wanted to say something, wanted to rob him, but something prevented him from doing either. Visa suddenly felt very tired. He lay down next to the bumper.

Steckler wheeled the engine hoist over to Visa and put the hook around his belt.

"What the fuck?"

He pulled on the chain, tightening the slack in the hook. The steel links rattled through the pulley, and Visa, like Peter Pan, slowly began to rise.

"Hey man, this a cheap belt!"

Steckler kept pulling the chain with such force and speed it seemed he was throwing it to the floor. Visa, rising further off the floor, felt obliged to beat his arms in the air, as if it was that motion that kept him off the ground.

"Sheeet."

The hoist had been raised to its fullest extension. Now Steckler began to wheel it across the room. Visa, hanging sideways from the hook, twisted around trying to hold on to the chain and disengage himself from the hook. His frantic wriggling motions shook the hoist, bouncing it back and forth on its wheels but not slowing its motion.

Reaching the end of the room, Steckler opened a window, the one without the fire escape. Visa, still dangling from his middle, watched him. He noticed it was the top half of the window that was opened.

Steckler started to tip him through the window.

"Hey man, I told you it was a cheap belt!!"

Steckler was several stories up. It was problematic as to whether a body thrown from his window would die. It was not problematic about that same body being hurt, the degree of hurt corresponding to the quality and amount of garbage that cushioned the body's fall. But these were theoretical considerations, and Visa, having been pushed through the window and dangling outside the building from a hook attached to a chain hoist, was in no mood for theory. The ground, to his squinting eyes, seemed miles away.

"The Charge did it," he yelled, "he done most of the fucking, I done just a little."

Steckler had no idea what he was talking about. Nor had he any interest.

"Charge's the one that got his rocks off. Me, hardly any."

Visa, lying on his side, hardly moving because of the single eyelet that held his belt, cursed his choice of belts and wished he had taken the time to put on his cartridge belt with its many hooks and eyelets. He looked up and saw the clouds moving, and he thought the Building was tipping over. It became a fact of mind that the Building *was* tipping over, and that either way he would fall. I'll die having fucked only four times, he thought, and the last one didn't count because she was only half a woman, she said that herself. Then he looked down at the sidewalk. It didn't seem that far away. In fact it seemed closer than it had before. Very quickly he decided that he didn't want to die.

"Hey man, what you want? Get me in."

Steckler had no plan to drop him, or not to drop him. Seeing Visa lying next to his car, the idea of hauling him up with the chain hoist just came to him. But the follow-up, what to do with him once he had him up and hanging out the window, hadn't. He waited for the thing to come to him, just as he had always waited for the right move to appear when he fought someone. There was no right move. Nothing came to him. Anything was right. He could drop the bastard or haul him in; either made no difference.

"Hey, motherfuck . . ."

Visa could not finish his sentences. Still over the sidewalk, he now had the idea that his belt was slowly loosening, that the eyelet was being pulled out of its hole, that the small piece of metal that held the bar of the belt was bending. Grabbing the chain, he might be able to haul himself in, if that bastard didn't let go of the chain altogether and drop him to the street. He wondered how he would hit, feet or head first, and if he would lose consciousness before he hit the ground. Steckler let the chain out one link, then two. Visa got angry, wanted to yell at him but couldn't, then started to cry. There were whole sentences he wanted to say, but when he began forming the words in his mouth they seemed to melt, his tongue seemed leaden and uncooperative. He lay perfectly still on the hook, afraid to shake it, but the wind was blowing him back and forth in arcs of increasing length. He didn't want to be here. He wanted to be somewhere else. He wanted this, whatever this was, to be over. He could feel his pants coming undone, the snaps loosening, the zipper pulling down. He grabbed ahold of the chain. Do it now, he thought, do something, do anything. He started to moan.

Steckler heard him singing. He didn't wonder about it. Whatever men did, no matter how strange, he took at face value. A thing existed at the surface for him. There was no underneath.

He looked at Visa, swinging on the chain, black knuckles white as he gripped the links of the chain.

"What's your name?" Steckler asked.

Visa said nothing. His mouth, his tongue, were glued together, were one. He eyed Steckler frantically. He now had visions of falling on his back, of his lungs, stomach, and heart exploding on the sidewalk, pieces of fleshy shrapnel flying everywhere. He will have to be sewn together.

"Can you weld?" Steckler asks.

13

WHEN the story was first told by Tyrone's grandmother that he had been born twice he never believed it because he never believed anything his grandmother said, which was strange because everything she said he later found out was true, even the story about his grandfather and the one-legged rabbit. But he heard the story again from his aunt, always sober, and then from his uncle, rarely sober, and when he mentioned it to his father, who wore his gray Postal Service cardigan and smoked a sweet nutlike tobacco, flecks of which got caught in his nose and were discharged like shotgun pellets in a violent storm of sneezing, his father stiffened, looked slightly outraged, and coughing, shifted the pipe to the other side of his mouth. It was a signal that he wished to talk no more about the subject, and he felt it strange since his father had not talked at all about it. His cousin taunted him about it and they settled it by fighting; they bloodied each other's face methodically, as if they were painting a canvas with their fists, and when they stopped fighting they had not settled the issue but settled their need to settle it.

"It was the dignity of the thing," his father said, looking off into the distance as if he had seen a stray special-delivery letter wedged in an inhospitable crack at the post office.

"The woman had great will . . . oh yes, such a will."

It was longer by a sentence than anything the man had spoken to him in the last month. His father rationed out his words to him as carefully as he drove, a process that occupied him about once a week. Last month his father's sentence had been, "Watch out for the screen door." This, after the door had banged in his face, and he had learned later that it was not the banging in the face that so preoccupied the man but the fact of the screws being loose on the bottom hinge of the screen door, the inference from which was that he should tighten the screws.

"Well, what the deal was, like I told you, about grandpa and the rabbit." His uncle rambled on and he stopped listening because his aunt would stop the man shortly and he had heard the story many times· over, though in the retelling it always changed. First the one-legged rabbit had raced dogs and always won, his grandfather betting on the rabbit, until the rabbit had been caught and eaten by a blind three-legged dog, a story that he had never believed, and his uncle, a large, mocha-colored man, thin at the top and bottom and immense in the middle, would change his story when he saw the look of disbelief on his face so that the one-legged rabbit only raced dogs with one leg missing or dogs with two legs tied together, or didn't race dogs at all but climbed trees and caught squirrels. His uncle watched his reaction, waiting to have the truth of the tale confirmed. The rabbit was on special exhibit at the Smithsonian; the rabbit toured with Barnum's circus; ten thousand, twenty thousand had been refused for the rabbit; it had been kidnapped, ransomed.

"You puttin' a chill on the boy, Dwayne, you stop that."

He bristled at the word, but his aunt called anyone under fifty "boy," not caring about the reaction. She was as immune to public opinion as his uncle was a slave to it. She spoke two words to his five, and after she had contradicted him, which was quite often, he would turn to her and say, "Is that so?" ready to take back what he had so passionately proclaimed just a moment before. His aunt was also long, but thin, and thin in all the places where you expected a person to be thin. They were childless; nevertheless, he was of the opinion that his aunt and uncle fucked often, much more often than his mother and father had and much more energetically.

"So tell him about the borning part."

She ignored him. He felt that in public his aunt rebuffed his uncle on purpose. In private she was all over him, running her large hands up and down his pants.

His father said nothing, never did when they came over, which never stopped them. They had a duty to perform, much like Meals on Wheels, only instead of food they delivered conversation, enough to last out the week, or to last until their next visit. It was expected that the conversation be stored in the pantry of their minds, to be used during the week, and he always felt that every time they came he would be given an examination on what they had said on their last visit, a sort of blue book exam of the sort he took at the University of Chicago.

"The boy has education. Don't need to be told about no twice birthin'."

His aunt looked at him and almost winked, as if they shared some sly conspirators' plot. Her large bony face, heavy with shadows, was rubbed constantly by her hands until the skin lay open in its grain. The room revolved around their conversation, he and his father an alien presence.

After they left, a residue of what they had spoken about settled in the room, and his father, uncomfortable with the stray vowels and consonants scattered about the room like so many dead letters, post office failures, moved from room to room in the small bungalow, re-arranging the framed pictures of his dead wife on the dresser, checking to see that his gray gabardine suit with blue piping was cleaned and pressed and hanging in the closet for next week's work, and disap-pointed that it was because that would mean less to fuss about, con-tinued to walk about the house, chased by the sentences his aunt and uncle had left.

Shortly after that his grandmother appeared, in what purported to be an occasion. She was over one hundred years old, or so it was said, and turtle hard: a small, stooped crustacean sort of person who walked with a cane that looked like the hindquarters of a deer. She stood in the center of the room opening and closing her mouth many times, like a fish, before she spoke, and when she did speak, she seemed to taste each word as it came out, snapping the corners of her mouth, and he could hear, but not see, the elastic of her spittle crackle against her lips and the insides of her mouth. She swallowed and reswallowed air, needing to taste the atmosphere before she could speak.

His cousin stood by her side, sneering, he thought. He steadied her when she walked, brought her chairs, drove her around to her ceremonies, and handled the sales of the Florida Water and the Dream Books. His father hated her in that dry, silent way of his. She was his mother's mother, and his mother's death, many years before, had found her deep in a trance that had lasted days. She could not be told about it while she was in the trance because if she were disturbed she would never wake up and never go to sleep, landing instead in some region between the two: a blank, wall-less, horizonless zone, a crack between the two worlds.

"About that birth," she said, and then waited, as if she expected him to finish the sentence, or had forgotten what she had said and let her mind slip fifty, seventy-five years back when she raised her own children and her husband, a Pullman porter (he had one leg, and so had a special affinity for the rabbit, saved it when his brother was going to shoot it, and so they had one more meatless meal), was off for days at a time on the Roanoke & Western, the Silver Streak, being sure to carry his shoeshine kit and the gray silver-polish paste that all porters had to buy out of their own salaries.

She gummed the words, new words, silent words, and he couldn't hear them, but he could hear the elastic snap of her spittle as it rattled about in her mouth, sounding like the crackle of cellophane. She looked around the room, seeing things that he could not see, and she was not frightened of the faces she saw in the shadows, the dead relatives, the murdered Indians, nor was she bothered by what they said.

He felt dizzy, wanted to sit down. His body was in the right place, and he could feel its steadiness, but his head, not his physical head, but another one, the one inside his physical head, was banging around as if it were trying to get out. He found a chair, slumped in it, looked up and saw his grandmother still standing, leaning on her deer's leg cane, looking over his head, opening and closing her mouth, and he could hear the story she told but not the words. It did not seem as if she were speaking, and yet the story became clear in his head, it unfolded as it happened.

His mother's water had broken in the drugstore across the street from the hospital, and she leaked on her dress and the plastic vinyl of the booth she was sitting in to sip an iced frappé. Rushed across to the hospital, oblivious to the stain in the skirt, the interns found she was already dilating two centimeters, so they wheeled her into the delivery room. It was here, while he was being born, while she was giving birth, that she had an epileptic fit, eyes widening, nostrils flaring (flared to begin with), mouth set in a grimace, and before she could bite off her tongue they had stuck a tongue depressor between her teeth, upon which she clamped with such force that they tried to shove several more in there. Her vast body shook uncontrollably, a hidden motor pumping to its own mysterious agenda, and while the baby was being born, her legs wildly thrashed about and then clamped tight around both him and the doctor, holding them prisoner in her great sweaty thighs. They were clamped together: the baby tiny and black, the doctor young and white. The doctor was both embarrassed by the embrace and worried for the life of the baby, who seemed to breathe slowly between the drenched thighs, pressed like freshly washed clothes between two laundry wringers, squeezed not to death but flattened in the manner of wrung clothes, narrowed, attenuated. The doctor struggled for forty-five minutes, turning slowly in his patient's vise, pulling the baby gently forward, sliding it along the inside of the mucus-coated thigh, his elbows braced to give himself space to breathe, and when he managed to free the baby (that was him! that lump, that bit of dark flotsam!) from his mother's coils, the epileptic fit subsided and the afterbirth followed, expunged, like foul air. The mother relaxed her legs, and the doctor was released from her hetaeraical embrace, staggering back to look at the baby who was in the arms of a nurse, who was barely in the arms of the nurse. She sat up, angry, feeling cheated, and then in a series of motions (all too quick, too blurred, hard to be precise about the accomplishment) she scooped up what came from her and replaced it, him too (the warmth, the safety of dark and wet, the quiet), and got up, holding everything in, the doctors, nurses, unbelieving, too startled to act, having never run across such a situation, she walked, swelling belly again, legs not waddling but pinned tight to themselves, as if she was holding a notebook between her thighs, walked out of the delivery room, took the elevator downstairs, into the lobby, past the admittance desk (no longer startling anybody since she was now relegated to the status of pregnant woman), with her husband trailing behind, confused, ashamed, thinking that the delivery had been such an embarrassment to all that it had been postponed, or else it was suggested that she "do it in some private place," and so he never dared walk ahead or even with her, never dared question her motives, not quite understanding what had happened, afraid to ask because of the will of the woman (she frightened him) and watched her walk down the street, walking as if she had to keep her feet within an eight-inch-wide strip, walked for at least eight or ten blocks (he would have remembered if he could, feeling the gentle bounce of her walk, the muffled sounds, blindly groping for the umbilical cord and not being able to breathe inside her pool, but then, not needing to) until she came to another hospital and walked in, seemed to know just where to go, on the elevator (her husband unable to follow, never able to follow) and got off at the second floor, walked into the delivery room, empty, followed by a young intern who was eager to achieve his first unassisted delivery, lay down on the table, feet in the stirrups, a quick succession of contractions, so quick they were continuous, and this time the doctor barely had time to position himself between her legs when he shot out, propelled into the hands of the doctor, who had expected to gently guide the baby out (wanting to reserve for her a gentleness between the legs she had never been able to consummate with any man) and so was shocked at finding him (still this bit of black flotsam) in his hands, suddenly, as if by sleight of hand, a magician's whim had placed him there, and this time she sat up, satisfied that the second birth had not cheated her, that the expulsion was conscious. The doctor placed the baby in her arms, leaving the umbilical cord (somehow reattached) in place, and he nuzzled her nipple, working the most advanced part of his body, his mouth.

He did not remember that, but his grandmother did.

"Whatever you do," she said, "you got to do twice."

She looked around the room with short, jerky movements, as if her head were part of an animated film.

"Maybe more than twice."

They were the first words she had spoken that he could remember. He remembered her telling the story, but he couldn't remember how she had told it, the words she had used. The only thing he was left with was the story. Now her words seemed to snap and crackle, possessed of a burnished quality, as if they had been polished by her long dead Pullman porter husband.

She tapped her deer's leg cane on the floor three times, listening to the wood sound.

"There's more to the story, but you ain't ready to hear it yet. You too dumb."

She stood gaping at him, opening and closing her mouth.

"You gonna be in bricks," she said, "lots of bricks."

She talked to many people, the living and the dead. Among the latter were Catholic saints and African queens.

"Sit down," he said. "Sit down, let me bring you some tea."

He didn't know why he had said that, but then he did. He wanted her to stop talking. He wanted her to shut up.

She sat in the chair he brought, and his cousin looked around for another chair, expecting him to offer one, which he didn't. His cousin went into the next room and dragged a chair in while he and his grandmother had tea. As soon as the cousin had dragged the chair in, he had to leave the room and find himself a teacup.

She drank tea by hiding her teeth, curling her lips over them, and though she was a hundred years old (he thought), perhaps only eighty, perhaps one hundred twenty, she had all her teeth (he thought) or perhaps had none of them and had in their place a cleverly designed set of false teeth, made none too perfect to replicate what aged teeth would look like.

His cousin sat in a chair next to her, snarling at him, picking his nose and flicking the balled-up mucus on the floor.

"Whatever you think you know," she said, "you don't. Same thing with the snotnose here."

His cousin jerked his head around.

"Get yourself some manners, boy."

He stiffened, and watched his cousin climb up the chair, or try to, his back rising up the wooden back of the chair.

"You got to find the light," she said. "Every evening when I go to bed, I gets up and looks for the light. I been looking everywhere, since I was a child, eight or nine, must be 'bout hundred years now. Go to sleep and get up, search for the light every night, hundred years of being up all night and looking."

The light in the room was beginning to fade, either from the sun or the New Jersey pollution, and his grandmother, a red-brown, began to glow in the light. Her gray hair was almost yellow, or white.

And then she caught fire. He saw the small flames, like tiny snakes, that flickered outward from the circumference of her hair. He could smell the burning hair, see the tiny melting ends, hear the crackled hush as the fingernail-sized flames engulfed her head. He got up. Behind his grandmother's head the sunlight, or what there was that the New Jersey sky allowed to filter through, framed her flaming head in an afterglow. He could duplicate the sound of her burning hair in his throat by gathering saliva at the base of his tongue and blowing air around it. The flames, growing no higher on her head and yet consuming her hair with a vicious regularity, cupped her skull like a cap, a halo of heat. She sat stiff and upright, her eyes widened, and her mouth opened and shut, still like a fish, but a burning fish, a glowing fish, phosphorescent from the depths. He wanted to douse the flames, throw tea or some other liquid on her head, but he hesitated, stung by some odd sense of decorum which mitigated his fear of her burning head. As soon as her head had started to burn, his cousin had left the room. And he, no longer sitting but standing, watched her burn.

He tried to speak but couldn't. Her gray hair melted, burned, the huge ball that was the mat of her hair kept getting smaller. He watched her skin glow, turn red, perspiration form on her upper lip. The flames now completely covered her head. She got up from her chair.

"Ah," she said. "Ah . . . ah."

She stamped her deer's leg cane on the floor, demanding an explanation from the floor about her burning head.

"Ah," she said again, and this time the flame seemed to have consumed her hair, and began eating away at the loose folds of skin that enveloped her skull. She opened and closed her mouth again, her eyes bulging, and small charred scars appeared on her forehead and in front of her ears.

"Goddamn," he said.

He threw lukewarm tea on her but failed to douse the flames. He looked for a coat, blanket, shawl to wrap around her head, and finding none, wrapped her in his arms, burying her burning head in his chest, the heat melting the plastic buttons on his shirt before he could smother the flames.

He released her, and she looked up at him, bald, thoughtful, her head a mass of furrows, pink and red showing through, something white and clear oozing out from the wounds.

"Ah," she said, as if she had just been released from bondage, the skin hanging in flaps from her skull and the sides of her face, which itself looked startled, almost young, the intense heat having seared away thirty, forty, fifty years, melting creases and folds and furrows and exposing the skull underneath, the muscles, the tendons, the jawbone.

He held her, but she pushed him away, swaying, remembering her husband who had died in his sleep in an empty upper, traveling from

Chattanooga to Tallahassee, his silver-polish kit at the ready, and having to sign for his coffin and being presented not only with the silver-polish kit (wrapped in a small chamois ditty bag) but also a silver Waltham Railroad watch, a sewing kit, an unopened letter she had written to him (complaining about their daughter), and a box of condoms.

She took one step, and remembered again her daughter, his mother. She looked up at him, surprised, smiled, and he saw her cry for the first time in her life. Before he could reach her, she fell. After the funeral, he moved to Brooklyn, into the Building, into an apartment that had thirty-seven radiators, especially put there by Haber for his sister who suffered under the illusion that tiny men were making her live at the North Pole.

14

TUBBO Rivera was a dope dealer who moved into the Building. His motto was: If you can sniff it, smoke it, jab it, swallow it, or stuff it, I sell it. Before he got into dope he got onto welfare, all four hundred pounds of him. His caseworker suggested that he have an operation, at city expense ($40,000), where part of his intestine was stapled off so that his body wouldn't be able to digest all the food he ate. He did, and it didn't, and Tubbo slimmed down nicely, keeping his name and several hundred pounds of his old weight. Now that he could walk instead of waddle, the caseworker suggested he find a job. He stole steaks from supermarkets, but the aggravation threatened the staples in his intestine, and he decided to get into a more rewarding line of work. He fenced four-cylinder German and Japanese cars but gave it up and turned to dope. He found the small amounts of dope and the large amounts of money particularly appealing, especially for people like himself, with an ethnic background. "Hey, brother Dope don't care where you come from," he'd say.

Tubbo came up the hard way, working for a dope dealer on the Lower East Side, first as a spotter, someone who looked out for the police, and later as a steerer, a street shill for his dealer's brand of dope. But Tubbo was ambitious, despite his having been on welfare and gotten an Ivy League M.B.A. He forgot to load his boss's nine-millimeter automatic, and during a raid by a rival drug dealer the ammunitionless gun proved little help against some heavies with sawed-off shotguns. Tubbo took over his dealership. He hired his crew, made his connection (his supplier was a man who owned a string of community newspapers), and operated out of an abandoned building on the Lower East Side, which he reinforced with steel plate, state-of-the-art sensing devices (used on jungle trails in Vietnam), and laid up a supply of weapons. Tubbo brought innovation to the profession. The girls he hired to cut the raw stuff into nickel bags were notorious for the amount of heroin they stole while performing this valuable function. They stuffed the powder into bras, handbags, shoes, whatever they could. But they were professionals, and Tubbo liked dealing with professionals. So he increased their wages, high to begin with, and made them perform in the nude. Stripped, there were few cracks or crevices they could jam the clandestine powder into, and those few that were available were unsuitable for obvious reasons.

He had two cars: one a beat-up ten-year-old Chevrolet, a rust bucket that blended into the decay of the neighborhood, and the other, for trips outside the neighborhood, a 4-4-2 Olds coupe with a Hurst shift, tricked-up suspension, and a quick-change rear end. The Olds was so fast he frequently couldn't remember where he was going. But at speeds over one hundred ten, the rear end had a tendency to lift. One rainy afternoon on the Henry Hudson Parkway, going one hundred twenty, absorbed in Mozart's *Requiem* which came booming out over his one-hundred-thirty-watt car stereo system, the rear end lifted, and the sudden loss of weight caused the big Olds to spin, flip the guard rail, and land, wheels first, on a sailboat that was anchored in the boat basin at Seventy-ninth Street. Boat and car both sank, the former first, and while Tubbo was settling into the frigid waters of the Hudson River he wondered about the meaning of his life, the contribution he made as a dope dealer, and world hunger. What was he doing to solve world hunger? He pondered this as the water rose to his neck, chin, and then swirled about his nose. With tremendous effort he pushed open the car door, and popped to the surface of the river, swimming, despite his stapled intestine, the few strokes to the shore.

Dripping wet, beyond what the rain called for, he stalked the Upper West Side, looking at the lush fruit and vegetable stands jammed with rainbows of produce. He gazed through the window of Zabar's, his mouth watering at the sight of beluga caviar, Schimmelkase, and Finn Crisp crackers. He thought about that rich slurry of protein bypassing much of his intestines, and its ultimate destination, the great watery gulch that he had just been dipped into. He decided there was too much food in Manhattan, that it would cause too much pressure on his staples, that there was nothing he could do about world hunger, and that he would sell dope in a more congenial neighborhood. He moved to Brooklyn.

He approached Tyrone and offered him a job. "Dope," he said, "is an equal opportunity employer. I even toss in a car, a flashy Lincoln with an ax stuck in the roof and some minor scuffs on the grill." Tyrone turned him down. "Hey, I understand," Tubbo said, understandingly. "No hard feelings, it's okay with me. Plenty of young studs in this neighborhood anxious to make good bread. You know?"

Tubbo's speciality was suburban junkies, kids whose fathers owned garment factories, were divorce lawyers or practiced liability law, were cardiologists, headed city agencies, owned chains of stores that sold jogging shoes or computers. They arrived nervous, flustered, uneasy in Brooklyn, in large black Oldsmobile Ninety-eights or Buick Rivieras, and they jockeyed for parking space on the block and the favored spot at Tubbo's front door with Wall Street lawyers, new venture capitalists, bond traders, fashion designers, and hotshot procurers, all of whom would not trust a go-between but did trust Tubbo to deliver to them the latest drug of choice, preferably something they could sniff or swallow or smoke (they left mainlining to the kids). They were professionals who had learned long ago not to trust anyone, and so for the drugs they kept for parties and those they used for themselves they were willing to make a foray into Brooklyn, into a neighborhood that was barely fashionable, a neighborhood where the number of muggers equaled the number of muggees. They arrived with guns and bodyguards, the kids with barely enough sense to make it back to where they came from.

Tubbo gave honest weight and honest adulteration with his dope, and complained about "those greedy fucks from Bensonhurst who adulterated the hell out of everything or else forgot to, which was worse," and in general gave dope dealers a bad name.

Tubbo was a true professional. He worked long and hard to build up his clientele, was concerned about his product, and contributed to several Hispanic-American organizations. He was a pillar, if that is the word, of his community, regardless of the fact that his was a highly mobile community with a highly underdeveloped sense of delayed gratification. Loyalty was not one of its strong points, so the fact that Tubbo was able to develop a loyalty of sorts from his customers and also suggest to them that whatever they did to get the money to buy his product they not do in his immediate neighborhood was testimony to his persuasiveness. On the other hand he had little trouble enforcing the latter part of this arrangement because most of his clientele came from outside Brooklyn and had no desire to stay in the borough any longer than they had to.

Success, however, did have its drawbacks. Competition was one of them. Out of necessity Tubbo became a weapons expert: weapons that were machines and weapons that were tools. He used the latter, in a series of grisly butcherings, to drive home the point to rival dope dealers. Then he relaxed his standards somewhat and expanded his clientele to take in local junkies, and one night was invaded by a local gang high on amphetamines who ignored his reinforced door and swung in on ropes through his windows, guns blazing, forcing Tubbo behind a couch where his M–16 jammed on him, and they carted off the half-dead overweight dope dealer to the basement and left his bottom half to freeze in the flooded cellar. As soon as they heard that Tubbo was half a Popsicle, the neighborhood junkies became frantic. They broke into the local brownstones and stole expensive pasta machines, sixteen- and thirty-two-bit microcomputers, Nikons, Betamaxes, tiny TVs, Atala and Peugeot ten-speed bicycles, gold jewelry, Swiss watches, money, anything easily pawned. With the junkies desperate, the brownstoners went crazy. They took karate courses, bought .357 Magnums, called the police at odd hours, banded together to form block patrols, and bought large, nervous dogs of unstable temperament and trained them to bite anyone not wearing a suit and tie.

A truce of sorts was established when a new dope dealer moved into the neighborhood and met with the brownstoners and promised to enforce Tubbo's old rules.

Tubbo's car, the Lincoln with the ax in the roof, was left on the block for months, collecting tickets, cats, garbage, its windows progressively smashed, tires and engine parts disappearing until the only thing left was a frame and body that sat on wire-framed milk cartons, the doors, hood, trunk, open to the universe. Neighborhood people touched Tubbo's car for luck knowing that its owner was a frozen TV dinner in the basement of the Building.

15

S TERN paints with urgency because he knows the Building is doomed. It has a smell about it, something damp and mixed with urine, and he knows that smell, just as he knows the smell of flaking plaster and gritty broken marble, frayed electric lines, puttyless windows that rattle in the wind, and doors that never quite close. The Building flows through his brush and onto the canvas, onto the madonna series that he is trying to finish, the series of big rawboned women, nudely sprawled, each attending to some hidden task. In his paintings the object of their work is never clear, but their bodies, their long limbs and thick elbows, their red-veined noses, football-shaped breasts, and ham-hock thighs, are all quite solid.

The intermittent heat, the sporadic water, the electric blackouts are not hindrances to Stern but minor inconveniences, a small price to pay for the vividness of the Building and his apartment. If he needs heat he will burn wood in a small Norwegian stove. Water he will lug up from the street. Stern revels in the decay of the Building. He loves the abandoned buildings next to his, the empty lots once full of apartments, the weeds and wild trees that grow in these lots. It is this decay, this vacant space, that finds its way into his paintings: huge open areas of flesh indicate what once was—the sagging breasts that once were firm, the varicose veins, the shiny, cracked, callus-infested feet, the tiny spiderweb of capillary veins that cover the cheeks. He can paint them nowhere else. The flaccid bodies of his models melt in formal studios. But here they are exalted, here their very looseness seems to set his mind free, seems to excite his brush. Magentas and ambers agitate for space on his canvas. Reds and greens butt up against yellows; the borderline between them rises, like the swell in a swirling sea. Browns, blacks, and grays hammer the paintings together.

It is a good neighborhood for madonnas. He can find them in the bodegas and the Haitian fruit stands, in sleeveless blouses, pushing a baby carriage, teetering on high-heeled shoes, old-young faces heavy with an astonished blankness and shaved eyebrows replaced by pencil-thin stripes carefully arched over the eyes. He can find them in the candy stores, whose insides are caged in by thick plastic that covers all the merchandise and small armorlike doors where money for the candy and dope is passed through. He can find them in the Building, though often they are reluctant to pose in the nude, having, Stern thought, little appreciation for the rigors of art.

For the *Madonna of Broken Plaster* he found a Puerto Rican mother with three children who was desperate for money. She refused to pose in the nude, but she was willing to expose every part of her body. Stern took her in pieces: head, neck, breast. She would only expose one breast at a time, bra strap undone, and each breast in its turn, an orange effulgent globe, seemed to stare at Stern from the clothes that swaddled it. It bobbed and dipped and jiggled impatiently, as if reluctant to be disturbed, uneasy in the air, and he continued to paint her in parts, including her vulva. Of the latter he got only the tiniest glimpse. Pants and panties were slipped down only to where the legs joined the hips, and Stern was presented with a vertical band of flesh punctuated by a shield-shaped vulva, maple-colored hair, a fingernail of labia exposed. Ultimately she exposed every part of her body, front to back, a process of changing and unchanging that required a precise orchestration of zippers and hooks and snaps and buttons, coordinated to an astonishing degree. She was most embarrassed at showing her feet bare, especially the bottoms, and Stern feeds off this embarrassment, painting the rest of her body in her feet, as if breasts, arms, shoulders, hips had all collapsed there. He is amazed at her toes, at the way the bones in the feet separate, the angularity of the ankles, and he forces her to expose her feet longer than she would wish. She squirms while he paints. He is fascinated by the lines in her soles, the thick white callused skin, and its meeting point with the light-brown skin of her foot. It is the cobalt blues, the titanium whites, the ochres that celebrate these lines and whorls and cracks, and the *Madonna of Broken Plaster* becomes the gaps and cracks in her feet. Painted underneath, she becomes a crucifixion of decay. Stern reproduces her as a plaster-of-paris madonna, repeats it many times over the canvas, and the plaster-of-paris madonna also becomes the broken-plaster madonna, she who oversees cracks in apartment walls, who watches roaches crawl out of cracks, the madonna of smooth surfaces, of things that work, of clean floors and botanicals that heal, lighter than the bleeding cross, more merciful than the wrath of God, the madonna of meat on the table, warm clothes, and jobs. "May your blessed presence grace this home and all those in it."

It is this giantess that Stern has come to paint, and after many false starts she begins to take shape. She is tall and broad, wide, cylindrical, a totem. She is Christian, Indian, Buddhist. She is wise in her way, which is the way of the madonna, the mother, and the earth springs from between her legs. She is the mother egg. She becomes immense, wears a sombrero, has legs the size of garbage cans, squashes evil between her thumb and forefinger, strides the earth in boots as big as boats, punishes those who prey on the poor. She is touched by the hand of God; the painting becomes a vertical Sistine Chapel, awash in blues and grays and whites that swirl about in a muscular chorus. She smashes capitalists, gives food to peasants, restores the land stolen by giant corporations, and Stern shows this with a flair for the dramatic, disavows subtleties.

But the Puerto Rican woman, in bits and pieces, will not do as the *Madonna of Heat and Hot Water*. For that he finds a black woman, tall, a model and poet, Butterfly McQueen's daughter out of Clark Gable, bitter as nails, "who is only doing this for the money." She speaks of herself in the third person, and Stern feels that he will never become one of the elect who are allowed to speak to her in the first person. He does not take her bitterness personally, and she has no intention of giving him that luxury. Upon entering his apartment she immediately strips, thrusting her pubis forward, as if to batter him with it. She has large breasts for a woman of her thinness, and narrow hips. She poses as she pleases, and Stern is afraid to ask her to adopt certain positions, a feeling made all the more complicated by the fact that he does not know what pose he wishes her to adopt. He refuses to let her see the painting, feeling that her criticism would unnerve him, take away a prop he needs for this madonna. But then, he has no indication that she wishes to criticize the painting or even look at it. Most of her poses have to do with her gazing off in the distance, dreaming. She puts one leg up on his chair, wearing shoes that make her look naked instead of nude. Her elbow rests on her knee, pressing one breast toward the other, and Stern wonders who has kissed those breasts, who has made love to those chocolate cherries. "You living in a dump," she says. It is the third sentence she has spoken. Stern trots out the browns and vermilions and ochres. There are stretch lines on her breasts and around her stomach. He is afraid to ask her if she has any children.

The madonna does not go well. This woman bathes in hot water, scads of it, has Niagaras of steaming, scalding liquid she can order up at the touch of a finger, and Stern resents her for this, resents her warm, composed presence and the dreamy look in her eyes—a bitter, dreamy look. The wildness presses in on him. He is bored, angry, given to technical niceties in the painting that look out of place. But nothing looks in place because there is no place. The *Madonna of Heat and Hot Water* is a shivering presence, a banger of pipes, a caller of plumbers, a lighter of stoves, a bundler of children. She knows how to repair furnaces, call for oil, turn on the pilot light; she is the fire of the planet, the warmth of the womb, the savior of children. She gives suck to the starving, there is fire in her loins. She is elemental. If the landlord won't do it, she will. The painting changes. She becomes the *Madonna of Betrayal,* the bitch goddess of despair, and in that a connection is made. This black bitch knows only too well how to turn aside the good intention, how to promise without delivering, how to put up a temporary front, and Stern can feel betrayal oozing from her pores. He puts her in a cross-legged stance, seated in the painting, though she refuses to adopt that pose for him, and this betrayal only excites his brush; it shakes to paint. This madonna will not just break hearts, she will burn them, fry them, scorch and sizzle them, grind them into powder, and drown them. She doesn't laugh, she cackles, she crows, she caws, she has claws for feet and red-veined eyes that look like spiderwebs across the whites of her eyeballs. She spits out broken promises. This madonna is black and yet pink, brown and yet light blue; she is soft in her hardness, and it is in this softness that betrayal finds its nest, in these ruined edges, in these flawed borders. Stern paints her in this glory, shouting at her excess, and the woman shows puzzlement at his cackle. He paints laughing, pushing her into poses that she refuses to adopt, until she finally stands looking at him, hands by her sides, hips thrust forward as if they were disjointed.

For the *Madonna of Ruined Dreams* Stern finds an Italian whore, a Jew whom he grows to hate (Can only Jews really hate Jews? he thinks), an Iranian grandmother whom he finds in a nudist colony in Piscatawny, Pennsylvania, and a Druse from Pakistan. All are of middle height, with similar features, square lips, sharp noses, black hair, skin ranging from olive to pale yellow. Stern begins to confuse them and berates the Iranian grandmother for something the Druse told him, complains to the Italian whore that she isn't Jewish enough, and the painting begins to pattern itself after the Stations of the Cross, though in each instance there is a flaw, a purposeful mistake, and Stern grows to hate the women even though this flaw is part of the painting, part of the ruin. Stern feels that the painting is decaying in front of him, that if he doesn't hurry up and finish, it will disintegrate. He believes the women are quickly growing old and soft, hanging folds of flesh appear on their bodies daily. The ruined dream becomes bitter, he begins to cry, and the painting seems to disappear. The Iranian grandmother chucks him under the chin and tells him not to worry, the whore tries to make love to him, the Druse tells his fortune (which he does not want to hear), and the Jew doesn't complain, which bothers him. The painting lacks focus, the *Madonna of Ruined Dreams* becomes her own prophesy, and the thing turns in on itself. Stern feels that a more successful painting would have been a failure, that this failure is his success. And yet hardly anything is clear in the painting; it is a swirl of colors and shapes, signifying nothing, a collapsed presence. The other madonnas have form, religiosity, vibrate with a wretched spirituality.

The next madonna, the one he has high hopes for, is the *Madonna of Sex.*

He had approached a big blond woman, who subsequently fell from the roof. There were madonnas of every kind in his painting, but he had no blonds, and he knew that the painting needed one, needed a blond's cowlike presence. She was languid and enticing in her movements, and Stern thought she was easy pickings. She talked as if she had something else on her mind, that she would do anything if it wasn't too much trouble, and yet when he tried to exploit the latter he was put off by her line of conversation, as if gaps, whole minutes of talking had been left out, and Stern sometimes wondered if he had fallen asleep on his feet and missed something. She kept asking about his pregnant wife, "Now two years pregnant," she said, "and what about the child who moans in the night?" He had no idea what she was talking about, but there was something about the way she talked and the way she put a smile behind every sentence and the slow way she let her tongue roam around the inside of her mouth after she finished talking that led Stern to believe she would pose, and that posing in the nude was nothing to her, that she had none of the hang-ups about her body "that all those Mediterranean types have." She explained to him that she was in her body but not of it, that she inhabited it much as they did this Building. My body is merely a front for what I am, she said, and not a very good front at that. "If all you want is my nipples and my hair," she said, "I can send you a picture." Stern emphasized that that was *not* what he wanted. "If all you want is something to jack-off to . . ." He repeated what he had said. "It costs money," she said. "I am very expensive. You don't get me for cheap." Stern said he could pay, not a lot though. She seemed to lose interest in the conversation.

He met her again in the hallway. Steckler was welding and the lights were flickering, as if brown moths were beating their wings around the light bulbs. "Come in for tea," she said. She was standing by the door wearing three bandannas in her hair: red, purple, and brown. She had on a white blouse and a purple print skirt, a brown cotton sweater, a red vest brocaded with gold fleurs-de-lis, high-heeled skintight boots made from the body of some long, elegant lizard, and twenty silver bracelets that dangled from one arm. She stood by her door, one hand on the doorknob, as if about to enter. But she made no motion to go in. She was waiting for Stern to say something. He already had, and once again thought he had fallen asleep and had missed something. "What do you think?" she asked. "About what?" She ignored him. It was, in her opinion, not a question one answered but rather a question one asked, and the answering was in the asking. "Just what is it," she said thoughtfully, "what is it you artists want?" Stern didn't know. He had never been asked the question before, and was afraid to ask himself, afraid that he might find an answer. "Bodies," he said, "we look for warm bodies, breathing bodies, nude, that will hold uncomfortable poses for hours." He noticed how heavily made up her eyes were, as if she had used a Magic Marker to deepen the outlines. "I thought so," she said, somewhat softly, "I thought we were being used in some way. Do artists fuck their models?" "Sometimes." "Would you want to fuck me?" "I want to paint you." "That will cost you extra."

He found a waitress from Staten Island, blond, older than he wanted, but he painted a younger face in place of the coffee and dough-nut lines in her cheeks. He made her pose as if she were reaching for something, her body twisted around, and when her trapezoidal muscles didn't pull her large breasts tight enough to suit the needs of the painting, he made her stand on a pipe over a tub of ice water and, turning her body around, hold onto another pipe to keep from falling. The room was cold the day he painted, and the waitress complained, and all the while Stern painted, carefully reproducing the moles on her thighs and the fist-size knobs of bone that protruded from her pelvis, he thought of the blond downstairs. "He's got shingles," the waitress said. "My horse on Staten Island has shingl—" "Shut up. I don't give a fuck about your horse on Staten Island. Shut up." "What kind of a painter are you anyway?" "Shut up." For Stern, painting was an obligation, forced on him for the same reason and in the same fashion as rocking back on their heels is forced upon penguins. "Why aren't you pregnant?" Stern asks. "I was," she said, "once. Do you want to hear about the child?" "No." The best news, Stern thought, is no news at all. He didn't want to talk. He didn't want to explain the array of madonnas, why they were grouped this way instead of that, whether they were examining each other or merely smiling through each other's legs, and if the painting, which by now covered several walls and was too large to be shown in any gallery, and probably any museum (and would be unlikely to be shown there anyway since no one had ever heard of Stern and he had never heard of anyone, priding himself on his ignorance, like the high-school dropouts he paid to help him lug his paints upstairs), all these explanations merely served to give some reason for the painting, some reason to the painting, when none in fact was needed, wanted, or desired. Indeed, reason was the enemy of the painting. If he had stopped to think about the why of the thing, it would cease to be. The painting, he knew, was not merely the enemy of the outside world but a devil to the one he was in. Cuzz, he was convinced, was burning the Building so he could destroy Stern's painting. He had made the mistake of showing Cuzz the painting, and had detected a critical comment, something muttered under the breath, some curse that escaped Stern's ears but still floated about the room, coating the room and his painting with its shellacky presence.

He met the blond downstairs once more, by the broken elevator. "I have to go to the doctor," she said. He said he was sorry. "Don't be," she said. "Men are never sorry. That's why they're men." He asked her if she had a good doctor. "I wouldn't go if I didn't," she said. "A woman, she has no degree, she knows more about the body than doctors." Stern said he didn't think that was wise. "What's wise, anyway? You? A painter? Let's see your wise. Show me your big wise.

Otherwise." He felt as if he had been accused of something, as if gnomes should ring bells warning people away as he walked down the sidewalk. She stood by the elevator, either just having ridden it or waiting for it to come, both of which were impossible since the elevator had been broken for many years. "I'm pregnant," she said, "I'm fucking pregnant, that's all." She said it as if she had a flu virus. "Well," Stern said, "at least I'm not the father." She leaned against the wall, pressing the elevator button, which still lit, for about thirty seconds, when pressed, and was often the only light in the hallway. She was wearing a one-piece white jumpsuit with a small gold pin in the lapel. Attached to the pin was a tiny chain, which was pinned to a different spot on the jumpsuit so that the chain formed a half circle under her nipple. The pin said "Magna Cum Laude." She noticed Stern reading the pin.

He had asked the waitress from Staten Island to hold a dead chicken over her head. She stood on two piles of bricks in a tub of cold water. The blood from the chicken ran down her arm, wriggled through the hairs in her armpit, continued down over her naked breast, riding the roller coaster of her nipple, and then descended down her belly, following the groove made where her leg joined her hip, rushed toward her pubic hair, and then dripped into the tub, so that it looked as if she, shivering and goosebumped from the cold, was peeing blood. As Stern turned away from her to get another tube of paint, he faced the window, and saw the blond from down below flying by, peering in, and Stern, certainly not expecting to see her falling by his window, registered mild amazement rather than surprise, and it seemed to him as if she was trying to say something to him as she flew by. "What," said the waitress when he had turned around again, not believing what he had seen, "was that?"

"Nothing," he said, "less than nothing," and worked with a fury that surprised him. The waitress hadn't been eating well and was beginning to look a little gaunt. "I can't stand food anymore," she said. "I'm around this swill all day, the smell of vinegar and mashed potatoes, I feel like vomiting when I think of food. They don't pay me to eat it, just to serve it." "Shut up," Stern said. "I'm too fat anyway," she said, ignoring him. "It wouldn't hurt to lose some bulges. Jesus, it's cold in here." Now he could hear the sirens and the commotion down below. "I like heavier women," Stern said. "If you don't eat I'll get someone else. You look like hell." There were several sets of sirens: fire and police, then ambulance. None of them were applicable to his painting. "I want you to twist more," Stern said, "I need the muscle that runs across your ribs." "I'm twisted as far as I can," she said. "Anyway, you don't pay me enough to twist more. I'm no damn acrobat." "Twist more or I won't pay you at all," he said, "and shut up." Footsteps on the stairways, running through the halls, knocks on doors, including his own. He was running out of Cobalt Blue. Damn! "Open the door! I know you're in there!" Stern finds another tube of Cobalt Blue, stiff with age. His door is rattled. "Open up, police." He mixes the Cobalt Blue with Magenta, working the colors with his thumb. "Open up, now!" The tinned-up door rattles. Someone is kicking it. "Why don't you answer the door?" the waitress says. "I told you to shut up," he says.

Though he had told her he would only use her once in the painting, he had in fact used her several times: looking at herself, looking into herself, looking beyond herself. She has taken up more room in the painting than he had intended, and it extends to more than three walls so that he must fold up one end of it, like a Japanese book, keeping the folded end in the closet while he sews more sections of canvas onto more ends. But he is tired of her gauntness, her stringy muscles, the goosebumps on her flesh, the way her nipples tighten in the cold, the red bumps on her knees, the thinness of her legs and the thickness of her hips, the fact that her nose is red and always runs. He does not like women who have horses. There is something of themselves they have given to the horse, and it is that much less they have to give to his painting. He has talked to the flying blond's daughter, Lisa, and she agrees to pose. She comes up in a frayed blue bathrobe, says very little, and is willing to assume whatever pose Stern desires. Her silence bothers him. She never mentions her dead mother. She undresses as if she were dressing, as if in the casual display of her body, somehow, she were wearing clothes. She has a small vulva, rich with hair, and her breasts, though small, are quite firm and weighted down with large nipples. She finds nothing that Stern does strange, is indifferent to the painting and to her place in it, barely acknowledges his presence. She moves her long legs and arms with quiet composure, with a certainty that suggests that she, more than Stern, knows which pose to adopt for the painting, though she has never seen it. Her eyes seem foreign to her face, and Stern cannot accept them. He paints her long body, follows faithfully her curves and bumps, the elegant length of her neck and chin, the sort of tennis ball shape of her cheeks, the dip in her nose, but when he comes to her eyes he must borrow. This he does from the dead woman. He hardly remembers what her eyes looked like, but his hand and brush remember because they paint what he has forgotten. Painting her, Stern feels like a father, and Lisa, the girl, sensing this, laughs at him, ringing a tiny gold bell she wears around her neck. She refuses to remove this. The madonna painting, recently peopled with older blonds, now becomes younger, and the circle of women who dance around the center (though in reality there is no center) arm in arm are taking the painting from him, making it become something else. What started out as a heavy, ponderous thing, huge women with babes suckling at breasts, is now full of long-limbed lusting women who have banished children and babies to another portion of the painting, will have no commerce with those heavy curved mothers who preceded them. And all this because of Lisa, Stern thinks. Without knowing, she has changed the painting.

He has no idea where the painting is going, and yet his hand is so sure of the direction that never for a moment does it hesitate to paint, and Stern feels as if he is being dragged along by the hand, chained to his brush, and that somehow he is an innocent bystander to the myth-ridden thing he sees unfolding before his eyes. Women flying, women fornicating with bats and donkeys. He feels as if he has painted all this before, as if the outlines of the painting are there on the canvas. Lisa smiles at him. He lusts after her, is quickly ashamed. Even in her smile he can detect her indifference, and this excites him. He will not consummate it. Human beings (perhaps) couple with creatures in such a way that each merges with the other, becomes confused with the other. Hands devour feet. High plains with long veldts appear, hemmed in by steep bluffs. Herds of long-haired ungulates, and caves with signs, paintings. Stern is a prisoner of the painting, and each day Lisa sets new poses for him, as if the outline for the piece were known to her. There is no longer any creative effort, no longer any struggle to determine the shape of this thing. It flows from Stern with certainty, with Moses-like rigidity. He is merely the chief rabbi officiating at the ceremony. He is no longer painting; he is performing a ritual, a sacrifice.

16

THE lunatic had never made a conscious decision to become a lunatic. It had been thrust upon him, an honor of sorts, a quirky occupation. He had never known anything else, having been born in the Building (the laundry room, when there was a laundry room) from parents who, both to him and to the occupants of the Building, were, and remained, hazy, insubstantial. One day someone noticed that both parents were no longer around; the lunatic was the sole occupant of the apartment. No one knew where his parents had gone, and no one asked the lunatic. He was not concerned. Their function had been to give him birth, bequeath him the apartment, and then vanish, troubling people as little with their going as they had with their coming.

It was the lunatic who knew about the river that flowed through the cellar of the Building and the other rivers that lurked in the Building, hiding, biding their time, waiting to spring forth from unsuspecting pipes and crisscross the entire Building, holding it in one vast watershed, a rain forest, and it was the lunatic who first saw the man who loved chickens consummate his passion on the roof, and though the lunatic had never considered chickens in quite that fashion, he did feel the terrible loneliness of the chicken man, since he had it himself, and was glad that chickens had been put on the face of the earth to relieve his loneliness. It was the lunatic who first noticed the fireflies, and kept quiet about them, since their presence, in huge glowing numbers, humming about the vacant apartment they took shelter in, was the body, but not the blood, of our Lord, and signified the holiness of the Building and its occupants. It was the lunatic who had seen Mary Smith start her Cadillac dream ride late one night, when the streets were unusually still and the moon had been caught in an old clothesline that was slung between the Building and the one next to it, and it was the lunatic who, unknown to Mary Smith, had found Shanker broken and bleeding in a Williamsburg tenement and carried his battered body, slung over his shoulder like a rug, back to the Building and up to Mary Smith's apartment where she found him when she got back from her dream ride. It was the lunatic who had dreamed that the exterminator was coming, and had warned the fireflies, or thought he warned them, and it was he who considered all creatures great and small who lived in the Building somehow blessed and was able to cry in their presence, as if these animals were certified and duly authorized to hear confessions. It was the lunatic who had seen Singiat-Sing Dan Dinphuir's demon ghost dragon, and knew that the creature appeared in dark doorways and on ceilings, a powdery film, like moth dust, spilling off its horned head and spiked feet and tail. It was the lunatic who knew the sounds the Building made at night, and could imitate them at will, and also knew about the Indians who lived on the banks of the river, and it was the lunatic who saw Eschopf in the cellar carrying his chess pieces and who watched as Steckler came down to hot-wire his welding equipment into the main junction box, running the thumb-thick cables alongside the silent and rarely used steam pipes, and it was the lunatic who knew that the Building had been built on the foundations of an old Indian burial mound, the bones dug up and thrown in the mortar to help calcify it, giving the cellar walls the pale-green glow that emanated from them when the weather was humid, and it was the lunatic who, sitting in the cellar late at night, watched what happened to these walls when the people whose bones had been put in them came back to claim them. Even Eschopf stood aside for them, and made sure his head, which he sometimes carried in his arms, was in its accustomed place, on his neck.

The lunatic was on speaking terms with sanity; but he was buried in it, mired, trapped. He turned it over and over in his mind, questioned its premises, sucked at it like a piece of licorice and found its aftertaste just as unpleasant. He was the first to notice the flaking plaster and crumbling marble, the first to tell Mr. Tontine, the Norwegian wood-worshiping super, who promised to fix it but seemed to have a prejudice against nonorganic objects.

The lunatic, with the dwarf on his back, went down to the cellar and fed bits of meat to Puff the Magic Dragon, a giant German shepherd, who lived on rats and small dogs and stray cats and who was at one time owned by a family of gypsies who stole roofs from apartment buildings and sheets of copper from the tops of public buildings and bred German shepherds in crowded apartments and sold them to Puppy Land Pet Stores. Puff lived in the electrical supply room, a pitch-black room that contained few supplies and no electricity. The dog growled as it ate, feasting a nervous and erratic eye on the lunatic, and the dwarf howled with glee and jumped up and down on the lunatic's shoulders, wishing that the dog would explode in just the way he had seen dogs explode in Kenya after having been "witched."

They watched Tonton Tute lead his three concubines down to a mudhole in the cellar and watched them strip and frolic in the gray paste, lathering their bodies with the oily sheen until their breasts and thighs glistened in the unearthly cellar light, and later in the night they saw the computer designer lead the Haitian ritual of the dead in which three men were shrouded in white, laid out on white sheets, their nostrils stuffed with white cotton soaked in ether and spirits and then ceremoniously buried, only to be dug up three days later, forever under the spell of the voodoo priest who conducted the burial. They saw a protesting Tubbo Rivera, his leg almost sawed off, the lower half of his body frozen in a cake of ice, a look of placid cocaine cool in his eyes and a twisted grimace on his lips, saying good-bye to life, his dope, his record collection, his beige Lincoln Continentals.

And when the professor was home and demanded the company of the dwarf or was not at home but had chained the dwarf to the radiator with a twenty-foot-long chain so he could reach the kitchen, the bathroom, the bedroom, but not the front door, the lunatic roamed the Building alone, sometimes sitting on the greasy parapet that leaned dangerously toward the courtyard filled to the second story with garbage and the rusted skeleton of a Buick Roadmaster, and if he waited long enough he could watch the grayish purple and yellow sunset that set a halo around the Watchtower building along the waterfront. Or, tongue to the air as if to receive Holy Communion, he waited for the sooty rain whose first drops in summer sizzled on the cracked tar. José had painted his name on the chimney, and the lunatic followed the letters with his fingers, then followed the outline of the letters. He listened for the sounds of the Building, and smelled everything that was wafted upward in the air: chicken and onions, stale sweat, the fuzzy carbonation of beer, the peculiar odor of love, broken marble, the salty smell of screams, the burning smell of hate, blood (tangy, somewhat sour), wood, popcorn, ammonia, roach spray, salt, soda, urine, perfume, death, birth, women's legs and what they hide, men's genitals, ice cream, rice, and the perpetual scent of tears.

The Building was an idea in the mind of the lunatic, and he knew that if he should forget about the Building it would simply cease to be, collapse. The sinew that held it together was the idea of the Building in his mind. And it was because of this that he lugged the bushes on the subway at four o'clock in the morning, twenty bushes, bagged in plastic, all transported on the I.R.T. to Eastern Parkway (or was it Franklin Avenue, yes, it was probably Franklin Avenue), the subway clerk objecting when he handed the bagged bushes over the turnstiles, all twenty of them, and then arranged them neatly on the edge of the subway platform, the first car, and propped open the door with a two-by-four until he had gotten them all in, and then propped open the door again until he had gotten them all out at his stop, either Eastern Parkway or Franklin Avenue, probably Franklin Avenue, but that was after the transit cop wanted to know what he was doing with twenty bushes on the subway, and the lunatic, despite the handicap of lunacy, immediately recognized the stupidity of the question and mentioned it to the cop, who then wanted to arrest him, with or without bushes, and the lunatic, recognizing that he was on a mission of sorts (not of sorts, a real mission, the bushes were being transplanted to a more congenial atmosphere, somewhere where they would not get stepped on, burned, pissed on, dug up, stripped of leaves, carved, shit on, rained on by beer, soda, transmission oil, furniture polish, floor wax, indeed by every liquid except water), and explaining to the officer the nature of his mission and the categorical imperative that demanded their transmission by subway (who had the money for a taxi, and more to the point, who could find one at four A.M. in Brooklyn?), an answer that somehow did not suffice, despite its reasonableness, which made the lunatic think that reasonableness was precisely the problem, so he explained to the policeman that bushes were a form of wealth and he was looking for a bank where he could deposit his bushes, and it was during this explanation that the policeman seemed to become offended by the presence of the lunatic, and the lunatic, recognizing this, locked the policeman in the conductor's booth before his stop, placed the two-by-four in such a way that the doors were held open, removed his bushes, and proceeded on his way. And that way was to carry five of them for half a block, go back and get another five, and so on until all twenty had been moved half a block, after which the twenty bushes would take another half-a-block step. And so on to their destination. After reaching their destination, the Building owner's front and rear yard, and digging twenty holes, and filling them with fertilizer, elephant dung from the zoo, and then watering the elephant dung, and then planting the bushes, packing the soil tight but not too tight, and then watering them again, and then putting the shovel back in the owner's garage, he shot himself several times with a pearl-handled pistol of a low caliber, the bullets burrowing lazily in his skull until he dropped the gun and sank to his knees, in a reverie, aware suddenly that the mind that had taken the bushes to save them had in fact taken them from the Building where they had been for years, and if they had not thrived had at least survived, amongst piss and shit and Popsicle wrappers, the scraggly things blunting and softening that hard outline of the Building, the roots of the bushes caressing the foundation, supporting it, and he had yanked these same bushes, rudely, from the only soil they had known, planted years ago by Eschopf, arriving by freighter from Istanbul one frozen March day. He apologized to the bushes, still bleeding, though less profusely than the Scandinavian whore who was thrown from the roof and split apart like a watermelon on the sidewalk, the lunatic the first to reach her, cradling her head in his lap, on his knees alongside her, trying to hear what she had to say, the words coming out in bubbles of blood, other parts of her body scattered about the width of the sidewalk, still trying to speak, her heart furiously pumping blood through the many openings that suddenly appeared in her body. Still on his knees, still bleeding, he could see the bushes bleeding with him, the soil a deep red, and by the time he had gotten to the hospital (with the loss of surprisingly little blood) he was crying, not in pain as the doctors thought, but because of the bushes. This, he said, deeply to himself, between sobs, is why I am a lunatic, and the bitterness of this spurred not tears of pity but anger, a general rage at the bushes and then at the Building for having gotten older, for having sagged, for having cracked mortar and hallway lights that didn't work and elevators that fell to the first floor and a roof with holes like the holes he now had in his head, beyond the customary number. Afterward, he thought, it's a great way to get rid of a headache.

When he recovered he carried the dwarf with him and listened to the dwarf prattle on in a language he could not understand, a language that seemed to consist of a series of clickings of tongue against teeth, so that when the dwarf spoke he ignored him, a reaction that seemed to spur greater verbosity, a shower of consonants, from the dwarf. As the dwarf talked he seemed to chew at his teeth and to spit out bits of them as he spoke. A fine white porcelain spray covered his conversation, a sort of gritty talk.

The dwarf rode on his shoulders, and the lunatic held on to his foot as if he were holding on to a subway strap, the dwarf obliging him by swinging his leg to match the sway.

Together, lunatic and dwarf climbed the stairs in the Building to the roof and examined the holes in the roof and made sure the José chimney was still there and standing on the edge of the crumbling parapet had a peeing contest into the courtyard below. Then with the dwarf bouncing on his shoulder he ran down the stairs to the courtyard and determined the length of their streams. Overturning the grocery cart that was draped over the statue of the boy nymph with the broken finger in the pool clogged by garbage, the lunatic dumped the dwarf in the cart and raced him through the lobby, bumping over the broken tiles and spilling him out when they came to a big gap in the marble. The dwarf had many things to say about this, spewing them forth through the sand of his teeth, and the lunatic, who listened intently, remained ignorant of their content. The dwarf jabbed him in the chest with a wizened, shrunken finger to make a point, and the lunatic nodded, agreeing with the emphasis.

Sometimes he dragged the dwarf around by the foot, as if he were pulling on a huge doll. The dwarf strongly objected to this and, twisting frantically until he was freed, hobbled, bounced, ran to the professor's apartment and let himself in.

Temporarily freed of the dwarf, the lunatic began to take down the brick wall that fenced in the concrete-hard dirt which used to hold the bushes. Chipping away at the wall brick by brick, he carried them to the basement, not by the side of the Building, which had a sunken entranceway that was now flooded and floated a carpet of newspapers, puzzle pieces, food boxes, condoms, and stolen Social Security envelopes, but through the lobby, down the basement stairs, past the electrical supply room, past the living graveyard of voodoo corpses, past Puff the Magic Dragon, past Eschopf and the green wall, and into a small room that smelled of old manure and duck shit from the time Glasho, the excrement artist, kept ducks and goslings and turkeys in pursuit of his art, and began to pile them neatly in one corner, overlapping them in the fashion he had seen the wall built, so that the bricks began to form their own foundation wall. He carried them down six at a time, two across the width of his body, two the other way, and two the bottom way. The dirt was harder to take apart than the wall; he had to use a hammer and chisel and break it into chunks which he broke again and again, ending up with lemon-size pieces that he put into a canvas bag and emptied into the courtyard, where he cleared a space in the garbage, finally reaching the courtyard floor, and on this floor once again pounded at the dirt, striking the lemon-size chunks of old earth with his hammer until they gave up their "dirtness" and returned to dirt: hard, gritty, pee-soaked, oil-clogged bits of broken glass, beer can rings, and soda bottle tops surrounded by shells of dirt. Into this silt he dropped some seeds he had sent away for in a *Green Lantern* comic book, seeds that promised to come up in days and sprout tall shoots of flowers and fruits and vegetables and then turn into shade trees from which tasty nuts would drop, and since he had sent away for these seeds immediately, and had also sent no money now, he had received a special packet, at no extra cost, of sea urchins, which came in powder form and only needed water added to them to grow into delightful pets, as tiny as the eye could see, and fully trainable. Every day the lunatic carried water from the flooded entranceway by the side of the Building. For fertilizer he sifted through the garbage to find fish and chicken bones, which he smashed between bricks and dumped on his garden, first clearing off the air-mailed garbage that had landed the night before. The sun only struck the garden for a few hours, peering over the Building and into the well of the courtyard during midday.

He scratched the part of his head where a bullet still remained that the doctors could not remove, and worried about the rain and the sun, whether too much or too little of one or both, or whether through this air either could come. The air seemed too heavy for sunlight, it was too solid, the particles that floated in it would refract the sun away from his garden, and the rain, by the time it reached his garden, would not be rain but something else, some kind of acid, bleached and leached by cooking odors and the salt air and the brick dust that wafted upward from the crumbling buildings of the city.

Every day the lunatic could hear buildings falling in the city. There were huge explosions with bricks and mortar flying through the air and parts of people flying after them. He could hear his Building moan in the night and wondered if they embalmed buildings like they embalmed people. What did you call a building when it died? People had funerals but buildings never had funerals. It would be fitting if, when a building died, there would be some ceremony, some special occasion marked by an event everyone would remember, perhaps a sacrifice of some sort.

He put crosses on the roof for everyone who had died in the Building, stone crosses that he cemented in place with tar, and spray-painted their names on the roof in front of the crosses and said three Hail Marys and two Our Fathers. "Our mother mary, full of grape, bestial fat cow . . ." He could never remember the words but he knew that words had to be said. "Our father, who art in Heuvelton, hollow be thy fame, thy fill of sun, thy silly bun . . ." He said them over again, using different words. He thought he might teach the words to the dwarf and then copy what he said. He wondered where the dwarf came from, and why. Why did God make people like that? Why did God make him?

He carried the bricks up from the cellar and made an altar on the roof, holding the bricks with tar. The altar had a wall and a tiny bench and places for votive candles and a brick frame where a picture could fit. He spit on the bricks and shined them up, trying to make them all the same color. His finger was raw from rubbing on the bricks, so he used his elbows, and then his shoulders. He couldn't get the bricks to be the same color. He thought about painting them, but he didn't know if God liked paint. God liked blood. He needed blood for his altar. He scraped his arm on the edge of a brick, squeezing until he had enough to spread around the altar. Now he needed someone to consecrate the altar, some spiritual person, or an animal with an exalted sense of honor, like an owl or a coyote.

He thought about the dwarf again. The creature was made from parts of different people. That explained the ill-proportioned limbs. Somewhere else, he thought, there was someone with long arms and legs and a short body and tiny head. He wondered who made dwarf clothes.

How old was the dwarf? He didn't know, and suspected that neither did the dwarf. Dwarfs are born old, and die scarcely older, though they may live for a long time. Dwarfs and witches.

He could see dwarfs and witches flying across the moon, the one with its tiny legs pumping furiously, the other, large black hat and flowing cape, cackling at the moon. A witch lived in the Building. He was sure of that. A pair of them. Twin witches. He missed the dwarf; he wanted to hold him. The dwarf made him wonder about people. Dwarfs carried stones in their pockets they sucked on. Dwarfs carried amulets and frogs' legs. Dwarfs could start fires by looking cross-eyed. Dwarfs rode on the backs of pigs and spit on spiders. Dwarfs had warts and humps and their piss was green.

Now that he had built the altar, the Building will not have died in vain. He wondered if his parents had died in vain, and tried to remember where the laundry room was, and who did laundry in it, and if, when the Building collapsed, when it turned to dust, when the plaster had crumbled and the termites had eaten the timbers, if anyone would remember. He remembered the Building, door by door, brick by brick, so that when the time came for it to go, it would, if he remembered hard enough, still remain. But a witch could make the Building keel over, or explode. During the meeting about the rent strike, he had asked about exploding buildings, but no one would tell him about them, and he felt as if he had said something he should not have.

On days that the professor kept the dwarf locked in the apartment on a dog chain, the lunatic grieved. He missed the comfortable weight on his shoulder and the incessant stream of chatter that the dwarf kept up, and the lunatic would pause in front of the dwarf's door, expecting to hear the scraping and scratching the creature made as it went from one room to the next, or fixed its own supper. The lunatic found a rotted teddy bear in the garbage one day, and propped that up on his shoulder and carried the tiny cotton carnivore around with him for several days, holding him by the leg. But this stuffed dummy was no substitute. The lunatic grew dull and listless, like a dog starved of its nutrients, and even the growth of his garden, which under his careful tutelage had sprouted tall and amazingly sharp-leafed plants, failed to excite him. He listened for the dwarf every day and was rewarded by the faintest of sounds, sounds that he took to be those made by the dwarf but that could have been made by water running through the pipes or rats clacking their way across the linoleum on tiny clawed feet. He did not know if the dwarf missed him, and he knew there was no way he could know, and that knowledge was an uncomfortable gap in his head, as if one of the bullets he had sent through his skull had bruised, but not destroyed, his memory. The problem was, he told himself, I forget nothing.

The dwarf produced an ache in his body, made him feel like a familiar part of himself was missing, as if he had awoken to find a bone gone from his shoulder. He imagined the little brown man, knuckles scraping the ground, in the apartment, talking to the TV, speaking the strange clucking sound that went down his throat as often as it came up, as if he were speaking to someone in his stomach and then being answered.

The ache was in different parts of his body; sometimes his shoulder, sometimes his stomach, sometimes his groin. At night the lunatic dreamed about his parents, who were small and brown.

One day the professor, late for his class on classical philology, forgot to lock the dwarf in, and as soon as he left the little imp scurried out the door and hopped up on the shoulder of the gleeful lunatic. They raced up and down the stairs, threw bits of tar off the roof, ransacked the cellar for garden dirt. With the dwarf chattering away, the lunatic tended his garden, which was now producing swollen squash in colors unimaginable in seed catalogs. Using his pocketknife he cut off narrow strips of squash which he fed to the dwarf, who consumed them as if he were eating bananas.

That night, seated on the roof, they watched the moon rise and change colors in the smoky night air. Someone screamed from the apartment below. Three blocks away an apartment building went up in flames, room after room exploding like a string of firecrackers. The police had to push two vandalized cars away from the hydrants. There was a chill in the air. The dwarf shivered, and offered his hand to the lunatic, and feeling the warmth of the other hand around his, he hopped into the lunatic's lap and embraced him. The lunatic held him tightly, rocking gently back and forth. They talked softly, neither understanding the other.

The dwarf was by turns quick, shy, forward, voluble, and quiet. He had a monkey quickness about him, and indeed some mistook him for a monkey, but he was a monkey only in height and color. His eyes were too large for monkey eyes, his nose too narrow, his mouth too thin. He was not monkey thin; he was misshapen like a dwarf, with the out-of-proportion limbs and the rocking gait. But wrapped in the lunatic's embrace, and at a distance, there were those who mistook him for a monkey.

He was quick to anger, though no one ever knew what he was saying, least of all the lunatic, who was slow to anger, and slower to forget. After the fire had turned to smoke, and the smoke to steam, and the steam to a slow hissing, and the firemen began to coil their hoses and put them back in the trucks, the lunatic and the dwarf jumped up, as if on signal, and began throwing rocks at the moon. Dipped in salad oil, a greasy brown, the moon hovered over the Building as if it were pregnant and about to drop moonlettes. The rocks flew over the roof and clattered in the courtyard below. The dwarf howled. He jumped up on the lunatic's shoulder to be nearer the moon, and threw with a vengeance that bordered on lust. After each hurl he pounded the lunatic's head and pulled his hair while he howled. And the lunatic, with this weight on his shoulder, threw with a sidearm motion. They threw broken bits of mortar from the José chimney, and each time the lunatic threw, the dwarf bounced, holding on tighter to prevent his being tossed off. They were near the edge of the roof, and the sidewalk was six stories below. The lunatic imagined the dwarf falling, pitching over his head in a great semicircle and plummeting to the ground, only to bounce up again, with one side of his head caved in, falling again, bouncing up to the roof again, this time a shoulder and arm hinged in an unfamiliar place, falling, bouncing, coming up, other parts of his misshapen body broken, bleeding, nerves and organs exposed, the mashed, battered bits of flesh splayed about the ends of his arms and legs and the broken points of bones poking through his skin until the final bounce, when he came up as a ball of flesh and splintered bones meshed with blood and skin.

The lunatic laughed. The moon was red, bloody, dripping. It would set the roof on fire. They would burn like tissue paper and rise in the air like fireflies. They would burn in pieces. The sun was burning the moon, which would burn the Building. They would explode in a huge crescendo of fire, an aurora of flame. The Building would puff outward, a balloon of bricks, and rain stone on the sidewalk. Flaming timbers, sofas on fire, children in burning diapers would fly through the air and fall softly with a whisper of ash. Walls would collapse, people shouting, crying, the fire engines with eight-story ladders would tilt toward the Building and the ladders telescope out to touch a wall, firemen would rescue screaming mothers and dogs with burning backs. The gas mains and the boilers would explode; destruction and death would democratically level his Building.

The lunatic embraced the dwarf once more, and they kissed, lip onto lip. A slowly growing warmth enveloped the lunatic. He let out a sigh, and lifted the dwarf high over his head to the tip of his long arms. The dwarf howled. The lunatic began to imagine the flames that would engulf the Building and the parabolic arc the dwarf would take if he flew through the air to the street.

17

M R. Tontine, the super, the Norwegian wood worshiper, had an apartment on the first floor and inherited the job from Gustafsen, a Swede who was stabbed five times by a four-hundred-pound woman living on welfare who objected to the way he looked at her. It was Mr. Tontine's job to answer all questions about the Building, and he was delegated by the owner to deal with bodies tossed off the roof and those found in the cellar, in addition to any stashed away in closets. It was Mr. Tontine who dismantled the crosses the lunatic had put on the roof and took down the altar because he thought it was sacrilegious and put the bricks back in the cellar. It was Mr. Tontine who cleaned the eyedroppers and hypodermic needles out of the empty apartment in 4B so it could be rented, and it was Mr. Tontine who disappeared around October when the heat did not come on and the tenants banged the pipes, sending Abdul Karim into a frenzy. Mr. Tontine was good at repairing door frames that had been kicked in, bad at plumbing and electricity, uninterested in stone, plaster, lathing, linoleum, glass, and a variety of other materials that covered walls, windows, roofs, or floors. He was chosen by the owner because he spoke mostly Norwegian. He was designated to answer all questions about tenants' leases, and any other questions that might arise about the repair and maintenance of the Building, asked either by tenants or by building inspectors sent through the city's Department of Housing Preservation and Development, formerly the Department of Housing and Development Administration, and was also delegated to answer questions by the city's Department of Real Property and by the federal government's Department of Housing and Urban Development. Mr. Tontine liked to answer questions. He would launch into elaborate, incorrect explanations for all questions directed at him.

Unaccustomed as he was to plumbing and electricity (Mr. Tontine came from a village in Norway where toilets were considered a luxury, indeed a sign of ostentation, and Tontine, while voluble, was basically a modest man), Tontine spent most of his time carving wood faces in railroad ties. These he placed along the walls of his apartment and decorated with pine boughs and spruce limbs and lit candles that fit in hollowed-out cups he carved into the tops of the heads. His wife was a big-boned woman with blazing white skin and penny-sized patches of red on her cheeks who liked to have sex on top of Tontine and crush his head in her arms. She went to all the Tupperware parties the Wilson Sisters gave, bringing home quantities of plastic snap-lid containers of every size and shape, which she loved and Tontine hated.

"My dear Tonti," she called him, and Tontine would come running, as well as he could run in wooden shoes and wool iceman's pants that were several sizes too large for him, because she was quite "dear" to him, and he to her. They had three children so far, all blond, the only blond children in the Building. The children played with the lunatic and threw bottles at the purple lady and went to the local public school, where as the only white children in the school, they liked to touch the curly heads of the black children, who also delighted in feeling the cornsilk straightness of their blazing yellow hair.

"Tonti, bring down the cheese," and Tontine would run up to the roof and bring down the goat cheese that was curing behind the José chimney. "Tonti, bring up the cider," and Tontine would run down to the cellar and fetch the cider that was cooling in the river that ran through the basement. The cider was kept there because the river ran more consistently than electricity in the Building, and Tontine's wife was a stickler for cold cider, properly cured goat's cheese, indeed all the items of food she put on the table.

The table was wood, the walls were wood (wood boards nailed over crumbling plaster), and the Tontines heated with a wood stove, knowing the unreliability of the oil furnace and the fact that the cellar frequently flooded, flooding the pilot light and the burner, and also knowing that strippers frequently came over from New Jersey and stole the pipes, which Tontine did not know how to replace. Tontine did not like to replace anything; he would rather repair, but he was partial to repairing organic objects. He was confused by things that crumbled, or bent without breaking, and while he could trace the course of water as it flowed through the pipes behind plaster, or knew just where in the wall the electric lines were by running his hands along the wall, he was loath to do any repairs on these conduits, and would have to call a plumber or an electrician who had been first cleared by the owner. There were few individuals who fit this category.

Once a month, Tontine went around and knocked on each apartment door and asked in Norwegian if everything was all right. He was answered in a variety of tongues: Vietnamese, Haitian, Spanish, Cambodian, Chinese (Canton), and sometimes English. He was sometimes answered politely, most often not at all. Mr. Tontine was not bothered by this. The United States was a new country, and he was a new citizen in the country who was willing to make his way, to take what comes and make the best, to put his shoulder to the wheel, assuming he could find a wheel. He never frowned. If he couldn't smile he looked blank. Most of the time he looked blank. It was, he knew from experience, the perfect reply, a reply that, unlike Gustafsen's, was not liable to get him in trouble.

Trouble was what he tended to avoid. So when bodies began turning up on the sidewalk, or in the cellar, or hanging from laundry hooks in clothes closets, Tontine had explanations: some had strokes, some fell asleep and managed to catch their collars on unseen hooks, some went swimming in the cellar and hadn't realized how deep the water was. His explanations were ignored by everyone, except the lunatic, who while unable to understand Norwegian, thought that it sounded similar to the language the dwarf spoke.

There were many other complaints that Tontine was forced to listen to: someone was driving a car in an upper-floor apartment, a school of eels was living in the toilets, the electricity only worked intermittently, someone's wall was turning to sand, faucets frequently failed to work and the heat had been turned off since last month (the owner sent around a note saying he was installing a new boiler), and doves were living in one of the top-floor apartments.

All the complaints were true, Tontine knew, and there were many more he hadn't heard yet, but knew he would. The complaints were waiting for him, like old age and faulty wiring. The eels he caught with an old horse head for bait and then cut into strips and fried in batter and served with asparagus and zucchini in a béarnaise sauce. He nailed screens over the broken windows in the top-floor apartment, but the pigeons seemed to be able to find a way in. He tried to shoo them out with a stick, a broom, a shovel, but they only flew around the room, or into the other rooms, and Tontine, racing after them, could only move them from room to room until exhaustion forced him to drop on a pigeon-shit-coated couch. The chalky white blobs of excreta felt like velvet, like soft buttons of fur. At night in bed, his head crushed by his wife's strong arms, he thought about pigeons, the throaty sound of their cooing, the flutter of their wings, sometimes loud and explosive, other times as soft as cotton being pulled over silk. He never found eggs, but feathers were everywhere: on the sofa, clogging the vents in the broken refrigerator, in the stove, in all the holes in the plaster.

There were hundreds of pigeons in the apartment. They drove the rats down one floor into the apartment of Tonton Tute, the Haitian computer designer, who fumigated and drove them into the apartment of the Wilson Sisters, where they were dined on by twenty-seven cats and two parrots. At night, their cooing caused Abdul Karim to think that a dozen camels were fornicating, and he did the only sensible thing one does when plagued by a dozen lusting camels: he set out buckets of rancid grease to drive them away. The grease attracted mice and roaches, which frightened Mary Smith, so that when she jumped from her kitchen table she, and her three hundred fifty pounds, fell through the floor to the apartment below where a Vietnamese family were sitting huddled around a charcoal fire made in sand which sat inside an iron pot which rested on a layer of bricks under which was a four-by-four-foot piece of sheet metal. Tontine repaired the floor, but he could do nothing about the pigeons.

They invaded the hallways, and people coming home from work (those who did work) or those who liked to roam the hallways like the Puerto Rican deaf-mute or the lunatic who raced up and down the stairs found themselves attacked by pigeons, their heads and sanity pummeled by pigeon wings, their foreheads stained by milky pigeon feces, their nightly noise bombarded by the soft rustling of hundreds, some said thousands, of pigeon wings folding and unfolding, the clack of pigeon claws over linoleum, the cooing of contented pigeons, happy as pigs, who were prepared to cluck their way to eternity in the Building.

Tontine, apart from dining on an occasional pigeon, did not know what to do. Pigeons had never been a problem in Norway. Pigeons, as far as he knew, were sweet plump things who paired off for life and liked to live around statues of war heroes on horses. Tontine knew his Bible, having searched it for references to wood, and knew about the plague of locusts, and thought that they were being visited by a plague of pigeons. It was, he thought, the prelude to some disaster, some ominous event that would somehow involve wood, and that he, Tontine, would have to prepare for. It was one of life's little lessons, a calamity, something that Norwegians were well aware of. He told his wife to stock up on food, mainly canned goods, though precisely why they should he didn't know. It just seemed sensible, the Norwegian thing to do.

The owner was upset that they weren't paying rent. He had never allowed pigeon coops on the roof, unless he could get rent for them, and he certainly wasn't going to allow a pigeon coop apartment unless there was profit in it. When rent day came and the owner came to collect from the people, he also tried to collect from the pigeons. Failing that, he felt they had no right in the apartment, they should be evicted, and he set about to do that. He had as much success as Tontine, which was to say very little, if any. The owner was sure the pigeons belonged to someone, however, and expected his rent. But even if they knew, the pigeons were silent on their ownership.

At night, in bed, Tontine whispered to his wife.

"What's happening?"

His wife was silent.

"Something's happening to this Building. I can't fix things here anymore. Too many things break. Too many things made out of strange materials."

"It's the pigeons," his wife said.

"No, it's the language. English I can learn. Those others I can't."

His wife clucked at him. She always made little of big, tiny of small. She was a smoother-over, a tucker-in of corners. If Tontine couldn't solve a problem, he turned his back on it. He let it crawl up on his shoulder, hoping it would go away.

"The pigeons will leave. They'll get tired, they'll leave."

"I'm not worried about the pigeons."

"Roll over on your back."

"It's the little yellow people. They're making fires on the floor."

"Move your legs."

"What if the floor burns? They don't seem to understand. They think they're still in the jungle."

"Your breath stinks."

"The blacks are always tossing things in the toilet, the browns toss things out the window, and the yellows don't toss anything out. I try to get them to toss out their garbage, set it outside the door, they won't. They save their garbage. The place stinks."

"You're not hard yet."

"They collect garbage. Someone else puts out garbage, and they take it in. I tell them that garbage is to throw out. They smile and nod their head. They have a separate room set aside for garbage. It stinks."

"Am I too heavy?"

"Some of them nail the door shut. They go up and down the fire escape like monkeys."

His wife grunted.

"They're growing things on the floor. They think they're in the jungle. They put seeds on the floor and water the floor. The water leaks into the next apartment, shorts out the wiring."

"Yes," his wife said. "Oh yes."

"They turn off the radiator valves in the winter. They build fires instead. They don't believe the radiators will ever get hot. I try to tell them, once in a while the radiators get hot."

His wife was breathing heavily, her eyes rolling up into her head.

"Did you hear what I said?" Tontine asked.

His wife, busy with her own fire, was lost in the jungle.

"This guy keeps running up and down the stairs, carrying bricks, building altars on the roof. I tear one down, he builds it up, it goes down, it comes up again. He likes to toss things off the roof. Can you hear me?"

No longer in the jungle, his wife was riding a wave in the ocean; she was the wave, then she was the ocean.

"The pigeons are the least of my worries. The owner wants me to fix everything. With what? He doesn't give me any money to fix. He says, 'See if you can make do.' 'Make do with what?' I ask. 'A little here, a little there. Borrow from wherever.' 'Borrow from where?' I ask him. Then he threatens."

His wife moaned, like a sea bird miles from land, like a lake-bound loon.

"They've got pets in the apartments. Pigs, snakes, lizards. They feed the garbage to the pigs, let the snakes and the lizards take care of the rats and the roaches. Snakes and lizards don't smell. That's one thing I'll say for them."

A long sigh escaped from his wife, a sigh close to death and ecstasy.

"The whites in the Building are the worst of all. Where do they come from? Countries I never heard of, around the Balkans and the Mideast."

Tontine couldn't stop talking. He was like a broken alarm clock, forever giving off the incorrect alarm. He couldn't understand this country, the lack of order. He tried to find out who was above and who below. He was willing to take his place at the bottom, as long as he knew who was above him and who was at the bottom with him. But there was no bottom. The country was a bottomless pit, a huge hole with no dimensions. "Give me the iron boot every time," he often said to his wife, who, if she heard never acknowledged the metaphor.

Soon after he became super, "the yellows," as he put it, began moving into the Building. The first couple he encountered were so small and diminutive Tontine thought they were children, and asked them to bring their parents. "But we are the parents," the man replied, in flawless English. He was a diamond merchant from Phnom Penh, down on his luck. His name was Singiat-Sing Dan Dinphuir. "This is Mrs. Singiat-Sing Dan Dinphuir," he said, motioning to a little girl that looked eleven to Tontine. "And here are our children." Seven tiny children stepped from behind the bushes where they had been playing, and in which they would play for days to come, until the lunatic shipped the bushes via subway to the owner's mansion, after which they played in the floating garbage cans. Tontine could hardly imagine a child that size having seven children. "Please, we need an apartment," Mr. Dinphuir said. "My wife is pregnant." Where, Tontine thought, could she be hiding a baby in that tiny body? Her stomach, while not flat, was not especially big. "Seventh month," Mr. Singiat-Sing Dan Dinphuir said proudly.

Next came a Vietnamese rice farmer with thirteen children whose wife looked ten; a Cambodian, occupation unknown, single; three Laotians, brothers, who were working to save money to send for their families and whom Tontine relied on to help around the Building; and more boat people from Vietnam. Tontine had never known people could be so tiny.

Mr. Singiat-Sing Dan Dinphuir invited Tontine and his family over for dinner shortly after his wife delivered. "A celebration," he said. "Another male child. You will be satisfied. My wife will prepare the food."

Dinphuir's apartment was festooned with balloons, streamers, and crepe paper. Bells tingled, tiny mirrors flashed, and Tontine smelled incense.

"Please to seat yourself," he said.

"But there are no seats," Tontine said.

"Of course," Dinphuir said with a chuckle, "please to seat yourself." He motioned toward some cushions.

Singiat-Sing Dan Dinphuir's wife had given birth the night before. "She has been cooking all day," Dinphuir said proudly.

They all sat cross-legged on small silk cushions. The children had their own cushions against the wall. They watched the adults, giggled, and stuffed small round brown objects in their mouths. Tontine's children, unable to speak Cambodian, and the others, unable to speak Norwegian or English, were chattering away in a language none of the adults could recognize.

"I love the pigeons," Dinphuir said.

"Don't worry," said Tontine, "about the pigeons."

"Pigeons are not a subject for concern," said Dinphuir. "On the contrary, a house with a pigeon is a house with good fortune. It is a sign of wealth."

"We're working to get rid of the pigeons."

"Oh yes, they are quite beautiful. They are, how do you say, birds of a feather flocking beautiful together."

"They'll be gone in a month."

"Ah yes. I do enjoy when they bill and coo, and the rustle of their wings. A pigeon feather, you know, brings good luck. Every home in Cambodia has that, at the very least."

"Just give us time."

"Be lucky you don't have the demon ghost dragon," said Dinphuir.

His wife brought in the food. There were dozens of tiny bowls full of reds and greens and blues, short things in white paste and long things in green paste and red things in clear liquid and white things in a gel-like base, and steaming bowls of white rice and smaller bowls of green tea.

"What do you recommend?" Tontine asked.

"Oh yes," Dinphuir said.

Tontine nibbled on something green. A hand reached down and grabbed him by the inside of the throat. Its fingers were on fire, searing his trachea and mouth. Then the hand seemed to explode in his mouth, lifting him off the cushion. He staggered back, clutching his throat, his eyes beyond watering. He felt something liquid come out of his nose and ears before he passed out.

Dinphuir chuckled.

"Not the hottest, by the shot that is long," he said, "but then not the mildest either. I will run the water in the tub, if there is any."

In three days Tontine was able to eat solid food. His wife fixed him a dish of vanilla ice cream, which Tontine spooned gingerly into his mouth. Mrs. Tontine and the children had eaten and enjoyed all the tiny bowls of food, prompting Mr. Singiat-Sing Dan Dinphuir to exclaim that she was a true Cambodian, though a trifle large, with the wrong color hair and funny-shaped eyes. Mrs. Singiat-Sing Dan Dinphuir stayed in the kitchen during the meal, coming out only to serve, and smiling shyly from the kitchen door when they left. Three days later Dinphuir sent Tontine a lotus blossom.

Dinphuir smiled at Tontine when he met him in the hallway, and Tontine, if not quite smiling back, assumed a look that was partway between a smile and blankness. Each time they met thus, Dinphuir remarked about the pigeons, and Tontine learned that the Dinphuirs were not above eating their good-luck symbols. This he did not learn from Dinphuir but from the Laotians who helped in the Building. They said that Dinphuir was stringing together pigeon bones to ward off an evil demon that might plague the Building.

Tontine's plagues concerned plumbing and electricity. Steckler had hot-wired his cables so often that he had taken big gouges out of the wires that ran into the fuse box, threatening to short out the current coming in from the street. Finally one of the wires did short, electrifying the pool of water in the basement and stunning the creatures who lived in the water. When Tontine went down to check on the fuses, he noticed all manner of small, strange creatures gasping for breath on the banks of the pond in the basement. He pulled out Steckler's clamps, and minutes later Steckler had them on again. The pond buzzed a vivid blue. A carp, momentarily stunned, popped out of the pond and lay throbbing on the damp cellar floor.

The cellar plumbing was rusty, dripping in places because of condensation and leaking in other places. Pipes sagged, sometimes running for a hundred feet without a support. Valves refused to turn, or when they did, broke. Tontine told the owner about the pipes, and he told Tontine to "borrow a little here, a little there . . . do what you have to, fix, repair . . . but don't spend money." "Borrow from where?" Tontine asked. All the pipes needed to be replaced. The furnace looked like a small upended tank. The pipes leading into and out of it were rusted, one completely through. At times the burner sat under water. "See if you can find some tape in the garbage," the owner said. "Wrap here, wrap there, tape does wonders." But the garbage cans were usually floating in a pond alongside the Building, bobbing up and down according to the weight of the garbage in them. Once a week there was, if they were lucky, a garbage pickup. Tontine had to be prepared to retrieve the cans for the garbage truck and then leave them on the sidewalk when they were emptied.

One of the Laotians had done plumbing on an air force base in Vietnam, and offered to fix the pipes. He produced a maze of odd-shaped pipes, adapters, valves of every size and shape, and working without wrenches used steel bars, clamps, and rags. Slowly a network of pipes grew, producing, as far as Tontine could see, no discernible direction or focus. Huge pipes hooked into smaller ones, brass with lead. Sometimes a pipe would travel for ten or twelve feet and then double back on itself. When questioned about this, the Laotian said it was all a problem of the connectors. A maze of pipes grew overhead, so that Tontine had to walk with bowed head through the cellar. When he complained about it, the Laotians said it was fine for them, and showed Tontine how they could walk upright under the pipes. But as the pipes proliferated, multiplied, and expanded so that the cellar ceiling slowly disappeared behind a spaghetti network of tubing and piping, there seemed to be no change in the water supplied to the apartments or to the furnace. The Laotians said they had not yet found the right connectors, but were hopeful.

Moss grew on the pipes, mushrooms in the dirt. The cellar walls, flaking and brushed with a fine powder, seemed to give off a pale-green glow. The subterranean room became humid, the air was thick and full of vegetation. Orange spiders with large abdomens made webs in the corners and caught green moths whose powdery wings caught the weak cellar light and reflected it like a round ballroom mirror. Strings of winged ants crawled up and down the walls, disappearing behind the pipes. Fist-sized water bugs diligently patrolled the cellar floor, devouring bits of creatures the spiders dropped from their webs. Tontine thought he saw snakes, but he wasn't sure. The Laotians refused to go into the cellar. The overhead maze of pipes they had left attached to the ceiling, like tubing to train mice, had still not been connected, and weighted the ceiling, threatening to pull down what little plaster was left. Tontine asked the Laotians why they refused to go into the cellar. One of them mumbled something about a demon.

Then two of the Laotians died in their sleep, their eyes wide open. There were no marks of violence on their bodies. The third Laotian refused to come out of his apartment. He bolted the door, nailed it shut. After three weeks Tontine had to break the door down with a sledgehammer and pull the screaming, emaciated little man from his bed. Open cans of dog and cat food were on his kitchen floor, but there were no animals. After Tontine cleaned the apartment, it was rented the following week. A Mexican family moved in; they were clean, polite, and unable to understand Puerto Rican Spanish. There were rumors that they kept a burro in their apartment. Tontine dismissed the rumors, until he noticed empty feed sacks in their garbage. If they had a burro, it was noiseless and odorless.

The pigeons left, as his wife had said they would, but Tontine had the feeling that he was being stalked through the Building by some large creature. The pigeon apartment was rented to a small pig-eyed man who complained about horses. At night, Tontine could hear him nailing something in his apartment. Tontine reminded him that nailing into the walls was prohibited. He cursed, and spit into his hands.

From the street, Tontine noticed the Building sagging in the middle. From the side, it looked like one of the outer walls was leaning forward. The walls of the Building looked wavy.

"Something is eating the inside of the Building," he told his wife. "Nay. You think about the Laotians too much." "I think I hear chewing or chomping." "That's the pigeons." "They left." "Some are still on the roof, still next door." "It's not pigeons."

The next day, his wife never left the kitchen. She cooked all day: stews, goulashes, pies, cakes, baked meats, succotash, mashed potatoes, custards, puddings, gels, rolls, bread, flatbreads, roundbreads, johnnycakes, soups, soufflés, quiches. She broiled fish, baked ham, put up preserves. Day after day she continued to cook, until the kitchen became filled with dishes of food they couldn't possibly eat. She gave away as much as she could, but her culinary efforts outpaced her charity. She invited the Dinphuirs in for dinner.

They marched into the apartment single file, Singiat-Sing Dan Dinphuir first, the children by sex and age, and then his wife. Mrs. Tontine served them white and green foods: soups, breads, puddings, cakes, stews, fish, squash. The large table was crowded with food of every sort of consistency. Plates crowded plates and threatened to push bowls on the floor. The Dinphuirs ate as much as they could, and then more. Singiat-Sing lamented the loss of the pigeons. Tontine mentioned the unfortunate incident with the Laotians. "Ah yes," Singiat-Sing said. Tontine was not sure if he approved or disapproved of their death. "A most unfortunate occurrence, most unfortunate. I understand the man occupied the apartment for three weeks, depriving your landlord of the rent. A most unfortunate occurrence." Tontine learned that Mrs. Dinphuir was pregnant. The due date was three months from the evening of the supper. (Shortly afterward Tontine learned his own wife was pregnant.)

The next day Tontine began hearing complaints about animals that had entered the Building: rats, roaches, mice, ants, termites, bees, spiders, cats, dogs, sparrows, starlings, grackles, bats, raccoons, and snakes, but no pigeons. Someone asked him about the donkey. There was a complaint that a Vietnamese family was killing chickens in their apartment. The animal kingdom seemed to have overwhelmed the heat-and-hot-water kingdom, and Tontine wondered why animals would want to make their home in a building so poorly heated as this. October was fast approaching. He would soon be unreachable.

18

Mr. Singiat-Sing Dan Dinphuir, formerly of Phnom Penh, now of Brooklyn, formerly a diamond merchant, now a dealer in stones rare and not so rare, gems, metals, glass, indeed any hard object that could be shattered with a hammer or bent with a pair of tongs or melted down in a crucible and crumbled into powder, was a man of some importance in his former country. More than a diamond dealer, Mr. Dinphuir turned his hand to whatever would supply him with money and trinkets. He was inordinately fond of the latter (not that he despised the former), and was always on the lookout for "interesting pieces of dirt," which was how he described what he wanted to those who sold to him, while those to whom he sold he called his stones "rare and exotic gems, power objects."

He built shrines, for a price, throughout Southeast Asia. He uncovered archeological finds in the Mekong Delta, arrowheads and strange stones that felt like velvet, which he was advised by a local Shinto priest to get rid of immediately, which he did not do but kept in his possession for a number of months before he sold them to some officials from the Fogg Art Museum at Harvard and then used the proceeds to finance a "buying expedition" up the Mekong, where he purchased more arrowheads, spears, bows, glass beads, uncut diamonds, opals, sapphires, turquoise, and his wife. Mr. Dinphuir liked to travel in the old style. He was carried, in a sedan chair, by porters from a local tribe who also carried his food, clothing, medicines, portable music box, screens, tents, camp chairs, and other miscellaneous objects. By dhow he sailed up the river, and then by sedan chair he, or rather his porters, made his way through the underbrush. He was protected, he thought, by an amulet he carried with him, an amulet given to him by a Shinto priest who had warned him that its powers were unpredictable. Most often he would buy passage through hostile territory, and when he couldn't he would shoot his way through, sometimes losing a few porters in the process. He traveled during the dry season, when the weather was hot but not muggy and the ground somewhat dry.

Singiat-Sing Dan Dinphuir liked the brush country, as long as he could buy his way into and out of it and create around him the proper environment to enjoy it, an environment that would allow him to select what would enter his world. This usually included sounds, but little else. He kept the jungle at bay with a glittering series of nettings, cots, chairs, tinned goods, rifles, pistols, liquors, and, on occasion, ice packed in sawdust.

During one of his trips he constructed, for a handsome fee, a suspension bridge for a tribe of headhunters. Unfortunately for Dinphuir, the bridge collapsed under the weight of seven of the old chief's eight concubines. Most unfortunately for Dinphuir, the chief was not on the bridge, and when he learned of the tragedy, decided to detain Dinphuir while the tribe gave counsel as to how Singiat-Sing should be cooked, and eaten. Bribing the guards with liquor, Dinphuir left the tribe, and his porters, cots, chairs, tinned goods, and so on, and made his way on foot, and hands and knees, back to his dhow on the river. When he was discovered missing the next morning, the chief ate Dinphuir's porters instead. Somehow, Dinphuir managed to make it back to Phnom Penh, even picking up his stash of goods and wife in Saigon. Unfortunately, one of the chief's sons, by a fluke, followed Dinphuir back and laid plans for his death. It was, the son decided, necessary that

Dinphuir die a ritual death, the Death of the Seven Wounds: death by poison, knife, strangulation, fire, drowning, weights of many tons, and curse. Starting with the last first, Dinphuir became aware of a strange oppression, a leadlike liquid that seemed to invade his body and weigh down his lungs and heart. Consulting the priest, Singiat-Sing learned of the curse, and it was suggested that he use the amulet to rid himself of the person who was the originator of the curse. The priest, however, warned that the methods by which the amulet worked were capricious and, while usually successful, capable of some unforeseen side effects. Brushing aside the warning, Dinphuir proceeded to employ the amulet, and was soon able to tell the priest that the weight in his body had been lifted, "the lead turned into nectar." Then one night the demon ghost dragon appeared. It was small as these things go, being the size of a large tiger, but so hugely white and glowing, with such sharp scales, a swordlike tail, and smoldering eyes, that Dinphuir was terrified. It made no sound, but stood in his doorway for a minute and then faded. Consulting the priest, Dinphuir learned that having called such a creature forth, it now had to be appeased with new victims, otherwise it would feast on Dinphuir. "I believe this creature is specific only to Phnom Penh," said the priest, "but the more it feeds (the chief's son having been its first victim), the hungrier it gets, until there is no end to its appeasement."

The next week Singiat-Sing Dan Dinphuir moved to Brooklyn. He used the stones as bribes to get out of the country and to buy airline tickets. He arrived the perfect immigrant: literally destitute.

Like a ferret, Singiat-Sing sniffed the city for profit. Neither an optimist nor a pessimist, Dinphuir, like the Tao, like water, simply flowed to where the money was. He had his own magnetic north that honed in on profit, and he was content to walk the streets of the new city and let his blood tell him where the money was. It was seemingly a casual walk, with his hands behind his back and his head in the air, eyes darting from one side to the other watching where sales were made, watching the sidewalks, the peddlers, the trucks that delivered dry goods, the merchandise sold in stores.

He bluffed a landlord into giving him six months' rent and opened a store in a poor neighborhood that bought gold chains snatched in subways and sterling silver burgled from apartments. He melted down, converted to cash, and moved on to gems and stones when the price of gold and silver went down. When diamonds went down, he moved into topaz, turquoise, and opal and did a side business in molybdenum which was used to strengthen the metal in jet fighters.

He was suspected by everyone in the Building because he smiled too much. But the smile was not the smile of a congenial personality; indeed, he had no personality at all. The smile was simply a convenient pose he adopted to see where advantage could be taken. He was not a mischievous man, nor a vindictive one, nor an ingratiating one, nor was he one who liked to foment trouble, someone who enjoyed building empires of tumult. He moved as water moved, seeking the profit at hand, satisfying his senses but not dragged around by them. He bossed his wife, but was quite willing to take orders from her. He chastised his children, but when they became bold, in the American way, he accepted it. There was nothing he found unusual, no invention that surprised him, no attitude or habit that shocked him. He was curious, and inordinately fond of his hands, which were tiny even for a man of his size. He kept his nails trimmed to a slight point and wore no rings, though he had ample opportunity to. He wanted nothing to overshadow his hands.

"Mr. Singiat-Sing Dan Dinphuir," the owner shouted through the locked door.

"At your service, sir," he shouted back. He was respectful of authority, but quick to notice when that authority had been superseded.

"You are building no cooking fires in your apartment."

"Sir, I am not one of your Vietnamese," he shouted back, making the owner feel he had committed a grievous error in renting to Vietnamese.

"I was just checking, Mr. Dinphuir."

"We cook on the stove, sir, a habit common among most civilized peoples."

"Do you have the rent?"

"At the ready, sir. Do you have a receipt?"

"Of course."

The owner took Dinphuir's money, counted it after Dinphuir suggested he count it to make sure it was all there, a superfluous gesture, both men knew, since the owner always counted the rent money.

The owner begrudged Dinphuir his hostile politeness, but in the face of steady rent, it was an annoyance he could put up with. Indeed, the owner had a grievance with every tenant, no matter how long it took him to find it.

Shortly after Dinphuir moved in he noticed the services in the Building begin to deteriorate. He talked to the owner, who brushed aside his complaints, or said he was getting "it" fixed. After this happened several times, he realized that the owner had no intention of getting anything fixed.

"Pardon me, sir," Dinphuir said, "but about the business of the elevator . . ."

"What do you need an elevator for?"

"Sir, the point about the elevator is . . ."

"The elevator is on order. It comes from Switzerland. There's a dock strike."

"It would seem to me you have a capital investment here."

The owner, having finished counting his money, was gone. Singiat-Sing Dan Dinphuir watched him walk, if that was the word for it, down the hall, knock on the next door, and shout, "One hundred seventy-five dollars and sixty-three cents!"

To one who was not easily shocked by foreign customs or habits, Dinphuir found the owner's attitude puzzling. Here was a man with a sound investment who was willing to let it fall to pieces. "A splendid Building," he explained to a fellow Cambodian who used to fight for the Khmer Rouge, "all brick, of many stories, large apartments with finely crafted floors, all made of wood fashioned into squares, quite handsome, the Building sitting on a corner lot, close proximity to a park, surrounded by handsome brownstone four-story buildings . . . a capital investment, one to keep in one's family." In Cambodia, a good commercial property was kept in a family for generations. In times of pestilence, famine, war, and revolution, one held on to one's buildings, and one's farm, if possible.

"Ask him if he wants to sell," said the former officer in the Khmer Rouge.

"I did. He wants many thousands. But I don't think he really wants to sell. I don't think he wants anyone else to have it."

It was, Dinphuir reasoned, one of the customs of the country, perhaps accounting for the great number of disposable items one found in the stores. He felt that dealing as he did in nondisposable merchandise, gems that were as old as the planet in some cases, that he was missing out. "I am used to dealing in items that last centuries," he told himself, "a habit I grew up with, the custom of my country. Here, in this country, nothing lasts. All is temporary, all is illusion.

Perhaps only in America have they found the true Buddha nature."

He walked around Brooklyn and found the roads crumbling, the sidewalks cracking. Even the trees looked as if they were about to fall apart: the leaves rusty and blackened, the bark cracked and carved on, scratched bare in many spots. He noticed dented cars, abandoned buildings, vacant lots piled high with garbage and bed-springs. The sights filled him with enthusiasm, as if he were about to make a discovery.

A sea of black faces made him think he was in Africa. He had never been there, but he knew it was filled with black people, and he thought perhaps that Brooklyn was part of Africa. Perhaps he could procure a sedan chair and hire some of them to be his porters, carry him to remote corners of the borough where he could trade for gems and other items.

He went home and lit a joss stick and sat on his heels for half an hour. The moon, of which he was inordinately fond, rose and sliced across the greasy night sky. He thought he heard a cicada, did hear a cat howling, and garbage being tossed into the courtyard. When the smell of incense had permeated the room, he rose, on bare feet, and rang two tiny brass bells, shaped like claws with geometric designs etched in red, which he held cupped in his hands. He circled around the incense, softly ringing the bells and repeated five sutras and several other chants. His wife watched from the doorway, wearing several veils which she began discarding as soon as Dinphuir had finished his chants. The last veil she kept on. She dropped to her hands and knees and began crawling over to Dinphuir, a trip encumbered by the veil, which caught at her knees and threatened to pull off. Dinphuir, fully clothed, was standing, holding the burned joss stick in his hands. When his wife reached him, he flipped off the veil with the stick. She undressed him. The light of the moon was obscured by some sludge in the air from New Jersey. The room, previously bathed in moonlight, was plunged into darkness, acutely disappointing an amateur astronomer across the way who was watching the affair through a telescope. Singiat-Sing Dan Dinphuir and his bride were small and nimble, and well disposed to showing the advantages of their size. From vertical to horizontal they explored all degrees of positions. There was scarcely a position, a coupling, a gyration they could not enter into and withdraw easily from. They emitted no groans or grunts, no sighs, only a slight cooing sound, like the sound that pigeons might make. It was a liquid sound that seemed to circle the room and bathe the walls in its wetness. Their yellow skin was soft, without calluses or wrinkles or bulges to catch, and arms and legs slipped as easily as snakes across one another. They coiled and uncoiled with a fluidity that reminded one of fish, or sea serpents.

As Dinphuir finished with his own liquids, he felt first a drop, and then many on his head. It was raining inside. He looked up and saw a snake of water wiggling across the ceiling, settling at a low point where it discharged itself, just as Dinphuir had discharged himself, from the ceiling and onto Dinphuir. How could it rain inside the apartment, Dinphuir thought. One engages an apartment to be free of the rain. Dressing quickly he took a broom and poked at the low part of the ceiling, which now was bulging ominously. It was like poking a hole in the eye of a cloud. He was rewarded with a gush of water, the recipient of a waterfall. Dumped onto his floor, the water appeared puzzled. The levelness of the floor confused it. But as it continued to gush onto the floor the confusion quickly gave way to certainty, as it found the lowest level of the floor, made for it, and continued its downward motion. Dinphuir watched it with interest. A river was running through his apartment. He thought a curse had been placed on the Building. The water demon, having not been placated, had lifted a river up from the ground and dumped it onto the Building (which floor he didn't know, all he knew was that it was a floor above his) and then let it run its natural course.

Dinphuir ran downstairs to Tontine and shouted, "The water demon." Tontine, crawling out from under his wife, appeared at the door in a bathrobe. The rattling of the door frame alternated with Dinphuir's shouts. Tontine opened the door and cursed him. Dinphuir shouted that the water had invaded his apartment, had continued to invade his apartment, and was now invading other apartments as well.

"That's on your side of the Building," Tontine said.

"Yes, but you are superintendent for the entire Building."

"It's too dark to see anything now."

"The water is immense, it is a river."

"Sleep in another room."

"Mr. Tontine, you must act with dispatch. Otherwise, I fear the entire Building will be washed away to sea."

"The plumbers are asleep at this hour."

Tontine shut the door and turned out the light. Dinphuir climbed the stairs back to his apartment. The water had retreated to the side of the ceiling, but it still poured down with as much, if not more, force. Dinphuir knocked on the door of the apartment above him. When the occupant came to the door, after repeated poundings, Dinphuir mentioned the water. "Is that all you wanted to tell me, you dumb asshole? Get the hell out of here." The door slammed. In the apartment below his, the language was worse, but the message was the same. Dinphuir went back to his own apartment. The water, it was true, was not running in the bedroom. He went to bed. His wife was already asleep. She turned toward him, curling alongside of him, under his arm. Dinphuir could hear the sound the water made in the other room. It was not a drip-drip-drip, but more of a quiet roar, a low rushing sound, like a hiss, as if steam were escaping from a teakettle. There are demons in the Building, he thought. Certainly a water demon. He remembered the water demons of Thailand. They looked like round mossy balls of leeches. Some of them were small, the size of a fist. They lived in creek beds and made the creeks climb over rocks and up trees. If you didn't appease them, in regular ceremonies, they would invade your house. Those that lived in rivers were bigger, browner in color, and sometimes had fins or legs, but never arms. Instead of moss they had tentacles with suckers. Often they attached themselves to boats and rode for long distances. He had never seen an ocean demon, and had no idea what it would look like.

The next morning the water looked like a shiny coat of varnish that ran down the side of the wall, behind the baseboard, and down to the apartment below. The water had invaded just about everyone's apartment. No one had any idea where it was coming from. Tontine called the owner, who relented and allowed him to call a plumber. The plumbers came in the afternoon, and spent several hours roaming through the apartments, after which they reported to Tontine that they could not find where the water was coming from. Tontine asked if they could shut the water main. They did that, and still the water came.

"I told you," Dinphuir said, "it is the water demon. Shutting the water will do no good. If the water demon gets it into his head to alter the course of a river, he will throw the river wherever he chooses, and there is nothing you can do about it."

One of the tenants shouted at Tontine to do something, and Tontine shouted back that he was. They were, he informed the tenants, certainly going to find the source of the leak and fix it. The plumbers would come back tomorrow, perhaps with some officials from the Water Department.

"That will do no good," said Dinphuir. "You must consult a Shinto priest."

"Fuck the Chinese plumbers, just stop the fucking water."

But there was no stopping the water that night. Everyone went to bed edgy, the sound of gushing water rushing through their apartments. Some slept in raincoats, others with umbrellas over their heads. Some had to move beds, others sleep in the living room or kitchen. Some found that the bathroom was the only dry spot in their apartment. Curiously, the water in the faucets did not seem to be affected. It ran as well, or as poorly, as it always had.

The next morning the water looked a light tan, sort of like weak tea.

"The water demon is shedding his scales," said Dinphuir.

Two teams of plumbers had arrived, along with the owner and several officials from the Department of Water. "Marvelous," said Dinphuir, "a whole department devoted to water. They will be able to help in such matters."

The city did tests on the water and speculated that it was coming from the Catskills Reservoir. They, along with the plumbers, followed the course of the water, and could find no beginning, no source.

Dinphuir speculated that it was a continuous loop of water. Some water demons, nasty ones with great powers and a huge grudge against someone or something, could sometimes take a river or a stream and "loop" it, making it run like a loop over itself again and again. These were difficult to get rid of, and sometimes the only solution was to abandon the area where the water loop had settled. A platoon of Shinto priests had failed to remove one from a temple in Bangkok, though they had tried with bells, gongs, incense, chants, and dragon dances for over a month.

The suggestion was made that they rip up the entire top floor, but the owner vetoed that. The following day the color of the water changed once more, to a tepid green. "The water demon is pissing," said Dinphuir. For the second night, and the third, umbrellas and raincoats were put up or on. The entire Building now vibrated with the roar of the water. It filled the ears of all the tenants, like a perpetual buzzing that would not go away, like a permanent seashell held to the ear.

A mist hung over, and in, the apartments. Mold grew in corners. Bread, even with calcium propionate added to retard spoilage, developed spots. A smell of dampness, of moss, of the jungle and seashore hung about the Building. Some said it was an improvement.

Dinphuir watched the water in his apartment. The green seemed to be changing to a pale yellow. It ran down the wall with undiminished vigor, leaving little bubbles at the edges. Dinphuir expected to see fish and other sea creatures, or turtles and snakes, eels and crabs. He tasted the water. There was no taste to it. It tasted like water. He wondered where in the Building the water demon lived.

The third day the water turned a rusty red. It had increased in velocity and amount, fortunately, because there was no water in the pipes. Mrs. Dinphuir cooked rice in the rust-colored liquid, and that evening at dinner, to the sound of the rushing waterfall in their living room, neither Dinphuir nor his wife, nor any of the children, could taste anything unusual. Toilets were flushed by holding buckets in the course of the water and then dumping them in the toilet. Water for drinking and cooking was got the same way. As far as Dinphuir could tell, the water followed the course of the walls from floor to floor. There was a rumor that it collected in the cellar, and at night ran up the outside of the Building and gathered in the pigeon apartment. Dinphuir doubted that, since the pigeon apartment was rented.

Teams of plumbers scoured the Building, but were puzzled as to the source of the water. Water mains were turned off and on, but to no effect. A nasty one, this demon, Dinphuir thought. Every night, he and his wife made love in the living room, the only room large enough for their gyrations, with the sound of water in the background and a fine watery mist that settled on their bodies as they coupled and uncoupled, lubricating them to an oily sheen. Dinphuir glistened in the moonlight, and his wife looked like a brown eel.

In the evening the Building was shrouded in mist. It looked like a temple rising out of a lagoon, a Shinto shrine set in water. Even on sunny days the mist was apparent, but strangely, there was never a rainbow. The water demon hates rainbows, Dinphuir thought; it likes oily, scaly things that live in the slime underneath the pond. It likes putrescence and decay, brown mud, leeches, and river rats. It likes carp and suckers. It is the enemy of sunlight and air.

Then early one morning, Saturday morning, when Dinphuir was watching a cartoon on TV (a coyote was trying to catch and eat a bird, but the bird was a magic bird, because it made the coyote fall from great heights, turned him into a piece of paper, made him fall apart in pieces like a house of cards, put electricity through him, blew his hair and eyebrows off, and using him as an arrow shot him up in the air), he heard a strange hissing noise. It was not water, or the sound of water. It had a sharp, hard sound, a crackling sound. Dinphuir looked around. The wire that brought the magic bird show to the TV was on fire. But the wire was not burning. He noticed a small ball of sparks running from the wall to the TV and back again. It was orange-red in color, and sizzled and crackled as it rolled along the wire. It seemed to be bristling with sparks, like an electric pincushion. Back and forth it went, growing bigger, then smaller, louder, then softer. Now there was a rabbit on TV who could pull people through small holes, turn dogs into pancakes, make boards smack people in the face so they fell apart like sand, trick people into eating sticks of dynamite, which blew up in their stomachs, and could run faster than an express train, a racing car, or a jumbo jet. In short, a magic rabbit. Dinphuir looked at the ball of fire that was racing back and forth on the wire, pulsating in size and color and sound. It was small stuff compared to the magic rabbit and talking bird. When the rabbit was finished with his tricks, Dinphuir turned the set off and the ball of sparks retreated back into the wall socket, making a huge sucking noise, like a shovelful of mud lifted from a damp garden.

The following evening Dinphuir turned on the TV and watched a man flying through the air, when he heard once again the sharp, crackling sound, and walking around behind the TV saw the tiny ball of sparks dancing on the cord. Then he went back to the TV, and the pincushion of flame jumped into the TV program and flew through the air, chasing the man who was also flying. Then the man chased the pincushion of flame, which disappeared, and jumped back on the cord, dancing with feet that sparkled and sizzled.

Dinphuir thought that the demon ghost dragon may have followed him from Phnom Penh, but if so, had changed size and shape. It was hard to imagine this fist-size ball of flame as the demon, but perhaps he had shrunk in the journey. He remembered feeling hot on his left side on the plane flight over, and somewhat nauseous, and he thought that the ghost dragon may have hidden itself in his intestines. Ghost dragons could compress themselves for short periods. He knew of an instance in Thailand where an elephant rode in a tea chest for twelve hours.

The lights in the apartment flickered. Appliances turned them-

selves off and on for no reason. Sometimes there was no current from
the wall outlets, and at other times there was a torrent of electricity that
threatened to burn out bulbs and overheat electric motors. The wires
hummed and glowed, and the pincushion of flames danced on the end
of TV antennae and up and down lamps.

"It is definitely the demon ghost dragon," Dinphuir told the former Khmer Rouge officer, who scrunched up his face like an old betel
nut as if Dinphuir were crazy.

"We leave all that behind when we come here," the political com-
missar said. "There is no room for demons in this country. You imagine it all. It is simply a problem with the water and the electricity. Find
a new apartment."

"Nothing at the proper price, nothing suitable."

"Being particular gets you nothing here. Take politics. I, for one,
have no politics."

"You told me politics was everything."

"It is. But not here."

But Dinphuir knew the demon was in the Building. It accounted
for the attitude of the owner, who didn't seem to mind if the Building
fell apart as long as he collected his rent. It accounted for the river that
ran through everyone's apartment, and the water that often did not run
through the pipes. It accounted for the electricity that sizzled from the
wall outlets, sometimes on, sometimes off, sometimes coming through
in a torrent of power that threatened to fry appliances and lights. He
knew the demon frequently picked the most grand, the most luxurious
building to act out his devilish whims, and this Building, with its magnificent face brick, its floors of many woods and high ceilings, its elevators that once worked, its lobby the size of a shrine with fine marble
that once was not cracked, its courtyard with a fountain that must have
worked (the garbage was surely the work of the demon, they delighted
in refuse), its statuary embedded in the exterior walls, all these things
bespoke a structure of opulence and stature, a substantial building, a
peerless pantheon. The demon had even seduced people to live here
who argued and fought, clogged toilets, tossed garbage out the window, broke walls, set fire to apartments, and made trouble whenever
they could. Demons love chaos; they rub their hands in glee whenever
there is tumult, bickering and fighting positively thrills them.

There will be no end to it, Dinphuir thought. This Building is
cursed. It will not fall down and become abandoned like the others. It

will stand and torture its tenants. It will howl and laugh and grow hateful. It will choke laughter, cause the plumbing to fail, and stifle the miserable amount of heat the boiler manages to send up. The Building, Dinphuir thought, is the demon. The Building itself. There is no demon ghost dragon nor any other kind of demon, because the entire Building, every brick, every pipe, every wire, every piece of lathing and plaster and wood used in the flooring and marble and steel used in the elevators, it is all demon material: fashioned by a devil, designed by a sorcerer, built by a magician, and owned by an evil sprite. That explained why he had never seen the demon ghost dragon. That explained the glow that came from the cellar. Late at night, in bed, he explained all this to his wife. She was a hill woman, from a tribe that believed in magic, and governed its entire life around magic: planting, building, giving birth, caring for the sick and dead. She belonged to a hill chief who owed Dinphuir a sizable gambling debt, which he paid off with her. Dinphuir had marveled at how quick she was. When he got her, she could only speak her hill language, but she picked up his tongue with amazing ease. She seemed to have some foreknowledge of English which enabled her to speak it better than he.

Dinphuir smacked his head (it was something he had seen people do on TV when they realized something).

"Of course," he said to her, "that explains it."

She curled underneath his arm.

"The Building," he said, "is the demon."

"No," she said, "it is simply an unfortunate building."

19

BETH and Ester. Two separate beings, and yet somehow paler apart, something removed, something sucked out of each when they were apart, like jellyfish whose colonies have disbanded. Not twins, sisters, one the younger and one the older, though which belonged to which was not to be told. Beth and Ester Wilson, vaguely athletic, as old, thin women can be, women who when younger could twist their bodies into every knot in the *Boy Scout Handbook:* half hitch, bowline, timber hitch, double half hitch, and, of course, the Danish square knot.

The Wilson Sisters, spoken of in the plural, and when spoken of in the singular, the Wilson Sister, always acknowledging the brooding presence of the other, like dovetail joints in a fine chest of drawers. But not Danish. English. Father a respected merchant in Boston where he dealt in imported green and black teas and hemp rope from a four-story building near the old Boston Wharf. Drove a horse and cart from Boston to New York in 1912 and set up a wholesale silver and china emporium on Pine Street in Lower Manhattan, which he sold soon after and invested in ship anchors, nine hundred and thirty-six, which he stored under the West Side Highway. A man of regular and precise sexual habits, which he exercised every Sunday afternoon, following the Methodist service, in a huge mahogany bed that had a double canopy, his wife in attendance. After seven years the results of this habit were Beth and Ester (or perhaps Ester and Beth). Finally sold the last fifty ship anchors and bought a dancing bear, which would defecate in the living room and dance on the dining room table, a practice not looked upon with favor by Mrs. Wilson. The bear swallowed a Brooklyn Brick and died in the bathroom on the pull-chain toilet, but not before Mr. Wilson had taken a picture of the creature, muzzled, on the front lawn of their home in Brooklyn Heights, balanced on a huge leather ball, Beth and Ester flanking both bear and ball, and the bear, not only balanced on the ball but himself balancing a ball on his muzzled snout.

Years after the bear had died, Beth and Ester, "the girls," as Mrs. Wilson called them, rolled the heavy and now cracked and moldy leather ball around the front lawn, taking turns being the bear, each riding on the ball for brief periods before tumbling to the ground, still smelling some of the bear's musk on the ball. During the winter the ball was kept under the front stoop, acquiescing in the damp that hung around the cold stones, and grew molds of various colors that had to be scraped off in the spring. Mr. Wilson sold furs and then sailors' shoes, highly buffed, with a mirror finish. The girls were loved by Mr. Wilson until they became teenagers, at which time their long, gangly bodies awed him. They had huge knees and elbows, and when Mr. Wilson examined those on himself and his wife, he could find no similarity, and he began to think that perhaps the bear, in the mysterious way of those creatures, had somehow done something to them that caused their knees and elbows to grow to a size which menaced him. Beth and Ester were able to crack not just the joints in their fingers but also those in their wrists, neck, shoulders, elbows, hips, knees, ankles, feet, and toes. Mr. Wilson was of the opinion that they had been assembled rather crudely, and for that he blamed Mrs. Wilson, saying if she had taken more time she could have gotten the joints right. The girls grew up quickly. They never became twenty, nor any of the numbers up to twenty-nine, but jumped directly from nineteen to thirty. It was a leap they had been practicing all their lives. Their mother still called them "the girls." Their father didn't call them anything. When they came over to visit, he had the feeling that he was being bumped around the room, elbowed, kneed in the groin. The girls tried to roll the leather ball out from underneath the stoop, but it fell apart, like a tomato that has been sliced but left intact, waiting for the slightest jar that would allow it to separate.

They had lived under the spell of wealth for many years. This had little to do with money, which may or may not have been present, according to the fortune of their father and the extravagance of his business ventures. But he had created an aura of fluidity, a sort of graceful cushioning that allowed the sisters to float through their early years, as if both had been placed in highly varnished wooden canoes and set drifting down narrow, placid creeks. Debts were consolidated in new houses, paid off by selling old ones. The sisters were never so jolly as when moving from one house to another, regardless of the fact that the new house may have been much smaller and felt pinched. They moved from Brooklyn Heights to Dean, from Dean to Pacific, from Pacific to Vanderbilt. All the houses had stoops, and all of them had front yards that got progressively smaller, like debts that were paid off.

"When did we lose father?" Beth asked.

"That was after the pig fight," Ester said.

"Are you sure?"

There were those who swore it was the most astonishing event of the thirties, certainly the greatest cause for celebration Brooklyn had seen since the British landed on the sand flats and chased the Continentals all the way to Manhattan. After the bear died, Mr. Wilson developed a longing (if that is the proper word—some might say lust) for large mammals, creatures that weighed at least several hundred pounds. He went into the business of breeding fighting pigs. A few of the better fighters would hit four and five hundred pounds, lean and mean, and if given the chance could tear a wolf to shreds. Their squeals, which sounded like a car with locked brakes being dragged over pavement, could be heard for blocks, and the fight usually ended when one of the pigs had the other's intestines. Most of the fights took place in large garages in Flatbush, or any other area with a drain that could be hosed down. It was after one of these fights, when one of his favorite porkers had his eyes chewed out, that Mr. Wilson had a stroke, turning by degrees pink, red, blue, purple, and finally white, as if in a last effort he had turned to patriotism and mimicked the colors of the American flag, expiring in a magnificent technicolor death.

Then, by prearranged signal, the Wilson Sisters turned to acrobatic dancing. They performed in clubs and cabarets, on glass-smooth tables, the discreet sound of a drummer and a bass player in the background. They kept the house on Vanderbilt, even after their mother died, merely shutting off more rooms, until they only used two out of nine rooms, not counting the bathroom. In the other rooms were stored memorabilia from their father's investments: the pieces of the large leather ball, a link of chain from a ship anchor, harnesses for the fighting pigs, and several shoes, all for the left foot. There were stacks of newspapers in the rooms and bags full of empty tin cans. Glassed-in portraits of past Wilsons hung from the walls, tilting forward, glaring down at the floor. Many years later a distant relative tried to have the sisters committed, hoping to get the house for himself. The judge seemed partial to his argument, the Wilson Sisters having turned in toward themselves as they got older. They had decorated their character with the small sort of harmless eccentricities few object to when practiced by the very rich. Before he could claim the house as his own, the sisters sold it, and gave the money to the Fenster-Feeniman Cat Foundation, a nonprofit group devoted to the care and feeding of crippled, stray cats.

Set adrift on the streets, several cats in plywood cages with leather handles, a crippled parrot, one wing eaten by an enraged pig, shopping bags full of clothes, the sisters trudged around the borough, looking not so much for an apartment as for some piece of shelter, a quiet alcove where they could practice their acrobatic dancing, have rooms for the animals, and some extra space for whatever would come along.

It was the parquet floors that attracted them to the Building; they cherished the expensive hardwoods of different shades and hues, the borders cut into exquisite geometric patterns. There were five rooms, more than they needed, but they were familiar with excess space and unused rooms. They rode the elevator when it worked, and when it didn't almost sprinted up the stairs, lugging cat boxes and kitty litter, parrot cages, newspapers, acrobatic costumes, and groceries.

Age had narrowed their already thin bodies, producing skin that hung loosely in fatless folds. Their elbows and knees, always a prominent feature, became even more prominent, so much so that it looked like they had small cushions tied around their arm and leg joints.

They talked in sort of a sly shorthand.

"Well, sister," Beth said.

She was the younger one. She had known that all along, only not wanting to upset Ester, had never said anything about it, any more than she would say anything about the fact that she was also prettier, had more acrobatic ability, and in all probability would never go senile the way her sister had.

"Yes," said Ester.

She was the younger one. There was no need to get doddering old Beth bothered, otherwise she might swallow her false teeth and pee in her pants. Let her think she was younger. At the rate senility was creeping up on her, had in fact embraced her, she needed something to cling to. Ester, of course, still had her good looks. Heaven knows she wasn't one to brag or poke fun, but poor Beth had not one but two warts on the end of her nose (the end of her nose was large enough to support several more), which made her quite ugly.

The conversation ended there. The two sisters circled around the room, wary as mice, glaring at each other with black sharp crow eyes. Small objects flew from their hands, clattering on the floor.

Beth, of course, had insulted Ester. That was obvious. Or else Ester had insulted Beth. That too was obvious. Each of them, insulted in their own way, hurt by the sly invective her sister was so well known for (hadn't father commented on it, said "Your sister can be mean and nasty and cut you up fourteen ways to Tuesday"?).

She would throw an iron at her, she would carve her up with a meat cleaver, she would stick her fingers in the blender.

They circled the room for an hour, almost dancing, feeling the other's hate.

Toward noon they slumped to the floor, chin to knee, tongues lolling about in their mouths. Abdul Karim was banging on the ceiling beneath them, convinced that they were about to release ten thousand moths into his apartment that would flap their wings, blind him with their moth dust, and then smother him.

Ester woke up first. Poor Beth was lying on the floor in a pool of spittle. The dear was drowning in it. Papa had made her promise to watch after her sister. "She's quite demented," he said, "stark raving mad, a lunatic, not to be trusted with anything sharp, animal poisons, or anything of a like nature." Papa had told her that one night after a pig fight, on the front porch, a cicada buzzing in the Brooklyn dusk, a plate of scrapple on the table from the losing pig. It was a quiet Brooklyn night. Ester could hear the trolley cars rumbling up and down Flatbush and looked across the street at the wooden shutters on the brownstones.

Now a boarded-up building meant it was abandoned. Now the nights were noisy with those animals and their music, and they used buses, which were much better at knocking you down in the street than trolley cars. Then, too, they could kill better these days. She counted fifty-seven new ways, including some new diseases they wouldn't dare have let loose in the old days. Ah, the old days. How she hated them. She was glad that Mama and Papa were gone. She liked the mean way things were these days, she liked to watch people jumping on cars and other people, liked to watch fires and bombs exploding on television, big bombs, the kinds of bombs they never had when she was a child. She hated Beth, and loved her, and she had to look after her. She remembered the day the pigs got loose and ran down the block chasing and eating the cats and cornering dogs and tearing them to pieces and how frightened Beth was and how she had to comfort her and how Papa and several other men had to club the pigs and tie them up and how tough their skin was, like leather, like shoes, like pigskin.

Beth woke up and noticed Ester at the table. What an ugly bitch she was! Beth could have been married many times over if she didn't have to take care of this troll, this troglodyte, this clucky, smelly, piggy cunt. Ester smelled of vinegar, of old underpants, of rotten tomatoes. Her hair smelled, her teeth smelled, liquids leaked from her body, she had acne, dandruff, open sores with oozing pus, athlete's foot, carbuncles, gout, arthritis, boils, ulcers, sour breath, passed gas, had pink bleached-out skin sprinkled with pimples and nits that erupted oil, her eyes watered, and little bits of things hung from her nose, which was many sizes too large, her gums bled, her fingernails were cracked and yellowed, her feet turned inward and her knees outward, and because she sat on a toilet seat that Beth had warned her against sitting on, sat on it and not wiped it, had not waited long enough when she had gone into the stall despite the fact that Beth had shouted to her in the next stall to wait thirty seconds before she even began wiping off the seat since you never knew what sat down before you and a lot of the women these days were just bitches who didn't care who or what got into their pants, and there were a lot more social diseases around and venereal diseases, including some from Asia that would make your breasts and hair fall out, and Ester had sat down on this awful crawling seat that was thick with VD germs and clap bugs and gonorrhea slime and who knows what else, and now the dear had VD and gonorrhea—only she hadn't had the fun that usually went along with getting it.

Beth remembered when she had many suitors, men with money and power who brought flowers and chocolates, handsome men, athletes with lean and graceful bodies who played chess with Papa and winked at Mama and took her boating in Prospect Park while Ester sat in her room and tried to learn how to crochet but could never learn and always got the needles stuck in her sweater or else sat on them and bent them. The men who took her out were poets and painters and doctors and owned their own businesses and were attentive to a fault, always polite, she never let them get familiar and knew where their hands were at all times, but still with some of them . . . In the summer they wore boaters and had white shirts with tiny wingtip collars and heavy gold watches on fobs that stuck in a tiny pocket on their waist. These were men who would jump in ice water for her, who drove all night from Boston just to see her, who got up out of sickbeds in Chicago and flew in for the weekend, men who sailed from Spain, climbed impossibly tall mountains in the Alps. They all courted her, held doors open for her, took her to tea at Schrafft's, bought her hot chestnuts, and gave her rides in fast, open cars, took her out to dinner in places where the waiters sang and the menus were printed on glossy paper and the tablecloths so thick they were comfortable enough to sleep on. And all the while Ester sat in her room never learning how to crochet, bitter, envious, jealous: a mean, spiteful, vindictive creature who tried to rip all the clothes Beth owned and bit into every one of her chocolates and then stuck the pieces back together with her spittle, smudging the chocolate with her fingers.

And then when the suitors stopped coming, they developed their act.

They were older than anyone in the nightclub: older than the owner, the man who worked the spotlights, the stylish couples who came and seated themselves in the front row to see a pair of old ladies whose tights sagged in unusual places twist themselves into a series of Houdini knots, panting and straining, the skin on their faces pulled smooth the instant they got into and out of the knots. Once in the knot it was impossible to tell which arm belonged to which face, which leg to which trunk. Sometimes they were able to scurry across the floor of the nightclub, still holding their knots, like demented crabs with human limbs. At other times they looked not so much like knots as like a ball, as if huge hands had squashed them into a snowball. A few times they were unable to get out of their knots. People in the audience would come up, and with careful instructions ("You see that arm there? No, the other one. That's it. Now pull on that at the same time you tug on the foot with the ballet slipper") would push and pull, tug, twist, bend, and suddenly the old ladies would pop out of their knots, so quickly that most people thought it was part of the act. There was a quick round of applause, and the sisters would bow, perspiring, and exit.

While they were in their knots they would talk to one another in low whispers the audience was unable to hear. They complained about the other's breath, smell, lack of fluidity. They talked incessantly both going into and coming out of the knots, as if the words loosened their limbs, limbered their joints, coated their bodies with a sort of verbal grease. They talked to each other's arms, legs, heads, torsos, feet; sometimes talked to their own limbs. Indeed, in an especially good knot, one where the limbs were truly stretched and locked into place, muscle pressing against bone, tendon in danger of tearing, joints almost displaced, in one of these knots it was truly impossible for Beth or Ester to swear what in the pincushion of limbs were hers and what her sister's. Sometimes they felt that each owned all the limbs in the tangle; at other times they felt as if they were all head and that whatever happened below the neck was happening somewhere else, to someone else, at some other time. At times, face to face, nose to navel, ear to stomach, they felt part of a colony and hesitated to come apart, the very act of the unknotting separating them with unbearable finality. Knotted together in one of these especially good knots, the sisters often experienced an oceanic feeling sweep across them, followed by despair, followed by waves in which they felt they were levitating, lifting off from the earth, lifting off not the way a helium balloon would but more in the manner of some extraterrestrial object, something that would simply remove itself from the earth. During these moments a feeling of indescribable joy would sweep over them, as if the sea were churning in their blood. What one felt, the other felt, or soon would feel, when twisted together like this. When this happened an excess of light seemed to lodge in their eyeballs, preventing them from seeing their surroundings, and a great hissing sound, a rush of water, filled their heads. They did not bicker when twisted in this fashion. They did not talk at all. Pressed so close, there was scarcely a "they" to hold a conversation. "They" had become "it." A thing called the Wilson Sisters.

Once they were unable to be separated. Despite the instructions (or perhaps because of them) and a half dozen frantic people onstage pushing and tugging, the sisters refused to come apart, and the club's owner, sweating ferociously through his Dacron shirt (unbuttoned to the navel to show off his chains filled with gold cocaine spoons, chest hair, and a tattoo of an electric chair), wanted to get chains and tractors and pull them apart, fearful of the awful spectacle that two knotted old ladies would have on his club (still, he thought again, perhaps they could be exhibited, for a stiff fee, and draw people into the club). The sisters were brought to a hospital (trundled off in a forklift truck since no stretcher was large enough to contain their knotted bulk), and the doctors, skilled in such things, pushed and pulled and tugged and jerked and then, as a last resort, thought of amputation. Finally they were brought home and simply deposited, knotted, on their bed, with a practical nurse to visit them three times a day. The sisters were like this for three days, happier than they had ever been in their life, rolled up into a ball like the cracked leather one the bear would stand on and balance, balancing his ball (and perhaps there was a smaller bear on that one, and so on). Father and mother appeared to them, father's favorite fighting pig was back, cheerfully eating into opponents and snorting, his snout full of blood, and the dancing bear, having regurgitated the Brooklyn Brick, was busy working his way across the Brooklyn lawn by ball, the leather of the ball still new and shiny and not yet scratched up by the carnivore's claws. Then light and sound filled their head, a brightness and a sort of undifferentiated sound that blocked out all other noise. The third morning the sisters awoke and found themselves lying side by side in the bed. They could scarcely remember the preceding three days. A feeling of great peace and relaxation had invaded their bodies, as if their arms and legs belonged wherever they put them. This feeling lasted twenty-four hours.

The sisters were briefly in vogue with their act, a two-line mention in *Billboard* and *Cue,* one line in *Vogue. Life* came to see them. It became the thing to do among those who liked to see people put themselves in jeopardy. Nightclub owners were fearful that the sisters would have a heart attack and die onstage, twisted together in an impossible mélange of limbs, having to be buried in a double coffin. But as long as the sisters drew a crowd, they buried their doubts.

Then the fashion in nightclub acts changed, and the sisters found themselves on the street with the farting seals and the dancing dogs and trainers who had spent a lifetime teaching animals to do what children could do. It was, they felt, a fall from grace. Without knowing how or why, they had committed something dishonorable.

Without money, possessors of an arcane skill that was no longer negotiable, the sisters assessed their situation, and one word crept across their minds, like the inexorable march of a Times Square message blinking its way across a field of electric lights.

Tupperware! Bowls with lids that snapped tight! The sisters knew instantly that this was their salvation and that they could hold their Tupperware parties in the very Building they lived in, later expanding to apartment buildings nearby. There was something inevitable about Tupperware, they felt, as if it were the culmination of civilization.

The two of them, together, such ancient haughty queens, loaded down with Tupperware containers, plastic lids and jars, bowls and tops that snapped into place, popped shut, trudged from apartment to apartment, from Tupperware party to Tupperware party, spreading their wares on the floor like sidewalk salesmen, opening and closing containers with the sharp crackle that demonstrated an airtight compartment.

They were invited into apartments by women who were amazed by their age, by their being sisters, their living together and never having married, by their earning a living. Out of politeness someone always bought several tops and lids, all overpriced, and then someone else decided that she really did need the containers, so she bought a dozen, someone else bought a half-dozen small, colored plastic containers with ridged lids that snapped on, mix and match if you want, keeps tomatoes, peas, potatoes, even soup, Jell-O, tuna salad, why you can even turn it upside down with milk in it and nothing will spill, not even a drop, though it's not advised to keep it upside down for long; a demonstration of the importance of a good seal.

The sales came, good sales, the sisters knew their product, and then when they collected money Beth, or was it Ester, began to imagine what her sister was thinking.

That look on her face, she thinks she did the selling when it was me. They bought because of what I said. She can't even remember the sales pitch, doesn't know how to put the lids on tight, makes the wrong change.

Long, thin hands reaching out for the money, transparent hands, look through the flesh and see veins and bones and strings of muscles. Takes the money as if it were some delicate object, fragile as a spider-web (both money and hands) and cradles the money in her hands as if protecting it, makes change slowly, deliberately, as if there were a great hesitancy in handing over coins. They wrote out receipts in pencil on small pads of light green paper, making the loops large, with great flourishes, the way they had been taught in penmanship classes. No-where on the receipt did it say Tupperware; nowhere did it even say the Wilson Sisters. It was a standard business form, with no mention of the seller. No one seemed to mind.

They gathered the leftover Tupperware and stuffed it into shop-ping bags and carried it back to the apartment and leaving the contain-ers in bags by the door emptied the change purse on the kitchen table. Dimes, quarters, five and ten dollar bills were counted and placed in neat piles that were nevertheless raggedy and bumpy because it was old money and didn't lie flat like new money. Beth accused Ester of mis-counting; Ester accused Beth of leaving some money at the party, of not taking enough, of undercharging.

"Bitchwhore!"

"Cuntliar!"

The table overturned, the money falling to the floor, the dimes and quarters rolling around on the linoleum, describing ever wider and wider circles, the bills fluttering slowly, like snowflakes. The sisters, on hands and knees, pick up the money and stare at each other, hissing as they retrieve their cash. They spit at each other, soft globules of saliva that splatter on the floor. Neither can reach the other with spit, and the floor in front of each becomes a filmy, sudsy dampness.

"Smellycunt!"

"Assfuck!"

A chair is between them, they both reach for it, wanting to hit the other with it, but they can't pull it from each other's grasp, so the chair seesaws back and forth on the floor, until they try to push the chair into each other, at which point the chair seesaws back and forth on the floor with no discernible change. Beth lets go of the chair. So does Ester.

In the apartment below Abdul Karim goes crazy. By now the sisters have released the moths, and this very moment they are crawling through the floorboards and through the cracks in the ceiling, poised for the attack. He can see the thousands of tiny antennae pushing their way through the holes in his ceiling, and grabbing a broom he frantically begins to sweep his ceiling, at the same time and with the same frequency that the chair has been pulled back and forth, and it was that scraping he took for the sisters prying up the floorboards to release their moths. When the scraping stops, he is convinced that the moths, all ten thousand, have been secreted between the floor and the ceiling and will wait for night to come out and coat him with moth dust before they suffocate him. He will sleep in the bathroom that night.

Each of them has one corner of the change purse; they tug at it like puppies, old-lady eyes and veins dancing in their heads, mouths open, tongues out, drooling, sweating. Beth's panties have slid down around her thighs; Ester's stockings are in loose ringlets around her ankles. They sit on the floor facing each other, thin legs with huge knees pointed at each other, tugging at the change purse. They have forgotten about the money, which has been counted once more and stacked in a corner of the room. Now the battle is to see who will take the money to the bank and who will stay and feed the twenty-seven cats and the crippled parrot. They spit again, and this time, being closer, the spit strikes home, the fronts of their dresses become coated with saliva.

Abdul Karim has left his apartment. He will sleep with an uncle tonight and escape the deadly moths and their assassin masters, the Wilson Sisters.

Barely time to get to the bank. Barely time. If they don't finish fighting soon, don't put the money in the purse, don't walk the two blocks to Flatbush and the bank, it will be too late. They had expected to put the money in the bank today. For some reason, no other day would do.

One of them gives in. They both give in. Standing up, dresses hiked up to their knees, and beyond, stockings below calves, hair a rat's nest, barbed wire, a beard of white, they walk over to the money, each holding on to a corner of the change purse. Someone counts the money again and puts it in the purse; the other writes the amount of money on the back of a Con Ed envelope. At the bank one of them will take a deposit slip and examining all three parts to see that they are truly blank and that no cheating figures have been written on the second and third carbon copies, or false addresses, or magic words that might implicate the sisters in something not of their doing, one of them will write the amount down on the deposit slip, doing it in a corner so that no one in the bank can see what they are doing, and then take it to the teller, holding both the money and the deposit slip tightly in both hands, so tight that a thumbprint transfers onto both carbon copies. The sisters are always suspicious that the bank only gives them one receipt and takes the other two. Bank shenanigans. And then there is no one to walk them to and from the bank. More bank shenanigans.

They live on what they earn. They live on no more than what they earn. There is no Social Security (none for acrobatic dancing, none of the nightclub owners ever paid Social Security or ever paid for anything else). There is no pension because they never had a job with a pension. There is no welfare because they are the Wilson Sisters. There is no charity, no Mothers of Mercy or Fathers of Friendliness, because no one in the Wilson family ever accepted charity and no one ever would. Father and mother had made that quite clear, not that they had to (but both father and mother had left them nothing, except for the house, which had to be sold since it appeared it would go to their lawyer nephew who chased ambulances and worked one day a week on radical cases).

Ester opened the cat food with the wall can opener. The cats sound like wolves in the next room. Beth puts on an old cloth coat, pink, takes a hatpin and pins her purple straw hat with the paper flowers (mums, daisies, forget-me-nots, and stock), and takes her brown purse, inside of which she puts her change purse. She is mad at Ester. She wanted to feed the cats. (Ester is mad at her; she wanted to go to the bank.) She opens the door and walks toward the stairway. The elevator is stuck on the first floor. There is sand or gravel or some kind of stone on the stairs; she grinds it down as she descends, making a sound as if she were milling flour.

The lobby is dark. A stripped Buick Roadmaster is jammed into the double doors that lead out into the garbage-clogged courtyard. She can hear the sound of water dripping somewhere in the lobby. Why are the lights out? Why are the lights always out? There was a hole in the outer door. The doors used to be glass, and when they were broken regularly the owner replaced the glass with plastic, thick plastic, which took about a day longer to break. The mailboxes were ripped open. She didn't care. No one wrote to them, no one sent them checks; all they got were bills, which always came whether the mailboxes were ripped or not. The buzzer system had also been ripped out, the buzzers taken and the wires exposed, like dozens of baby snakes coming out of a den, their tongues sticking out to feel the air.

The only sound is the sound of her feet grinding broken glass and stone as she walks through the lobby. The only light is the dim light that comes through the scratched and broken plastic. It is a long walk from the stairway to the lobby door. At one time it was a magnificent walk, with carpeting and marble floors and indirect lighting that made bolder the extravagant stone busts that lined the lobby and showed off the rich grain in the polished hardwood tables that flanked either side of the lobby. There were no mailboxes then. Mail was sorted and laid out on the table and left there, and you came and took yours. Of course the doorman read the postcards and then announced their contents to everyone in the Building.

The only thing left from that scenario is the marble floor, though parts of that have been cracked and other parts pried up and carted away. Now there are strange objects in the lobby, objects that were never meant to be in lobbies: broken bottles, ripped purses, garbage, cinder blocks, tin cans, wet tennis shoes, bicycle chains and bicycle frames, envelopes opened and strewn about the floor. Sometimes it is impossible to see the floor.

She never saw who hit her; never heard who hit her. Suddenly she was down on the floor, the lobby floor, her head in a pile of torn envelopes, her hat somehow still on her head. She held on to the purse. Someone was trying to take her purse. She yelled. It was dark. Someone kicked her in the head. She opened her mouth and wanted to cry. Held on to the purse, someone pulled it, and she yelled again. An apartment door opened. A head stuck out. "What's happening? Who's out there?" "Get the fuck back into the apartment." The apartment door slammed shut. Another kick to the head. Blood. Her hat would not come off, but the hat was now muddy, and the flowers muddy and crushed, pressed against her head, cushioning the first kick to the head but not the second. She wouldn't let go of the purse. "Kick her again. Kick her until she gives us that fucking purse, man! C'mon, kick the shit out of her!" Another kick to the head and one to the ribs. Beth can't cry now. Something breaks. More blood, don't know where it's coming from. Another kick to the head, a lead pipe hitting her hand, breaking her fingers to get the purse, and the fingers, now broken, still hold the purse, and Beth, who was really the younger (or maybe the older), who was really seventy-five (would have been sixty-five but both she and her sister refused to be in their twenties, had gone directly from nineteen to thirty), was somewhere else now, her body broken on the lobby floor in a pile of bloody opened envelopes, and her mind, what was left of her mind, a spark, a small ember, the kind of thing you would need to blow on to start a fire, that flickered somewhere in her head. Pried open her broken fingers and got the purse. Wanted to kick her once more, but she wasn't moving, so they left her (two of them), took the money out of the change purse and threw both change purse and Beth's purse on the lobby floor with all the other ripped-open envelopes and purses and walked through the front double doors, kicking the plastic as they went through.

Ester had finished feeding the cats, cutting her finger on the edge of a tin can. She sucked on the finger. She felt sick. She cursed Beth. Beth always got to do the important things, while she was stuck with feeding the cats. She sat down at the kitchen table. She felt sick, her head hurt. She lost more blood from the cut than she thought she had. She tried to remember where the bandages were. Maybe they didn't have any. She walked, staggering, to the bathroom, and opened the medicine chest, took out some Band-Aids, tore the little orange string down the side, and was left with two pieces of paper she didn't know what to do with. She let them fall on the floor. She put the bandage around her finger. It didn't feel as if it would stick. She pressed tighter on the bandage. It hurt when she pressed. Her head hurt. She walked to the bedroom and lay down on the bed and tried to sleep. Something kept pitching her up and down. It felt like she was on a roller coaster. The cats howled in the next room. She was going to make Beth clean the cat boxes when she got back. That was only fair. Then she went up and down again, sometimes sleeping, sometimes awake, unable to tell the difference.

20

THE mistake was not Jonsey's, who had driven her down to the welfare in his Pontiac (a four-door hardtop, the rear doors didn't open, which she didn't mind because the only space big enough for her was the front seat), nor in a sense could it be said the mistake was Willy's, who had to go down to the police station and get Goodchild, Leroy, who had let a bunch of boys take his clothes off and then poured honey and feathers on him and set him walking in the middle of Atlantic Avenue during the evening rush hour, but the mistake was the welfare lady's who made the appointment that she had to keep if she wanted to stay on welfare and Willy, William, always came along and translated for her; she spoke perfectly good English but somehow they couldn't understand what she said, or else they didn't want to understand, and she always brought Willy along to help with the speaking, and now Willy couldn't come with her.

She came by ramp. Hard to lift three hundred fifty pounds upstairs, don't care how strong you are. Used the railing to help pull herself along; the guards never bothered her, they knew where she was going and knew she knew. Down the hallway, first door on the right, don't have to knock, just walk right in. Uhuh. See that look on their faces. Know there's going to be trouble.

Welfare lady (W.L.) spoke. Mary wished Willy were here.

The money, something about the money they wanted to know, where it was, who was touching it.

"Ain't no goddamn secret. Jujubee man got it for the chickens. Dexter, that's Dorah's second, told me about the man with the chickens. Uhuh."

Dorah was her oldest, had two children of her own, one of whom was just eleven months, the same age as her youngest, Dorita (by Jonsey, the parcel post man). Dexter was Dorah's second man, the first was Baines, a family man they only learned later. Dexter was a friend of Baines, or Baines's son, and he told them about Baines and then Dorah got sweet on Dexter, a shy boy, good-looking, had a good line and smooth patter, re-bop, crackerjack salesman, who was always over quota on his Xerox sales and drove a Z–28 Camaro with a Blaupunkt stereo and wanted to make a nice home for Dorah and her children as soon as he could find a place. (He was living in a small one-room apartment in Brooklyn Heights, hardly room for Dorah plus two kids.)

W.L. says something again.

"Had to take Goodchild back to Virginia, use the chickens, get the curse off so Goodchild can get some of his natural sense back."

Goodchild, Leroy, fell out of a window when he was younger, bouncing off some bushes that used to be there but now were gone and hit his head on the ice, and up until then he had always made perfect sense and as a youngster knew his times tables and played the piano and never wet his bed but now you go into his bedroom the smell of urine on his sheets, plain old piss, is so strong you want to throw up, and no matter how many times she washed the sheets and the walls, the bedroom smelled and Willy, William, who had to share the bedroom with him, complained. Willy was a smartass, old enough to be out on his own but couldn't find a job, and he helped out at home though he didn't want to, and his friends always kidded him about it and kidded him about his brothers, Goodchild, who just needed some sense knocked into him because the sense was knocked out of him, not like James, who was retarded and liked to set fires, and Shanker, who was doing things with the dope, a bad boy to have around, but she loved him even though she knew that he was stealing them blind and sticking the needle in his arm, which got Willy so angry he used to beat up on Shanker, punch him in the stomach and head, but Shanker was beyond feeling much of anything, and he hardly moved when Willy beat on him.

W.L. speaking, something about the apartment and the Building and how many violations the landlord had.

"Used to be thin as a jackrabbit. Daddy never let us have much to eat," Mary said.

Now she had the eating sickness. Oh Lordy, how she could eat. Corn chips, Tang, bread, the soup that's left in the bowls, and the ends of sausage and peppers the children don't finish, the tiny tips of ice cream cones that they throw away, spaghetti scrapings that stick to the sides of the aluminum pot, leftover french fries (lick the grease off the paper it comes in), dregs of soda, cake crumbs, and, Oh Lordy, the specials, cents off this and that, the free samples they passed out (a new chip, a new dip, a new cheese, a new spread), save the banana peels for banana bread, flakes from the dry cereal that settle at the bottom of the cardboard box, old fish, fruit, damaged cans, broken and bruised and battered boxes where the noodles, linguini, and beans spill out, stuff that's loose in supermarkets that you can fill your pockets with and even if they catch you can't do nothing about because it's all loose (rice, peas, the little itty dried stuff, mouse turd food she called it), what sticks to the table, the counter, powdered drinks that come in the mail, food that's left in the corners of jars and stuck between the threads of lids, anything left on the edge of the knife, chew the bones down until they glisten, suck out the marrow, tips of carrots they were going to throw away, bread crusts, that rubbery stuff that covers cheese, dried drippings in the oven, stuff that falls to the bottom of the refrigerator, lick everything before you wash it, lick it twice, lick it clean. And then there were the dishes of rice and potatoes, spread thick with mayonnaise, the glasses of rich, creamy milk, the cauliflower, the cream of wheat, chicken, veal, pasta piled high and steaming, whipped cream, angel food cake; white food from a white world, which she stuffed into her black mouth. She carried her savings account inside. The food was safely stored, deposited in layers of fat that wrapped around her like a boa constrictor, her suet savings. Soon as she got the money she put it all in food and then put that food in her so she carried her investment around with her. Her bulk was her bank, her armor, her defense. She was a human battleship; she was her own fleet.

"Why the goddamn hell I got to move?" she asked the welfare lady.

There was Edna Lee, the brightest girl in her class (and that included the white kids in the class), and Jonsey promised that Edna Lee was going to college, and he was going to set something up for her but had a hard time with Shanker around and told her she had to get rid of that boy, he was no good and never was or would be. "He gonna put you all in that needle and stick you all in his arm," Jonsey said. She couldn't put him out on the street. She knew what he was doing, but he wasn't no cat you could just push out; if she put him out on the street he wouldn't take care of himself, wouldn't wash and wouldn't eat, would get sores. She cried when she thought of him huddled in some doorway, shivering, begging for junk. At least here he was warm, and she made him eat and wash. Dorah and William wanted to throw him out. "We ain't runnin' no fuckin' social welfare agency."

W.L. said Willy had to get a job.

"God bless Willy," she said. "That sweet boy is around when you need him. He look after Goodchild. And that's okay he beat on Shanker, but I don't like him to."

She cursed Willy for the beatings and cradled Shanker in her immense arms, his head dwarfed by her upper arm; and Shanker, his head buried in fat, was either high and constantly dropping his head and lifting it up again, or nervous, like a gerbil, nose twitching, eyebrows going up and down, a sort of frown/smile working its way across his face, followed by a series of twitches that seemed to fall across his forehead and cheeks like rain.

"I used to work," she said. "Used to be thin. I would be out in the fields before sunup and outpick and outpull the men. Couldn't stop me. Couldn't marry me off 'cause the men ashamed I work more than they. Used to carry a feed sack home from the store, sling it across my shoulders and walk down the road whistlin', no shoes, just a piece of a dress. Them men bother me, I used to whup 'em good. Uhuh."

Came up from Virginia because she had a dream, and the man hated to lose her, but you had to listen to a dream so she left, her daddy still down there, and not his daddy but his daddy's daddy was a slave and then free and then doing the same thing when he was free as when he was a slave and the old women used to sit around and have a laugh over that.

W.L. say they can't pay for Willy no more.

"God bless Willy. Uhuh."

She started to sing. She had a good voice, but her phrasing, her timing, was her own, always a little off, as if she was slowing down and then catching up to the song and going beyond it and then waiting for it to come along again, and she would stop in the middle of the song, just dead stop, like she couldn't remember the words or couldn't remember where she was, and then start singing again, only this time the song was in another part and she was back in the earlier part of the song, which didn't bother her but was the reason why no one could accompany her, no one knew how, so that despite her fine voice she always sang alone, a rich creamy contralto, like beef gravy, which bubbled right up out of her throat and filled the air. She could feel heaven in the song, in her singing. God filled her with that song, and she sang with every ounce of her three hundred fifty pounds, every gifted, exalted, honorable ounce.

W.L. said they couldn't pay the rent no more 'cause the Building had too many violations, and the landlord was not making any good-faith effort to fix them.

Mary Smith had come to the end of her song.

"God bless the home, praise the Lord!"

Soon as they kick some sense back into Goodchild, Willy could get a job. Willy could handle just about any job, but he was too much a smartass for his own good, too quick, too clever, and they don't want him around.

W.L. say the check be reduced by the rent amount and that Willy have to find work and contribute to the family—they taking him off too.

This time she started to hum, keeping her lips closed, building up a sweet foundation in her throat that keeps threatening to go higher but never does, and then starts to, closing her eyes, starts to sway back and forth, the chair creaking, and the W.L. afraid the chair will break (they keep an extra braced chair for her visits), but this time she is leaning back and forth on the chair, first the back legs take her weight and then the front, and the W.L. wonders if the legs will buckle, if Mary Smith will fall, if she falls will she be hurt, and if she goes down, can they pick her up again, or will she just have to stay on the floor and several people get behind and roll her out of the office, down the hallway, and down the ramp.

She will go home and gently pull the feathers off Goodchild, wash the honey off his chocolate skin (so soft that skin) and then rub him down with talcum (Goodchild love talcum) and then feed him something warm and hot, soup, yams maybe, chitlins, some hot milk with a little bit of cocoa sprinkled in it that he loved so much, put him to bed on clean sheets, which Jonsey got back from the Laundromat still smelling of soap with lemon that might hide the urine smell, hum him to sleep, hum him with the same hum she humming right now, uhuh.

W.L. asks her if she understands.

She understands.

The dream got her up here, but the dream wasn't a dream but real. "You dreamin' it be real," she said, "and it be real and that ain't no dream."

She talked to Willy, William, who despite his impatience and his anger with her, at her, would sit and listen to her for hours, lost in some strange reverie he couldn't understand and had a hard time accepting.

"Call the dream lady," she said. "Dream lady ain't got no color but you call her and she come. Know what she look like?"

Willy didn't.

"Course you don't. If she ain't got no color, how you know what she look like? But once you seen her, you know what she look like."

(Still humming, the W.L. wondering if she understands.)

"Now if you're sleeping in a bed, she won't come. You got to be awake, but sleeping, she comes."

"How could someone be awake but sleeping?" Willy asks.

(The W.L. thought the same thing but didn't want to say anything.)

"Hush you mouth," she said.

Still humming. Could hum and talk. W.L. amazed she can do this but then not amazed at Mary Smith, who can do whatever she sets her mind to. Willy was not there, but she had the same conversation with Willy she was having with the W.L.—that is, the W.L. was listening to her the same way Willy did. Mary Smith liked to repeat her conversations with different people. It seemed to make them more solid, more real. It was like repeating a dream.

"Where we goin'," Mary says, "tha's what I want to know."

"We were talking about your welfare check," W.L. said.

"Oh, yeah. When I was younger I like to frolic. Kick up my heels a little. My daddy don't take to that. He lock me up, but I bust out, uhuh. They call me bustout. I was always strong. Daddy couldn't even whip me after I was twelve. Could whip my momma, but he couldn't touch me 'cause I show him the mule."

She doubled up a sizable fist and started to pound the desk. The W.L. could feel the tremors through the desk. They seemed to reverberate through the desk and into her body, into her bones. She felt dizzy. Mary Smith's arms, huge, which looked like she had sacks of rice tied around the upper and lower parts, shivered under the blows to the desk.

No longer humming, had stopped some time ago, but the W.L. wasn't aware when she had stopped, just that she had stopped, and she wondered if she had been sleeping or dreaming.

"We'll have to readjust your check."

"What do that mean?"

"It means that your check will be reduced."

Mary Smith stared at her, keeping the fist on the desk, her thighlike arm resting on the desk as if it was about to encircle the desk and pick it up, fling it through the window. Her arm seemed to expand the longer it lay on the desk.

"Ain't you tired?" Mary Smith asked.

The W.L. was exhausted. She felt like there were small drains at her elbows and knees and that a pale-colored liquid, something heavy and thick, was slowly dripping from her body and collecting in pools on the floor. If she didn't do something, her body would just drain out, spill onto the floor. She felt her eyes closing and her head nodding and then caught herself.

"No," she said.

Mary Smith continued to look at her through small eyes that seemed tightly bound, as if they were under compression in her head, buried in that great black rock she called her face: soft, solid, stony.

"I can fly," said Mary Smith.

"I'm not tired," said the W.L.

"Right through the air. Clap my hands. Praise the Lord. Uhuh."

"I'll have to get your signature on this form."

"Ain't *signing* nothin'."

"If you don't sign it I can't issue you a check."

"Willy got to look at it first. Don't sign nothin' without Willy lookin' at it."

"I can't issue you the check."

"How we gonna eat? You thought of that? The rent man come around. You thought of that?"

The W.L. was mesmerized by her arm, which seemed to swell up to gigantic proportions.

"Just sign this form."

"Don't sign nothin'."

"We'll make another appointment so Willy can come in and read it for you."

Mary Smith got up with what seemed to the W.L. incredible speed, as if a catapult had flicked her out of the chair. She was a tank of black, a boulder, standing rock steady on legs that could support grand pianos. Her hair seemed to have grown closer to her scalp, to have been patted down and rolled into her head, which itself was larger, the bones miraculously growing. The W.L. was no longer tired. In her conversations with Mary Smith there was always one sentence that should have gone unsaid, that set off some tiny explosion in her, and then kept growing. She feared for the integrity of the desk, the composure of the glass, and, finally, the solidity of her bones. She never knew the mistaken sentence beforehand, but after, always. The room pulsated, swelling and contracting. The W.L. looking at Mary Smith, not wanting to but knowing she had to and being a creature of duty always fulfilling her obligations, and Mary Smith, returning the honor, rarely staring at someone unless there was a reason to drill home some forceful point, and now, her eyes becoming so hard they looked dull, as if pounded into shape on an anvil, she kept looking at the W.L.—no, not looking, there was something beyond looking she was doing.

Mary Smith took a step back and started to hum, and to the W.L. it sounded as if she was saying "uhuh, uhuh," repeating it over and over until the W.L. felt she was getting tired again, and she could smell something sweet, perhaps incense, or something sweeter yet, honey candy or marzipan. She smiled, in spite of herself, and remembered Christmas, for some strange reason, surrounded by relatives, rich desserts, and presents in huge boxes with large bows, none of which measured up to the majesty of the boxes.

Then Mary Smith started to sing, and the forms and the desk and the whole office swirled around the W.L. in a blur so that the only thing that presented itself to her senses was the rich contralto of Mary Smith that sounded like chocolate butter being slowly whipped with a metal spoon in a stainless steel pan and the blur of colors that represented desk, typewriter, pencils, pens, paper clips, carbon paper, thumbtacks, all the dull steel-colored office implements; and now Mary Smith's voice had a flutter to it, and what she had perceived as strength she now perceived as weak, vulnerable, a thing of beauty that was dashing itself to pieces on some hard and unyielding object (herself). *Praise the Lord,* but it sounded like *Crazy load, Paisley road, Pays elode,* and, through tightened lips, *Spacey loud.* There were many other words, and the W.L. figured it was an old-time gospel song, but the first three words were the only words she understood; the others she recognized as being English, but just barely, as if the language had been spoken by an isolated group of English shepherds who through the course of centuries had developed their own intonation, accent, and emphasis, until the new language could scarcely be called English.

Mary Smith stopped singing and took a step back, toward the door, a process that should have reduced her in size in the eyes of the W.L. but in fact did the opposite, filling the room with her presence.

"Who are you?"

The question kept revolving around in her head, a query that wouldn't leave no matter how hard she tried to make it leave, and after Mary Smith had left ("Praise the Lord, uhuh, and pray your blood don't quake, pray your bones don't break, pray your skin don't shake") she had to run to the ladies' room where she threw up, in convulsions that seemed to reach down to her knees and shook her head, so that her hair, which was waist length but pinned up in a bun, shook free and became awash with partially digested food. She washed her hands and face several times, rinsed her hair, pinned it back up without drying it, and went home for the day, feeling unusually relaxed and at ease with herself.

Mary Smith went home to find that Shanker had sold Goodchild to some teenage boys so he could get a fix, and when Willy retrieved Goodchild, he still had some of the feathers stuck to his skin but what held the feathers was not honey but some other sticky substance, something not edible. Goodchild sat in the tub while she stripped the feathers off and then tried to give him a bath but there was no hot water, again, and not too much cold water. She heated several pans of water on the stove and when little bubbles began floating to the top poured them into a washbasin and then added some cold water, took off her brassiere and tested the temperature of the water with her tit, sticking it nipple first and then the whole breast into the graying water, and satisfied that the temperature was right (her huge football-shaped breast now feeling warm and light) dumped Goodchild into the tub, him not complaining all this time, and began rubbing his body with an amber-colored bar of soap. The water was soon filled with feathers, and Goodchild, amused by the buoyancy and size of his penis, began laughing.

Shanker would be gone for the night. He would not come back when he was tired or hungry, he would come back when he was broke, probably in the afternoon, sneaking into the apartment by the fire escape, quietly, so as to avoid Willy and Dorah.

As she washed Goodchild, Mary Smith looked around the room, at the molding that was springing loose from the side of the wall, at the triangulated pieces of parquet that were curled and coming up, yellowed from Goodchild's urine, at the small network of cracks that began to appear one evening in the apartment, followed the next day by a widening yellow mold that covered the cracks, followed by the paint blistering, and then the huge gush of water that ran through the apartment for a week. The putty was dry and cracked in the windows, and some of the panes rattled, held in only by tiny glazier's points. The radiators had been without heat for a year, and now winter was coming again, and she prayed to Jesus to send up heat. Oh Lord, just send it tumbling up, in great waves, great steamy waves of heat. Praise the Lord, uhuh. Willy told her she was a fool, that it wasn't Jesus but Tontine and the landlord who should be providing them with heat, and when he said that, she became instantly angry, just the way she had been with the W.L., only this time she hit Willy. He had stepped back because he had known it was coming, but he had not stepped back fast enough, or she was faster than he thought, because the "Mule" came out like lightning and dumped him on his ass in the middle of the room, and Willy, cursing, got up and poured himself a glass of milk.

"Praise the Lord, child, uhuh, and watch for the dream lady."

Willy had hit her back once, and she had cried, not so much in pain as in shame, and Willy, the shame in him magnified, cursing, shouted at her and told her not to do that again and then hugged her, crying, tears running down his tight, athletic face and onto her broad face, and he couldn't stop crying, and carried the memory of that with him so that he never hit her again, only tried to step back to avoid her temper, which he could do quite often, especially if not backed into a corner.

"Got a job," Willy said, "and Dorah would have too if they hadn't cut the day-care."

"I had a dream, uhuh."

"Don't you want to know what it is?"

"Told you, I had a dream."

He finished his milk and put the glass in the sink and turned on the water to rinse it out. The faucet belched and bubbled, and a rust-red water emerged from the faucet, sounding as if sand were running through the pipes.

"I'm the chicken man. I dress up like a chicken and run through the streets squawking, handing out cards for the Chicken Shack."

"Uhuh."

"It's on a trial basis. To see if the owner gets more customers with some asshole like me dressed up like a chicken running and squawking through the streets."

He stopped. The dignity of the job no longer concerned him. Not when there had been fifty other applicants standing outside the Chicken Shack on Bedford Avenue, practicing their squawks to see who could do the best and loudest, and the owner, a fat black man with several Chicken Shacks spread across the ghetto, listened attentively to each of the applicants, finally choosing Willy, and Willy felt that a victory of sorts had been achieved, a milestone reached, and that submerged so long he was finally coming up for air, and it didn't make any difference if the life preserver was chickenshit.

"Dorah would have had a job as a secretary. She some typist. But no one to take care of the kids."

Mary Smith had tried once to take care of Dorah's children, but for some reason, they had confused her, as if her own children had been simple and straightforward, easy to care for, but grandchildren added a layer of complexity, were complicated personages with whims and needs that were far from those she recognized. Dorita, her own young one, she barely managed. Sometimes she dreamed that she was taking care of her, feeding her, cleaning her, and thought that meant she really had done these tasks and could not be convinced otherwise. When that happened, Dorah simply took Dorita as one of her own and did for her what she did for hers, while Mary Smith "dreamed," lying in bed with her eyes open but asleep, so that she could hear and yet not hear, talk and yet not talk, as if she were in some zone between sleeping and waking.

Shanker came back that night, swinging in lightly through the fire escape window. There was a restless quiet to the apartment. Shanker roamed through the rooms looking for paper money, then change, then something he could hock. James was the lightest sleeper and would probably wake up, but he was too retarded to say anything, he would only moan, and Shanker would give him a piece of bread soaked in oil to keep him quiet. Shanker moved quickly, almost noiselessly through the rooms, continually wiping his nose on his sleeve, the shoelaces to his sneakers undone and dirty, one sneaker tongue pulled out and flapping on one side, his fly half zipped. Shanker moves with the ease and the ferret glances of a man with one thought on his mind, and there is something almost beautiful in the natural quickness about him, the thoroughness with which he probes drawers and envelopes, crock jars and purses, like an anteater pushing its sticky tongue into the farthest reaches of the ant nest. Shanker pauses, sniffing the air, sniffling, takes out a handkerchief that once was white, wipes the back of his head, wipes the dirt, the spittle, the bits of paper, gum wrappers, and sewer flotsam that have found refuge in his hair. He wondered if he could sell James, then decided he was too retarded to sell. He put the handkerchief back into his pocket, and then putting his finger alongside his nostril, he blew the contents of the opposite nostril on the floor and then alternated the process.

Mary Smith sits up in bed. She has just had a visit from the dream lady, who is dressed all in white with white cream all over her black arms and legs so that her skin looks not black, not white, but purple, like some Mexican cactus.

"Shanker, that you?"

Shanker is quiet, except for his sniffling; his nose will not stay dry. He weeps through his nose. He turns his head from side to side in short, jerky movements, like a hand puppet or some mechanical toy. If he is quiet his mother may go back to sleep or back to whatever she was in before.

"Shanker, you there?"

Mary Smith is awake, not dreaming now, the dream lady, the purple lady, Matilda, Matty, now a shadow on the wall, a moth beating its wings against the window trying to get out at the street lamp.

Shanker extends his chin, as if he had a nose on the end of it and was sniffing the air, which felt close and quiet, felt as if the room were stuffed with black cotton.

"Shanker?"

One more time. Perhaps she had been dreaming; perhaps what was there was not Shanker but the wish of Shanker, the wish filling the room with its presence and its aped smell of Shanker. Mary Smith rolled over in bed. The dream lady, the moth, becomes bloated and drops to the windowsill, grows, keeps splitting out of its skin. Shanker moves again, searching the kitchen for silver, underneath the beds for socks knotted at one end, opens drawers, searches wallets, looks behind pictures, on the backs of high shelves in closets, beginning to get frantic now ("This fucking family doesn't keep shit around!"), his eyes dancing in his head (as if they were watching an invisible tennis match), his fingers soiled and overly soft, like old, spoiled velvet, the lobes of his ears dirty, his shirt, clean a week ago when Mary Smith took it out of the laundry for him, smelling of sweat and vomit, the seat of his pants dirty and ripped ("The fucking barbed-wire fences, they got no fucking business putting those goddamned barbed-wire fences there, and that broken bottle, who the fuck put that broken bottle there? I didn't put the damn needle in her arm, she did it, problem with that shit that comes from Iran is that it's too cheap and they don't bother cutting it so much anymore, hardly worth the fucking time, and the price is down, so you get the powerful shit, you got to watch out. I didn't put that shit in her. She stuck the needle in herself, she had spaces between tracks. I told her to go easy with this new shit, that it was much purer, but she wants this big rush, greedy bitch; they get that way when they get pregnant, looks like she got a basketball under her shirt, she keels over with the goddamn needle hanging out of her arm, head hits the floor like a melon"), and Shanker, now having an anxiety attack, which is a kind of a high, only it makes him jittery, he has these enormous feelers he puts out, and he knows what you're going to say before you say it.

The dream lady, enormous, purple, with a purple-flowered hat, sits on Mary Smith's chest, and Mary feels this huge burden with her labored breathing, and it is only relieved when the dream lady waits for Mary Smith to inhale, and with one great burst is sucked into the nose and body of Mary Smith, and the burden is both relieved and taken on, removed from her chest, swimming through her mind.

Shanker now becomes the thing he is searching for, becomes the junk, becomes the needle; there is only the flow through the veins that teaches him about time, that loosens the great chain of being and shows the links, that lets him lie floating inside his body, lets him swim through his arteries, strips the room of its illusions to show the reality beyond that, the floating, rushing, tumbling, jumping, diving reality. Dope is his friend, dope asks nothing in return except for the chance to *always* be a friend. *In the name of the Father and of the Son and of the holy Dope.*

Mary Smith is breathing slowly, her lungs burdened by the mountain of fat they must lift every few seconds, her heart pumping through an Amazon and its tributaries. The dream lady has taken her by the hand and leads her along her legs, along her eyebrows, through her scalp (twitching, doing a nervous little dance) and, standing on her forehead, jumps, hand in hand with Mary Smith, and the two of them leave the body of Mary Smith behind, leave these great fleshy clumps of black hills that rise and fall to the gentle tremor of her breathing.

Shanker has found what he is looking for, and if you look at him now he will smile, a benign sort of smile, a soft moon look, as if melted butter had been spread over his face.

21

"I am the exterminator," he said.

He exterminated, caused to fall over and die by poison things that bit and sucked, nibbled, chewed, munched, or otherwise gnawed, things that crawled, scurried, scuttled, climbed, slid, rolled, flew, waddled, or otherwise transported themselves in a fashion other than upright, and things that had fur, hard shells, feathers, skin too smooth and skin too rough, skins with bristle and skins covered with clanking armor, all manner of creatures who did not walk upright but otherwise transported themselves with a variety of legs or in ways not involving legs.

He was a tall man who smoked a pipe and always had a reassuring smile on his face, as if he were sucking on honey apples, and strapped to his back were two stainless-steel tanks, shining, polished to eye-itching brightness, with a rubber tube that extended from the tanks and looped around his waist and a nozzle that he could adjust by turning the serrated edges of a brass fitting on one end.

"I am the Pa Kettle of Pests," he announced. "I follow the water pipes, the drains, the cabinets, the sinks, baseboards, attics, cellars, closets. I lay down the stink, my brown liquid, wherever the pests are apt to congregate. I lay down a heavy stink; it does not pay to stint on stink. I lay it down thick and heavy, chemicals that clog the pores, that short-circuit the central nervous system, that shut down the automatic nervous system, that break the bond between oxygen and blood, that cause internal bleeding, that lacerate the intestines and cause heart seizures; all these things and more, as newer chemicals are found, I do. Flee when I come. Remove yourself from the apartment. I put down a heavy stink, and those of you with weak hearts, those of you with breathing problems, asthma, emphysema, diabetes, those of you with flu or smoker's cough, those of you who have a recent infection, eye trouble, are prone to sores, bleed easily, or have a history of other medical ailments, however remote, are advised to remain away for a week. My stink goes on strong, is laid down heavy; living things are around it at their own risk."

Abdul Karim had complained to the owner about moths, had described it in such a way as to make the owner think that there were masonry-eating termites that flew with furry wings and ate bricks and cashmere sweaters, able to pass through small cracks in otherwise impervious walls, and that these moths, who in the telling of it had become termites and then in the thinking of it by the owner had also become roaches, ants, mice, and a flock of vultures that the owner was convinced made their home in the José chimney and defecated into his furnace, which was the cause of all his heating problems, so he called the exterminator to get rid of the vultures. He also could hear the din of millions of tiny insects gnawing at *his* Building, rats who were chewing through the lead pipes, cockroaches who were busy eating the insulation off the electric lines, bees who were dying in the drains and clogging them, goats who ate the windowsills, dogs who peed on the floor and short-circuited the wiring beneath, birds whose excreta slimed up empty apartments. There were raccoons who had escaped from the park and were chewing their way through the doors in the basement and bats whose tiny claws brought down the plaster in the ceilings and a bag of black snakes let loose in the neighborhood by an enraged naturalist who had found their way to the basement and were winding their way up the drain and water pipes, appearing in apartments disguised as wiring, spiders who layered web over web in unused spaces, and small gecko lizards who had escaped from someone's apartment and scampered about the hallways, frightening the tenants and causing an oily sheen to be laid on the stairs, a slippery film that made footing precarious. These, of course, were only the smaller creatures.

But it was not Abdul Karim and his man-eating moths, nor the Wilson Sisters and their cats, nor the meat dealer and his divine dog who crushed the skulls of smaller animals, nor Tontine's pigeons, nor even the vultures that may or may not have lived in the José chimney and feasted off the bodies that appeared in the Building, and the fact that the vultures may have caused heating problems did not really concern the landlord since heating and the problems attendant with it did not concern him.

It was the fireflies. It was the appearance in the fall, much beyond normal expectations, of a cloud of fireflies that settled on the roof, a huge glowing presence, like a bonfire that swept through the air and settled on the owner's Building, and the synchronicity of their glowing produced a cyclic conflagration: first the roof was burning, then it wasn't, and so on. The landlord, a man of established habits and regular practices, was alarmed by the suddenness of the insects, the uneasy possibility of fire (when his fire insurance had lapsed and he was finding it difficult to renew, and he wasn't sure if he wanted to set the Building on fire and collect the insurance or set a small fire to drive the tenants out, paint over the soot, and rent out the apartments for several times what his current tenants paid him). The fireflies adopted various shapes and postures, and at times their glowing presence signaled a huge bird on fire, a flaming pine tree, or a bear that breathed fire. The owner, watching this cloud of insects and their blinking fire from across the street through binoculars, became alarmed, thinking that the fireflies had been sent by the gypsies who sold him the stolen roof and were trying to buy the Building from him, paying not money but something they called *Romany Script,* paper debentures they claimed had magical power.

"I am the exterminator," he shouted in the hallways, ringing a bell, and warning the tenants that the lives of all creatures below waist level, small things that breathed close to the floor where he laid down his stink, were in danger, and that all such living things who wished to be saved remove themselves from the apartment, from the Building, for a period no less than twenty-four hours after he began laying down his smell.

"I am the exterminator," he yelled, his almost yellowed face breaking into a series of smiles as he shouted his warning, and promised that he would cleanse the Building of all organic life and that the bodies of those left could be unceremoniously swept into the cellar and burned, warning that the smoke was not to be breathed since the toxic chemicals that leveled undesirable organisms did not decompose but were wafted up in the smoke, dispersed in the air, and deposited somewhere eastward, following the prevailing winds.

"I am the exterminator," he yelled, and he began laying down his stink as promised, and the putrid smell drifted into the apartment of Abdul Karim, who, fearing for his life and believing that the paraplegic was about to set another army of moths on him, fled screaming, but not before he had taken a list of periodicals he needed to restock his subway newsstand, and Steckler, caught in the basement hot-wiring his arc welder after he had burned up a set of electric lines on one side of the Building, cursed and tried to kick the exterminator, who as an exterminator was used to being kicked at and who dodged the kick, one of the few who had ever dodged a Steckler kick, and continued to lay down his stink, so that Steckler decided to leave, locking the apartment and locking Visa in the apartment with the admonition to guard his welding equipment.

Floor by floor the exterminator spread his foul brown liquid, and the sickly sweet smell entered the dreams of Singiat-Sing Dan Dinphuir, who left with his monkey wife and their many children to stay with a cousin who lived in Queens and imported sisal hemp. Tontine gathered his wife and children and all the wood objects he could carry and left via the back stairs, fording the moat that protected the side of the Building, which had resulted from a broken water pipe and the drain being clogged by ripped-apart purses. Hobson gathered the heavier-than-imagined paraplegic in his arms and carried her down the stairs, setting her at the bottom in the wheelchair with a tenderness that was part concern and part lust, though exactly what the proportions were no one, especially Hobson, knew, and wheeled her over the broken marble and gritty stones and glass in the hallway out to the front, where she blinked at the energy of the sun and shivered in the chill air, and Hobson, thinking of the cockroaches, those he had trained and listened to and spoke to and those that were his enemies, shivered at the thought of their dying bodies, rolling helplessly on their hard-shell backs, imagining the crackle and crunch that would be made when walking over the corpses of their brown shells. The Wilson Sister, Beth (or was it Ester?), gathered her cats in plywood cages and ferried them down two by two on the front sidewalk until she had a menagerie of cats in boxes, which attracted other cats not in boxes, who sprayed over the boxes and hissed and clawed at the cats inside, who in turn sprayed and hissed and clawed, and the Wilson Sister, Ester? Beth? ran around with a broom chasing the unboxed cats away and called a cab, which refused to take twenty-seven cats in plywood boxes. Stern refused to leave. He put on a gas mask and locked the door to his apartment and put a mask on his naked model, who tried to exit via the fire escape, caught only at the last moment by Stern who was not bothered by one or one hundred naked women climbing out of his apartment and down the fire escape but was bothered by not being able to finish his *Madonna of Cocaine Dreams,* a nine-foot-by-twelve-hundred-foot canvas of the Blessed Virgin in poses of surreal expectancy. The lunatic stayed in the cellar, hiding in a cave next to the river and watching the glow of the Indian bones that made up the foundation of the Building and listening to the moaning that Eschopf made when he couldn't find a chess piece that he had dropped in the mud. Mary Smith left, lifted out through the window by crane, her three-hundred-fifty-pound broken-boned body (the result of her ride with the dream lady) unable to negotiate the stairs, and Willy, Dorah, James, and Dorita left with her, but not Goodchild, who had wandered off with the lunatic, and not Shanker, who was high somewhere in Williamsburg, lying behind the metal stairs in the hallway of a tenement, pants soaked in urine and blood from a beating administered by muggers soon after they had helped him shoot up and too numb, too high, to understand why they were hitting him or what they were hitting him with or where they were hitting him (though days later, when he tried to hobble back to Mary Smith, he would remember, quite painfully remember). Tonton Tute, fearful for the health of his zombies, dug them up from the mud in the cellar and dragged them up the cellar steps and into the trunk of a sixty-three Lincoln Continental, still drugged, rearranging their limbs so that he could fit two of the zombies in the trunk and then put the third in the back seat, spreading newspaper so that the mud did not dirty the leather seats, and drove off to a Haitian beauty parlor, where in the back room religious services were held and the zombies could be safely stored until the moment of awakening had arrived and the zombies could enter the world once more, having descended into the underworld and come back, hopefully to tell what they had seen and provide instructions for those about to descend and for those who would remain above but needed instructions in living. The T'ai Chi master left with Glasho, the excrement artist, who was preparing an exhibition in a Soho gallery and spent most of his time prowling the street for material and who, since his self-immolation, had been practicing the art of levitation, a skill taught by the T'ai Chi master who, as a Taoist, was continuing a tradition that had been handed down for thousands of years, before the time of Lao-tze. The meat dealer-turned-sniper preferred to stay and shoot at things that moved in the street, occasionally lugging up a bathtub, which he dumped from the roof on visiting social workers or firemen or the owner when he came to collect the rent, the bathtubs falling to the cement below with a great clang, as if some huge bell had been rung, sometimes shattering, sometimes merely denting, and the pile of bathtubs that accumulated at the entranceway grew until a path to the door had to be cleared and the bathtubs were shoved to one side where the bushes used to grow, which the lunatic had lugged in the subway to the owner's house. The deaf-mute left, along with his family, but not before he walked all the halls and felt the walls with his fingers, as if saying good-bye, wanting to reaffirm a past nostalgia, hearing the lapping of the ocean on the walls and the cries of sea birds from the ceilings and feeling that the Building would soon spring a leak, be underwater. Cuzz left, along with his torches and his friend Truth. The professor of linguistic philosophy packed up the dwarf's clothes and put them neatly in the baby carriage and wrapped a pink knit-wool blanket around them, tucking in the corners, and packed some of his own clothes in an overnight case with a strap so the case could be hung from his shoulder and wheeled clothes and carriage out the apartment, bumping them down the steps, over the piles of garbage in the lobby, and out to the sidewalk where a Black Pearl Cab ("We are not yellow, we go everywhere") driven by a suspicious-looking heavyset black man chewing a week-old cigar was waiting to take him to a run-down apartment in Red Hook over a garage that dealt in stolen Mercedes Benz and Cadillac parts.

Vigorously pumping the brown slime that coated the floors and wallboards and stairs, pipes and radiators, moldings, baseboards, stair risers, kickplates, and cellar, the exterminator shoved his hose into every nook and cranny of the Building, until the flushing of rats and mice, the scurrying of cockroaches, the startled, asphyxiated breath of cats and bats who plummeted to the floor in convulsions, the dizzying death circles made by termites, the impassioned writhing of snakes, the seizures of turtles, the psychotic web spinning of spiders, and the howling of soon-to-be-dead dogs set up an animal hum in the Building which the exterminator ignored, accustomed to the rebuttals of insects and the complaints of creatures whom he poisoned, used to the noise and surreal din that accompanied their death throes, as if they held him personally responsible and were making their testimony now, registering it with him, so that he, who herded them in death as the tenants had supported them in life, but done it silently, simply put earplugs on and went about his killing business, his deathly profession.

The fireflies had invaded the pigeon apartment and had turned the interior into a Broadway sign, flashing off and on at regular but not discrete intervals, like a signal of distress, as if the purged Building, being forced to take a laxative, was crying out for help. The exterminator went floor by floor, his killing slime trailing him, the smile of death on his face and reincarnation in his eyes, knowing that the chemically poisoned creatures whose tiny hearts he had stopped were now being transformed into another karmic wheel, to reappear soon as landlords or laborers, whales or mayors, walruses or avocados. The exterminator was simply an instrument of the wheel, a cog that helped turn the wheel, not himself the mover of death, not the kicker but the kicked. The exterminator also knew that someone, not he, would have to come after him and clean up the corpses, sweep up the tiny rigor mortis bodies and dump them into the incinerator, or plastic bag them; the sign of his work was often neatly spaced rows of plastic bags, black, stuffed with the meat of his business.

He rarely had to enter an apartment; the crack at the bottom of the door was large enough for the entrance of the brown slime, the viscous liquid that soon coated the entire floor like some oily gelatinous slick, as if an oil tanker had broken apart in a sea on the roof, and while the fumes wafted upward through holes and cracks, a sort of anticooking odor, the liquid leaked through holes in the floor, dripping down in long wavy strings into the apartment below, itself a pool of the brown that was leaking into it. Trucks brought more stainless-steel tanks filled with brown liquid, which were placed on the landings, until hundreds of them had been discharged into the Building, until its double set of wings, its cellar, its stairs and landings and hallways and lobby were awash, dripping in virulent brown.

"Death to the living, and life to death," the exterminator sang, who as a lapsed Hindu had constructed his own religion and invoked the devils of some thirty separate religions of India.

Stern had stuffed the crack between the door and the floor with rags, backed that up with a strip of wood nailed to the floor, stuffed pencils in the keyhole, locked the windows, sealed up the cracks in the ceiling, and nailed flattened tin cans around the steam riser and water pipe holes. The exterminator was unable to shove his hose under Stern's door, so he banged on the door and told Stern to get out so he could take care of business; but Stern, ears plugged, gas mask in place, a fire burning in the tiny cast-iron stove to ward off the fall chill, ignored him and rearranged his angry nude model, readjusting her gas mask, partly to show that he did have her interest at heart (would only have it if it coincided with his). While the exterminator banged at the door, first with his fist, then with his shoe, then with one of his tanks, and finally with a small hammer he carried with him (which did little good since the door was steel lined, a precaution Stern had demanded when he first rented in the Building), Stern ignored the sounds, proceeding with his *Madonna of Cocaine Dreams,* a soiled sort of brownish painting in which the Virgin Mary, having just discovered Christ on the cross, is about to pass on to the drained body of Our Lord a potion or potions unknown, or is about to cradle her Son's head in her arms, an act befitting a mother, or is performing some other vague function that involves arms and hands and the limbs of the Lord, or doing none of these, is by herself, enveloped in a burning bush, unable to scrape the haze from her head, a heady anesthetic that confuses her, and somewhat dopey, she makes her way through the flaming vegetation. Stern is unhappy with the way the model poses, and despite her severe protestations, ties her with heavy rope that seems to separate her body into several sections, the rope framing and suspending breasts, dividing arms in two and three, surrounding pubic hair (the flaming bush of the painting a replica of the model's), cutting across waist and upper and lower thighs, presenting Stern with sections of flesh, a series of bodies and sections of bodies, the repetition of which is caught in the painting and provides it with both its decisiveness and its indecisiveness.

The exterminator tries the transom, which Stern has taken the precaution to nail and brace with two-by-fours. He bangs long and loudly on it, moaning and crying. "I am the exterminator," he yells, but Stern barely hears him, ears stuffed with Q-tips, nor does he hear the accusations of his model, whose nipples, despite the wood-burning stove, are tinged in blue. She yells at Stern, who is inspired by her anger, thinks he may make the room a bit colder, have her jump around, suspend her from a hook in the ceiling, show her as a piece of meat, talking meat, and she wonders why she must pose nude while the madonna in Stern's painting is fully clothed, indeed seems overclothed, and Stern knows she is thinking this, knowing that all his models question him thus when his madonnas are fully clothed, and he will not answer them, believing that it is beneath an artist to explain his reasons or his work to models, to the public, to critics, to anyone, and that to work in confusion, in mystery, in paradox, is a gift of art.

The exterminator, determined to gain entrance to Stern's apartment, climbs up to the roof, searching through the many holes to see if one leads to Stern's apartment. He sticks his nozzle into any hole he can find, spraying the apartments below with a brown cloud that condenses into a sea of brown, a brown waterfall that descends slowly, as if in arrested motion, through apartment after apartment. But none of this reaches Stern, who, gas mask in place, has dangled his shouting model from a hook in the ceiling, and while she sways back and forth, the vivid shadow from her nudely tied form rushing across the wall with terrifying speed, paints her terror and anger with a transcendence that amazes even him, that transforms the madonna into an angry Amazon, a womb-carrying, spear-wielding, snarling, naked-breasted virgin consumed with lust and death, determined to tear at the heart of existence.

The exterminator appears at the fire escape window, tapping on the glass. "I am the exterminator," he yells again, as if this magic incantation were the open sesame to Stern's apartment. He raps on the glass again and tries the window. Stern waves him away. The painting is almost finished. He will not stop. Consumed by thunderbolts, betrayed by monsoons, he would still finish this painting. The exterminator takes out his hammer to tap a small hole in the glass and insert his nozzle to discharge his deadly brown. Stern sees his intent, but caught in the flow of the brush he continues to paint, the distraction, forcing him to continue later, a deadly interruption. He must not derail the train he is on. The painting already exists in his mind, in the oils, in the brush, and now it must exist on canvas. The flow must not be stopped. This vision is too eager to get out, and if he stops it will continue to come, escaping through his head into the air. The painting is on a projector he cannot turn off, cannot rewind, cannot show again. He will paint in a pool of brown, he will let the swill congeal around his legs, he will slosh in this poisonous oil until the painting is absolutely finished.

The exterminator has a reverence for art but also one for business, and he understands that the latter supports the former. Stern can work in slime. That is not his concern. He taps a small hole in the bottom of the window. A large chunk of pane falls several stories, through the bars of the fire escape, and shatters on the sidewalk. The exterminator unsheathes his tool, adjusts his nozzle, and prepares for the discharge. He does not consider what he does to be a violation. It is merely his duty.

The cloud of fireflies, having settled in the pigeon apartment, are restless once more, and ascend through an opening known only to them, clustering around the José chimney, illuminating it with their blinking presence, and then take off once again, as if by signal, a cloud of light. They buzz around the edge of the roof and descend the fire escape. The exterminator looks up, is confronted with organic light, a blazing insect presence. He swings his hose around, preparing to drive them off, to dispose of them in the same manner that he has disposed of so many other organisms in the Building. But they descend upon him, thousands, tens of thousands, and no longer blink but stay lit so that the exterminator is surrounded in pure light, a heatless light, and suddenly confused by the presence of white on this dark fall afternoon, thinking perhaps that the sun has retraced its steps or the earth suddenly stopped and was spinning in reverse, forgets his hose or remembers it but for a moment forgets how to use it (as one might forget a familiar object in a moment of pressure or confusion), and the insects, now bathing him in pure light, motiveless, slowly pick him up, or he feels that they pick him up, perhaps something else does (he hesitates to suspend his belief in gravity), such that he rises, either to a standing position, or perhaps much higher, his feet not quite touching the fire escape, then clearly not touching it, and then the cloud of fireflies, now providing a steady source of unblinking light, lift him up and carry him higher yet, above the roof, where he can look down on the Building, the holes in the roof, the battered-in doors, the broken syringes, the torn shoes and ripped purses, and then he is lifted higher yet, until not only Building but borough is in view, and he rises in a cloud of pure light, escapes in a ball of white, the prisoner of fireflies, and the Building is still a part of gravity, hooked to the earth and the city, but the exterminator, now one with the fireflies, an angel, has lifted himself into one of his karmic wheels, leaving behind his killing brown and the Building.

22

TEN years ago, while training for the Olympics, Lowell married a
woman who weighed what one of his arms did. Picture this. Him,
a beer barrel above the waist, arms like truck tires, a round face, features pressed tight with the strain of lifting hundreds of pounds of iron.
She came up to his armpit. She was a dancer, thin as a leaf, a pale,
energetic woman tired from exhausting workouts. Wide hips pared
lean with diet soda, tight legs that dreamed of fat. She danced until
she was drenched, dragged herself home, fell asleep in front of the
eyeglass-size Sony TV.

Lowell worked out in the parks on the Lower East Side, ran to work
in a sweat suit, kept a towel around his neck, bench pressed three,
maybe four hundred pounds. Although immensely strong, he got sick
easily: colds, flus, chilblains, sore throats. He kept the apartment like
a sweatbox, oiled the floors, left sandals outside for visitors. He had
three skylights with steamy vermin-ridden plants that hung from the
apex of each. A blender, before he smashed it, mixed the vegetable
juices that they lived on: his mixed with yeast and steroids, hers thinned
out with water.

They lived in the lower part of the city, over a firm that recycled
wooden skids. On Sundays the rocky streets were hushed. Paper littered the broken sidewalks, wooden skids were piled up in doorways.
He walked the streets in a British army sweater with patches on the
shoulders and elbows and broke wooden slats with his fists. Coming
upon parked VWs, he lifted the front ends and placed them on the
sidewalk. Often he felt like smashing anything he could wrap his hand
around. The air was too clean, the city too quiet. Sundays, for some
reason, felt like death. Water bugs, captured coming out of sewers, he

threw against brick walls until he could hear their brittle shells snapping under the impact. Then something else snapped.

He did something strange to his wife.

Now she was gone.

He stripped himself naked and shouted into the toilet bowl. He slept and shouted for three days and then crawled over to the phone and knocked it to the floor, managing to dial the operator. But when the operator came on, the only thing he could remember after years of studying Hegel and the phenomenology of Husserl, after years of Walt Disney comic books and Jesuit training, weight lifting and bio-energetic feedback, was his mother's phone number, which he shouted into the phone, at the receiver, as if the receiver were Kant, while the operator patiently explained to him that he could dial the number. How could he dial the number? He wanted to, but he had fins instead of hands.

He passed out on the floor, the phone off the hook, a shrill wail from the receiver a reminder that the phone was off the hook.

His sanity had frittered away its welcome, had been advised to pack its bags and get moving.

He lived in the left eye of a whore, believed passionately in stainless steel, made some deposits and some withdrawals.

He was good at finding things that were lost, was consulted on a random basis, and made money with this gift. He was giddy, strong, clear as ice, could divine logarithms, and conjure up, when necessary, calculus. (Lowell: "Now, I am no expert in madness, any more than a frog is an expert in frogness, but one of the things I have observed about people in this state is that they, we, are obsessed with things we don't like. It is as if we coat ourselves with flies and spend our lives trying to brush them off, having forgotten what it was ever like to be free of them.")

He slept in a friend's basement apartment for a month, ate Hostess cupcakes and drank apple cider from a high-priced natural-foods store around the corner, read the collected works of Mark Twain, and watched people from the knees down. Then he wanted to watch people from the head down. He sat on roofs and watched the city, the silty sky, pondered the gray and brown hazes and the dirty sunsets. He watched fat, gouty pigeons and tiny cement-colored sparrows flitting about from branch to branch in auto-exhaust-stained trees. He watched roof tar crack, grow dusty, flake into the gutter, and then bubble up in the sun, like oil, becoming all sheen and glisten. He watched toy fires flash up in buildings, tiny fire engines thread their way through the streets, smoke billowing into clouds that refused to leave the horizon.

In the late afternoon the city began to puff itself up, growing fatter as the dirty sunset filled out the buildings with huge shadows and gave immense depth to shallow constructions. Lowell could imagine himself as one of those buildings: breathing out, growing fat, gaining corners and edges.

Then he no longer wanted to sit on roofs. He wanted to find the surface, the floor, the crust. His geometry collapsed a dimension. He wanted to hobnob with streets ("Curbs became my guidelines, lane dividers my symbols, stoplights my catechism"). He was a mole flooded out of his tunnel.

Though he did not exercise, his strength did not go away. It remained inside his body, waiting. He was strong, fat, tired, puzzled, anxious, full of good intentions but doubtful of those of others.

Something was missing. Not just with him . . . with other people. Pieces. Parts of buildings fell. Other buildings collapsed. He wondered how they managed to stay up so long.

He walked.

He consulted sidewalks and curbs, traipsed through vacant lots, ambled through parks, waded in fountains, pondered statues, stood transfixed before clocks. His head became filled with buildings: empires of steel and glass, some with sloping fronts like ski runs, others that looked like grids, pointing the way to some vague and mysterious plan. He saw great stone slabs that looked like hymns to permanence being torn down as quickly as possible, as if someone were embarrassed by their squat dignity. He saw tenements, row upon row of disemboweled caves scrawled with a spaghetti of twisted pipes, frazzled wires, cracked and shattered porcelain. In the summer, squatters who used them clubbed out the marauding dogs and slept on filthy mattresses laid down on diseased floors. In the winter they fled. No one knew where they went.

Where was he? Which borough? Which city?

Perhaps in the Bronx, staring at a population that didn't exist, that got sucked out, floor after floor vacant with broken windows and empty dreams, doors banging forever against scarred walls and the wind scattering paper through echoless rooms.

And then in his madness, a plan.

He would fix the broken buildings. He would hire himself out to a city agency that fixed such buildings.

23

THE cripple hit Sanchez in the neck with one of his crutches, holding on to a paraplegic for support, and as Sanchez dropped to the pavement the other protesting tenants cheered, not realizing that the cripple (on disability insurance) had deprived them of the speech Sanchez was about to give, a speech that he had prepared especially for them in his capacity as deputy commissioner, or as assistant director, or as deputy director, or perhaps as all three, depending upon the shifting nomenclature so peculiar to his department (H.P.D., Housing Preservation and Development), a speech he had been practicing for weeks and had committed to memory, and now the blow from the crutch had popped the speech out of his memory, like a piece of stale toast sprung loose from an old toaster, so that when Sanchez was in the hospital recovering, immobile in a yellow cast, he remembered everything that happened that day, remembered too their chronology, had even remembered the color of the sky and how cold the pavement was, everything but the speech. Not a word.

Lowell had a meeting with him his first day out of the hospital.

When Sanchez interviewed him his neck was in a brace, he could only look straight ahead, and if he wanted to turn he had to turn his entire body, doing it slowly, as if his head were a broken eggshell held in place by gummy cellophane.

"What the hell kind of name is Lowell?"

"I don't know. It's mine."

"Is that a fruitcake name or what? I mean that sounds like a girl's name. It sounds vague, like it don't know what to do with itself."

"I didn't choose it."

Sanchez said nothing. He kept trying to look behind himself, a rotation he could not perform. Lowell wondered what he was looking for; perhaps the other crutch.

It was difficult to describe Sanchez. He seemed to change from moment to moment. Looked at face forward, Lowell thought he was slight, almost thin, and somewhat apologetic. But sideways he seemed to take on weight, become gruff, sloppy. Sanchez asked him if he had any experience in housing and was pleased when Lowell said he didn't.

Lowell was confused by the way he talked. He thought that Sanchez had only recently learned English and approached certain phrases with a virginity that left Lowell startled. He thought that perhaps Sanchez enjoyed the effect, that he made certain statements with the same degree of ease as a man putting on a condom for the first time. The more he talked, the fatter he seemed to get. Above and below his neck brace he swelled up like a pouter pigeon. Lowell was afraid he was going to float to the ceiling.

"You have to take a test to get hired by the department," Sanchez said, "even if your name is Lowell. You go for a physical, security clearance, recidivist-record clearance, loyalty oath, conflict-of-interest oath, drug detox analysis, multiple-choice questionnaire, several other things."

Sanchez walked him around the department. It covered many floors. This floor was huge, a semi-open room, a hall, bathed in acoustical tile with bathtublike segments of fluorescent lights in the ceiling. At the ends of the hall and at various spots in the middle, walls had been erected to house offices. Desks surrounded the offices, and partitions, chin high, surrounded the desks. Sanchez walked through the hall tapping on the glass, as if trying to awaken the occupants. Everyone was working, Lowell noticed: head down, pencils moving, typing, moving papers, opening drawers, looking up at the ceiling to count the acoustical tile, answering the phone, moving the chairs back and getting up from the desk. Everyone except one man with an olive complexion and a purple cap who sat eating a pencil and spitting out the wooden bits at Sanchez. He smiled at Sanchez, showing as many teeth as not teeth. His desk was clean. He shrugged his shoulders and looked at Lowell. "I can't type, I can't read, I can't write, what do you expect . . . ¡eh! muchacho, ¿que pasa?"

Sanchez quickly swept Lowell into an office.

"This is your office," he said, "but you won't spend much time here. You'll be out in the field. I'm going to give you your building tomorrow. It will keep you busy. Don't mind the tenants. Just collect the rent. Don't pay any attention to what they say. Just collect the rent. If anything happens, you'll get disability insurance. Collect the rents, note the repairs needed, don't worry about the tenants. Don't take what they say seriously, even at the tenants' meetings. They won't do half the things they threaten. Just collect the rents. You'll be judged by your rent collections. Don't worry about the threats. I'll give you a list of contractors you can use. Don't use anybody not on the list."

Sanchez thrust a grimy mimeographed sheet in his hands and then ran. He bounced down the hall as if his head was set in gelatin. Lowell had never seen a cripple move so fast. From the way he was running, he thought Sanchez might injure his neck, break something in it, or bounce his head off his neck.

Sanchez stood at the end of the hall, panting, his eyes threatening to escape his head.

"Tomorrow!" he shouted.

Lowell had no idea what he meant by that. The pencil eater looked at him and winked. Lowell winked back and knew immediately it was a mistake.

The pencil eater rolled over to him. He had a stainless-steel wheelchair, with a small electric motor under the seat.

"You new, hey?"

Lowell looked down at him. He had an urge to jump on his foot to see if he would shout.

Lowell said yes.

"My name's Hector, Puerto Rican. They can't touch me. They know it, I know it. They're under quota for spics."

He laughed. Bits of pencil stuck between his teeth.

"I can do what I want to. I can even work if I want to. What about that, English?"

"I'm new."

"Of course you are. I know. Think I'm dumb like you, English? Wear a helmet. You got a helmet?"

He laughed again until he started to cough, doubling over in his wheelchair. Lowell wanted to hit him in the base of his neck with a sharp glass ashtray, but he didn't smoke.

"Wear a flak vest. Vietnam. Something that covers the balls. They like to go for the balls. That and the head. They'll hit you with anything that's got a point on it and a lot of things that don't."

He looked over his shoulder. Sanchez was coming back.

"You'll take Washington's place. Ask Sanchez to tell you about Washington."

He rolled away as Sanchez arrived, looking like one of those grayish white puffballs found under dead logs. He tried to say something, but his face looked so fat and featureless that he couldn't find his mouth.

"Don't pay any attention to him," Sanchez said. "He doesn't know anything. He's going to be fired shortly. He knows that."

Lowell said nothing. He wanted to be left alone to dream about putting buildings back on their feet, to order bricks and mortar and get tradesmen on the phone, tile cutters and carpenters, pipe fitters and glass installers. Lowell wanted to look at the plans of his building, he wanted to see where the beams were, where the wiring went. He assumed he had been hired, though Sanchez had never explicitly said he had, and having been hired would have the resources of the city behind him to fix ravaged apartment buildings, a fund for development (hadn't one of the brochures said as much?), and the help of many city agencies (or he should have, the brochure hinted at this, though rather vaguely, and left open the provisions for implementing it, but still in all, the implication was there). He was surprised to find Sanchez still in his office.

"Just stay in your office," Sanchez said. He turned his body to look behind him.

"And wait. Just wait."

"For what . . . when?"

Sanchez ignored him. He seemed to have discovered something under his neck brace and was determined to crush it with his fist.

"What about Washington?"

"What about him?"

"I heard . . ."

"He's fine, just fine. You should be so lucky."

"What happened to him?"

"Nothing. Who told you? Hector? Don't believe anything he says. Washington is comfortable, very comfortable."

"Is he hurt, is he in pain?"

"What are you talking about? What do you mean? Get back in your office and start to work."

"On what?"

"On whatever. Don't let the commissioner see you not working. That's bad. He shouldn't even see us talking together."

"Why?"

Sanchez left. This time he walked slowly, majestically, treasuring the balls of his feet with delicate, pigeon-toed steps, as if he were threading his way among egg cartons. He wore pointed shoes, as sharp as ballet slippers, the leather dyed a pale blue. A tiny, dotted, perforated design decorated the front of the shoes. Lowell could imagine him spending many hours behind his desk, legs curled up, rubbing first one shoe and then the other. It was a job he must have looked forward to each day.

The desks in the department were a gun-metal blue, but the tops of the desks were made of some kind of rubber composition that formed a very slight cushion. If you pressed down hard enough you could feel it give. It was wonderfully adapted to filling out forms with ballpoint pens because if the pen skipped ink, which it did, then pressing harder would allow the ink to flow without scratching the paper. Pencils also left a good impression. Hector had taken apart his stapler and was using one corner of it to gouge out a piece of the desk top. "My initials," he shouted over to Lowell. Then, seeing that Sanchez was gone, he buzzed over.

"You notice his shoes, don't you?" he asked.

Without waiting for an answer he continued.

"Well, his shoes is too thin to walk anywhere. He can't go out in the field because the rocks would cut up his little feet. So he sends someone else out in the field. You. You got a club?"

Every time he talked about the field, Lowell kept getting a picture of a vast field, full of wheat or straw or hay or whatever the hell else they grew in fields, which was something light tan in color, that grew on the end of a stick, clusters of something hard like in breakfast cereal, repeated for mile after mile. Lowell couldn't imagine what a building would be doing out in the field.

"He's afraid to go out in the field," Hector said.

"He's gun-shy. He got kicked in the head, hit by some cripple, and now he won't go out there anymore. Sends suckers like you. Ask him why he don't go out. It's his job. Says in the manual he's got to go out. You could look it up. Me, I don't got to go out; but him, he got to, says it in his job description—you could look it up."

He buzzed back to his desk.

"Nam vet, Purple Heart," Hector shouted over to Lowell. "I don't got to do nothing, and you can stick that where there ain't no light, English."

Nobody looked up when he said this, even though he looked around to see if anyone would. "Motherfuckers all of you," he said to the tops of their heads.

"Something else," Hector shouted over to him. "I can't get my pecker up, paralyzed from the waist down, shot, Nam, saving all you motherfuckers so you could go on pushing pencils. What do you think of that, English?"

There was a sudden silence, as if everyone were listening for a toilet to flush. And then the buzz of the ceiling lights was drowned out by a low growl, a dozen throats gargling, noses blown, or feet shuffled about the floor.

Lowell wondered how many buildings Sanchez would give him. He wanted ten, in the same borough. He wanted big buildings, fat buildings, buildings with face brick and marble, stone terrazzo entrance foyers, and shimmering brass elevators with elaborately hinged gates gilded with seraphim, and tenants who . . . who what? He knew nothing about tenants. Though he was one, he never thought of himself as a tenant. He had always thought of himself as a social worker. He had gotten a degree in English and philosophy from a small New England college, knowing he wanted to do social work and try out for the Olympics. He wanted to make a change and had been to places where he had seen people making a change, to Cuba, to China, parts of the South and West.

He thought that because of the things he would do for the building, the tenants would be eternally grateful, like sea turtles would be if untangled from fishermen's nets, like slugs would be if saucers of beer were set out for them. He wanted to redeem Hector in Sanchez's eyes, he wanted to take Sanchez's neck brace off, get him a pair of sturdy-soled shoes so he would get out in the field. He knew it was absolutely hopeless and counterproductive to save everybody, and he wanted to do it.

24

"I am going to give you one building," Sanchez said.

"Just one?"

Sanchez looked small, shrunken, the neck brace having imprisoned his head. He sat opposite Lowell in the chair, rubbing his shoes and trying to turn around while he was seated in the chair.

"Would you like a swivel chair?" Lowell asked.

He turned back, annoyed. Lowell could see stains on his neck brace and the soiled spot at the back of the brace where his hair kept rubbing it. The filthy brace disgusted Lowell, and he felt that the stains might rub off on Sanchez's body and spread, becoming as heavy and large as manhole covers, and that if pricked would break and release millions of wind-borne spores.

"One building, that's enough to start. I won't make any promises."

Lowell didn't know what he was talking about, but he wanted many buildings, he wanted to survey them, console them, and put the hand of plenty on them; he wanted to paint, fix, prop, repair, support, and otherwise restore them to citizenry.

He gave Lowell the address, written in pencil on the back of a xeroxed form. Lowell wanted to shout after him, but he had left, with his pointy shoes, his pigeon walk, and his gait of the barely-having-been-there.

Lowell had wanted to say to him: *Give me something official, your titles, your deeds, your mortgages, your chattels, give me your letters of debt and your bills of procurement. Something more official! Something glorious, with state seals and stamps and embossed circles, the arabesques and swirls of notary publics with large, florid handwriting.*

But he had only gotten a sheet of paper, half a sheet, the front side xeroxed, with three typewritten addresses, the last two X'ed out because of mistakes in typing and written over in pencil after the faint scratch of a ballpoint pen that ran out of ink or was defective had been thrown away.

"You got Washington's Building?" Hector asked.

Hector had appeared, somehow mysteriously, at his side. Lowell was amazed at how Puerto Ricans could leave and arrive so quickly, as if they were interchangeable units flown in and yanked out for obscure reasons. He was beginning to hate Hector; no, had long hated him, had disliked him long before he had known him so that their initial meeting and greeting, if it could be called that, was for Lowell merely the continuation of a long relationship, a relationship that was oblivious to the parties involved but ran on the ratio of its own gears.

Now this olive pit, this bit of dark fluff was talking to him. He wanted to jab his eyes out but knew that would do no good; Hector would simply grow eyes somewhere else.

"Lemme see."

He grabbed the paper out of his hand. Lowell reached after it, but Hector buzzed his electric chair away.

"Don't hit cripples, especially spic cripples," he shouted. "And I'm a noisy ratfuck. I'll have the whole department down on you if you do, but only after I take a razor to your balls, ¡eh! muchacho, hombre muy loco muchacho."

He read the address.

"I thought you couldn't read."

"I can't. But I know numbers. And you, my dear English asshole, got Washington's Building. That one is going to take up all your time."

Hector readjusted the purple wool cap on his head. He stuck a pencil between his teeth. It stood out from his mouth like a pipe. He smiled and bit it off.

"Look, I'm trying to help you, asshole. Trust me. You know what they did to Washington?"

"No."

"Look, Washington is black, and that neighborhood is mostly black, though the whites are starting to move in. You know what they did to Washington? Should I tell you?"

"I already know."

"Fucking bullshit you do. Fucking liar."

"How would you know?"

" 'Cause even we don't know. All we know is that he can't walk, can't work, won't be back for God knows how many months, if at all. That poor shithead."

"Which one is . . ."

"*The Building.* Burn that in your fucking head. Nobody else will take it. Look."

He motioned his arm toward the center square. It was crammed with desks, gray desks, and people behind them.

"We got wops, spades, spics, kikes, chinks, all on quota, everything on quota. We got cripples, fruitboys, bulldykes. We got welfare, hop-heads, junkies, boozers, perverts, ex-cons. We got it all, and it's all on quota because they say we gotta hire minorities and so we do, but this whole fucking city is one big minority. They're ain't no fucking majority anymore. So everyone here knows they're on quota so they work a little but not too much, and me, I don't work at all because I'm three minorities rolled into one. I'm a fucking bonanza—a vet, a cripple, and a spic. Hell, they fill up half their quota with me alone, plus my skin is dark so they list me as a boogie, a spade, a nigger. I'm Mister Minority. I could have a parade all my own any day of the week. But only you, Mister English, are dumb enough to take the Building. The rest won't take it. Even that Hasid sitting over there, see the one, with his fur hat and his curlilocks . . ."

Hector picked up his pencil and started to stab his hand with it.

"Damn, damn, damn."

He put it in his wool cap.

"For starters, let me tell you about Brooklyn. Brooklyn is like a guy I saw on a street corner in Sunset Park getting his leg sawed off. Who knows what he did? Stole from a numbers runner or a small-time dope dealer. Bunch of guys holding him while one guy saws his leg. He screams, the sound cuts through the backfire of the trucks. They got four guys holding him and one guy trying to take his leg off at the knee. Now I ain't no doctor, but that must be a dull saw. They can't get it off. So they try an ax. Guy really starts yelling. They whack away, like beating a watermelon with a baseball bat. They didn't even bother to take his pants off. That's Brooklyn for you. But this guy is tough meat, an old turkey, his leg won't come off. They walk away disgusted with him. Course his leg isn't attached as well as it used to be, but most of it still dangles from his thigh. Lots of blood, though not as much as you might expect. I saw him later. He limps. Has a hole in his leg. He bears no grudges. Hell, he's from Brooklyn. He understands why they did it. He's only sorry they can't get it off."

Hector fingered the pencil in his cap.

"Hell, no one knows who owns the Building," he said. "Whatever you do you gonna be fighting the old landlord, he still thinks he owns the Building. Maybe he does. Sanchez is bluffing when he says the city owns the Building."

Hector spits into a paper cup.

"Brooklyn is a fantasy, English, Brooklyn is a subterfuge. It is a piece of jism that hangs off the pecker of Manhattan. It is unreal. Brooklyn blew its wad years ago, English. Let me give you some advice about the Building. For starters, they got a sniper in the Building. The cops are there every week. Don't spend much time in front on the sidewalk. And don't spend much time in the Building either. That Building is the sieve before the drain. It collects those who are about to be flushed down the toilet—loonies, weirdos, dingbats, crazies, psychopaths, and just plain off-the-wall assholes."

Lowell asked someone else in the department, someone who was rumored to have published a poem in the late forties, about the Building and about Brooklyn. The aging poet told him that first the landlord, then the city, then the landlord, and now perhaps the city owned the Building. "But ownership of the Building is an illusion, a sleight of hand, an ontological chimera. There may be a mortgage; it may be paid off. There may be back taxes owed; they may be redeemed. The crazy, the maimed, the forlorn, those smitten with a calling for paranoia, and those blessed with psychosis live there . . ." His voice trailed off. He uttered the last sentence with a sigh, envious.

"Brooklyn," said the poet, quite patiently, as if he were talking about another planet, "has its own sense of time. There is no linear time in Brooklyn. There is parallel time, events happening simultaneously. And there are events that reverse their order the second time around, as the mood strikes them. The deaf speak, the blind see, the lame walk in Brooklyn."

Lowell learned that the Building was in limbo, never quite owned by anyone. Its physical presence was definite, but its legal status was hazy, a shuffle of conflicting papers, torts, deeds, wills, documents testifying to parties of the first and second part, disclosures that the title was held by one person and the mortgage by another (on the verge of losing the building, Haber had sold the title to someone on the block, kept the mortgage, then tried to sell the mortgage, and failing that had sold a second mortgage and kept back a purchase money mortgage, then sued the holder of the deed, claiming that any liens on the property due to nonpayment of utilities were his responsibility, and the holder of the deed told Haber that he bought with the understanding that the Building was free and clear of liens and countersued, while a longtime relative of Eschopf showed up claiming that she in fact owned it and that Eschopf's deal with Haber was null and void and that she was going to turn the Building into an animal shelter, which some thought it was already).

"Hey, English," Hector shouted, "at least the old dope dealer is gone, but some faggot artist with a Doberman got his apartment and that dog is primed to kill. Better skip trying to collect his rent. I won't tell you about the rest."

He took the pencil out of his cap and started to stab his hand. After three or four tries he drew blood. At the fifth, it stuck in his hand. He cried without tears.

"Damn this fucking country anyway. Damn it all to hell."

25

To get anywhere in New York you ride the subway. To get nowhere in New York you ride the subway. And to get somewhere in New York, you ride the subway. The subways are filled, thus, with those going somewhere, those going anywhere, those going nowhere. Lowell belonged to the first category.

He was on the "ratfuck" train. At other times he had ridden the "fuck yo momma" train, the "shabazz" train, the "kid bang" train, the "proletarian punk" train, and "ratfuck II." But "ratfuck" was one of the older trains, having been covered with graffiti long ago in the yards at 148th and Lexington, scoured and painted over by the Transit Authority, "ratfucked" again with spray paint, hastily, the edges dripping before the artist was set upon by killer wolf dogs the Authority had let roam loose in the yards, scoured again though not painted, the "ratfucks" showing through dimly, and then touched up again in the yards (by a celebrated graffiti artist who had his own gallery in Soho along with a criminal record for extortion) with a fresh can of spray, this time the letters fresh and heavy thanks to a new improved variety of spray paint that adhered better, resisted wear and weathering, and never cracked.

"Ratfuck" was a D train, a double R, an F, or a B train. It was impossible to tell which, since at one time or another it displayed signs that claimed allegiance to all those lines. In reality it was all those trains, since the Transit Authority could never make up its mind which line it ran on, changing its mind in midline so that the train was diverted from the D to the B line, and if it was the QB it only ran during express hours, except between 34th and 42nd, the exception being that since repairs were being done on the bridge, during off hours the train ran through the tunnel, for six weeks or six thousand miles, whichever came first, or if the repairs took longer than expected, the dispatcher had a headache, the engineer was seeing double once again, or the train had been derailed, a regular and programmed occurrence meticulously planned by the Transit Authority to keep repair crews and passengers on their feet, alert and concerned about their subway.

He sat next to a man who wore a thick, gray, pin-striped suit, a stiff white shirt, an immaculately patterned Countess Mara tie, Gucci loafers, and a gold button in his earlobe. On his other side sat a man who wore three shirts, four jackets, and was rendered somewhat immobile by seven pairs of urine-soaked pants, none of which were completely buttoned or zippered or without holes, rips, stains, tears, or tatters. Below his neck there was no single word to describe the smell, but above it he was freshly shaven and smelled of Paco Rabanne. His graying hair was done up in a pigtail, his eyes were red and rheumy, and between his feet (grotesquely swollen to the size of miniature hams, the skin, once white, now the color of shoe leather) were three canvas bags tied at the top by a single rope, which then continued around his waist, acting as a belt for one pair of pants.

"Ratfuck" had stalled in the tunnel due to a short circuit in the modern outmoded wiring, and the engineer had bolted from his cab and ran screaming through the cars, claiming that alligators were crawling along the track, huge beasts with green bellies who lived on rats. The conductor pulled him into an empty conductor's booth and locked him in, then walked down the aisle calming the by-now hysterical passengers by saying that if there were alligators there was only one, that it was small and could in no way threaten the train, and that as soon as the short was repaired they would be on their way.

"When is that?" asked a passenger.

"Who knows?" said the conductor.

Most of the passengers ran to the window to see if they could spot the alligator and were rewarded for their efforts by seeing a pile of Wing-Ding wrappers by the side of the track. The lights in the train flickered and went out, leaving only a double-digit bulb burning at either end of each car. The trains were air-conditioned, which meant that the windows didn't open and the air-conditioning didn't work. The man wearing seven pairs of pants took out his penis and examined it. The man in the pin-striped suit took a penlight out of his briefcase and opened a copy of *Barron's* on his lap.

He sat between the two, the bum and the broker, thinking not of them but of the train's destination, wondering if it had one.

The conductor came through and asked if anyone knew how to drive the train. He raised his hand, not because he knew how to direct the train but because he had a question.

"Is this a D or an F?"

"It's a D, but it's running on the RR line making RR stops. However, we've run into a bit of a problem up ahead, so by the time we get out of the tunnel we'll either be a B or an F. Can you drive this thing?"

"No."

"Too bad. Ordinarily I would, but all those flames give me the heebie-jeebies."

The conductor walked swiftly toward the front of the train. Soon they heard a voice come over the speaker. *Attention, passengers. Thank you for your patience. We will be moving shortly, as soon as we rectify the indication.*

The train, however, refused to follow the conductor's instructions and sat, becalmed, in the tunnel. Mysteriously someone had turned on the heat, an oddity for August. He felt the seat under him warm up, then get hot. His calves felt as if they were being cooked by a hot-air drier. And then, he smelled smoke.

Attention, passengers, we will be moving shortly. Thank you for your patience.

He heard screams. The engineer was pounding on the door, screaming to be let out. There were two large alligators inside the compartment with him. More were coming in through the windows. Passenger safety, he shouted, could not be assured.

More smoke, this time acidic, smelling not of an ordinary burning but of electricity run amok, voltage gone berserk, amperage out of control.

"There are no alligators in the subway! That fuckhead ought to shut up. Someone ought to shut him up!"

Alligators in the subways were a myth, he knew that, and yet he could sense their presence, could almost smell their lizard dry skin, or could have if there were no smoke. It was not the kind of smoke you could see but the kind you could smell, invisible smoke, the worst kind because it kills you without your knowing it so that while you are up and walking around you're really dead, a victim of invisible-smoke inhalation.

The man with seven pairs of pants stood up and with his thumb and forefinger tried to touch his nose to his ear. He pulled and tugged, searching for the inherent elasticity that would allow these two appendages to stretch, touch, and perhaps join one another. Failing to do this, he grabbed his tongue and tried to yank it from his throat, making short choking sounds. Then he blew air into his cheeks and looked down over his balloon-shaped mouth at the seated passengers.

Just then the door at the other end of the car opened and a man appeared with a sign. "My mother is an epileptic, I am a deaf-mute. We are being thrown out of our rent-controlled apartment. Read about us in the newspapers." The sign was printed on paper with the letterhead of a Brooklyn trucking company. It was pasted to a blue board that the man wore around his neck, and alongside the sign were newspaper clippings with headlines that said "Tone-deaf violinist always playing 'Melancholy Baby,'" "Landlord tosses out epileptic and deaf-mute," and "She shakes, he can't hear, they get boot."

The man with the sign walked the length of the car, looking upward, sideways. When he came to the center of the car he found his way blocked by the man who wore seven pairs of pants. They briefly looked at each other, one mute by choice, one mute by chance, one temporarily mute and permanently blighted and the other permanently mute and temporarily blighted. Their eyes touched in hostility (one nut to a car, one loony per train). The man with seven pairs of pants felt that his territory was being invaded, and though he hadn't put the touch on any of the passengers, didn't even have a tin cup to thrust under the avoiding eyes of the passengers, nevertheless he felt that the option to beg was his and his alone on this D train, this RR train, this B or this F train.

Lowell watched the two of them, bantam cocks, dipping and duck-

ing, their feet pushing away imaginary dirt on the subway's worn linoleum. The pants man stuck out his chin and put his hands on his seven
pairs of pants. The deaf-mute looked away, read or pretended to read
the subway posters (Keep Hands Off Doors, Watch Your Handbag, An
Exciting Career in Business Awaits You). Both of them looked so
preoccupied, he thought, so intent on their own deliverance, as if they
were immune to pit vipers, could bend iron if called to. The pants man
thrust out his chin in a manner that suggested he was about to announce a secret weapon. Firmer than ever, in control of his madness,
he dared the deaf-mute to continue, to beg, to be in that train.

The mute, puzzled, feeling things slide about the surface and make
noises he could not hear, syllables he could not understand, thrust
forward his begging cup. The pants man looked at it, startled, attacked
by coins, and then, searching for his prick in the multifarious folds of
his pants, withdrew it and directed a stream of urine in the mute's cup.
It rattled grotesquely, heard by everyone in the car except the owner
of the cup. The mute's eyes widened; he kept the cup extended, watching nickles, dimes, quarters slowly submerged in piss.

Attention, passengers, we will be moving shortly.

Lowell watched the urinator sit down, and the urinatee stared at
his cup, the change swimming in pee. The subway train jerked, moved
a few feet, stopped. Some static came over the speakers, drowning out
what was an attempt at speech. The engineer was still banging on the
door.

He watched the pants man make another face while the mute
remained impassive. Looking out the window he thought he saw a huge
green face staring back at him: a great, toothy, snout-filled face with
bumpy eyes and warty skin pushed together in great pustules. It reminded him of a man he knew who could not bear to have anyone look
at his face and walked around with a scarf wrapped around his nose and
jaw. The green face outside the window opened and closed its mouth,
showing rows of teeth and an inside that looked like chewed-on cocoa
puffs. Who, he thought, was desperate enough to live in the subway,
on the tracks? What sort of creature could abide the rushing trains,
their erratic schedule, their tunnel-filling presence?

Attention, passengers . . .

The train jerked forward a few feet. The man in the pin-striped suit
bumped into him, he bumped into the seven-pants man; the mute, on

his feet, struggled to balance his cup of liquid. The train stopped, and they reversed their bumping.

Outside, the green face appeared at another window, biting the glass. He noticed it, but no one else did, and he also wondered if anyone else noticed the smoke, the smell of which now was pungent, like burning hair. He had the sense that somewhere along the tracks electric wire was burning, slowly, glowing like punk, sputtering like a long string of knotted-together pee-soaked socks that had to be constantly relit.

He knew they had been deserted by the crew. The engineer's banging had stopped. He had been let out a side window, as had the conductor, leaving the doomed train to bake in the tunnel. He heard the labored breathing of the passengers. One of them was not breathing at all.

The train jerked forward again, stopping with a screech as sudden as the jolt that propelled them these few feet. He thought that at this rate they would reach Brooklyn in 1995, dead people filling the train, like those trapped on the *Titanic,* their mouths agape, hair floating in the underwater arctic. The green face outside had opened its mouth and laid its teeth alongside the glass. The white puffy insides of its mouth coated the window with a yellowish mucus. What frightened him most about the mouth was the lack of a tongue. What sort of creature was allowed to roam the subways without a tongue? Had it been removed by Muslims for some infraction of the Koran? He tried to think of himself as a Muslim. If he had been one, he would never ride the subway.

Suddenly the train sprang forward, as if jolted from the rear. The lights flickered, and then flashed on, the passengers startled to see their neighbors. The train picked up speed, thrashing about on the track like a nervous snake. The mute stumbled forward, his precious cup in jeopardy.

Attention, passengers, attention, passengers . . .

He couldn't pick up what else was said, the voice disintegrated into static. The screech of rubbing mechanical parts on the train, the bump and clang of out-of-round wheels, the whine of steel wheel against iron rail erased all other noises. Almost malevolently picking up speed, the cars were flung from side to side. He saw them pass a slew of stations: Lawrence, Whitehall, Rector, Wall St. People waved arms, fists, newspapers, umbrellas at them. Rocks were thrown. Sirens sounded.

Attention, passengers.

A young man, quite portly, wearing a suit and combat boots was lying on the floor. An old lady who looked like a frozen turkey screamed. A young girl, blue jeans, sweatshirt, sneakers, jumped off her seat and began to give the portly man cardiopulmonary resuscitation. The turkey lady screamed again.

"She's kissing a dead man. Stop her!"

The turkey lady jumped up on the plastic seat, waving a shopping bag that said *I'm a Princess, I shop at Mintzes.* As the train rounded a curve, she tumbled off and landed on her shopping bag. Her hair, elaborately coiffured and sprayed into submission, tilted to one side. Sprawled over her shopping bag, she seemed to have forgotten where her arms and legs were. Like an overturned beetle, she waved what she could helplessly in the air, thinking that a miraculous motion of air currents would deposit her on the subway seat.

The young girl kept working on the portly man, breathing life into his flab. Another man, older, had loosened his shoes and tie and offered to relieve the girl when she got tired.

The turkey lady, rolling along the floor as the train seemed to thud from side to side, was helped to her feet by the seven-pants man who, as soon as he had seated her, made a face at her. She propped up her hair, taking several large hatpins and spiking her hair to the side of her head.

Attention, pa . . .

Now they were in the open, but what open he couldn't tell. He could see streams of lights, avenues of sparkling bits of white and yellow, and broad swaths of black. The train seemed to be laboring uphill. He looked at the subway map, the parts of it he could see that peeked around the edges of black graffiti letters that smeared the glass over the map. They were either by the *e* in *motherfucker* (but which *e* he couldn't tell) or the *r* in *ratfuck.* He had a sense that the train would soon leave its tracks or that it would travel beyond its tracks and plough through to the ocean, ignoring subway stops, the end of the line, and the sand on the beach. He had a sense that the entire train would be washed out to sea like the poops in millions of New York City toilets that, salmonlike, headed for the cold, protein-rich waters of the Atlantic.

The turkey lady had gotten into an argument with another lady who was barely a year her junior but at least one hundred pounds her senior. They were separated by a Puerto Rican who was reading *El Diario,* trying to ignore them, whose legs somewhat impeded the resounding thwacks on the legs the turkey lady was administering to the fat lady. Growing more exasperated with her ineffectual blows, the turkey lady stood on her seat so that with two hands she could drive the fat lady's head deep into her shoulders. It was a fitting-enough punishment, she felt, for someone who disagreed with her, for someone who outweighed her, and for someone who was probably of a different persuasion, religionwise. She beat the fat lady with the handle end of the umbrella, feeling that that was where the weight was and so that was where the punishment lay. But she did not scream or yell, feeling that this would take energy from her task. She wished someone would hand her a baseball bat so she could do the job with proper justice.

The fat lady, pushed-in face, stockings rolled up to just below her knees so that Lowell could see the acres of fat that clung to her thighs (he thought that any man who attempted to climb that mountain would require some rescuing), stuck up a heavy arm, grabbed the umbrella, and broke it over her knee, tossing the pieces out the window. She did this with resolute calm, Buddha-like, and went back to her Eastern European newspaper that reported out-of-date news.

The portly man, though still on the floor, was sitting up and sported a reasonable shade of pink. He was helped to his feet, slowly, with almost infinite patience and kindness, by the young girl and the older man, and he returned to the paper he had placed on the seat when he had keeled over.

They were underground again. He could feel the hot oppressive motion as the train slid through the tunnel. They were in a different country, a different borough, and whatever happened to them now could be easily excused. Faces flashed by the window, subway workers in awe of the runaway train.

They rushed by unused stations: one that featured glassed-in display cases with clothes from the forties (forever mummified in their underground crypt), another that was boarded up (encrusted stacks of yellowing newspapers, the *New York Sun,* the *New York Mirror,* the *New York Telegram*), another that moved at the same speed they moved and then disappeared, vanishing into the underground fog. He saw mastodons stuck in the walls of the tunnel, the bones of dog-sized horses, cave paintings on turn-of-the-century tile. The prow of an old leather boat stuck out from one wall. From another, the business end of a spear, its tip red. Bows, arrows, muskets, bayonets were scattered across the tracks, making a terrible clatter and crunch as they were crushed by the subway wheels. The train swung around a curve, leaving space between the tracks and the tunnel wall for an Indian in front of a teepee, his fire burning.

The train was slowing down. He felt it would stop, somewhere in Brooklyn. Then it was running mysteriously silent, as if the out-of-round wheels had rounded themselves, as if the rails had straightened out to avoid the horrible jetlike screech the train made when it pulled into a station around a curve.

Attention, passengers . . .

He saw the seven-pants man stand up, feet firmly planted in the center of the aisle, and face the rear of the car.

"Attention passengers," the seven-pants man said. "I am the king, the fountainhead, Ronald McDonald. I have come to rescue you. Follow instructions. Do as you are told. Keep hands off doors."

He paused, to scratch through several layers of shirts.

"I am Superman, the Pope, Charlie Chaplin."

He waved his arms in the air.

"Don't be fooled by imitators. This is the real thing. This is the real McCoy. I'm from another planet. I've got backing. I've got the army. Kissinger shines my shoes. Now listen, here's my plan."

He stopped and put his hand up to his ear.

"You want the subways fixed? I'll fix the subways. But I need money. Lots of money. Give me money and we'll travel first class. No more waiting for trains. Me and Kissinger don't wait for no trains. I'll put rugs on the floors, easy chairs in the cars, we pipe in music. All the food you want. I truck it in from Idaho. Oranges, apples, lemon meringue pies. Soda fountains in all the cars. You can sit on your ass and eat. I send little people around to wipe the drool from your mouth. I keep all the dogs out of the subway. Me and McNamara, we got the army behind us. We got Dean Rusk, Cyrus Vance, Haig. Heads of state, affairs of state, you get your shoes shined, drinks. I got the army behind me, a planetary army, a space army."

He started to sing "Nobody Knows the Troubles I've Seen."

"Shut the fuck up," said the deaf-mute.

"Sit the fuck down," said the Puerto Rican.

"If I sat down," said the seven-pants man, "then I wouldn't be able to stand up and talk. I wouldn't be able to stand up and walk. I wouldn't be able to stand up and caulk. But this way, I want to think it over. I want to mull it over in my mind, to ruminate on it, to speculate on the possibilities of my perambulations. I want to know what Ronald McDonald would say. What would Mickey Mouse say? What would Kissinger say? What would Isaac Stern say? What would Albert Shanker say? What would Muhammad Ali say? What would Kennedy say? What would TV say? What would my socks say? What would you say?"

"Sit down, just fucking sit down, you fuckhead."

"And then again, what would they not say? Knot say? Rot say? Got say? Dot say? Even if the unspoken, unsaid, not said thing . . . even if it was the collective head, the balloon head, the mummy head, the corporate head, the legislative head, the bony head, the penis head, the head on a bottle of beer, the headmaster . . . what if they not say?"

"Shut up."

"The army, Kissinger leads the army. I give F.B.I. orders, I give C.I.A. orders. I am watching Haig, who is watching Reagan, who is watching Carter, who is watching Nixon, who pardoned Kennedy, who laughed at Truman, who liked Ike, who feared Roosevelt."

"Fucking fuckhead."

"The boils, the roils, the goils who give you boils and roils."

"Sit down, you asshole."

"I am the president, the vice president, the secretary of statehood. I ride roughshod, scour the kitchen, direct armies, send battalions into the field. When I speak Castro quivers, Reagan realizes. I have been lifted by fireflies to amazing heights. I have seen soot control the city. I have ridden on the back of the beast. I have been deposited in vacant buildings, appointed prince of broken glass, king of crows, minister of mattresses. I have seen rivers run through fake buildings, been appointed fake superintendent, planted bushes, and watched bullets swim through flesh. I have eradicated, eliminated, flushed poisons through halls, boilers through walls, semen in stalls."

"Motherfucking cocksucker."

"Fothermucking socktucker, rockrucker, mockcucker. Eat the smut that sells the putt, hair pie on oysters. I have heard God speak through the asshole of a dog, seen the whore fly off the roof, supplied the excrement artist, dodged falling bathtubs, untied old ladies, sat in on the commissioner."

The seven-pants man interrupted his speech, looking at the passengers who were no longer looking at him but looking out the window at the slowing inky blackness. They were coming to a station. The train was going to stop. Everyone would leave because they felt this would be the last stop the train would make, that it was doomed to loop the city forever.

"I am the minister, the reverend, the rabbi, the priestess. I am the exalted, the anointed, the exonerated, the execrable. I float in the face of misfortune, fly in the face of ineptitude. I am chairman of the buildings, C.I.A. of the apartments, Chief of Staff of Supers. I control the bricks, direct the mortar, lay the foundation for rent control, bring up the heat, solicit the pipes, make repairs when and if necessary, prepare work orders for patch-up, tear-down, build-up. I am Captain of Sheetrock, Lieutenant of Joint Compound, General of Wallboard. I fix the subways, I fix the buildings, welcome to Brooklyn."

The train slid to a stop.

The passengers collected at the doors, which cranked open, spilling them out.

Lowell looked back and saw the seven-pants man, standing in the middle of the subway car, strangling himself.

26

LOWELL thought it wise to have an apartment in Brooklyn. He found one on a commercial street. It was a small, nondescript building with a front entrance door that didn't fit its frame. The apartment had recently been painted a chalky white that barely covered the cracked and flaking paint under it. The wooden-slat floors were uneven, bulging, falling away like a mildly disturbed sea. The hot water was lukewarm at best; sporadic banging in the pipes announced a gift of steam that warmed the radiators and sometimes the rooms they were in. The sink, on spindly legs, tilted toward the center of the room. Lowell turned on the taps and watched the bubbling, cloudy water spurt from the spigot, as if it had been trapped an inordinate amount of time in the pipes.

He decorated with furniture from the street and a cheap mattress whose newest ingredient was the brown paper it was wrapped in. At night, with the lights out and the sink leaking, he was oblivious to the little tap dance the mice did on the wooden floors, despite the fact that, with the mattress on the floor, they did it inches from his head.

It was home.

He considered himself lucky. His block had only a few apartment buildings—not like those huge cell blocks of apartment buildings that stretched for mile after mile in the Bronx. Here the buildings were never more than four stories. Private brownstones filled most of the block, with a few apartment buildings like his scattered about. The only thing that bothered him was a certain lackadaisical air on the part of the super. But the building was minimally clean, there was light in the hallway, and he could smell the ammonia on the stairs. Not much to complain about. Even the rent was right.

He went out to have his shoes repaired. He couldn't find a shoe-repair store but he did find a shoe store that sold jogging shoes and cowboy boots. There was no supermarket, but a deli that stocked European beer and sold half- and quarter-pound fried chickens that looked like they were covered in gold foil. He sat on one of his spindly kitchen chairs eating a quarter pound of chicken and wiggling his toes inside his new jogging shoes. Bad choice, he thought. Mugging shoes. They would frighten the neighbors.

But the neighbors seemed unconcerned. He barely saw them. In fact for the first three weeks he didn't see anyone in the building. Heard nothing. He took to watching out of his window at the entrance and finally, after several hours, saw an old lady, black coat, make her way into the building. He rushed out of his apartment to see if he could meet her in the hallway and introduce himself, but she had disappeared. He could hear nothing in the halls, not a whine, not a scratch, not a growl. And no one seemed to be cooking, or else they were eating fruit and uncooked vegetables.

One night, lying on his mattress, he heard a single scream, a long, drawn-out cry that seemed to be composed of two normal-size lungfuls of air. At first he thought it was a car siren, but there was a waver to it, a terror, that came from no mechanical object. Abruptly as it started, it stopped. No one seemed to take any notice of the intrusion, but long after the sound had died its echo lived in his head, and he propped up his pillow, tried different positions in bed, and still couldn't get to sleep.

The next morning he felt drugged. He couldn't shake the echo of that scream from his head. He listened to the news for stories of painful deaths in Brooklyn, but there were too many to tell which was the one he might have heard. The entire borough could have been covered with screams. He looked out his window and saw young men wheeling grocery carts filled with parts from BMWs and Mercedes Benzes. Where were the groceries?

He heard the scream again that night, twice, separated by what he thought was panting or barking. No one seemed at all concerned. This time he went back to sleep and woke the next morning feeling refreshed, greeted by a gray drizzle that seemed to rain oil on his windows. He opened the window and stuck his hand out, letting the liquid fall on it, and then smelled it. There was no smell to it, but he watched the water empty out of the drainpipe into the courtyard with a great swirl of suds, as if the contents of a washing machine had been emptied from the heavens. While he watched the swirl of rainy detergent, someone threw a brick off the roof.

The following day someone came by and wanted to remove his radiators. There was no reason offered, and when he protested the man offered to remove the sink or the toilet seat, whichever he preferred. He preferred neither and told him so. The man retreated, disappointed, as if he had been personally slighted, pipe wrench in hand.

He called the super, who knew nothing about the man but then admitted that they were upgrading the systems. The delivery systems for heat and hot water may have been among those affected, but he wasn't sure. The boiler, the super told him, would be shut down for repairs. Be prepared to make the best of the cold, the super told him. August had cascaded into October. It was cold. The leaves were coated with something slick and slipped to the ground, squishing underfoot. Sometimes cars remained in the same spot on the block for weeks. Hoods flew open, parts disappeared: batteries, tires, radios, carburetors, then entire engines.

A xeroxed sign appeared in the lobby. SAVE THE BOILER! Save it from what? For what? Before he could ask the super, the sign disappeared. He asked anyway. The super didn't know what he was talking about, waved him away, went back to watching "Fantasy Island." "The halls look dirty," he told the super. "Don't bother me," the super told him. "This is the part where Shelley Winters comes looking for Mr. Right, only she's the Queen of Sheba and she's looking for the king, played by Vincent Price. Only the guy that's right for her is Henry Winkler, playing the Fonz. Only, see, she's a secretary in a sex-aid factory in her other life, and the Fonz, Henry Winkler, is the janitor, and she don't want nothing to do with the janitor but he's really right for her but she don't know it. But here on Fantasy Island she wants the king, that's Vincent Price, only he's got some funny ideas about what he wants queens to do and, Shelley, she can't do them on account of she's fat, but the Fonz, Winkler, he don't care about her fat. This is the part where Vincent Price finds out that the Fonz is on the island with Shelley Winters, and he's set his monkeys out after him, except that the Fonz, being he's the Fonz, has made this sling out of old Boy Scout belts from the time there was a scout camp on the island and Price was the headmaster, before he became King of Sheba, and in real life he's the star salesman at the sex-aid factory and he's making eyes for Shelley, but we know they ain't fated for each other."

A note was slipped under his door. BOILER MEETING TONIGHT. "What does this mean?" he asked the super. "I don't know," said the super. "I don't know nothing about it." He was watching "Love Boat." "Three couples, only what they don't know is they got the wrong partners. This one guy is a salesman for a sex-aid factory, Sonny Tufts, and he's shacking up with this secretary from Planned Parenthood, Ella Raines. Only they don't get along too well 'cause Sonny Tufts he don't hear too well on account of the face-lift he had that covered his ears. So he takes up with this deaf-mute, Jane Wyman, who's being mistreated by this guy she's with, John Ireland, a gruff rancher from Alaska, who starts making eyes at Faye Emerson, who runs the studio band for the local radio station in Council Bluffs, Iowa. She's with Bruce Cabot, a Mormon missionary who made millions in forced religious education, and he's got some funny ideas about sex and underwear and contraceptives, so Ella Raines aims to set him straight on that score. Of course, they're dyed-in-the-wool enemies, but they fall in love despite their occupational differences, and the captain of the boat will probably marry them, if they can find the captain."

The tenants, armed with knives, were taking turns guarding the boiler. He learned this from Dado, a tenant from El Salvador. "This man, this landlord, this piece of excretion, he thinks that God wants him to rip the boiler out. He tells us that God told him that we should all leave so he can fix the apartments up and co-op them and make millions. He says that God told him this is going to be a rich neighborhood, no room for poor people here, and he believes it because God said it and that's that. Yes, and amen. Hallelujah."

Dado leaned toward him when he spoke.

"Look," Dado said, "we're in this together, like the sea is in the sand, like wildflowers are in the meadow. You cannot separate the smoke from its fire. How can they separate us? Tell me, how?"

But "they" did separate them. He and Dado pulled boiler watch at different hours. He was told to bring a knife, a long knife, preferably a kitchen knife for cutting roasts, something with a point and a long blade. The boiler room was flooded, and they wore galoshes and sloshed around in the darkened water that left a whitish oiliness around the walls of the room. He thought, what am I doing this for?

He asked the super about the garbage in the hallway, and the super said he couldn't be bothered. He was watching "This Is Your Life" with Ralph Edwards. "They got an all-star cast. Yvonne DeCarlo's mother has a farm in North Carolina, where she raises one-legged rabbits. One of them sleeps with Rin-Tin-Tin. Dog won't do anything without his rabbit. She got into an argument with Jack Warner over the rabbit, took her rabbit home, and ruined that dog's career. Things were never the same with that dog. All the animal acts dried up afterward, and most of the trainers went into the guard dog business, killer attack dogs hired by the studios. One of them bit Jean Harlow and she sued. Hired this famous animal lawyer. His brother, her uncle, married her daughter's sister, whose cousin on his mother's side was her aunt. They settled out of court, and Jean Harlow had plastic surgery done on her ass, some Styrofoam sewn in, and the surgeon who did it was friendly with Yvonne DeCarlo's mother's daughter, Yvonne DeCarlo, who did needlepoint for him and washed his socks. She got an invitation one night to have dinner at his place, and Jean Harlow was there, along with one of her boyfriends, Clark Gable, college boy from back East who was crazy about her because of the Styrofoam in her ass. He walked on airplane wings for a living. He was shacking up with Margaret Dumont, who gets jealous with the attention Clark is paying to Jean, so she climbs into a gorilla costume and takes the subway out to City Hall and tells the mayor she is the Queen of Brooklyn. Walks over to Jack-in-the-Box to order a burger and has a heart attack. Yvonne DeCarlo's mother drives her to the hospital. Margaret is crying inside the gorilla. No one knew. That's one advantage to being inside a gorilla."

He pulled boiler guard with an old lady, Florence Smith, an ongoing member for the past thirty years of the Great Books Club, who showed him how to use the knife. "This way," she said, holding the knife forward and slicing the air upward, "is your gut attack. It disembowels them, rips open the intestines, stomach, and with a little pressure you can reach the spleen and the pancreas." She raised the knife in the air. "Normally you don't want to cut from above, too easy to have the knife taken away from you. But if you must, make it short, quick" —she sliced downward abruptly—"and then drop into a crouch." She spread her legs apart and squatted, knife held close to her center. "Keep the handle in close to your belly button, protect your gut, and don't get suckered out of position."

There was a tenants' meeting at which the landlord showed up but couldn't speak. Three silver safety pins were stuck through his lips and snapped shut. An attendant, a small, wizened man, spoke for him. "The landlord is fasting, it's part of his religion. He wants you all out. That's all I got to say, except that be sure and pay your rent or we'll kick you out." The tenants went on rent strike and put their money in an escrow account. Dado and the Great Books lady went around and collected the money for the account.

A dope dealer moved in on the first floor and ripped off the entrance doors to reinforce his own door. The super, when approached, was unconcerned. "He's a tenant, he's got rights." He was watching "Happy Days." "Lovable pops, Turhan Bey, he's not doing so well in the old in-and-out department with moms, Gloria De Haven, so he goes to this store to buy a sex aid. Only the clerk, see, is an old high-school friend of his, and he asks the clerk not to tell anyone, he's a little embarrassed. But the clerk has this spinster sister who learns about lovable old pops and his sex aid to help out in the old in-and-out department with moms, and of course she blabs it to her cousin, Virginia Mayo, who works in the same office as pops. So the boys in shipping, they start up a lottery to guess the size and displacement of pops's artificial whango. Only pops's daughter, Corinne Calvet, learns about it in her high-school class and her boyfriend, he won't have anything to do with her until she brings it to school, she's too upset to tell pops, who in the meantime has lost it. A couple of kids, Russ Tamblyn, Lon McCallister, find it, paint it red and green, and enter it in their class art project, and of course pops, when he sees it on display in the school auditorium, with its blue ribbon . . ."

There were screams, shouts, and gunfire from the dope dealer's apartment. Someone counted one hundred twenty-five people in one day going in and out of the apartment. Junkies passed out in the hallway, sometimes with needles hanging from their arms, or legs, or ankles. Small fires, bonfires, were set in the halls.

Well-made cars with out-of-state license plates circled the block, double-parking in front of the building. One night someone appeared at the fire escape window and emptied the chamber of an M–16 into the junkies and the dope dealer. Bleeding through the mouth, the dope dealer took out a forty-five and shot off the top of the M–16 owner's head. The police sealed up the apartment.

"That guy with the M–16," said Dado, "I know him. He lived on the top floor. A veteran. Married to a Vietnamese. She can't speak English, and they got a five-year-old girl."

When questioned by the police, the super recited the plot lines of the "Flying Nun" and told them who was on "Celebrity Bowling for Dollars." During the confusion the landlord slipped in two men with acetylene torches who made a piece of modern sculpture out of the boiler. They also managed to cut the water and sewer lines. It was a day or two before anyone went to the basement and noticed the contents of the sewer spilling onto the concrete floor. "Mary Mother of Joseph," said Dado, "it's like a duck farm down there."

The landlord wanted to hold a revival meeting in the hallway. He told the tenants (the fast was over, the safety pins safely snapped through his ears) that he was inviting the Miracle Lady, Sister Sarah, and the Five Virgin Tabernacles, and that next Sunday, the entire Sunday, would be given over to Sister Sarah and the redemption of all the damned souls in the building, which meant, he said, everyone. "You are all invited," he shouted through a bullhorn in front of the building. "The only price of admission is your rent." But Sister Sarah and the Five Virgins played to an empty hall, albeit a somewhat freezing one. The landlord, resplendent in a white ermine coat, three diamond rings, two gold teeth, a pearl-handled cane (and a silver-handled .357 Magnum he kept in an inside pocket), managed to hide his disappointment. But late that night someone raced through the building shouting *Fire!* followed by the fumes of urine-soaked wood blazing in the hallway. The fire had been set under the stairwell and soon engulfed the stairwell itself, rising up to feast on the ceiling, licking at the doors to apartments.

Lowell found another apartment in Brooklyn.

27

WHEN he rounded the corner and turned onto the block of the Building, Lowell was unprepared for the bloody body that lay before him. It was flat against the sidewalk, as if sleeping, cheek pressed to the cement. The start of a river, something dark that looked like crankcase oil, something heavy and slow, flowed from the head and followed the tilt of the sidewalk. Several squad cars were there. No lights or sirens. A few heads out the window. Someone outlined the body in chalk. Pictures were taken.

"Motherfucker came flying through the air."

The police were questioning someone.

"What's your name?"

"Call me Cuzz."

"How do you spell that?"

"C-U-Z-Z."

"You live here?"

"Right."

"Is that your first or last name?"

"Both."

"What happened?"

"Motherfucking broad just came flying off the roof, like a bird. Arms and legs spread open. Crazy broads ought to tell you when they go jumping off the roof."

"How do you know she jumped?"

"I don't."

Several cops were on the roof, looking over the precipice. They called down, shouting something unintelligible. A platoon of men, in various shades of uniforms, went into the Building. A voice yelled out from the hallway.

"Fucking elevator doesn't work."

"Walk up like the rest of us."

The elevator isn't working! That would be one of the first things Lowell had fixed. Walking into the marble entrance hall, he stepped on broken glass. He was confronted by a huge hall, forty by one hundred feet, lit by a single bulb. A set of magnificent marble steps, each one chipped, led up to the rear bank of apartments. The marble railing had been knocked off and lay shattered on the floor. Off to the left, through a set of doors, was a courtyard with a marble fountain, the fountain presided over by a cavorting boy nymph, also marble. Scattered around the courtyard was garbage, broken refrigerators, a grocery cart, a television set with a busted picture tube, and a teddy bear.

Lowell had the name of one of the tenants, the head of the tenant association. Apartment 3H. He walked up the stairs. Gray, fuzzy things were stacked in the corners of the stairwells. Magic Marker on the walls. "The girl in apt. 3 does it to a T." The steps felt wet, coated with something that looked gray and slick. At each landing he felt as if he were on the edge of a cliff or a pile of rocks, delicately balanced, awaiting an avalanche. The doors to the apartments were covered with sheet metal, bolted in place. Most of them had three or four locks.

He knocked on the door of 3H. Someone opened the door, two inches, where it was stopped by a chain. The person he wanted wasn't in; they didn't know when she would be in, didn't know if she was ever coming in. No, he couldn't leave a message; they had no paper, no pencil. Lowell dug a piece of paper from his pocket. No, they couldn't take it. Have a nice day. Good-bye. The door shut.

A door opened at the other end of the hall, then slammed shut.

The doors were gun-metal gray, the frames rust red. Small brass peepholes were welded in the center. He could hear apes behind the doors shuffling around on padded feet. There was a smell to the Building: pots left in the sink, rusty SOS pads, wet cement, newspapers left in the rain. The halls were dark, painted a musty yellow, the ceilings the color of old cobwebs. More smells. East European vegetables, overcooked, smelling of garlic and old socks. A casserole of smells: urine, tar, roaches, bandages, fire, salt, cat shit, popcorn, something old and sweet.

He walked down the steps, alone, followed by what he could hear. His ears trailed him by ten feet.

He could feel the Building vibrate. A buzz seemed to circle the Building and settle in the walls, then run up and down the stairs. The buzz was a hymn, a tone poem to the Building. The smell of food, garbage, the sound of shouts, music, the feel of gritty plaster, flaking, crumbling, almost oily. He put his hand on a pipe and felt a vibration. The hum had settled in the pipes. He looked at his paint-flaked hand, bits of metal mixed with the paint.

Outside, the police had left, the body scooped up, sawdust sprinkled on the sidewalk, the chalk outline of the body on the sidewalk. Two men stood in the doorway. They seemed to resent Lowell's being there, and Lowell was furious at them for loitering in the hallway of *his* Building.

Back at H.P.D., Lowell explained it all to Sanchez.

"What?" said Sanchez.

He seemed to be in physical pain. Lowell expected to see needles sticking out of his neck, a vise-grip pliers on his tongue, his scrotum knotted with fishing line.

Lowell started to tell him, and Sanchez interrupted.

"No, the other part," he said.

"The death?"

"The murder."

"She was blond. She came off the roof."

"How does one 'come off' the roof?"

"Who knows? Fell, pushed."

"Oh damn."

Sanchez walked around in a circle, scratching his neck brace. There was a slight irregularity to his walk, as if with each step he had to go over a stone. Lowell noticed his leg twitching, starting down at his ankle and ascending his leg, until his entire body seemed to shake loose of itself.

"The reports," he said, "you'll have to fill out all the details."

He fell to the floor, his head hanging over the edge of the brace. Lowell felt that if he picked him up he might flow apart, like spilled liquid. He reached under his arms and gently lifted him into a chair.

Hector whizzed over in his wheelchair.

"You could take off his shoes now that he's out. Them pointy shoes is expensive. Cut the laces with a razor blade, and they come off quick."

"They're not my size."

"Who got murdered?"

"The blond."

"They'll probably take you off the Building now."

"How could I have stopped it? I came around the corner and she came off the roof. Flying. Before I got there. Before I stepped into the Building. She never got to know me. I do not believe this was some form of greeting."

"There's a trick to writing the report," said Hector. "You got to say something without saying something. You got to be precise, but vague."

It was the first of many reports he would write.

28

THE Building was in a coma. Even the activity of the sniper, the Festival of Bullets, was not enough to drag it out of the doldrums. It was a freezing honeycomb of caves, full of cold-damp, mildew, boredom. The tenants huddled in their own apartments around turned-up gas stoves, the oven doors open, newspapers stuffed in cracks under the doors.

Huge cracks appeared in the mortar between the bricks, great jagged lightninglike scars that tore across the side of the Building. The front door, made of kick-proof glass, had been kicked out, and one of the doors torn off its hinges. There was a pool of water, or some other liquid, in one corner. Broken marble littered the floor. In the courtyard, miraculously intact, was a marble statue surrounded by garbage stuck in the center of a pool that spouted nothing. Overhead, fluttering like gulls, flapped the washlines of those apartments that still held people. In this dark cavern Lowell could feel his footsteps before he could hear them.

He was there for a tenants' meeting. His instructions were to organize the Building. The meeting was held in a yellow apartment with voodoo dolls on the walls. Usually the meeting was held in the basement, but because of the fact that someone had tied Tubbo Rivera up in the basement and the pipes burst and he froze in a pool of ice and they emptied a twenty-two in his head and tried to take off his arm with a carving knife or his leg with a saw, this was inconvenient. The junkies didn't understand that Tubbo couldn't help them anymore, ever. They wanted to hack through the ice and get him out of the basement. They pleaded to the frozen Tubbo through the ice in the basement.

The meeting began.

Did Lowell know the elevator didn't work?

Yes.

Well, because the elevator didn't work the rabbi got peed on. The rabbi rode the elevator up to the fourth floor. Some kids were standing on top of the elevator. They cut the wires, opened the hatch in the top, and peed on the rabbi. What are you going to do about that? And what about the deaf-mute rapist? He lives with his family on the first floor. What are you going to do about that? And what about the artist in 3B who sets himself on fire? And the kid who lives on the roof and drops chimney bricks on us? And the Mormon missionary who is never home and leaves the water running. And the seven-year-old who got raped on the roof. And the dwarf and the professor. And the cockroaches. And why does the landlord come around to collect the rent?

The city owns the Building now.

The landlord comes around to collect the rent. Some pay. What are you going to do about that?

Don't pay him.

He says he'll kick us out if we don't pay him, and we got no place to go. Sure it's cold and there's no hot water, but where can we go? And I got a seven-month-old kid. It's so cold I got to push his bed next to the gas oven, which I keep on all night to keep him warm. What if it explodes?

We're working on the boiler.

And what about the pipes?

Are they gone?

The strippers from New Jersey took them.

Naw, they burst in the cold. All you gotta do is fix them.

There's a work order out on the pipes.
Are they gonna throw anyone else off the roof?
I hope not. How many tenants are in the Building?
Fifty apartments, probably one hundred fifty tenants.
But only fifteen of you are here tonight. Where are the rest?
You crazy? Everyone knows it's not safe to walk these halls at night. Muggers live in one of the apartments on the fourth floor. They're like roaches, they come out at night. Only they got razor blades; they mug in the streets and run up to the roof and leave the empty pocketbooks there.
What apartment?
4D. We told the cops, it don't do no good. They won't pay no rent either. Look, the hell with the muggers. Just give us heat and hot water and we'll take care of them. But if you don't give us that, you can kiss this Building good-bye. So long, José! Adiós, motherfucker! How smart you got to be to see that?
What about the sniper?
Fuck the sniper, man. Ain't you been listening?!! Fix the mother-fuckin' pipes and boiler, motherfucker!!!

Lowell went home and hoisted his weights, something he hadn't done in years. It was a bad habit, he knew, like too much masturbating, and yet he couldn't help himself. His sanity seemed to be invested in those weights, and with each pound he lifted he felt as if he were pushing something off his shoulders, the muscle ache a delight, the exhaustion a vacation.

The following week Lowell went around to collect the rents and found that a "small man in baggy pants" or a "large man with a derby" had preceded him, collecting rents. He was the previous owner of the Building, and the tenants paid him out of habit. He promised them he would fix the elevator, fix the stairs, and as soon as he collected enough rent he could get the fuel tank filled with oil. But the basement was now flooded beyond hope (a river no longer running through, but a lake, an ocean), the oil burner submerged, and pipes sprayed various water designs around the boiler. Lowell explained to the tenants that the city was now the landlord, not to pay the former landlord, and the tenants agreed, at least to his face, but he felt they secretly thought that if they didn't pay rent to the former landlord, it would go against them in some mysterious way.

He reported what happened to Sanchez, and when he finished he
realized that the only thing he heard at the meeting was complaints;
nobody had put forth a plan or a proposal for organization. Sanchez,
however, was not concerned.

"We put them in the T.I.L. Program," Sanchez said.

"What's that?"

"Tenant Interim Lease. We give them a new boiler, we fix the roof,
we plaster the walls and do some fixing of the mechanicals, plumbing,
wiring. Then we turn the Building over to them and let them manage
it to get the damn thing off our backs."

Sanchez scratched his neck brace.

"We've had the boiler order in for months," Lowell said.

"I know. D.G.S. has it. We got to bust some butts down there."

The "busting" was evidently successful because within a week they
had knocked a hole through the basement wall, drained some water in
the basement, and by the end of two weeks the new boiler was installed.
Oil tanks, however, had not been installed. It was January, February,
chilly months. Lowell was cursed at through partially opened doors. He
couldn't get a tenants' meeting organized. The tenants were angry at
the lack of heat and refused to meet until the city finished the boiler
work. Several weeks later the oil tanks arrived, were hooked up, filled
with oil, the furnace turned on, and steam spouted through dozens of
cracks in the heating pipes that served the Building, drenching it in an
oily white fog. It took three weeks to fix the leaks, and during that time
the tenants still refused to meet. Sanchez berated Lowell and told him
they had to meet so they could understand that the Building was being
turned over to them, they would be the landlords, their Building would
be co-oped and they could buy their apartments for just two hundred
fifty dollars apiece.

("I don't want to be no fucking landlord. You the landlord now,"
a tenant told him.)

With the heat on and the radiators hissing in everyone's apartment, Lowell was able to call a tenants' meeting. He explained the new
proposal to the tenants.

"What am I paying two hundred and fifty dollars for?"

"Your apartment."

"I already got my apartment. You gonna try and take it away from
me?"

Lowell explained the proposal once more.

"How can I buy my apartment? I can't take it with me. Can I sell it?"

Lowell said that the details of selling one's apartment were being worked on.

"What good is that?"

Lowell went back and told Sanchez that the tenants didn't seem to want to buy their apartments. Sanchez was furious.

"They got to! They got to buy 'cause we got to sell! A new ruling come down. We got to sell, we got to get out of having so many damn apartments!"

The following week he went back to the Building and none of the tenants would open their doors to him. He found out that someone had stolen the boiler. It was done without knocking a hole in the wall. The day after the boiler was stolen, the basement began to fill with water. A thin film of ice spread over the surface, broken only by small creatures who scampered across.

"How the hell they get the boiler out of the Building without knocking a hole in the wall?" Sanchez wanted to know.

"They cut it up."

"I know that, dummy."

Sanchez spat out the last word, as if it were a tiny slug of metal he hoped would implant itself in Lowell's chest.

"I think someone in the Building stole it," Lowell said.

"Oh yeah?"

"They do things like that."

The city put another boiler in, which took another month, and posted a boiler guard in the basement. They chained the boiler to huge iron rings that were buried deep in the walls, drove spikes into the sides of the boiler, and set the ends in cement columns that reached down below the foundation. A burglar alarm was put on the boiler. Then the boiler itself was wired, like an electric chair, to jolt whoever touched it.

"They steal the whole building from you," Hector said, "brick by brick, door by door. They take the walls and the ceiling and the floor and grind the boiler down into iron filings and take that out until you got no fucking building left. They stick it to you, English."

Why would they do that, he thought. It's their Building or could be very easily. How could they steal what was almost theirs, and where would they put it?

"They do it out of spite," Hector continued. "They'd sell their own arms and legs if they could."

He sounded as if he were speaking through an amplified voice box . . . a high, tinny voice that seemed to be on the verge of turning powdery. Lowell wondered why Hector worked in the department if he hated it, hated the people in it, hated the tenants. He asked him.

Hector smiled.

"Hey, English, don't take it personal, but I hate this whole fucking country, hate you and everyone in it, hate it all. Bunch of motherfuckers, every one of you."

He started to turn purple and reached around for a breathing apparatus at the back of the wheelchair. A fat rubber tube, with steel rings every inch, projected from the bottom of a stainless-steel box that had a small glass tube half filled with a clear liquid, and Hector held one end of the tube against his mouth and nose. Lowell watched him suck the contents of the tube, his chest heaving, the purple blotches that first appeared on his face fading, replaced by red and then pink splotches, until the normal mottled color of his face returned.

"Your first mistake, English," he gasped, "is that you think someone gives a shit."

He stuck the tube back over his mouth and breathed heavily from it.

"Everyone in this country is a greedy fuckpig."

Lowell wanted to argue with him, but for some reason couldn't, and then decided that he wanted to kick him, stomp him, punch his face.

"It's capitalism, man," Hector said. "The whole thing runs on greed. They sent me to Nam so the gooks could shoot my balls off. They sent all the spics and niggers to Nam so we could get our balls shot off, get our spines shot up so we couldn't move, get our knees blown off so we couldn't walk, get our intestines carved up so we couldn't eat, get pieces of our head blown off so we couldn't think. Then all you kikes and wops and micks and fuckpigs that fucked up enough so you had to go to Nam, they made officers. Always the last ones to lead a charge. Always sending us up first so the gooks can blow us away. So we frag you. We get killed on the line, and officers get killed in their tents. We had a whole regiment of officers spooked. Why do you think they ended the war? Protest? Bullshit! They ended it 'cause they ain't got no more sane officers. They're all scared out of their dorks not knowing when we would frag them. Easiest thing in the world. They pay us to kill. We kill."

The purple blotches appeared on his face, and Hector sucked at his tube. He watched Lowell breathing. Lowell's eyes followed his, which jumped and danced erratically. He had a 101st Airborne tattoo on his wrist.

"I can't get the goddamn thing off," Hector said, and Lowell didn't know if he was referring to that or to the tube, which dangled from the front of his shirt.

"Once you understand how the system operates, English, you got it made. You look for someone or something else to work over. You find a place to stick your dork before someone sticks their dork in you. That's capitalism, English, economics 101."

He pressed a button on the arm of his wheelchair and whirred away, the electric motor making a high-pitched whine that accompanied the sound of the cross-treaded hard-rubber wheels that rolled over the linoleum. Back at his desk, which was clear, unblemished by paper, he opened his drawer and dumped the contents on top of his desk. Then he took out a penknife and started to stab the paper, collecting a wad of scrap paper and forms on the knife blade until there was no room left on the point. He took them off, spread the speared papers around his desk, and began again.

Sanchez called him into his office.

"You been talking to Hector again."

"He's been talking to me."

"You should know about Hector."

"I thought you said he was going to be fired."

Sanchez looked up, somehow surprised that Lowell had remembered what he had said. But having remembered, Sanchez decided he could ignore it, the statement meaning nothing as long as it had not been committed to paper.

"He was in Vietnam."

"I know that."

"He told you?"

"Yes."

"What else did he tell you?"

"He was in the front lines. He got shot up."

"He told you he was in the front lines?"

"Not in so many words."

"Before he went he was a clerk here."

Lowell didn't know why, but that piece of news shocked him in some strange way.

"He never carried a weapon. He never got out of Saigon. He was a clerk typist over there. Worked in a supply depot typing uniform clearances. Private first class."

"But . . ."

"He was in a brothel when the Viet Cong staged a raid. Humping this fourteen-year-old girl when they burst through the door. He got shot in the ass. The bullet hit his spine. Several other bullets hit him before he could roll over and pull the girl on top of him. They picked about twenty slugs out of her body, all meant for Hector."

Sanchez paused, scratching the stubble on his chin.

"They started coming for him and he was frantic. He was stuck in the girl. He couldn't get out. This gook had used all his ammunition so he takes out a knife. He pulls the girl off Hector."

Sanchez paused again, took out a long, thin cigar, and lit it. He looked at Lowell, and Lowell knew that he wanted him to ask what happened, to give him, Sanchez, permission to continue.

"How do you know all this?"

Sanchez puffed on his cigar.

"I was his supply sergeant. I was humping this broad at the other end of the room."

He looked up at the ceiling. The smoke had gathered in layers, slowly swirling above the windows.

"Gook was just a kid, or looked like a kid. You can't tell. You never could. Didn't look no more than twelve."

"What happened?"

"I always liked guns. Even then I liked guns. But they didn't allow you to keep your own weapon. Against regulations. And I was a supply sergeant. What did I need a gun for?"

He took another puff on the cigar and watched it rise to the ceiling and join the slowly revolving cloud that hovered over the top of the room, dulling the fluorescent lights. The ceiling, made up of old squares of acoustical tile, had pieces gouged out of it, from knives and thumbtacks thrown at it, and was yellowed, probably from Sanchez's cigar smoke.

"Still, I had a .357 Magnum. Gave it away when I got back to the

States. I used to wear the damn thing strapped to my waist, like Patton. I loved Patton. Still do."

He stopped, as if to remember what really happened, or else, as Lowell suspected but would never really know, as if to create what happened.

"I had it hanging over the bed. I didn't get off the girl. I'm still in her. I take the gun out of the holster and point it at the gook's back. Just like the movies. Like some war picture."

He paused again.

"You know the funny thing? This gook was carrying pictures of his wife and kids or his mother and sisters and brothers. They all look young. You can never really tell."

"Why funny?"

"They usually don't carry pictures. Americans carry pictures. He must have gotten the idea from an American. Maybe he stole a camera and film from some grunt. But where the hell did he get it developed?"

Sanchez laughed.

"But that wasn't what spooked Hector. When I hit the gook, parts of him sprayed on Hector. Intestines, bits of lungs, I'm not sure what. He goes crazy. He goes absolutely apeshit. Stands up yelling and screaming. 'Get him off me, get him off me!' he yells. Not get *it* off me, but get *him* off me. You'd think the gook had syph or something. As soon as he stands up, the pieces of the gook fall off him. Course there's still some blood on him. He tries to brush it off. He can't. He goes crazy. Running around the room, yelling, screaming. We can't make out what he's saying. He sees the gook lying in pieces on the floor and runs out the door and onto the street. Now he's in his birthday suit, stark naked. He's yelling and screaming in the middle of the street, only no one pays any attention because the Cong have staged one of their attacks and rockets and small arms are going off all over the place. It's like a couple of Fourth of Julys all at once. Hector is running up and down the street, still screaming. He's got bullets up his ass and several other places, he's bleeding, and he's screaming. A medic tries to grab him, but Hector is not ready to be grabbed. He decks the medic. Still screaming, not yelling now, just screaming. A bunch of us run out and wrestle him to the ground. We get the medic's stretcher and strap him to it. That's the last time he walks on his own. You tell me how a man with bullets up the ass can run around and then be paralyzed for the rest of his life. What kind of paralysis is that?"

He laughed again, a high-pitched laugh, somewhat like Hector's but not as high, and every time Sanchez laughed he put his hand on his neck brace as if to reassure himself that it was still there.

"Of course, I could be making all this up," he said, "but you'll never know that. Anyway, it's not important."

Sanchez questioned Lowell about the Building, and after hearing some depressing answers, forgot what he heard and told Lowell that the commissioner had big plans for the Building. They are going to fix it up, put it in tip-top shape, and then have a big ceremony and turn it over to the tenants, who will own and manage it themselves. No more city involvement. Lowell's job is to see that the whole process runs smoothly, that the money is spent quickly and efficiently to do the things that need to get done, and then to rally the tenants around the Building and take responsibility for it.

Sanchez outlines the step-by-step procedure on the blackboard with chalk, wearing a woolen mitten (he is allergic to chalk; Lowell has seen him wear a plastic bag over his hand, a plastic medical glove, bandages, but this is the first time he has seen the woolen mitten, a bright red and green).

"The commissioner has his prestige on line with this program, Lowell."

He pauses. Lowell feels that Sanchez wants him to say something, give support, but Lowell feels a tightness around his throat, as if it were clogged with smoke, chalk dust, or blood.

"What I'm saying is that it's up to you, Lowell. Make this Building work, and there's no stopping you in this department."

Lowell had not taken the job to be stopped, to be disappointed. He had to succeed. That was his failing.

"Oh yeah, I forgot to tell you," Sanchez said. "One of the kids in the gook's picture, I adopted him. He's in high school now. You should see his grades."

29

EITHER to celebrate the entrance of the Building into the T.I.L. Program (the Tenant Interim Lease Program) or to celebrate the entrance of the Building into the Community Management Program, a ceremony was held in Williamsburg, neighborhoods away from where the Building was located, in an Orthodox kosher catering hall where each attendee was served a breakfast of baked apple and whipped ersatz cream, a wallet-size piece of fish, fried, nine peas, a half of a baked potato circumscribed by three onion rings, two cheese blintzes, which had no cheese but contained blueberries and cherries in a sweet, oily sauce, pastries, and instant coffee served in plastic cups, the meal dished out to a segregated audience, the women seated in the smaller side of the room under dirty lights and on one side of a green plastic screen done up to look like leaves and flowers, the men seated on the other side, burping with boredom, both separated sides looking at the speakers' table, which was also separated, a wall of plastic plants serving to mark off the demilitarized zone between the sexes.

There was an impressive list of people who did not come—both United States senators were not there, each expressing his regrets and pleading prior commitments, the mayor was not there, his schedule not permitting, the commissioner of Housing Preservation and Development was there and not there, and several State Supreme Court judges were also not there, but their letters were, and they were read, expressing their support for the project; and there was a not quite so impressive list of people who did come, an assistant commissioner of H.P.D., who gave a speech more serious than the occasion called for, the head of a community group, the president of a construction company, Sanchez, an official from the Department of Housing and Urban Development, a nonprofit housing expert, a rabbi, a priest, a mortgage officer from a savings bank, an assistant clerk in the mayor's office, and one man who mysteriously appeared on the podium because of a lifelong desire to make a public speech. Jockeying for position through the crowd of eaters and speakers was a photographer who made a special point of photographing whites with blacks (and blacks with whites), the pictures to be used in press releases to combat charges of racism that had been leveled by various radical groups.

Hector learned about the ceremony and wangled an invitation, but Sanchez, who arranged it, made sure the catering hall was not wheelchair accessible, and Hector arrived to find that he could not negotiate the wheelchair up the steps and could find no one willing to hoist the chair, his bulk, and his acerbic tongue up the stairs to the catering hall. He looked for the freight entrance, couldn't find it, and then decided to drive home over the Williamsburg Bridge, to the consternation of the cars who honked furiously at him as his electric wheelchair rolled over the center traffic lane at seven miles per hour.

Sanchez asked Lowell how he liked the ceremony, and Lowell said he thought it had the proper aura of dullness. The speeches were stilted and officious enough to make one feel uncomfortable; there were enough plaques and wreaths and "auspicious moments" and "bold steps forward" to reinforce the feeling of an official ceremony: acid indigestion. Lowell burped up an aftertaste of fish, an oily stew that reminded him of damp wool and sweaty socks, and quickly swallowed some lukewarm coffee that puckered the inside of his mouth. People looked around to make sure that everyone was as uncomfortable as they were, and satisfied at the signs of distress they perceived on other faces, they attacked with relish the barely edible fish.

"This is the perfect ceremony," Sanchez said.

He paused, looking as if he were about to suck on a pipe.

"Everybody yawns, they're bored, the speeches never stop, everybody's heard them before, the food is lousy, and the waiters look like they're trying to hustle you. It's a ritual. Everybody pays homage to the ritual. Excitement would make the commissioner nervous, get the politicians upset, and make the tenants think they were missing out on something."

"Maybe they are."

"You mean the program?"

"Which one?"

"We haven't decided yet."

"Don't the tenants care?"

"They'll find out in time. And what difference does it make? We pay to fix up either way."

"But shouldn't they decide?"

"You're talking like a liberal. All they want is warm and dry, heat and hot water; they don't care who they get it from."

Sanchez leaned back in his chair, changing from an imaginary pipe to an imaginary cigar, which he puffed, making a round little O of his mouth and alternately sucking and blowing his cheeks. He had his neck brace off and kept turning his head, quickly, as if he were watching a column of horses that kept racing around the catering hall.

"How do these decisions get made?" Lowell asked.

"We have strict guidelines."

"Who made them?"

"They keep changing. The thrust stays the same, but the details, the particulars, we experiment with those."

Lowell imagined a laboratory with toy buildings, people with white coats and test tubes.

"Of course," Sanchez added, "no one really knows what they're doing. We're all guessing."

He smiled at Lowell, and Lowell didn't know if he was serious and the smile meant to show an honest vulnerability, or if the smile was another one of Sanchez's cynicisms, a scathing denunciation of his job and the department. The smile hung there, an enigmatic warning, a sort of puzzling pose that dared interpretation. Lowell smiled back, a weak kind of thing that only turned up the corners of his mouth.

"Let me tell you a story," Sanchez said. "A short story, about Hector, about his dog."

He stopped, waiting for Lowell to ask him what kind of a dog it was so he could say he didn't know, that no one knew, that people who knew dogs had seen it and couldn't decide, that it was a dog that seemed to change from minute to minute. But Lowell did not ask him that question, so Sanchez could not tell him all he did not know about the dog.

"He's got this dog, see . . ." looking over at Lowell, this time with a real cigar, unlit, in his mouth, "this dog has special training, a very highly trained dog, very responsive, but very, very well trained. This dog does whatever Hector tells it to do. And also, like I say, very, very heavily trained. Hector has him trained to do his business, his poops, on the editorial page of the *New York Times*. Dog sees the *New York Times* masthead, underneath a headline, "An Acceptable Doctrine of Nonintervention," and right away this well-trained dog shits on it. Conditioned reflex. Well one day he can't find the editorial page. He tries another page, but the dog won't shit on it. This is a big dog now. He comes with lots of shit. But he's so used to the editorial page that he won't shit on any other page of the *Times*. Hector is frantic. He tries a *Daily News* editorial, "Lock 'Em Up and Throw Away the Key." No good. Not even a *New York Post* editorial, "Man Rapes Own Grandmother." No, that dog is very heavily trained, and he won't dump on anything but *Times* editorials. Hector in the wheelchair, it's hard for him to get out. Anyway, it's late at night. Newsstands closed. Where's he going to get an editorial page? What will he do?"

He starts chewing on the cigar.

"He starts knocking on doors. Asks for the *Times* editorial page. But he don't live with no intellectuals. No one in his building reads the *New York Times*. Meanwhile, this dog is back in his apartment, ready to explode. Did I tell you what kind of a dog it was?"

"No."

"I didn't think I did. Anyway, Hector's dog is dying of shit. The more he sits, the more it builds up. His whole insides is filling up with shit. And Hector can't get a copy of the *New York Times*. What does he do? Tell me."

"He could go to the library and get the editorial page on microfilm and blow it up, and the dog could shit on that."

"The library is closed. Use your head. Meanwhile this dog is filling up with shit. What is he to do?"

On the speakers' podium, the man who made the toilet seats that were going in the newly renovated Building was speaking.

"I really don't know."

"Of course you don't know. I'm telling the story, so how could you know?"

The man who made the toilet seats for the Building was now seated, and his place was taken by a steel-door manufacturer, who assured everybody that from now on no one would be able to kick in the doors, they were solid-core doors with double-gauge steel on both sides and a reinforced center, and they came with a tiny peephole made of bulletproof glass.

"This dog is blowing up like a balloon. He's two, three times his normal size, and his normal size is big to begin with."

"Wait a minute . . ."

"Look, who's telling this story?"

Lowell wondered. Sometimes he thought that Sanchez spoke in

directives, as if he had memorized the day's memos and then spewed them out.

"Now, one thing you may not know about dogs, and that is, they got two assholes."

He looked around for the effect this statement would have on the other diners and, finding none, continued.

"That's right. Don't look so stupid, that only shows your ignorance. They got two assholes. Now Hector has trained the first asshole and trained it well. But he forgot about the second one. It's hidden, underneath some hair, off to one side, hard to spot. Now the first asshole is sealed up tight. That's the trained one. Nothing can come out of there until it sees the editorial page of the *New York Times*. But the second one, that's something else. You know what happens with the second one?"

"Wait a minute . . ."

"Who's telling the story?"

A man who made intercoms was speaking. He mentioned "buzz-back" and "double buzzback" and the secure feeling of knowing who you let up before you let them up.

"Now this second asshole in a dog is rarely used. Scientists call it a vestigial asshole, kind of like an appendix. But all this stress is building up inside the dog, so that this second asshole is no longer vestigial, and it's no longer under the dog's control. But it operates different than an ordinary dog asshole. It's also a kind of defense mechanism."

"Wait a minute, Sanchez."

"Look, who's—"

"Telling the story? Not you. This is something you read. Hector doesn't have a dog. How could he walk the dog? He hates dogs, he told me so himself."

"Of course he hates dogs, especially after what this dog did to him. But hey, understand Hector. He's got to have the things around that he hates the most. Me, number one, for saving his life. The dog is number two. He's got to have a dog around so he can hate it."

The garbage cans in the Building were of the spill-resistant, vandal-resistant variety, in a new special size to hold more garbage (fewer trips up and down to empty the garbage) and with new improved handles. They would, of course, be delivered after the new compactor system was installed.

"Hey, Lowell, you got to understand the Spanish mentality. That's for starters, and then you got the overlay of the Puerto Rican mentality, which adds complexity upon complexity. You see, we understand you English very well, we have to, to work with you."

"What's that got to do with the dog?"

"I'm coming to that. Now, you take your average Spanish, Hispanic, spic, whatever. He comes home, he expects to be obeyed. He demands it. He's like dogshit outside his home, but inside he's the king. With you, English, it's the other way around, exact opposite. Now the Spaniard, he comes home, he expects to be obeyed. Instantly. But take when your Puerto Rican comes home. He expects to be obeyed beforehand. Take me. I like to be anticipated, before I give the order I want it obeyed, so that when I come home everything works and I don't have to go around the house shouting like some Spaniard."

"What the hell does that have to do with dogs?"

"I'm coming, I'm coming. Your Spaniard looks down on your Puerto Rican. They don't like the way we talk; they say we butcher the language, we talk too fast. But we talk a compressed Spanish, a little hard for them to understand, their minds don't work as fast as ours. All Puerto Ricans have fantastically high IQs."

"I don't believe that."

"Of course not. You English never do. We know that. We know you, know how you think, so we expect that."

"What about the dog full of shit?"

"I'm coming, I'm coming. That's another thing that we have that you don't. Patience. We wait a thing out. Ninety-five percent of all problems solve themselves in time. Four percent are insoluble. That leaves one percent you can do something about."

Having run out of door manufacturers and security-lock specialists and iron-grating installers, the podium was strangely empty, and an uneasy hush, like cold oatmeal, descended upon the catering hall, causing Sanchez to look up, as the other diners did, feeling somewhat uncomfortable over the absence of speech, the vocal wallpaper to fill in the edges around their conversation. A rabbi ran around frantically looking for someone to give a speech, hoping that a nail manufacturer or a cement supplier who had been overlooked was present, or failing that, thought that the woman who kept the attendance list could read that. A priest offered to say several Hail Marys and a brace of Our Fathers, but when reminded of the utter inappropriateness of the occasion for these, he sat down in a huff, thinking that the least he could do was recite the names of the CYO basketball champs for the last twenty-five years, being able to do the last twenty years from memory alone and then referring to a palm card for the rest. On the other side of the palm card was a glow-in-the-dark Hail Mary and the name of an Irish funeral parlor. The priest, knowing a little about science, wondered if his ass was radioactive since he carried the card in his wallet, which he kept in his rear pocket, and he had heard that glow-in-the-dark paint was made, at one time, with radium. A rabbi volunteered to offer on-the-spot mitzvahs for those who so desired, but there were none who so desired, and he too sat down in a huff, thinking that at the very least he could recite the names of all the doctors in his congregation and then the names of all the doctors' sons, with special emphasis on those doctors' sons who also were attending medical school, and then the names of all those sons whose fathers were not doctors but were also attending medical school, and then after that the lawyers. A minister got up and began to expound about how everyone was a brother to everyone else and that we all prayed to the same God (a chorus of boos) but that God in his wisdom had seen fit to let hundreds of faiths bloom, charging each with its special duties and obligations, and then he recited other bits of Protestant nonsense until a rising chorus of catcalls made him step away, red-faced, chagrined that his call to unity had met with so much hostility, such outright anger and resentment; and flustered at his flawed nobility, feeling that perhaps he had mispronounced a crucial word or unwittingly violated a canon of kosher banquet hall etiquette, stepped off the platform that held the podium into empty space, his foot frantically feeling for something firm, his body expecting it and then not finding it, tumbling backward, his head, arms outstretched, striking and overturning a plate of hot blintzes which scalded the minister's hands, causing him to sink them in two pitchers of ice water, both of which overturned and ran into a plate of peas so that the peas, lighter than water, floated to the top of their bowl and then rushed pell-mell in the temporary river of ice water along the banquet table, and the pitchers broke, the glass gashing one of the Protestant theologian's arms, causing him to wave both about quite frantically, droplets of the blood of Jesus being flung about the hall, and when the rabbi came up and attempted to comfort and steady him, the minister grabbed for his face, as if for a raft in a deep pool of water, and smeared blood over the rabbi's face and beard and then reached out and tried to grab the priest's tunic to stem the flow of blood, but the priest, sensing madness and anarchy and Martin Luther nailing his epistles to the front of his cassock, stepped back, bumping into a man with a machine gun who stepped up to the podium and announced over the loudspeaker that in the name of the people and in honor of the May Twenty-second Uprising the July Fifth Committee had taken over the banquet hall and that armed guards had the exits covered, so please, everybody, do not get excited, stay seated while we, meaning his committee, plan the rest of the activities. These included a five-hour speech by a short man in a red bandanna and combat boots, during which time no one was allowed to talk, a command that created more protest than the armed invasion of the July Fifth Committee. The speaker charged that the city and the local community leaders had sold out the poor people in the neighborhood, that the level of greed was running higher than usual, and that what was happening with the Building was that it was being renovated for those with higher incomes, as they would be the only ones who could then afford the rents, so poor blacks were being driven out, and that in the historical process those who committed these crimes and others against the poor would have to pay for them, that trials would soon be held in which certain people, capitalists and their toadies, running lackey dogs of imperialism, would be tried before a people's court out at Shea Stadium, found guilty, and sentenced to a winter in a heatless apartment until they confessed the errors of their ways. By the third hour of the speech, some of the audience had passed out, despite proddings by uniformed men with M–16s, their heads resting in a plate of congealed blintzes. For those with more self-restraint and cunning, an arm was propped up on a chair in such a fashion that sleep, under the guise of wakefulness, was obtained. At the end of the five-hour speech, the diners had to empty their pockets and put the contents in the center of the table ("to support the revolution"), being allowed to keep one subway token, and before the doors of the banquet hall were unlocked, the diners had to shout, in unison, arms clasped, three times, "Long live the July Fifth Committee, and death to their enemies, the fascist-capitalist-pig exploiters." After twenty minutes, when the shouted slogan had reached the level that the leader seemed to want, everyone was allowed to leave the banquet hall, single file.

Leaving the banquet hall, Lowell blinked rapidly in the Brooklyn air, feeling as if he had been deposited on one of Jupiter's moons. It was an area of Brooklyn he had never seen before: old warehouses, auto repair shops, crumbling brownstones. Women with bandannas on their heads pushed prams chock full of tiny children, Orthodox bearded Jews swarmed the streets, wearing no ties but a look, Lowell thought, of bemused tragedy, as if an event over which they had no control was unfolding before them.

"Where are we?" Lowell asked.

Sanchez looked puzzled.

They had come by car, but the tires on their cars had been slashed, and the bureaucrats did not know how to change a tire. Single file, in a trail that seemed to stretch for blocks, they slogged off to the subway. Heads tucked into their shoulders, bent forward as if expecting to be beaten, the officials walked desultorily toward what they thought was a subway station.

"Is it true?" Lowell asked.

"Of course it's true," Sanchez said. "Everything radicals say is always true. We have to raise the rents to cover the cost of renovation. But they get Section 8 subsidies, so they're covered."

"Will the poor get pushed out?"

"Those poor with Section 8 subsidies can stay. Those poor without will have to pay more rent."

"Or leave?"

"Or leave. Who the hell do you think we are? Santa Claus?"

Sanchez took out a cigar and lit it. It seemed awkward in his mouth, and he had a hard time keeping it lit.

"The poor, the dirt poor, don't have to worry," said Sanchez. "It's the rich poor that get hurt. Those with a few bucks put aside, those who work, they get hurt."

As if to emphasize his point he sent out a huge cloud of smoke from his cigar, a fog of blue that instead of dispersing into the air, followed him around, tethered to the cigar.

A gaggle of geese, a pride of lions, a bunch of bureaucrats, Lowell thought, as he watched the line stretch out before him, a line of patient public officials trudging toward one of their own masterpieces, the subway. After several blocks and after several more blocks, it became obvious that they were nowhere near a subway station. Lowell wondered if they knew what a subway stop looked like. On they walked, as if through snow, bracing for the inevitable wind.

They found a subway—the LL or the RR or the QB, Lowell wasn't sure which, but since all the bureaucrats seemed collectively to think that this was the right subway, that it would snake through the murky depths of Brooklyn into the finer, more rarified atmosphere of Manhattan, they descended upon it, several trying to bum their way on with an obsolete civil servant card and were subsequently arrested. Pushing onto the platform and then, when the train came, into the subway cars, which were already crowded because the train before had broken down and had to be taken out of service, the bureaucrats shoved and pummeled their way into the depths of the subway car, assaulted by the stale air and deadly gases stagnating in the car because an overhead rotating fan was out of commission (someone trying to jam a ripped-off fire extinguisher between the blades and the blade guard).

An elbow at his throat, a shopping bag that contained a sharp and possibly lethal weapon jammed against his back, a woman who looked embalmed standing in front of him, staring at him with dead fish eyes, a teenager, color unidentifiable, with a "box" that had treble, bass, and volume cranked up, Lowell searched for Sanchez. Able to turn just his head, Lowell was unable to find him and thought that perhaps he had gotten on the next car or had dropped between the cars onto the subway tracks. Then he noticed that the elbow at his neck belonged to Sanchez. Squirming, violently jerking his body, he was able to turn so that he faced him.

"What about the dog?" Lowell asked.

The embalmed woman looked at him quizzically, one dead fish eye lower than the other, which was surrounded by a huge lid that fluttered ominously and seemed on the verge of swallowing the eye until the eye turned outward and fell out, causing Lowell to gag, but not the woman, who calmly caught it and pressed it back into the empty socket.

"The second asshole, the dogshit," Lowell continued.

Sanchez stared at him as if he were trying to break a tiny web that had been ensnared over his eyes. His eyes widened, the upper and lower lids separating until they were no longer oval but round, causing the embalmed lady to stare at Sanchez.

The subway stopped; the lights went out, except for a dim yellow bulb in the center of the car and one at each end. Lowell figured they were somewhere underneath the East River. In the dim light he could barely make out Sanchez's face. A distorted voice came over the loudspeaker, its crackled syllables indecipherable. The garbled message was repeated a second time. Lowell felt he could go limp without falling to the ground: underneath one arm was the embalmed lady; under the other was the owner of "the box," who, undaunted by the fact that his radio wouldn't work underground, had inserted a tape and cranked up the volume so the booming base was in a position to rage against Lowell's ear. He twisted around violently, apologized, and the radio fell to the floor. Before the owner could retrieve it, Lowell moved again, shouting something and causing a minor panic, a whirlpool of passengers revolving around Lowell and the radio, and in the melee Lowell managed to step on the radio several times, breaking or at least damaging, he thought, part of the radio's tape-transfer system. He apologized again to the owner, mumbling something about an epileptic attack. In the dark he could not register the look on anyone's face, and he felt a sense of freedom he had never experienced before, as if he were not trapped in a subway with hundreds of tons of water rushing overhead but in a room where he was able to act out his most bizarre fantasy. He felt like a termite queen, in touch with her workers, who would scurry about obeying her orders simply by touching her abdomen, by sensing the chemicals she secreted.

The voice over the loudspeaker came on again, mumbling something different yet still indecipherable.

Then there was silence.

"What about the dog?" Lowell whispered in a voice that seemed to carry half the length of the subway car. Then the dim yellow lights, the last vestige of clarity in the car, flickered and went out. A faint odor of smoke drifted through the car. Lowell recognized the smell: it was electrical, burning insulation. The dark hid what Lowell and most other people in the trapped subway thought: there was an electrical fire somewhere up ahead, the exhaust fans were not working, the billowing smoke was slowly wafting toward the trapped subway car so that what would have been at most an unpleasant cloud a speeding subway train would have to go through, causing several moments of minor coughing until the moving train had cleared the smoke, was about to engulf them because they were stalled, because the train was caught in its own failed mechanisms. The inky black saved them from having to witness the progress of the poisonous cloud, but they would smell it, sharply at first, then more dully as their senses were used to it, and then, competing for oxygen, their lungs and the fire, the smoke would push, clog the air in their lungs, filling in the tiny sacs with a tight slime that prevented any passage of oxygen. There would be a panic of breathing and not being able to breathe, of lungs working in terror, filling with smoke, heaving faster as they searched for a stray pocket of air that would temporarily relieve the pain of oxygen deprivation. People would start clawing at each other, feeling that everyone else had used up the air that was rightfully theirs, trying to retrieve what little was left in the smoke-clogged atmosphere.

People shifted uneasily in the car. It was the calm of suppressed terror, a quiet roiling of the waters of panic. A buzz came over the loudspeaker, followed by a crackle and several more buzzes. The three overhead lights flickered briefly and then went off. Lowell heard the warning thump and hum of the subway motors; the train was briefly jerked ahead several feet and then stopped. The sound of the motors died. There was silence. The loudspeaker too was dead. It was the last part of the beast to go. Lowell felt immeasurably saddened at the death of the great electrical creature that had carried them through the mole holes of the city, a being they had always taken for granted.

There was a temporary stillness in the subway car, the relaxation before panic.

"The dog."

Lowell turned in the direction of the voice.

"The second asshole," Sanchez said, "was you."

Lowell stiffened. He could feel people moving in the car. It was very quiet, everyone afraid to voice what was on their mind, so that when Sanchez said "The dog," people turned abruptly, as abruptly as if someone had shouted "Fire," and when he added "The second asshole was you," they sighed, moving back and then forth, thinking that the term applied to them for taking this train when they could have taken any other.

"The dog could not shit," Sanchez said, "yet the shit was building up inside him. It puffed him up to alarming proportions. What was Hector to do?"

Lowell got another whiff of smoke.

"Let me tell you about this dog," Sanchez said. "The dog is dozens of years old, older than any dog has a right to be."

The lights, the dim ones, flickered briefly. Lowell heard the thump of the motors, and the train jerked forward for twenty feet before it stopped. But this time the motors kept thumping, an encouraging sign, Lowell thought.

It was during this jerky forward motion of the train and the brief flickering of the dim lights, which seemed to buzz on and off about a dozen times, that Lowell noticed a tall man in robes, with a staff, making his way through the crowded train. He seemed to glide through spaces that barely existed or, like water, flow around obstacles. Even with the lights out, Lowell had the sense of him standing in the middle of the subway car, and for some reason he thought the man had a beard, a long pointed one, a beard that was dyed purple, and had purple robes and purple hair streaked with white, though he had seen none of this.

With the lights still out, the train begins to move, then stops. Static comes over the loudspeaker, followed by more static. Then silence. Another encouraging sign. There is no longer a smell of smoke. The train starts up again, travels for fifty feet, and then stops. The lights, the full lights, go on. People blink uncomfortably. Lowell does not see the tall purple man. Then the lights go off. A voice comes over the loudspeaker and says something in a language that does not seem to be of this planet. They pull into a station.

Having finally made it, Lowell and Sanchez trudge back to the office, a gaggle of bureaucrats.

"That," Sanchez says, throwing off his coat and tie and settling back into his chair, "was one of the most successful ceremonies I have ever attended. The speeches, the food, the protestors, everything was perfect."

He pulled out a real cigar and lit it.

"I know the commissioner would have loved it too. He would have just gone ape-crazy over it."

"I thought the commissioner was there."

"That was his double. He always sends his double. You never know what's going to happen at one of these things. Once you get out in the neighborhoods, it's a jungle. But this went beautifully. I'll put it all in my report. I want you to make one out too."

He sighed and put the cigar out, sticking a piece of paper in the typewriter.

"The Building, sweet Jesus, we'll fix that Building up like new, better than new. The tenants will kiss us."

He relit his cigar and started to type.

"I don't know how to type!"

He tore the paper out of the typewriter.

"What about the dog?"

Sanchez looked at him as if he had no nose or had a potted plant in his head.

"That dog was older than it had any right to be. The dog kept filling up with shit and just exploded. Shit all over the place. The dog completely disappeared. Ask Hector about it. Hector, by the way, is my brother."

30

I T was bolted, screwed, spiked, cemented, riveted, locked, and otherwise secured by various forms of cement, steel, and iron, but the commissioner remained uneasy over the new boiler put in to replace the one stolen in the Building, so a directive came down, filtering slowly through several grades of civil servantry, like well-perked coffee, and Lowell found himself posted as a boiler guard. A cot was set up for him with a supply of blankets; he was given a hot plate, a tiny gas refrigerator (there was no electrical outlet, or at least none he could find), a flashlight, a supply of light bulbs, a carton of tomato soup, several cans of coffee, and a case of Wonder Bread (it used to build bodies eight ways, now it builds bodies twelve ways; Lowell pondered on the four additional ways it built bodies and wondered if any of those ways was significant for him), a metal box of Band-Aids, a twenty-two caliber rifle (for the rats or the mice, which were the same size as cats but it didn't make any difference what size they were since he didn't know how to fire the rifle and if attacked by rats or a herd of snarling mice planned to club them with the rifle or throw bullets at them), a construction helmet, a memo pad, and a reading lamp. Of course he need only remain down there eight hours a day, from four to midnight during weeknights and six P.M. to two A.M. if he pulled weekend duty; these were the times that the commissioner had determined, through computer studies, were most susceptible to boiler thievery, a rare but growing form of burglary that would soon rival pipe and roof removal.

Lowell was not the only one on boiler guard. There were several others, few of whom he met, except for Hector, who arranged his schedule so that it overlapped with Lowell's.

"This ain't so bad," said Hector. "I pulled pipe guard, roof guard; now that roof guard is a pisser, you're out there in the rain and snow, plus I got to get someone to pull me up the stairs."

"Aren't there elevators?"

"They never go to the roof."

He turned to Lowell.

"Hey, English, you pretty. Kiss me."

Lowell stiffened. A hesitant "no" stumbled from his mouth.

"Good," said Hector, "just want to see if you queer. Don't want to be down here with no queer, no fagboys, no fairies."

He waited for a reaction from Lowell, then continued.

"Not that I got nothing against them. Hell, half the department is queer; the other half has herpes. But we be down here together we got other things to worry about than kissing and sticking dicks in each other, hey?"

Lowell agreed.

"They want to set this fucking Building on fire."

Hector pointed to a corner of the cellar.

"See that spot?"

Lowell squinted his eyes.

"That's where they tried to thaw out Tubbo the dope dealer. The upper half of him decomposed while the lower half, balls and all, was preserved in ice. He could have lasted another thousand years, his lower half could; they could have shipped half of him in ice to the Arctic and dug him up later like the mastodons. But he's an iceberg. He floated somewhere else in the basement."

Hector made a face, twisting his mouth so that half of it reached the region of the lower part of his eye while the other half dipped down toward his chin, like a roller coaster.

Lowell shivered. It was damp in the basement. He could hear water running but could not find the source. It rushed by with a fury that sounded like a river, as if the entire Building had been built over a tributary of the Hudson. It was winter, but the temperature was in the seventies. December. Supposed to be one of the coldest winters on record. He shivered again.

"They torch this place, it goes up like a fucking tinderbox."

"It's brick," Lowell observed.

"No fucking difference, man. They know how to set fires. With enough gas they can get the fucking bricks to burn. We roast like ribs down here in our own grease. We be charred, man."

The prospect of frying in his own grease in some way calmed Lowell. He could imagine himself burning quickly, becoming instantly unconscious, and achieving a second life through flames. They would be found, as Hector said, like two burned logs, like grizzled sharks.

They were guarding a Weil McClean Boiler, oil-fired, with automatic water feed and two safety shutoffs, Model MA–S344. It looked like a steel box to Lowell, with two wrist-size pipes that entered and left and several smaller pipes, finger size, that were attached to the side. There was a pressure gauge, a steam blow-by valve, a drainage valve, and four small steel plates that had printed instructions for the boiler's operation. The boiler had an alarm system wired to it, with a beeper that Lowell and the other boiler guards carried with them.

"Is this where you found the dog?" Lowell asked.

"What dog?"

"The exploding dog."

"I never had no dog."

"The one that only shit on editorials."

"I never had no dog. What could I do with a dog?"

Hector picked his nose and tugged at his earring.

"Sanchez had a dog. A little rat-size dog. Used to shit on his shirts. You could put that dog inside a Buick on a hot summer afternoon, roll the windows up so that no air came in, and that little sucker would bark all afternoon."

"Sanchez . . ."

"Lies. Never believe the man."

"He said you were brothers."

Hector scratched a scraggy beard and made another face. This one involved a nose, one eye, a corner of his mouth, and his elbow.

"Don't believe that man. He's my brother?!! Ain't that a pisser!"

"He said you were in Vietnam together."

Hector snorted, picked his nose, snorted again.

"Jesus, let me out of here. I gotta leave."

He snorted again.

"Just roll me up the fucking steps. I don't wanna hear no more about Sanchez."

During the days that followed, Hector talked less and less. The number of times he called Lowell an *asshole* or *fucking English* decreased, and Lowell wondered if he was feeling well, if perhaps the cellar air had affected his lungs. For Lowell, the effects of the cellar were more subtle. The light bulbs hanging from the ceiling merely cleared the darkness from the center of the cellar and did a rather poor job of that. The cellar walls and the shapes that lay beyond the boundary of the light remained as mysterious as ever. He couldn't remember if he had ever seen the cellar walls, indeed if there were any, nor was he aware of the other rooms and objects that were in the cellar. At times he could see a strange glow that came from the darkness. It would vibrate, pulse, even dance. He thought he heard growls coming from somewhere. A large man carrying a smaller man, or perhaps a doll, came down once and then quickly left. Once, when he was sleeping, Lowell dreamed a man came down and dug up three bodies from the muddy floor, shrouded in white, and carried them one by one up the cellar steps. It was a bad dream, and he thought no more about it. One day, or night, he wasn't sure which, he came down to the cellar and found chicken necks piled in one corner. He swept them up and put them in the garbage.

Hector was gone for a week. He was sick. His place was taken by a man who wore a high-school varsity jacket and spent his time looking around the cellar for things he could take. He was an old man, who told Lowell he was out to "beat the system." "I'm in it for all I can get," he told Lowell, advising Lowell to do the same. "These fucking people want you to wipe their asses, do everything for them. I'm telling you that as one white to another." The following week he left, replaced by someone Lowell thought was comatose, and who, when he stood on his feet, which was extremely rare, kept his chin on his chest and his eyes rolled up in his head. He had just gotten out of Matteawan and was doped up on several currently fashionable drugs, he told Lowell in one of the three sentences he spoke the week he was in the cellar.

Lowell was made sergeant of the boiler guards. Sanchez gave him his commission, approved of course by the commissioner, and signed by him along with Sanchez. In the damp cellar air the ink faded and the paper began to fall apart, so that when the inspection official came by Lowell had nothing to show him, except for a laundry stub which for some strange reason he hauled out.

When Hector came back he told Lowell "some asshole tenants" were planning to burn the Building down. "We got to get outta here," he said, almost bouncing up and down in his wheelchair, twisting his earrings and the patches of beard that decorated his face. "This place ain't safe. They gonna torch it." He spoke with great certainty. Lowell had no reason to doubt him, but he wondered, why, with the city fixing up the Building, the tenants would want to burn it down.

"Don't think logic, English," Hector said. "That's your first mistake."

"It doesn't make sense."

"Hey, these tenants are animals. Only thing worse than a tenant is a landlord."

In the next several days Lowell noticed a lot of activity in the Building. Pipes were replaced, new wiring put in, replacement windows installed. Trucks loaded with Sheetrock pulled up in front of the Building, and mechanical hands swung dozens of pieces of Sheetrock into third- and fourth-story windows. Paint trucks pulled up. A new exterior door was put on. And slowly, week after week, an attempt was made to clear the garbage out, excavate and remove the fountain, pave over the courtyard and brick up all entrances to it. To keep people from airmailing garbage down, the windows that overlooked the courtyard were going to be bricked in until a housing code was found that prohibited it.

Then winter hit with a vengeance; the boiler did and did not work. Teams of maintenance men trooped down to the cellar, turning the boiler up, turning it down, replacing a pump, fixing a hose, resetting the thermostat, which was re-reset every night when shivering tenants came down and changed it again, only to have it changed once more by other shivering tenants, so that the boiler was not just re-reset, but dozens of re-re's, and Lowell thought that perhaps H.P.D. was running a boiler-maintenance school. The Building got hot, cooled off, became cold, got hot again, cold; ponds, frozen, appeared in the basement, and then mysterious streams of water (which Lowell could see this time) that ran up instead of down. Some apartments became steam rooms, others became cold-storage rooms. The super, trained by the department, had disappeared. A small yellow-brown man, Cambodian, Lowell thought, ran around telling the tenants that a river was attacking the Building. All this Lowell heard from Hector, who despite his immobility seemed to know more about the Building than anyone.

"Problem with the Building, English, is that it's several buildings. It's too big, makes no sense a building this size."

He was cutting his fingernails with a foot-long switchblade, a blood groove running down the center.

"Building like this just too damn big."

He put his fingernail clippings in his pocket, buttoning it shut. He patted the pocket, making sure they were still there.

The Building was put on cold alert, then heat alert, which meant that it was too cold and then too hot, and that H.P.D. felt it necessary to tell the tenants the heat conditions in their apartments.

There was a tenants' meeting in the cellar next to the boiler. Lowell presided over it and listened to complaint after complaint. The tenants told the city, which in this case was Lowell (Sanchez refusing to come, claiming that his neck hadn't healed properly and that he didn't want to risk reinjuring it), that they were not paying rent until the heating system worked. Lowell tried to work through the meeting in a rational manner, with tempers subdued and inflections low-key, but as the meeting progressed the sound level rose, coming to a crescendo, like a wave about to break, and as one little old lady with white hair got up and started using elaborate oaths, which not only called his own birthright into question but that of every city official connected with the Building, and then compared the city to some foul sewer disease, shouting through a bullhorn, containers for liquid were launched in Lowell's direction, and he was forced to find refuge behind the boiler while glass shattered at his feet, tin cans skittered against the wall, and several milk cartons, loaded with sand, bounced off the boiler. Feeling that the usefulness of the meeting had peaked, Lowell called for an adjournment.

After the tenants left he cleaned up the mess and then lay down on the cot for some rest. He wasn't sure how long he had slept, ten minutes or two hours, but when he woke, Hector was shaking him by the shoulder.

"What you do with it?"

"With what?"

"The boiler, stupid."

Lowell rubbed his eyes and looked in the direction of the boiler. For the first time he saw what the wall behind the boiler looked like.

"Where's the boiler?" Lowell asked.

"Where the fuck is the boiler?" Sanchez asked.

"Where's the fucking boiler?" the commissioner asked.

Lowell could answer none of their questions, any more than he could satisfactorily explain how the bolts, screws, straps, locks, security alarms, concrete, and barbed wire had been severed, cut, drilled through, sawed off, bypassed, and otherwise removed and the boiler dug up. There were no holes in the walls.

"Spontaneous evaporation," was Hector's answer.

"It just disintegrated," he added. "The voodoo people hexed it away."

Lowell, brought up into the light after weeks underground in the dark, began to think that he had dreamed the whole six weeks in the cellar. It seemed unreal to him, and when he questioned Sanchez about it, Sanchez shrugged his shoulders, first one and then the other, as if to neither confirm nor deny his feeling. You were down there, he said. That, however, did not answer his question.

"You got to find the boiler," Sanchez said.

"Where?"

"That's your problem."

As bitter cold swept the city, the department brought in an emergency boiler, oil-fired, which sat outside the Building heating water, turning it into steam, which was piped into the Building through large insulated pipes that were strung up over the sidewalk. For the first time in many months frigid apartments slowly lost their chill, became warm, and Lowell's knocking at doors asking if anyone had seen a boiler was greeted not with angry snarls or hoots of laughter but with mild derision or questioning grimaces, and during a tenants' meeting that Lowell held a few weeks after the temporary boiler was put in, there was a round of applause for Lowell and for his decision to "evaporate" the boiler and bring in a temporary one. Lowell protested that none of that had been his doing, but such protestations fell on unbelieving ears. The pitched glass and cans had turned into cheers and compliments.

But the emergency boiler would not remain forever in front of the Building, cooking heat for apartments. Lowell reminded the tenants of this, and someone suggested that they cut a hole in the cellar wall and drive the emergency boiler into the cellar and then brick it up again. There was, Lowell assured them, no provision to do that.

While the heat was gone from the Building, construction had stopped, the workers saying they couldn't work without heat. The shivering tenants watched them walk off the job. When the heat came back on, construction did not start because the company that was doing the work had another job to complete, and the contract the city signed with the construction company was vague as to a completion date. Half the Sheetrock was up, and half of that was taped but unpainted; stacks of four-by-eight Sheetrock were piled up in the hallways, scratched and pissed on by cats, nibbled by mice, cracked by baseball bats. Rolls of roofing paper lay in their packages on the roof. Some of the holes had been fixed. When the roofers left the sniper returned, dumping the roofing paper on social workers who came to the Building to determine if the housing conditions met Welfare Department regulations. They did not. Rents were held up. H.P.D. said they could not finish the renovations until they were partially financed by the rents. No rents, no renovations. The Welfare Department suggested that those tenants on welfare move to a building owned by a neighborhood slumlord.

"We got to find that fucking boiler," Sanchez said. "The commissioner's ass is on the line with this Building. Now the mayor knows about it, there's publicity, and the head pimp at Welfare would love to work us over. Thing they love to do best is hold up a check."

Where do you look for a boiler?

Lowell began with the Building. He searched the basement and found not a boiler but a savage police dog locked up in a small supply room (empty otherwise), piles of chicken bones (and other bones), three beds of mushrooms, a used roof, one wall that glowed green, a pile of bricks, a bush that grew mysteriously, three freshly dug graves, and a family of four who fled as soon as Lowell shone a flashlight in their direction. There was, he also discovered, much water in the basement: running water, standing water, and walking water, water that seemed to flow uphill over obstacles.

He thought he found it under one of the elevators, but it was a crumpled Buick Roadmaster he found, pressed into a cube from the weight of the elevator, which had turned into an outhouse due to a hole in the floor, and years of compost underneath the elevator, fertilized by the Buick, had produced several strange yellowish plants with long tendrils that shot up the sides of the elevator shaft and climbed to the roof, creeping over the tar and wrapping the José chimney in their embrace, and now that the boiler had disappeared and no heat was coming up the chimney, had snaked their way down the chimney, doing a complete loop in the cellar when they came to the elevator shaft.

Then Lowell began to hear rumors about the boiler. It was sighted on the roof, it was stuck in the chimney (sucked up by a tornado), it was in the Cambodian's apartment where they used it to steam rice (it was in the super's apartment to boil potatoes), it was in the courtyard in a grocery cart, it had been airmailed to Turkey, strippers from New

Jersey had it, a go-go dancer in a bar on Canal Street was performing on it.

In the dark Lowell noticed how the Building seemed to swell, to puff up, as if to swallow its own boundaries and push beyond them. Walking the halls he kept hearing a hum, a vibration that throttled the walls and floors, and he felt that somewhere in the Building there was a huge engine that ran a cranking machine that jarred the Building, lifting it up slowly and then just as slowly dropping it on its foundations. He had not discovered the room where this machine was kept, but he had the feeling that when he did he would also discover the boiler and learn how, and why, the boiler had been "disappeared" from the cellar.

Even in the debris and with the renovation only partially completed, Lowell could see that this Building could never be duplicated, that whoever tried to build like this would not be making a building but a monument, a thing whose spiritual message was eternity. He had seen oak beams and oak doors and fleurs-de-lis on the ceiling, gold leaf and cut frosted glass (those few that were left, which were high up and hard to steal), stamped brass door handles (the few left), traces of a marble fireplace, traces of a tile floor. Oak doors were replaced with steel-clad doors with spyholes, oak beams with pine, fireplaces bricked over and covered with Sheetrock; not that he objected to the replacements, they were practical replacements, but somehow . . . Goddamn, he did object to the replacements! Let them replace like with like.

A large man with a shovel-shaped face as black as boil salve stood in the hallway and motioned him inside. He seated Lowell at a table in the kitchen. Dozens of floating candles in short, wide glasses were placed about the kitchen, throwing a soft-glowing yellow light that seemed to pulsate. White shirt, white pants, black socks, and white shoes set off his black skin, made it glow and burn brown, purple, magenta. In the flickering light of the candles, Lowell noticed some books on the kitchen table: *Theory of Functions of a Complex Variable, Asymptotic Analysis, Point-Set Topology, Zermelo-Fraenkel Set Theory, The Cantor-Bendixson and Morley Derivatives,* and *Godel's Constructible Sets.* Other books, whose titles he could not read, were thrown open on the table with passages and formulas underlined and numbers and formulas written in the margins in pencil and continued on sheets of paper that were scattered about the books. The icebox door was open, and in the light of the twenty-five-watt bulb Lowell saw an opened jar of mustard, three half-eaten Jamaican meat pies, an opened can of sardines of which two were missing, several cups of coffee, and three books, all open, with more pencil marks in the margins. The man in white shoved the icebox door shut with his foot, startling Lowell. He got up and walked around behind Lowell, who thought he might be holding a knife, a long, ragged butcher knife with a chipped blade that could be plunged, with some difficulty but with extreme effectiveness, into his neck, shoulders, back, or sides, and he was so sure that the black man was standing behind him with his knife-upraised arm that he didn't turn around, feeling that this was some kind of test and that to pass it he had to go to the door of death and peer in. He could feel the breath of the man behind him on his head, a warming breath that seemed to fall about his ears and neck like a cap, extending even down to his shoulders. At some point Lowell couldn't tell if that was his breath or a kind of warm liquid, a warm, heavy wetness that fell about him. Fear filled him to the point of drowsiness, and he started to nod off.

The man shouted, and Lowell jumped to his feet and in the same movement spun around, surprising himself with his own agility, as if he had planned this movement hours, weeks before, and had practiced it diligently.

He stood looking at Lowell, his face screwed up into a series of wrinkles that looked like mud flats, dry gullies in the mud-baked plains of Kenya. Lowell, now startled awake, stared back and felt that somehow he was omnipotent and far from danger, the problem with the man being not safety and danger but simply bad breath. It was an overpowering stench that reminded Lowell of the day the sewers in his hometown backed up. He stepped back, as if he had been pushed, and sank into a chair opposite the one he had been sitting in.

"The boiler," he said.

Lowell looked up, expecting the boiler to pop out of his mouth.

"The problem," he continued, "is that there are city voodoos and country voodoos. The latter are afraid of boilers."

He stopped to gauge the look on Lowell's face.

"If it was just chickens, with their heads twisted off so the blood could be swallowed, that would be one thing."

He picked up a book from the table.

"Here we have partially ordered sets, cardinal numbers, Zorn's lemma, well-ordering, and the axiom of choice. Do you know what I'm talking about? Of course not. Neither does Mama Jujubee. She is country voodoo. She knows nothing about the theory of sets. She knows plants. Did you see the plant in the elevator shaft?"

Lowell said he did.

"Did you notice anything strange about that plant?"

He shook his head slowly, as if he were afraid it would fall off.

"Notice the color of that plant, notice its length, and then tell me if you think it's a plant."

Lowell felt that whatever answer he would give, it would be the wrong answer. It was the same way he felt in grammar school with his third-grade teacher who, he felt, expected—no, demanded—the wrong answer, and Lowell, sucker that he was, eternal optimist, was always able to provide it.

"That plant took several months of ceremonies to grow the way it did and to do what it did."

"And what was that?"

The man looked at him as if he had worms crawling out of his nose.

"For several months the plant grew, but it didn't grow. Country voodoos know how to do that sort of thing. Then it shot up through the elevator shaft, crossed over the roof, came down the chimney, and spirited the boiler away."

"How?"

"Do you know topology theory?"

"No."

"You'll have to ask Mama Jujubee, who also doesn't know topology theory, but then, she doesn't have to."

"So she has the boiler?"

"I doubt that."

"But she knows where it is."

"I also doubt that."

"But she knows where it might be."

"That I don't doubt. The boiler had become an unpleasant shape for her."

He blew out the candles and left Lowell sitting in the darkness, his presence in question. Lowell felt a wind blow against his legs, as if a door had been opened, but he noticed no door opening, and the darkness felt as if it extended for just a few feet, and in some sense was very comforting. Suddenly the door was opened, a slice of light through the black, and Lowell felt as if he had been intruded upon, caught doing some nasty business with his pants around his ankles.

Lowell jumped up and made for the door. The slice of light widened. He found himself in the hall. The man was behind him. The boiler had now assumed proportions he could hardly imagine. He had lost sight of its size, its shape, and could only imagine its function, a bubbling cauldron supplying steam to convoluted pipes, a sort of fancy stove to heat water. He felt someone was using it to make tea, to drown cats, to wash cars. The boiler, once a friend, once a warm respected lap dog, was now some prickly teasel, braided with thistly flowers that caught and tugged at flesh. It reproached him; it rubbed him raw. It left him open and bleeding.

But then, he could no more complain about the boiler, or its lack, than he could complain about the Building and the things it was missing, or Sanchez and Hector and their monomaniacal desire to extract some admission of failure from him. Sanchez wanted him to say: you could do it but you can't. Hector wanted him to say: you can't do it *and* you can't.

Then the boiler reappeared in the basement, surrounded by leaves. Smears of rust-colored blood streaked the flat gray sides, and when it was reattached to the pipes it worked perfectly, as if some ceremony, some blessing, had been performed on or over its innards. It must have been, Lowell thought, a ceremony with great power.

31

BEFORE it had been the Department of Housing Preservation and Development, it had been the Housing and Development Administration and before that the Housing and Redevelopment Board, and Sanchez, who had been the Assistant Commissioner at the Office of Rent and Housing Maintenance, Division of Evaluation and Compliance, and then moved over to the Department of Real Property, which superseded the Department of False Property, after he had been in charge of Code Compliance and Deviation Acceptance, but before he had been a Building Inspector Department Head, Bribes Division, had overseen the Participation Loan Program, which was now defunct, and had also been in charge of the Management in Partnership Program, which was now largely dormant, and then put in charge of the 312 Program before the money ran out, and had spent time in the Homesteading Program, which had sold about a dozen buildings a year out of the more than four thousand H.P.D. owned to qualified tenants (poor, but with a good income), moved over to the Community Management Program before moving on to the Tenant Interim Lease Program. Sanchez, neck brace removed and his neck exposed, a thin white affair that seemed to have the ability to telescope, is reading a report. It is Lowell's boiler report.

Lowell can't remember what he put in the report. He knows Sanchez will ask him questions about it, but his mind is vacant when it comes to the report, as vacant as if he had to give a talk on asymmetric slopes in Lorentz transformations. He wonders why the department is concerned about the boiler now that it is back. "The boiler went on a visit. It visited some other boilers. It was lonely. Now it is back." He might have put that in the report, and then again he might have written about boiler thieves. He knows that whatever he puts in will be unsatisfactory to Sanchez.

"This report is bullshit."

Lowell nods.

"But the commissioner loves it. He just loves it. I don't know why. I don't even know how he saw it. I never gave it to him. How did he see it? How?"

Lowell shrugs his shoulders.

"Did you give it to him? You gave it to him!"

Lowell answers no twice.

"So he snoops. I've got to stop him from snooping. He can't snoop at my desk. I'm claiming discrimination."

Lowell nods again. He seems to have been stricken by an attack of nodding, his involuntary nervous system having grabbed ahold of his head and neck and shaken it thoroughly, in regular intervals, as if to remind him that his body is not under his control.

"How did you do it?"

Lowell shrugs his shoulders. The nod seems to have settled down there. He can't stop shrugging. He thinks a cable-knit cardigan and a pipe and slippers go with someone who shrugs.

"I mean that part in the report, it's all bullshit, of course, but I must confess it's rather charming bullshit. You know, that part where you allude to the opposing forces in the Building?"

He can't remember that part, any more than he can remember what the opposing forces in the Building are. Hector had advised him to be specific but say nothing in his reports.

"It's amazing how you manage to be both specific and general, morally outraged and yet objective, compassionate and yet removed, even though, of course, it's bull—"

"I know, I know."

"The commissioner goes for that stuff, the theoretical with the real, the hands off with the hands on."

"It's a trick I learned in school."

"Where did you go to school?"

"Maine."

"I didn't know they had any schools up there."

"The University."

"Maine?"

Lowell sighed. He was fast depleting his supply of nonverbal communications. Now he was groping at the very bottom of the bag for the last in a series of twitches, moves, jerks, motions, throat sounds, and finger movements he could use.

"The report remains, of course, inadequate, except that the commissioner—"

"—likes it."

"You've been listening!"

No more sighs or shrugs.

"I listen, Sanchez. I heard."

"The commissioner might want to talk to you. Not now but later, later. Now I want you to deal with the contractor. We got a problem, caused by Hector, with a roofing contractor. I want you to get it straightened out. Don't tell Hector. Don't get him involved. Don't even talk to him."

"What's the contractor's name?"

"Ask my secretary."

An order had gone out to put a new roof on the Building and indeed a new roof had been put on, but on the wrong building, an empty building (vacant, a shell, gutted), and the department refused to pay while the contractor claimed that he had put the roof on the building whose address he had been given, but Hector swore up and down (sideways too) that he had not given the contractor that address, that he had, in fact, given him the Building's address. Hector shouted at the contractor over the phone and then passed out, a signal that Lowell should take over. Lowell picked up the phone, dangling over the edge of Hector's desk, while Hector, dangling over the side of his wheelchair, tried to reach for his breathing tube, making feeble, erratic grasps, and as Lowell talked to the roofing contractor, Hector kept grabbing at Lowell's pants until Lowell, unable to talk over the phone and have his leg grabbed, perhaps mauled, tickled, or scratched at, was forced to push Hector to one side, and Hector's face turned the color of his hair, purple, while the contractor offered to split the cost of ripping the roof off the other building and putting it on the Building, and Lowell said that he was not authorized to make such an arrangement and doubted whether a roof could be removed and reapplied, the contractor saying that yes indeed it could, he knew, because he bought all his roofs from gypsies and that was the only way they sold roofs.

The dispute could not be settled over the phone, and nothing would do but that Lowell had to go out to the contractor's office and come to some settlement. It was around the corner from the Building, a storefront in an abandoned building, the crudely painted signs on the window proclaiming: Dondeen Heating Oil, Dondeen Insurance, Dondeen Real Estate, and Dondeen Contracting. Also Title Searches, Writs of Habeas Corpus, Dispossess, and Psychotherapy. Under that was another sign: Dondeen Exterminating (If It Crawls, We'll Kill It). Telescoping iron gates stretched across the front of the store, and in the dusty window there was a tiny grimy statue of a small plump boy peeing into the mouth of a frog. Sink fixtures, locks, the U-joint of a waste line, and a pocketbook entitled *Who Says You Have To?*, all coated with an indeterminate layer of some gray sort of grease, shared the window with the pee-er.

Dondeen was a man of medium height, sandy hair, and was, as he put it, "Puerto Rican from the waist down, Irish from the waist up." He greeted Lowell warmly and ushered him into the back office, paneled in plastic wood and covered with dirty acoustical tile that had yellowed in one corner. Several bullet holes in the wall were circled with a red Magic Marker and a decal was affixed to one wall that said: *Dondeen Car Service, You Pay We Go.*

He motioned Lowell toward a chair, a sofa of sorts, the front seat of a 1968 Plymouth Valiant Slant Six.

As soon as Lowell sat in the Plymouth, Dondeen slapped his forehead.

"Why did I do it, what a schmuck, a mistake!"

"The roof?"

"What roof?"

Dondeen looked at Lowell as if he were a Ubangi with a hubcap in his lower lip.

"The notes, I get these notes . . ."

"I don't . . ."

"You get involved, you get trouble. Waste of time. Teach them to read and this is what you get."

He blew his nose with such force that Lowell thought that one or both of his nostrils would come off.

"Literacy Volunteer. That's me. One of your West Side hand-wringing liberals. I teach this guy to read and what does he do? Writes notes on cards that he leaves on my typewriter, IBM Selectric with Correcting Ribbon, 'I hate you, I will cut you up, stay out of my life, I will kill you and your family, I will poison your friends, you are the worst kind of garbage, slut pig, and I love you.' He's always writing that kind of shit and leaving it around for me to read. Why do I put up with it? Better off he can't read. He should have stayed in the pits."

Dondeen walks over to his desk and takes out a pack of cigarettes. He offers one to Lowell and then withdraws it before Lowell can reply.

"That guy shouldn't even be on the streets, and they let him come in here and learn how to read. I say put him in the zoo, but do something to protect the animals. Say, am I boring you? You look flushed. Are you sick?"

Lowell answered negatively.

"Ten years of Adlerian analysis and I went into Literacy Volunteers. Lot of good it did me. Now, I question everything, look at motives, even my mother, God rest her. She's still alive, but look at her motives, when I was younger I couldn't bring myself to, my old man . . . but you don't want to hear about that."

He lit a second cigarette which he placed in the ashtray with the first.

"Geez, how that man could hit. I could have written him notes about how he hit, broke my teeth, my jaw never set right, bit my mother's ear off. He doesn't look violent. I mean this guy I taught to read. He lives alone, masturbates into a sandwich bag and leaves the stuff in his freezer—told me that one night over beers. I thought he was harmless. He worked with a company that moved heavy machinery, printing machinery, presses, linotype machines, big stuff like that. He's got a belt full of metal studs—what the hell, I'm not there to teach the swells how to read. Have you got a cigarette on you?"

He lit a third cigarette, which he placed in the ashtray with the other two so that the cigarettes and the lengthening ash on them looked like one of those Christmas tree stands where bolts hold the tree upright.

"This guy lived for his dick. He fucked banana skins, liver, caps, dogs, and more women than you can imagine. It all came out of his dick, but now I taught him how to read, it all comes out of his pencil. He complains he can't get it up as much; he writes instead of fucks. What I want to know, what I got to know, is this progress? I mean is this civilization and its discontents? Are we advancing the species with this creep who waves a pencil around instead of his dork? That is the epistemological question: He used to be his penis; now he is his pencil. Is this your higher order?"

He swooped down and picked up Lowell's legs and swung them up on the Plymouth bench seat.

"Look, free associate. Say anything that comes into your mind, feel sorry for your relatives who can't be here."

"The roof . . ."

"We'll have plenty of time for the roof later."

"We can't pay . . ."

"What's this thing with the roof?"

". . . on the wrong building."

"Are you from H.P.D.?"

Lowell nodded.

Dondeen stood up and plucked a burning cigarette from the ashtray and swallowed it. Smoke came out of his nostrils. He picked up a second burning cigarette and sent it after the first one. Smoke came out of his ears. The third cigarette, burning, he put in his pocket; it suddenly reappeared in his mouth.

"I thought you were here for therapy."

"The roof . . ."

"I heard you."

"I thought you were a roofing contractor?"

"I am, I am. I sell heating oil, repair roofs, do some nondirective therapy, real estate, shiatsu, some other things."

He slapped his forehead.

"You're probably here about the roof!"

Lowell heard several dogs barking.

"Dobermans."

"Yes."

"What can I say? What can anyone say? An honest mistake, I can understand what was going through this guy's head. It's a terrible burden, just terrible."

"I was sent to tell you that you'll have to give us a new roof."

Dondeen looked at him with one eye.

"And I know how you're feeling too. You're new in the department. You probably feel they're taking advantage of you. They send you out to do things they wouldn't have the guts to do themselves. They whisper behind your back. You don't have to nod, I know these things. You're probably still C–2. Right? C–3? These things I know."

He patted Lowell's hand, who noticed how small his hands were and how they were comparatively hairless and how the knuckles seemed to be flattened out, spread across the hand, and the tiny red splotches, drinker's veins, that had settled across the back of his hand.

"Who's your boss? Sanchez? They bounce him from failure to failure. He might not be there when you get back. And what about you? Look at you. You look awful. Who would hire you?"

Dondeen stuck his tongue out, put his thumbs in his ears, and wiggled his fingers. It struck Lowell that he was cleaning out his ears, or that his hands were in danger of leaving his wrists and would float upward unless he performed this ritual.

"I bet you're lonely at night. You probably masturbate to girdle ads and eat lots of ice cream. Tell me I don't have you pegged . . . of course. But you're turning over a new leaf, no more chocolate ice cream, read a serious novel a week, wink if I'm right . . . eh?"

"This is—"

"Bullshit, right?"

Lowell was about to answer him when there was a terrific commotion in the back room.

"The Dobermans found him, sonofabitch!"

He rushed into the back room, the dogs barking, something falling, Dondeen yelling. Lowell heard someone yelling back at him, a high-pitched Latin voice, very nasal, shouting something obscene, an impropriety regarding Dondeen's mother, which brought forth another clatter, something being dropped, something being stepped on, the sound of wood cracking, a window opened, glass breaking, boxes falling, the dogs now barking and howling, several "fuck"s and "shit"s coming from the back room, more boxes falling, and Lowell thought he heard lightning and thunder, the door was kicked open, and Dondeen came back, what little hair he had flying off in several directions, holding a Doberman by the scruff of the neck and kicking two others back into the room at which point he pulled the door shut, keeping hold of the Doberman.

He lit a cigarette and put it behind his ear.

"The dwarf gets loose in the back room, and he likes to diddle with the dogs, especially the females. I try to stop him, but the only way you can stop him is to kick him in the head. He has this thing with dogs, thinks he's a Mexican hairless; you got to kick the sonofabitch in the head to keep him outta there. When I kick the motherfucker in the head, they complain; people come out and give me a summons, I add it to the others."

Dondeen lights another cigarette, takes a few puffs, and puts it in his pocket.

"Motherfucks, those dwarfs. Gypsy roof people, bred small so they can crawl under the roof and strip off the tarpaper and kick it into a roll while they take the roofing nails out. Those sons of bitches once had a building with two roofs on it, and they stole the one underneath and put the one on top back so neat you never knew they had stolen the one underneath. But they are a heathen people, oh God, yes. The women diddle with the male Dobermans, and believe me, that plays hell with a dog; he gets spoiled, can't keep him around women and hardly around men, while the females attack anything in pants. They are a remorseless people. They do not cry, Lowell. Never trust a people who don't cry. They will not shed a tear over their own; they just pack up and move on. They have as much compassion as a dry sponge. I saw four of them sit and watch a fifth drown. After he went under for the last time, they went through his pockets, he had left his pants on land, and divided the money. When the body was recovered they reclaimed his watch, gold fillings, and two satin cummerbunds he wore around his waist. There was no funeral. They burned him in a fire of packing crates. Melted down his silverware; all gypsies carry silverware with them. Ate his walnuts. And ripped his clothes to make quilts. They don't care, Lowell, they truly don't give a flying shit.

"I buy all my used roofs from them; they lie, they cheat, they steal, but they do give a good price on used roofs. For another good price they will have their children install them for you, an unfortunate practice, since many of them are still learning how to nail, and I have gone up to inspect a roof the next day and found one of their children still nailed to the roof, the victim of an unfortunately placed roofing nail and a wayward hammer blow, and this delinquent, stoic despite the loss of blood, refused to cry or shout for joy when I approached, but merely hobbled off when I removed the nails that held it to the roof, cursing me over its shoulder as it stumbled off. The spawn of the devil, what human child could last twelve hours nailed to the roof and survive, have the strength to run away, indeed curse the person who freed him?

"They eat anything roasted, fried, boiled, toasted, baked, braised, or otherwise attacked by heat or gravy, preferably both, drink anything that fills a cup, bind their allegiance to no country, have a long set of customs which it is their custom to ignore, do not put off their need to relieve themselves."

Dondeen paused. He took the burning cigarette out of his pocket and began puffing on it. The smoke circled around his head and then slowly rose in ever-widening spirals until it caught the corners of the office in its huge corkscrew.

"You only see the one who sits in a storefront, the old haggle-toothed bitch who asks a dollar to look at the creases in your palm, a flannel bedspread separating her from the men playing cards in the back room in their underwear, the children crawling naked on the linoleum floor—but these are not your roof gypsies. Oh no. The roof gypsies do not speak Romany; they speak Finno-Ugric."

Lowell picked his nose. He always picked his nose when he was bored, rolling the residue between his thumb and forefinger.

"I don't care who is nailed to the roof, Dondeen. I only know we paid for a roof, and we expect a roof on the Building. Ninety-five-pound felt paper, a seam overlap of three inches, the old roof to be made flat with bubbles slit, the final product to be broom swept."

Dondeen cocked his head to one side, as if he wanted water to clear out of one ear or was listening for snow.

"Forget this Building. It's going down, it's doomed. I've seen the hole in this *Titanic.*"

For every hole, Lowell thought, there was a city program to plug that hole, and for every program someone to see that the program worked, that the money got to where it should get to, that the materials agreed upon were delivered and installed as per instruction. It was a very simple demand, and for the first time Lowell saw that what he was doing was not pacification or patch-up but simply making things work. It could be done. And it did matter. And people could make it happen and he was one of those people, and the principle involved was not one of superiority but simply one of efficiency—this was the way to make the housing machine function—the way to oil its gears and maintain its levers and keep roofs over people.

"It will work, Dondeen, and you will put on that roof or I will have you in court and sue your ass off."

"You are an idealist, Lowell."

"I don't care what I am."

"As an idealist you are dangerous. Idealists are those who deny others their ideals."

"Granted. And in your case it involves making an unconscionable profit."

Dondeen laughed.

"You think I make a profit on this?! I do it just to keep a hand in. The city pays too late for me to make a profit."

Lowell got up.

"Watch out for the committee," Dondeen said.

How pathetic this office is, Lowell thought. How tiny it is, how greasy the walls, how scarred the ceiling. It reminded him of an old unsmoked cigarette someone might have carried around in a pocket, a magnet for all the lint and dirt and grease one could collect.

"You think I'm the enemy. I'm not the enemy. You need all the friends you can get if you're going to make that Building work. You can't imagine how many friends you're going to need. I may run off at the mouth, but I won't fuck around with you. I'll give you your roof. It will cost me but you'll get your roof. Make some friends, Lowell. You'll need them."

32

RUMORS about the Building were simply facts that someone had neglected to verify. They were not vague, floating things whose substantiality could never be checked but chunky, awkward grotesques, gnarled things that clattered and clanged, made the hallways smell, the Building shake.

The man who walked on ceilings was one. Both Mr. Tontine and Singiat-Sing Dan Dinphuir swore they saw a man walking on the ceiling. Neither of them thought it was particularly unusual and hesitated to tell Lowell about it, mentioning it offhand in the course of a conversation about something else (in Dinphuir's case he had been explaining to Lowell the ritual to follow for ridding the Building of the water demon). Tontine said he saw the man (he thought it was a man but he couldn't be sure) walk up the walls on his way to the ceiling, but Dinphuir said that the man merely stood in the center of the room and conjured himself on the ceiling. Both swore that the man did not just stand on the ceiling but walked on it, back and forth, though with some difficulty, as if he were slogging through snow or lost in some form of thoughtful contemplation and hardly noticed that he was walking on the ceiling. It happened nearly every night, and the people who lived over the apartment of the man who walked on the ceiling were the first to know about it since they kept hearing footsteps on their floor but could never find the feet that made them. Lowell ignored the rumor until one evening, his curiosity piqued, he knocked on the door of the ceiling walker, was invited in, and found out that indeed the man did walk on ceilings, had been doing so for several months. He said that it was merely a matter of exerting one's will. As an aid to exerting his will, he had coated his ceiling with Velcro, along with his walls, and wore a pair of Velcro boots, strapped tightly to his legs, with which he slowly pulled himself up the walls and onto the ceiling, explaining to Lowell that walking on the ceiling was not the hard part but that walking up the walls had taken a year to perfect. He had been doing the other for years, starting by positioning a stepladder so that he could lie on his back and position his boots on the ceiling. Lowell neglected to ask him why he did this; part of the mystique of walking on ceilings was not asking why one did it.

Talking dogs were another. Some claimed there was only one dog that talked; others said there were five of them and that they spoke a very rudimentary language, clipped, using only simple words, no more than one hundred fifty (someone claiming to have counted them). Hobson, the man who talked to cockroaches, claimed that only one dog talked, and that this dog talked through its asshole and said things that were not for the squeamish or those afraid of blasphemy. He thought there might be a small man inside the dog (it was a large dog) who babbled constantly. But Mary Smith told Lowell, in confidence, that five dogs talked, but that they never talked when humans were around, and that the only person they would talk to was the dream lady, the purple lady, who sometimes told her what they said. It was not, she said, particularly revealing or even interesting, and so she would not pass it on to Lowell. It was, of course, absurd, and yet Lowell could barely restrain himself from cocking his head toward every dog in the Building, perhaps in the hope he could learn something about it the tenants had neglected to tell him.

There was an eight-hundred-year-old man who lived in the Building. It was not Glasho, the excrement artist, in whose honor a petition had been gotten up to remove the artist and his materials from the Building, a petition that stood on very solid grounds as far as hygiene was concerned but whose constitutionality, Lowell emphasized, was very shaky. The eight-hundred-year-old man was a Taoist, one of the immortals, who, it was claimed, had come by boat many years ago from India and had lived in a cave on the spot where the Building now stood and who now lived in an apartment that seemed to vanish and reappear with the same speed, and perhaps in the same manner, as the boiler had. Lowell never found this esteemed gentleman, but no one in the Building seemed to doubt his existence, though some claimed that he was not eight hundred years old but only two hundred, that he was not a Taoist but a Rosicrucian, not Chinese but Indian, not an ascetic but an old lecher who impregnated several widows who lived in the Building, all of whom gave birth to tiny brown shriveled babies that died within days.

The man who swallowed himself was another oddity of the Building. Indeed his unusual gastronomic feat was the talk of the Building for many weeks, disrupting tenants' meetings. The lunatic claimed to have been present at his last supper and to have witnessed the whole event, a happening, he claimed, that was accompanied by very large shrieks of thunder and a series of elephantine burps, until the trencherman had managed to completely swallow himself and so disappear. This, of course, could not be verified; nevertheless it held sway over the minds and hearts of the tenants for two months, and the lunatic claimed he had proof—the man no longer existed. The horror that accompanied this scene, the lunatic claimed, could hardly be imagined. Lowell dismissed this rumor, until one day the man reappeared, having, as the lunatic claimed, "burped himself up."

There were many other rumors about the Building, and Lowell took them all into account, some of them more seriously than others. One involved bomb makers. They were a group of young students, or ex-students, with wiry hair and flowery shirts that were loose enough around the chest so that it was impossible to tell who was male and who was female (the males seemed to have no need to shave, no hair on their face, or else arranged for it to grow inward where they could bite it off). They came to all the tenants' meetings, said very little, took notes, and always paid their rent on time. The other tenants were suspicious of them because they had no foibles, no weaknesses; they were not on welfare, had no quirks or oddities as far as anyone else knew, and so, being a tabula rasa, in effect, rumors quickly sprang up about them.

Someone claimed that they were hermaphrodites, had both sets of genitalia, and could do it with themselves or each other with equal satisfaction. The specifics of how this was accomplished were vague, and rather ill defined, and so the imaginations of the tenants jumped to more conventional roles. There were two women and three men; there were three women and two men. While one of the men or one of the women kept score, the others coupled and held orgasm contests based upon: number, quality, length, uniqueness of position, forcefulness of fetish, and other criteria too complicated to go into (one involved several dogs—certainly not those who talked—one cat, two jars of Vaseline, a length of hose, a pair of silk stockings, an Iroquois mask, a bag of marbles, and a bouquet of roses).

When the sexual rumor had lost its potency, another swelled up to take its place. They were making bombs. When Lowell first heard this from the paraplegic who heard it on the radio (a bomb exploded in Manhattan, the borough of bombs, and this had fired her imagination; the radio gave instructions on how to make bombs, cocktails she thought they called them, if you changed your mind about blowing something up you could drink them), he dismissed it but then couldn't, the tiny, little ticking the paraplegic had set off in his head kept running, a sort of background buzz that sounded like "bum, bum, bum . . ." He asked Hector, who said, "Sure they making bombs. What the fuck you expect?" Sanchez ridiculed the idea but had the bomb squad search the Building, pulling up in front of it with a huge barrel-shaped truck lined with wire mesh and search warrants for every apartment. They antagonized everyone and found nothing. "They got ears in the police. They know what's going down," Hector said. Tontine told Lowell he found some old fuses and the shells of alarm clocks in the garbage. Why did he go through the garbage, Lowell wondered. One night there was an explosion in the Building, and the tenants, instead of running into the street, converged on the apartment of the five and demanded that they leave immediately. But the five were as mystified as the tenants about the explosion, until they learned that the dwarf had forgotten to turn off the gas oven and then lay in the professor's bed smoking. The dwarf apologized for the explosion, that is, he apologized to the professor who translated for the tenants. Lowell had the feeling that the dwarf was only apologizing to the professor, not to the tenants, but that the professor, ever mindful of protocol, simply extended the apology. All this took place at a tenants' meeting, and after this it seemed as if a plague of apology swept through the basement room. The five, who up to now had been as silent as stones, began apologizing for being so secretive, saying that there was nothing they wished to hide, but they simply led rather prosaic lives and saw no need to impose their wishes on their fellow tenants. Now, in order to become a part of the Building, to share in its work, they felt compelled to apologize for their silence ("A good round of self-criticism is always in order . . ."). They pledged to work for the well-being of the Building and the justice of the tenants' cause. The tenants looked somewhat puzzled, not sure they had a cause, but the five went on to explain that one of them was a nurse and would be willing to spend one night a week to see that health problems were directed to the proper authorities; another was a lawyer who specialized in housing cases; another knew his way around the maze of the city's bureaucracies and would be willing to guide those who had been frustrated by city bureaucrats, turning toward Lowell as he spoke. As they spoke, Lowell took note that there were two women and three men; the men were all thin, from short to tall. Of the women, one was stocky, with large breasts that seemed to roam around her chest, while the other was thin, with wide shoulders and small lemon-sized breasts. Lowell wondered why he should pay particular attention to their breasts, and thought that if they all hadn't been wearing loose-fitting shirts he wouldn't have cared, but their choice of clothing had piqued his curiosity, and he reminded himself he was horny. His wife and children had been gone for a year; he was living monogamously, not out of choice but simply out of circumstance.

They invited Lowell in for tea. Peppermint tea, they explained, "because we have researched the product and found that it is the one unexploitive tea on the market." As soon as it was said, Lowell had the funny feeling he couldn't remember who had said it.

Their apartment was painted white and light red. Several Klee prints were on the wall, a mobile hung from the ceiling, paperback books lined one wall. Lowell squinted to read the titles, but from where he was seated he couldn't. There were two iron-framed butterfly chairs, a Formica table, and about two dozen folding chairs. A stack of newspapers stood in one corner, like a white chimney. There were typewriters, each with its own cover. Light bulbs, surrounded by paper shades, hung from the ceiling. A framed serigraph of a clenched brown fist hung on one wall. Lowell had the feeling that everything in the apartment was "correct," that even the randomness, the carefully scattered magazines and books, was carefully ordered.

The woman with the floating breasts was called Kazima. She kept crossing and recrossing her legs, pressing her great calves outward for Lowell's inspection. She never volunteered her occupation, and Lowell hesitated to guess. The other woman, talkative, a health-care worker in a clinic, was Estelle. She had the longest face he had ever seen, quite attractive.

Tea was served and drunk in silence. Estelle passed out paper napkins, and one of the men set out a jar of honey. An eerie silence. Lowell expected noise, but even the street sounds seemed muted and far away. Kazima recrossed her legs, and Lowell noticed a bra strap slicing into her ample shoulder.

One of the men wore a red bandanna around his head. He kept picking at a guitar. Lowell didn't know what to say, thinking that he would have to invent speech for the occasion, or that having invented speech he would have to teach it to the deaf-mutes who sat in front of him, who picked at their hair, their noses, guitars, feet, anything they could reach with their fingers and several things that were beyond the reach of their fingers. Lowell noticed that the floors had been sanded and varnished, and he was about to comment on this, to congratulate, when he was seized by a sudden desire to stare at the floor and say nothing, as if the reflecting pool of the floor had muted him, swallowed whatever he would have to say.

One of the men, wearing pin-striped overalls, got up and turned to Lowell, raising his hand as if to speak, then scratched his head, the thought evaporating out of his head or escaping through his hand, and he turned away from Lowell to watch the misty sentence floating in the air before it disintegrated, broke up into a spray of words, of syllables, of letters, of bits of lines, of dots, of nothing. Now would be the time to make an official pronouncement, Lowell thought. But he had none to make. He had only questions.

Estelle turned to him and pouted.

The tall thin man with several tufts of hair that had escaped his chin got up to speak, thought better of it, sighed, and sat down. Lowell suddenly panicked because he couldn't remember whether he was sitting or standing. In another life, he thought, I would know, and I would not think that I was dreaming now, or beginning to dream, or wonder if I was dreaming.

He could hear sighs in the room, and it reminded him of the boiler, which had sighed at the beginning of each heating season as it built up steam and then let some out, a small puff, testing the safety valve before it plunged ahead and poured hundreds of pounds of steam into the Building, sighing, Lowell swore, with the effort, but not stopping, merely pausing, until billows of water vapor steam-engined their way into radiators and sent hundreds of valves whistling and steam pipes clanking as the condensed water was shot through the pipes by the pressure, knocking against the bends in the pipe. Sleeping alongside the boiler, Lowell could hear it talking to him, the hisses and gurgles taking a human dimension. Now, when he looked around the room he could hear the boiler talking in the sighs of the five, the prolonged, exaggerated breathing, the clearing of throats, the coughs, the sniffs. In one corner of the room Lowell could see briefcases. Why? What did they need briefcases for?

"We don't make bombs."

Lowell turned his head quickly.

"Who said that?"

"We don't make bombs."

The tall man, now wearing a pin-striped railroad cap, was speaking, clutching a briefcase.

"Bombs end up hurting the wrong people. Counterrevolutionary, bad propaganda."

He sounded as if he were not so much addressing Lowell as making a speech, forming a major policy statement.

Well, that's a relief, Lowell thought.

He had no idea what a bomb looked like, but he thought it might look like a comic-strip characterization—a bowling ball with a wick in the thumb hole. He could imagine closets full of them, drawers filled with them, floors carpeted with them . . . and one, accidentally lit, setting off the others.

"I don't know your names," Lowell said. "The men, I mean."

"It's not important."

"We could tell you if you want to know. I mean it's also not important whether we tell you or don't tell you."

"We have no secrets."

"I never said you did."

"Just in case . . ."

They told Lowell their names, and he made a mental note to remember them, but soon, five minutes, forgot them, except for Estelle and Kazima. The men all had single-syllable names, he remembered that much, and two of them had triple syllables in their last names. He couldn't remember who signed the rent check. Perhaps it was a money order.

Lowell finished his tea, swallowing the goo of honey at the bottom of the cup and the little peppermint bits that had escaped the tea bag.

"You've done some nice things to the apartment."

"Are you the city's administrator?"

"For this Building."

He felt embarrassed saying it; he didn't know why.

"Has the Building ever been on rent strike?"

Lowell shrugged his shoulders.

A week later he discovered a set of tar footprints leading to the roof and found Dondeen, fourteen rolls of felt tar paper, and several dozen buckets of tar.

"Hey, Lowell, look. I got all tall guys working on the job. No more children nailed to the roof."

It was a warm, smoky day. The haze lay in thick rolls about the city, and the sun looked gray and tired, but the glare was as bright as he could ever remember. Several gulls were perched on the José chimney.

"You got a bad spot in this roof. Someone dragged their heels, made big furrows in the tar, probably the source of leaks, no?"

The furrows went from the roof door to the edge of the roof. Lowell shivered. He could imagine the screams that accompanied those furrows when the Scandinavian whore was tossed off the roof.

"Must have been a baby carriage or something that they rolled off the roof, eh?"

The gulls moved from the chimney to the parapet.

"Maybe a car wheel. Jackasses are always throwing car wheels off the roof."

"Something like that," Lowell said.

"Those commies still living here?"

"Commies?"

"Don't play dumb. The bomb makers, the commies, those pinko Reds . . . they still here?"

"You mean the five . . ."

"I mean the commies, terrorists . . ."

"Homosexuals . . ."

"Dope fiends . . ."

"Lesbians . . ."

"Alcoholics . . ."

"Child molesters . . ."

"That too?"

"No, they've gone."

Dondeen looked disappointed. He would have loved to see the Building explode, to see bodies and limbs, bones and blood blossoming in the air, alongside burning timbers and flying rubble.

"You don't know how lucky you are to get those fuckers out."

"Lucky?"

"Bombers. Look, I can spot a bomber, I'm Irish. I can smell them. They don't give a shit, Lowell."

"I thought it was the gypsies who didn't give a shit."

"Bombers, gypsies . . . lots of 'em don't give a shit. They don't give a flying fuck."

"There's more?"

Dondeen snorted.

"Jeez, you are dumb."

"I don't take that personally, Dondeen."

"Look, Lowell, there's a long list of those who don't give a shit."

"Are you the guardian?"

"I'll explain it to you. Israelis don't give a shit, Arabs don't give a shit, neither do the British, the hippies, anyone who drives a tow truck, a newspaper truck, nobody in Iran gives a shit, the Bulgarians don't give a shit . . ."

"Just who does?"

"Pretty fucking few, I'll tell you."

"Name some."

"Give me a couple of days, and I'll come up with some."

"Just finish the roof."

Dondeen did finish the roof, it was inspected, approved, and Lowell signed the order authorizing payment, which went out one week later, an all-time record for the department, and Dondeen thanked him for the speed with which he got the check.

One day he cornered Lowell in the hallway of the Building.

"Let me tell you how to spot a terrorist," he said, lowering his voice when he came to the end of the sentence so that he hissed the word "terrorist." Lowell noticed how dirty the tips of his fingers were. He pressed close to Lowell, speaking into his lapels.

"Start from the ground, the shoes. They like to wear work boots, something you'd find in the factory. They like overalls, pin-striped denims, the kind railroad people from Missouri wear. They like caps and coats with synthetic collars or else army-surplus jackets. And they always carry briefcases. Your average terrorist is very businesslike, fits right into the corporate life. I hope you're getting this down, making notes, getting it on tape, something, for Chrissake."

Lowell said nothing.

"I can't believe how dumb you are."

"There are five adults living together in one of the apartments."

"Jeez, I can't believe how dumb you are."

"They have a right . . ."

"Fuckin' commies ain't got no rights."

"You left footprints on the stairs."

"The entrance hall light is busted."

But apart from the roof, the work in the Building was slow. Sheetrock was up, some of it taped, but none of it painted. For every job there was always something missing: nails, paint, joint compound. Or else the Sheetrock was cracked, the pipes split, the electric wires the wrong gauge. No matter how many times they fixed the main junction box, Steckler always broke into it; the lock was busted, sawed through, the hinges cut off with a welding torch. Lowell called a truce and arranged for Steckler to have a separate junction box. He found him quite reasonable, beyond everything he had been led to believe. The only strangeness was the sight of the man hanging from Steckler's ceiling. Lowell did not ask him about it, and Steckler did not volunteer any information. The man hung by a chain wrapped around his waist.

Miraculously, the boiler worked, and every time Lowell visited the Building he was drawn to the cellar and to the boiler, listening to the hiss and gurgle of oil, steam, and water as each liquid wound its way around the innards of that great machine. Lowell wiped off a bit of dust he found on the brass pipes leading into the boiler, cleaned off the water gauge, flushed the rusty water that collected in the tubes. No one had tried to steal the boiler, or tamper with it, and the great chains wrapped around the boiler (decreed by the commissioner) and cemented into the floor were rusting in the corner. New heat risers were being installed.

The only apartment Lowell couldn't get into was Stern's. Stern had barricaded his door, which was reinforced with steel, so a hole was knocked through his wall for the new steam risers that were going up from the cellar, and Stern quickly built a wall around the area they had broken into. They broke down the wall to attach a radiator, and Stern quickly boxed in the radiator so that when the steam was up this small box that contained the radiator swelled up with the heat. As the nails popped out of the box and the joint compound cracked and fell off in chunks, Stern built another box around the first, yelling, "I don't want your fucking heat, I want cold, ice, snow." Stern was painting the *Madonna of Broken Dreams,* or so Lowell learned from Kazima, who had been the model for the madonna until she had gotten into an argument with Stern about the size of her breasts, Stern wanting to tighten them up with transparent tape and Kazima refusing, calling him a bourgeois artist pig, after which Stern threw her out in the hall, naked, and tried to push her down a flight of stairs, a procedure that was forcefully halted when she broke his nose and then sat on him and punched him in the groin. Feeling sorry for the painter she carried him back to his apartment, bandaged his broken nose, and they made violent, thrashing love on the floor, Stern bleeding on her huge, sweating body.

The Wilson Sister welcomed the steam riser and welcomed Lowell, inviting him in for tea and showing off a gallery of eight-by-ten glossies, frayed like cotton at the edges, taken in the kind of fuzzy focus that was popular in the thirties, and recited for him the litany of clubs they had danced in and tied themselves into knots for, and, as a special treat, Beth (or was it Ester?) wove herself into a bowline knot while he drank his tea, and the plumbers sweated the joints of the steam riser up through their apartment, oblivious to the contortions, twists, and bends the old lady exhibited. Ester (or was it Beth?) apologized that she couldn't do the double half-hitch knot for him but explained that arthritis was catching up with her, limiting the kinds of knots she could tie herself into. "It does limit our bookings," Ester (or Beth) said. "We're not the draw we once were." She spoke as if there still were two of them. Lowell asked if there were anything he could do, and she said no, thanking him for the boiler that worked and the heat and the new steam riser, which, Beth (Ester?) said, would be much appreciated by their twenty-seven cats.

The riser rose into the next apartment, that of Glasho, who Lowell thought may have been the man who swallowed himself but was assured by another tenant that this was not the case, that Glasho was a man enamored of himself, so much that he kept bottled specimens of himself around the apartment, and when Lowell knocked on Glasho's door and was let in by a smiling Glasho, who immediately asked if there were anything he could do for him, Lowell told him about the steam riser, and in the telling looked around at the shelves with glass jars, hundreds of them, that lined the walls of the apartment. Glasho said, of course, yes, he would personally welcome the steam riser, and hoped that more would come through his apartment, many more, and when Lowell explained that they only had need for this one, Glasho said, of course, he welcomed just this one and he hoped that just this one would come through his apartment. "If I can be of any help," Glasho said, "in any way, however humble . . ."

The riser continued on through the apartments of Cuzz, who glared at him, and Abdul Karim, who scowled at him, sure that the riser was but the opening foray of a plot hatched in Lahore designed to wipe out Kurds by steam asphyxiation and melt down their gold teeth as an offering to the Hindu monkey god. The meat dealer's apartment was empty, except for a huge Doberman pinscher chained to the sink, who barked, as if through a megaphone, at the plumbers. The dog ignored the meat Lowell tossed at it to keep it quiet.

One of the tenants told Lowell about a man who talked to cockroaches; another tenant remembered when the cockroaches were so thick he would walk in his apartment at night and they would be underfoot, as thick as a carpet, obscuring the floor, and that even stepping on them, slipping as the ooze ran out of hundreds of the little hardshelled creatures, as he involuntarily skated across his floor, greased by cockroaches, that even then they refused to move, so determined were they to occupy his apartment, adamant in their insect stubbornness that his apartment, his plates, his glasses, his silverware, his boxes of crackers, and saltshakers, and glue in the bindings of his books were theirs, and that he, the human tenant, was only there at their pleasure.

And then one day, just when Lowell felt the work in the Building was progressing, albeit slowly, with complications (one of the steam risers had been inadvertently connected to a gas pipe, forcing steam out of stoves and another explosion in one of the apartments, which separated a water pipe and caused a flood that ran down five floors into the cellar where it formed a pool, some called it a river, a waterfall, which flooded out the pilot light in the boiler, shutting off the steam, which cooled the Building, freezing pipes and angering tenants, causing another break in yet another water pipe, this one larger, so that one side of the Building was awash in water and a pumper had to be called from the fire department to pump out the cellar and the first floor while the pipes were repaired, the boiler pilot light relit, the steam riser disconnected from the gas pipe, the gas turned back on, and the water which ran through the apartments was slowed to a trickle, but could never quite be stopped), a huge banner unfurled on the side of the Building, flaming red letters on a white background: RENT STRIKE—THIS BUILDING ON RENT STRIKE. Smaller signs, white lettering on red, appeared in windows repeating the message on the banner. Lowell felt betrayed. The banner hung from the apartment of the five, and when Lowell knocked on their door they refused to open it, refused to answer, refused to do anything except issue mimeographed sheets, which they put under the door of every apartment, that said the city was ripping them off: "Withhold rent, refuse to pay, no services—no rent."

Lowell learned that at a clandestine tenants' meeting a rent strike had been called because some tenants were unhappy with the city's renovation—its progress or lack of same. It was unclear how many of the Building's fifty-six families had been at the meeting; most of the tenants didn't know anything about it, assuming that the other tenants had voted for it and they were willing to go along with the majority. But it was questionable whether there was a majority. Everyone Lowell talked to understood the city's position and seemed happy that something, anything, was being done. Lowell could find no one who had actually attended this "tenants' meeting."

A third of the rents were paid to the city, a third were paid to a group called the Tenants United Party, and the other third were simply not paid to anyone. Mimeographed sheets appeared in the Building. "Fight Racism, Support TUP, No Services—No Rent." A local newspaper headlined the story, "Black Tenants, White Bureaucracy: A Study of City Sloth."

The gunfire started during the third day of the picket line. (The first two days the picket line was in front of the offices of H.P.D. at 100 Gold Street. Lowell was burned in effigy, along with Sanchez and the commissioner; Lowell was at his desk when Hector wheeled over and said, "They burning you outside, English, come look." Sure enough, they burned him from the feet up: brown shoes, purple pants, a red shirt, pillowcase stuffed with cotton and drawn on with lipstick—a passable likeness, but he was scowling and his tongue reached down to his neck. The commissioner was dressed in an old pin-striped suit, hanging from a gallows, which also burned; while Lowell may have been amused, the commissioner was not, and Sanchez had to be restrained from attacking the demonstrators. After the three of them had been reduced to ashes and mailed to the newspapers as a warning to anyone "who tries to fuck around with the tenants," Lowell was called into the commissioner's office and told that it was very likely he would be transferred to H.R.A.—Human Resources Administration, a euphemism for the Welfare Department—and put in charge of recalcitrant welfare mothers if he did not clear this matter up. Sanchez was told it was likely he would be either a toll collector for the Brooklyn Battery Tunnel or a cage cleaner for the elephants, rhinoceroses, and other heavy ungulates in the Central Park Zoo. Lowell did not recognize the demonstrators, except for the five. When he went out to talk with them, the police kept him from the demonstrators, who, angered at his presence, brandished broom handles, stickball bats, and rocks. A tall thin man with pin-striped overalls spoke through an electrified megaphone and called him a "vicious racist pig who was deliberately denying services to the tenants so he could force them out and the city could sell the Building to a speculator, economic displacement at its racist worst.")

The third day the picket line was set up in front of the Building, with the same signs and the same about-to-be-burned effigies. Again Lowell could recognize only the five on the picket line, but this time a group of tenants from the Building, Mary Smith, Willy, Tontine, the lunatic, the Wilson Sister, Steckler (Steckler? Lowell was surprised to see Steckler. He wondered if he had brought the man who hung from the ceiling), and several others came out and confronted the demonstrators, demanding to know who they represented, told them to get the hell out, said that for the first time in years they were getting services. The demonstrators called the tenants pimp whores, enemies of the people, and what followed next, before the shots rang out, was Steckler back-kicking two demonstrators to the pavement, before a picket sign stapled to a one-by-three was broken over his head, Steckler punching out the man who had done it even before the blood began streaming down the front of his face and he began to feel woozy, falling backward, caught by Willy who was still dressed in his chicken costume, having just come from work. There was disagreement later about where the shots came from, but there was none about the dead chickens that were suddenly dropped from the roof, as if the shots had killed the chickens, which were then launched from the roof, but whether the shots were from the chickens' execution squad or were meant to intimidate the tenants or the demonstrators, everybody, tenants, demonstrators, bystanders scattered, tenants running back into the Building followed by the demonstrators, and the sound of gunfire could be heard coming from the Building. My God, Lowell thought, there goes the Sheetrock, the taping. What if a bullet hits a water pipe or a steam riser? He was on the third floor, crouched near the stairwell, and could hear shots coming from the second floor. He started to crawl down the stairs, stopped when two bullets dug into the brick at the end of the landing, started to go up when he looked up the stairwell and saw a man on the fourth floor aiming a weapon at him. Lowell could only see one eye, the weapon and hands obscuring the face, and for some unexplainable reason, instead of ducking back against the wall and out of the line of sight, Lowell stared at the barrel of the gun, as if his gaze could stay the gunman's finger, or as if, fascinated by the barrel of the gun, its octagonal shape, the gunsight bumps, he also wanted to see the explosion, the burst of powder, the bullet racing toward him. And just as inexplicably the hand withdrew the gun, and Lowell pressed back against the wall, the hand reappearing with the gun, firing, the bullets striking the metal railing and the marble, denting the railing and burying themselves in the walls, and the marble cracking, burying the bullet. Two more shots, three, four; and keeping close to the wall, Lowell descended the staircase. There was more firing on the second floor, a different sound, a different caliber, and he could smell smoke. He couldn't tell if it was from the guns or a fire. Trying to decide, he heard someone shouting, three more shots, and he looked up the staircase to see a man caught on the railing, the upper half of his body upside down, his shirt sleeve clotted dark red, the same red running under his shirt, over his wrist, down the palm of his hand, and off his index finger, falling drop by drop four floors, where it splattered in tiny droplets on the entrance floor. The bleeding man was grabbed by the ankles, which were heaved up, like a lever, and his legs followed the rest of his body, plummeting to the floor, but not before he hit two banisters on the way down, breaking a few bones but also breaking his fall so that when he hit the bottom he was broken in more places than any man had a right to be, bleeding, but still alive. Lowell, feeling trapped on the stairwell, walked down to the second floor and started down the hall when a door opened.

"Get in."

It was Kazima. She was wearing a T-shirt, revealing a set of large, pendulous breasts that seemed to fall forever from her chest, and a pair of blue jeans that strained to hold her in. She wore no belt, and Lowell expected the top button, clasp, hook, or whatever it was that fastened these pants above the zipper to pop open and the great expanse that contained the rest of her body to flow out, like a burst dam. She shut the door behind him. He heard shots in the hallway.

33

IT was the apartment the psychopath lived in, an epileptic who had seizures and used his head as a battering ram to butt holes in the wall and crack the wood door, denting the door when it was replaced with steel (which caused Abdul Karim to think that Pakistanis were bombing the Building with tons of bogus Muslim propaganda wrapped in five-hundred-pound cotton bales), the apartment of the whirling dervishes, the same apartment the pigeons lived in, swishing in from a hole in the roof and flying endlessly around the edges as if the apartment were an aerodrome and the pigeons hired to put on a show, or, brushing their wings gently against the picture-frame ledges that circled the room were clearing it of cobwebs and dust, and that was the apartment the fireflies had settled in, a Las Vegas of light, millions of insect Con Edisons, intent on putting that utility to shame, creating light without heat, a buzzing sporadic glow, a lighthouse that warned stray ships and planes away from Brooklyn, it was that apartment that had become home, a lair, to the dogs.

Stray dogs, six, eight, more, a female bitch in heat, and the others, perhaps all male or mostly male, who had followed the bitch across vacant lots and through junkyards, into abandoned buildings and over rooftops, down cellar stairs and across the streets of Brooklyn—Albany, Troy, Utica, Rodgers, Eastern Parkway, Flatbush, Plaza, Butler Place—the bitch leading these male dogs, or mostly male dogs, as if on a leash. They formed a triangle, the bitch at the apex, though often the triangle flattened as several of the dogs tried to station themselves on either side of her or scrambled for the favored position immediately to her rear, which caused commotion among them, snarling, biting, some bloodletting, the bitch indifferent to this fighting or slightly annoyed by it. When they roamed the streets, either as a triangle or as a flattened triangle, or a column, scarcely military in formation but remarkably quiet, except for the fighting, and intent on establishing dominance with the bitch, who for the moment was not about to let any of them mount her, humans, other dogs, cats, and creatures of any sort avoided them, and when they crossed the street even cars swerved, certainly not from compassion but more from fear, as if this pack of dogs had the ability to fling themselves at car windows and doors, hurtling through glass and steel to drag the protesting occupants from the car.

They had been Christmas puppies; all nuzzly and cute, mongrel and purebred, and as soon as they had gotten bigger and become not so cute, or the weather had turned bad so that walking them entailed some hardship, the dogs were turned out, taken to remote parts of Brooklyn, to the garbage dump on Pennsylvania Avenue, and let loose, most of them half-grown, and they were quickly abused by larger strays who were more experienced in the ways of the street, until hunger taught them to be aggressive, opportunistic, and made them see humans as obstacles between meals. Lice and fleas found refuge in their hair, which became scuzzy, matted, and dirty; tapeworms settled in the intestines and heartworms in the chambers of the heart; arthritis invaded bones and joints that had been exposed to too many freezing nights. For dogs hit by cars there were broken bones that never mended properly, ruptured intestines that never healed, eyes that sagged and constantly teared, broken ribs. The dogs limped around the borough.

The pack wandered through vacant buildings, found the Building, climbed to the roof, pausing only to claw at the tar until the bitch spotted not the hole in the roof, which Dondeen had patched over, but a spot where the hole used to be and attacked it, coming up with a mouthful of tar and then scratching and clawing managed to bite through the roof so that the apartment below appeared, the ceiling not having yet been repaired from the time the fireflies dug a hole in it, and, wriggling her body through (during which process several of the dogs tried without success to mount her), dropped lightly into the apartment, trotting around the rooms, doing her business on the pornographic pinups that slid to the floor, which used to cover the holes in the wall the epileptic made. Dog after dog dropped after her, racing around the apartment to cover her scent with theirs, until the strong smell of dog urine wafted through the halls and into the other apartments. There was a great snarling and yelping as the male dogs strove to establish dominance, tried to determine the order in which they would mount her, but the bitch, still in heat, would have none of this, not yet, and either drove them off or merely sat down, frustrating their efforts to couple.

Shepherds, labs, retrievers; mutts, mongrels, mixes. Dogs with wiry, grizzled faces and hairless bodies, dogs with hair the color and feel of cornsilk, dogs with thin legs and barrel chests, dogs with massive heads and short legs with long hair. Dogs who could bark, yelp, yap, yip, growl, and howl. Dogs who would go for the throat, the genitals, the hamstring, the kidney. Dogs who pranced, who slunk, who jumped, who crawled, who waddled, who ran. Dogs who could crack an ox bone, chew through a two-inch oak door, jump a six-foot fence, and who, together with other dogs, could chase and kill anything in the city and most anything outside the city. Dogs who were much more dangerous than wolves because they were not afraid of humans, as Lowell and others discovered.

The dogs were fed by the lunatic, who threw dead chickens (with their heads twisted off and the blood drained, from the voodoo rites of Madame Jujubee) through the hole in the roof and also threw some of the huge, unrecognizable squash that he grew in his garden through the same hole, the melonlike vegetables hitting the floor with the sound of someone diving head first into a drained pool. This act of charity on the part of the lunatic only reinforced the importance of the apartment for the dogs; they had access to the ground via a broken window to the fire escape, but when they wanted to return to the apartment, for some reason they climbed the stairs to the roof where they dropped, one by one, through the hole into the apartment. Several slipped from the fire escape, falling into the garbage below; one dog hung by its neck when it slipped and fell between the tread risers, dangling and howling, and was finally saved by the lunatic, who climbed out on the fire escape and, avoiding the jaws of the frantic dog, pulled the beast up by the scruff of the neck and then jumped out of the way as it made its way back into the apartment.

On some nights the creatures roamed the halls, scratching at doors, whining and howling. The tenants, frantic in their locked apartments, refused to come out, and called anyone who would answer the phone, so the Building was regularly visited by the police, the ASPCA, and sometimes the fire department, each time the dogs having gone, trotting back to the Building single file after the officials had left. After several fruitless trips, the police, the fire department, and the ASPCA refused to come. The dogs had free run of the halls and stairways and made regular forays down the fire escape, peering into windows at frightened tenants, growling at the cooking smells that came from the kitchens.

Suddenly the bitch decided to mate. Mounting privileges had to be determined, and this was accomplished by a monumental dogfight, accompanied by apartment-amplified barks, growls, howls, snarls, and cries of distress as the mounting order was established. As soon as she was mounted and the first dog had spent himself, he was unable to uncouple. The bitch, disgusted by this anatomical state of affairs, turned and bit at the male, still inside her, who by now was so twisted around that both male and female were ass to ass instead of belly to ass. At that point he collapsed in fatigue, pulling her toward the floor, but she would have none of it and dragged him around the room, the two still coupled, turning and biting him whenever the opportunity presented itself, and the other male dogs joined in her vendetta. Love had never wreaked such havoc. Each male dog, in its turn, suffered this indignity, the pleasure interwoven with pain, and each returned, like an addict, again and again to experience this exquisite hell.

The noise that accompanied these amorous bouts was substantial. In the apartment below they could hear not just the dogs fighting but this mysterious sound of something being dragged across the floor. The barks of the bitch rose above the other howls, disgusted as she was with the ineptness of the male anatomy. There was no accounting for how love's plumbing could go so awry.

This affair, or these affairs, went on for days, setting up sympathetic vibrations in the other dogs in the Building and vibrations of another sort in the tenants. The meat dealer tried to shoot the dogs through the hole in the roof, the bullets passing through several apartments below the apartment of the dogs, one lodging in the muzzle of an old blind cat, causing it to lose control of its bowels and empty the contents of its large intestine on a dining room table.

Lowell had Dondeen patch up the hole in the roof and blocked the entrance door to the roof, effectively sealing the creatures in the apartment, and then had second thoughts about the wisdom of such a procedure. The dogs, hungry as spring bears, took to the fire escape, drooling at meals being prepared in kitchens, pawing at the glass, the frightened cooks recoiling in horror at these diseased, limping dogs. Hunger heightened their sexual appetite. As the bitch was mounted, so was the male who mounted her, and he who mounted him. A surge of sexual energy shot through the room; an erotic conga line was formed, manned, or dogged, by pumping, heaving dogs, as if one long penis joined them, interrupted at various points in its plumbing. No longer warring over position, since all positions were the same, a hush descended over the creatures, broken only by labored breathing, the scratching of claws digging into the parquet floor, the whines of ecstasy, and the growls of labor. Uneven in its horizon, unequal in its structure, unsure of its color, this fox-trot of fucking scuttled about the room as each dog attempted to press closer to the dog in front.

It was this production that greeted Lowell when he threw open the door to the apartment. Too busy to be startled, too engaged to be frightened or angry, the brutes continued their sexual conga line, and Lowell, though not a dog lover, was forced to admire the intensity of their pageant. The room reeked of dog, a mingled scent of zoo and feces, urine and cockroaches, and as Lowell stood in the doorway he felt dizzy, bedazzled by the waves of energy that poured out the door. It buffeted him, and he stepped back to let the unseen wind rush through the opening. He had brought a gun to scare the dogs out of the apartment and also a club and a pitchfork. What he intended to do with the club and pitchfork he had forgotten. He propped them against the wall and took the gun out of his pocket. He was about to pull the trigger when he realized that if he fired in the air, and there seemed to be no alternative, he had no idea where the bullet would fall. The idea of an unknown bullet, an aimless, wandering piece of metal dropping through the atmosphere, unnerved him. There was something disorderly about it, something cluttered. He put the gun back in his pocket, closed the door, carefully picked up his club and pitchfork, opened the door to reassure himself that the fox-trot was still in progress, and then quietly closed the door and walked away.

34

ONCE the dogs had left, Lowell was able to rent the apartment. He turned down some gypsy automobile mechanics, an endless Chinese family, and finally picked the Multi-Gravitational Aerodrome Company, Inc.

"We're incorporated for tax purposes," said the small, compact man who seemed to act as the spokesman. "Though for all practical purposes, it hardly matters since we rarely touch the ground."

There were seven of them, or six and a half: small, compact people with short heads and knotted muscles. The seventh, or the half, was shorter than the others, and it appeared that half of him was missing, though it was difficult to say which half. At first Lowell thought his head rested on his hips, but one day it appeared that the creature had feet but no legs, and was normal in every other respect.

They were quiet tenants. No one in the apartment below could hear them walking around. Toilets were flushed and water ran twice a day, for a total of fifteen minutes each time. It was a relief from the howling dogs that used to inhabit the apartment and reminded Lowell of the time when the apartment was filled with fireflies.

"What's going on up there?" the tenant below asked.

"Nothing," said Lowell.

Theirs was a silence of absence, not a silence of presence. No one was waiting for them to speak; no one wondered what they did. They were simply there, paid their rent on time, rarely went to tenants' meetings (never in fact), were seen often enough to remain inconspicuous and yet not so often that they became a regular feature of the Building. The tenant below them thought they went out at night, but why, and to what effect, he did not know.

When Lowell went around to collect the rent, he put his ear to their door and heard a faint buzzing sound, like a spring-loaded motor or a recording of a tiny airplane engine. Sometimes the sound creaked, and then there was a series of creaks, as if someone were opening and closing a rusty screen door or playing with the bellows on a hand forge.

They paid their rent in bills of small denomination, crumpled, soiled, frequently old and worn. The money had such a soft patina it seemed it would turn to dust if rubbed together. Lowell, however, had been paid in stranger currency. They never complained about the dog smell, which Lowell could never get rid of despite Tontine's efforts at scraping the rock-hard piles of excreta. They never complained about the tiny white encrustations from the pigeons, nor did they mind the billions of firefly wings. The fireflies had left a yellow glow in the room, the pigeons some feathers, and the dogs, despite Tontine's efforts, had left their smell.

"Dogs don't bother us," the manager told Lowell. "They bark at us but they don't bother us. They can't."

Lowell watched them file out of the apartment in the morning and return in the evening, each carrying groceries and an Adidas bag. His curiosity was aroused and then muted. He had other concerns. The renovation in the Building had slowed, indeed halted, and though no one had attempted to steal the boiler recently and the chicken rain had stopped, there was an uneasy lassitude about the Building, a sort of solstice. The tenants seemed to be waiting for an event. The paraplegic phoned him daily about disasters in Newark or Hoboken, and Abdul Karim complained that he was being attacked by trained moths.

Someone said they were Norwegians; someone said they were Finns. "They dance to the beat of a different drummer," said Hobson.

But whatever dancing they did, it was silent, imagined, a thing done in the air.

Lowell felt they were part of a Canadian cartel that made wonderfully eccentric tractors in Ontario, great powerful tractors with single-cylinder engines, cylinders the size of garbage cans, engines that ran on alcohol and pulled huge combines across the wheat fields of Manitoba, and that this cartel, the Multi-Gravitational Aerodrome Company, had gone bankrupt and these seven, these six and a half, the board of directors, were escaping creditors by fleeing across the border. Late at night Lowell could hear a small propeller-driven plane flying across Brooklyn, bringing, he was sure, food and supplies to the beleaguered board of directors. But Dondeen said that was just part of the story. They make a flying tractor, the propeller on the bottom, a sort of well-muscled helicopter that pulls twelve-disc harrows across soggy fields inaccessible to ordinary tractors. "Picture a tractor with no wheels," Dondeen said. "Now picture a tractor with no wheels and a big propeller on the bottom, a kind of Canadian propeller." "I can't," said Lowell. "That's why they went bankrupt," Dondeen said.

But every night Lowell kept hearing the plane, and couldn't escape the feeling that whatever they did had something to do with food, with Canada, with engines. They don't mind the smell of dogs because Canadians have hundreds of dogs.

"They sell model airplanes at Macy's," said Dondeen. "I'll show you." But Lowell couldn't find them at Macy's. Dondeen claimed they had been fired.

Nothing mysterious about them, though. They were normal, smaller than normal, perhaps a little lighter, a little less attracted to gravity; a quiet, well-ordered group of people who went about their business out of the limelight, who needed some structure but abhorred rigidity.

Lowell believed their tractors looked like huge steam calliopes, great, bright, red-and-gold-eagle-painted vehicles, with whistles, bells, and pulleys for various accessories, and that these cantankerous engines dotted the Manitoba wheat fields for which they had been designed, their paint fading, their silver bells and chains and pulleys rusting, their magnificent innards stolen by gypsy ironmongers, who melted them down into pig iron and sold them to the Japanese. It was one of the last great Canadian inventions, a design so radical it seemed suited to the vast agriculture of that northern land, but a design doomed by its very Canadianness. When they worked, their single cylinders coughing out huge explosions, spitting fire, scorching earth and wheat, they presented a marvelous spectacle as they rushed across the Canadian landscape, a flame-belching, whistle-blowing, pulley-howling juggernaut that not only pulled dozens of plows but simultaneously planted the wheat, speeded up its growth, harvested it, separated it, ground it, baked it, and deposited the residue in the form of neat, round, brown-colored loaves of bread wrapped in shiny blue and white crinkly paper, which were deposited in the backs of small vans. It failed because it went against the grain. The Americans had to invent it, the Japanese had to perfect it; otherwise the thing would never work. Secretly, almost apologetically, the Canadians knew this; bankruptcy was to be expected.

"We have nothing whatsoever to do with agriculture," the manager told him curtly one day.

Visions of huge tractors silhouetted on the Canadian horizon melted from his imagination. He was left with a vast, bleak expanse of Canadian land, an endless tabletop of wheat, punctuated now and then by small, dull, earth-colored tractors pulling unattractive farm equipment.

"And we are not," the manager almost shouted, "Canadians. We never have been. We never will be."

The melting continued, and Lowell was left, not with bright, cheery Canada, but some caliginous, landlocked country in central Europe.

"And we are certainly not political refugees," the manager added, ending the conversation.

What were they?

It made no difference.

"They're small, they're regular, they pay their rent, so why complain?" said Sanchez.

"I don't complain," Lowell emphasized. "It's just that it helps me if I know the composition of my tenants."

"Let's worry about the elevator. The city doesn't have money to fix the elevator. We're thinking of turning it into a compactor."

"That," Lowell said, "is already what it is."

The roof was another problem. There were several dog-chewed-through holes, and Lowell invited Dondeen back to patch up the holes. Dondeen said he knew precisely what the six and a half did. "It's simple," he explained to Lowell. "They make aerodromes. Aerodromes hold the air. They cover acres of land, and are of particular importance in areas where the air is too light and is in danger of escaping. They hold the air down with special valves and spigots and pressure gauges, which equalize the pressure both inside and outside the dome and prevent it from flying off or being flattened. You can see them out in the country," Dondeen said, "in places where the earth is thin and hasn't much weight, where gravity is lax, where things fly off and disappear." A day later Dondeen had changed his mind and said they made reconstituted air—thick air and thin air, according to the demands of the particular situation—and piped it into those areas that had most need of it.

But the seven, or rather the six and a half, remained innocent of Dondeen's speculations and filed as unceremoniously into the apartment in the early evening as they did out of it in the early morning. There was a regularity and a calmness about them that Lowell admired, an easy orderliness, a sort of floating sanity, as if they were monks of the atmosphere.

He learned the name of one, McGarrity, who wore spats and a bow tie with a wingtip collar, and looked like the other six, or five and a half. McGarrity carried an attaché case with him, inside of which was a small machine-looking thing with several rheostats and a trip switch. McGarrity brought up the rear of the procession, closing doors, doing a fast jog until he was in lockstep with the others. He also paid the rent and may have been the spokesman for the group.

It was McGarrity who held them all out the window in a human chain one dusky evening. Lowell was standing on the sidewalk and happened to look up just in time to see McGarrity jump on the windowsill and hang outside the window by his legs, head down. One of the five and a half scampered down McGarrity, who grabbed him by the legs, and the rest followed until they were spread out alongside the Building, upside down, hanging several stories down. Then one by one, starting with the bottom, they crawled back up to McGarrity and into the window, leaving McGarrity holding nothing. McGarrity saw Lowell, waved, and then disappeared inside. He didn't pull himself in, or jump in, or crawl in; he just disappeared inside. Perhaps unseen hands yanked him in by the ankles, doing it so fast, while Lowell blinked, that he hadn't seen it. What he did see was McGarrity's top hat, rather his bowler, which floated slowly to the ground, rocking back and forth in the air as it fell, as if to mimic McGarrity's wave.

As he watched the bowler fall, he suddenly became dizzy, and thought, there are people who fly. It was a thought that frightened him. Some small people, those who were light enough, who were perpetually at risk, they were in danger of leaving the planet. They could float in air, could float beyond air.

He knew what they were. They were pilots, barnstormers, aerial duelists who flew short, stubby biplanes painted green and tan, and they were in the *Guinness Book of World Records*. They flew five tiny planes that looked like spray-painted bumblebees. One of them ran along the wings, jumping from plane to plane, from wing to wing, ten thousand feet in the air, and when he reached the end plane, as if on signal, the five planes flipped over, and the wing dancer was thrown into the sky, flipped higher than the planes, catapulted toward the sun, an aerial Icarus, a mere thumb of a man plunging through the sky. The five planes turned and dived, plummeted toward the earth, their engines straining to beat the fall of the wing dancer. As they raced him down toward earth, they dived under him, and because of exquisite timing and years of practice, he fell into the well-cushioned rear seat of one of the biplanes. A cheer went up from the crowd below, all the more remarkable because at that height they could hardly see him falling.

That, of course, was just the beginning of their show. They flew side by side, wingtip to wingtip, and at a given signal they jumped into each other's cockpit and continued flying. Still flying they landed on each other's wing and then took off. They put their planes into a stall and fell, not head first but tail first, pulling up at the last minute directly over the audience, causing them to scatter and signaling the end of the show. They wore puffed-up leather jackets packed with pounds of sheepskin lining and had silk scarves that never ceased to flutter. Tucked underneath the epaulets on their shoulders were World War II aviator goggles from doomed P–51 Mustang pilots, the nickel plating worn through in spots to show the brass.

The planes were hangared on a small farm in southern New Jersey, meticulously cared for by an old man with a limp, an ex-pilot who had lost his nerve. The planes had shellacked and painted canvas stretched drum tight over aluminum tubing; the engines were sixteen-cylinder radial Pratt & Whitneys, fuel-injected. They all had dual cockpits with sliding canopies, and immediately to the front were three small indentations that held synchronized machine guns, which were timed to fire between the propeller blades.

They were in China before Stilwell, flew the Burma Hump, fought Jap zeros in Manchuria before they escaped to the Philippines, where they were taken prisoner and made to bow in a particularly humiliating manner before the Japanese prison commandant. They built a road through the jungle, a road made of sand and crushed rock, a road designed to go nowhere. Liberated by the Americans, they were mistakenly shipped to Estonia where they were caught up in the treason trial of Lavrenti Beria. Pardoned shortly after Stalin's death, they escaped to the United States in a stolen Russian bomber, an Ilyushin.

They were septuplets, or a half more than sextuplets, abandoned in the snow in the Swiss Alps and nursed to health by an Italian wet nurse, rumored to have four breasts, an almost-mistress of the famous Italian aviator Bandini, who had died in a fiery air crash before he could substantiate the nurse's mammary apparatus. They learned about Sopwith Camels and Tiger Moths at the breasts, so to speak, of this legendary wet nurse.

Raised as Roman Catholics, they converted to Buddhism during their days in the Japanese prison camp, but once they got to America they saw the hopelessness of Buddhism and became Methodists. It was, they felt, a New World theology, a sort of hamburger religion that would stand them in good stead no matter where they went. Methodists, they were assured, were everywhere and had the right connections when it came to runway clearance and hangar space. Methodists were the fulcrum upon which the country balanced, firmly planted at the center of belief.

Lowell, the modern man run amok, a religionless fiend, marveled at their journey through the world's religions and the various shades of heaven. He imagined the different theologies as various types of cloud formations—cirrus, cirro-nimbus, stratus, and so on—some low-lying and billowy, others tall and puffy, still others high and wispy, all of them explored by the stubby biplanes of the Multi-Gravitational Aerodrome Company (Incorporated), a feat that would land them in the *Guinness Book of World Records,* alongside the man who had finger-nails twenty-four inches long and the lady whose pubic hairs spelled out the Gaelic word for love. He thought of them as monks, or priests, or rabbis, or monks *and* priests *and* rabbis. They were traveling evangelists, flying friars, barnstorming Buddhists, temporarily forced to fly a holding pattern as Methodists. They flew as high as faith and their tiny planes would permit, straining to get closer to heaven and the word of God (a faint voice at best). They had become blessed by the rarefied atmosphere, enlightened by the lack of oxygen, ennobled by the thinness of the air, and unexpectedly purified by the radiation from ultraviolet light, the heavenly end of the spectrum. In this sparse atmosphere they were sure to find God, or they were sure not to find him, which would amount to the same thing.

And perhaps they would take Lowell up, and he too could hear the voice of God or not hear the voice of God, whichever suited the Creator, and having heard or not heard the voice would arrive back on earth bearing the lightness of aviators, enmeshed in ethereal calm. All he had to do was talk to these miniature flyers, explain the urgency of his mission, if mission it was, and they would bundle him in leather and sheepskin, give him goggles and helmet, leather puttees, silk scarf (starched to catch the wind), gently hoist his twice-the-size-of-their-bulk into the cockpit, taxi out of the hangar; the heavy little planes would rattle down the runway and suddenly jump up, fleeing gravity, then slowly, gently, begin to fly.

But cornered one evening while paying the rent, McGarrity angrily denied they were flyers and told Lowell they had no planes, no hangars out in south Jersey, no mechanic who lost his nerve as a pilot.

"We are what we are," he shouted at Lowell and slammed the door in his face.

"That," said Lowell to the closed door, "is probably what I expected."

When Dondeen came back to finish patching up the roof, he told Lowell he had another theory about what they did. Lowell told him to stuff it. He did not want to hear Dondeen's theories; he didn't want to hear anything about the little men.

"They can be bushmen, for all I care."

"Pygmies, albino pygmies."

Whatever they did, it made no difference to Lowell. They paid their rent. They were quiet. His ear pressed to the door, Lowell could barely hear the soft creaks, or series of creaks, that came from the apartment. It sounded to him as if they were winding something up, a spring motor, or, if not that, something on the end of a pendulum. He tried the door, thinking of apologies when they found him in their apartment, but the door was locked.

Then he discovered that someone, probably Tontine or the lunatic, had rented the basement to the gypsy automobile mechanics, and the boiler room was filled with Buick Electras and Oldsmobile Cutlasses in various stages of disrepair, hoods open, the innards of engines, mechanical intestines, scattered over the floor. They showed not the slightest desire to speak English, or even thought that such a language would profit them. Lowell wondered how they managed to squeeze the cars in the basement. He also wondered how, once they assembled the engines, they drove the cars around in the basement (the largest room down there being no more than forty by forty feet) and how they expected to get the cars out of the basement. When he tried to evict them he couldn't find them. One day he found a bright yellow Oldsmobile Cutlass in the lobby. It was the first brand-new convertible he had seen in years.

While the gypsy automobile mechanics could be heard but not seen, the endless Chinese family could be seen but rarely heard. They had moved into the stairwells, from the first to the top floor, and though Lowell could see them when he walked into the Building, as soon as he went over to them they fled up the stairs, pots and pans barely clanging, babies softly crying, accomplishing this with such speed that wherever Lowell walked they were ahead of him, rushing up the stairs, out onto the roof, down the other stairwell, or else down the stairs, across the lobby, and up the other stairwell. They lived on the landings and on the steps, sometimes out the window if the weather permitted. They cooked, ate, slept, did everything, almost, on the stairs, and no matter what they were involved in, even if of a delicate nature, would cheerfully grab their belongings and flee at the sound of Lowell's footsteps, being able to discern the sound of Lowell's tread from that of the dozens of tenants. The other tenants avoided the stairs as much as possible, and if pressed to use them had to follow what openings were made for them by the endless Chinese family, who smiled like a spaniel that had just swallowed a pound of butter, and continued their cooking, eating, sleeping, or suckling the dozens of babies that would soon take their place on the steps. Lowell tried chasing them, but they were too fast for him, amazingly nimble; even the older members of the endless Chinese family could outrace him up the steps or down.

"Squatters," Sanchez roared. "Throw them out."

"They pay rent," said Lowell.

"To us?"

"To someone."

"Throw them out."

"I'll need tow trucks, police, riot gear."

"That doesn't look good," said Sanchez. "Let them stay."

The endless Chinese family expanded, spilling over into the base-ment, sitting in the corners of the boiler room, watching the gypsies do valve jobs on Buick Electras. Soon there were so many they crowded around the Buicks and Oldsmobiles until the gypsies hardly had room to maneuver, and one evening Lowell noticed the Electras and the Cutlasses were gone, and the basement and stairwell were filled with hundreds of Chinese, gabbing, cooking, eating, gesturing, nursing ba-bies, gambling, playing mah-jongg, practicing kung fu.

Lowell thought the Building would collapse, overburdened by Chinese, and made plans to have them removed. He would use the tactical police force, with a Chinese interpreter, and accomplish the deed at night, perhaps during a thunderstorm to mask the commotion. They would block all entrances except the lobby door, and the police, in their snappy blue uniforms and shiny leather puttees, with lacquered riot helmets, would come in through the roof, forcing the Chinese down the stairs and out the lobby door. Police would be stationed at every entrance with walkie-talkies. The commissioner would be over-head in a helicopter.

And then one day the endless Chinese family left. Just disappeared mysteriously. The absence of yellow in a building filled with black and brown and red and white. A shortage of Oriental, a surplus of Occiden-tal. Lowell missed them; he could not say why, not even if a knife, a long, sharp knife, were held to his throat.

"There's nothing mysterious about it," McGarrity said. Lowell was standing inside the apartment rented by the Multi-Gravitational Aerodrome Company.

"We asked them to leave," he said, "and they left."

But Lowell did not hear what McGarrity said. He was watching bodies flying about the room. Small men and one smaller man, the half, whizzed about the corners of the room in colored undershirts, in bright tights, leotards, with tiny towels wrapped around their wrists and foreheads.

"We had calculated that their weight had upset the geometry of the room," McGarrity said.

But the only set of senses that Lowell had working were his eyes. How did bodies stay up in the air like that? Even small bodies, bodies not so weighed down by gravity? As each body came flying across the room, a fine spray of sweat followed it, a tiny errant thunderstorm.

"They were quite nice about it," McGarrity said. "Quite pleasant. They understood."

Trapezes. There were trapezes in the room, hanging from a ceiling that looked higher than Lowell had remembered the ceiling looking, higher indeed than the natural line of the ceiling.

"It's our livelihood," McGarrity said, "the precise geometry of the room."

Bodies hanging upside down on trapezes flinging other bodies across the room, like Frisbees, sailing slowly from one wall to another, a dreamy look on their faces, and yet, a look of immense strain, as if they had willed themselves to overcome gravity. The throwers, those who flung them about the room, and the catchers, those who caught the bodies that were flung, stared wide-eyed at what was being thrown and caught, veins and muscles knotted and gleaming in their arms. Those who were flung about twisted and turned and circled in the air and seemed not to be thrown as much as pushed off, launched, projected into space.

"It all depends upon geometry," McGarrity said. "Just high-school geometry."

McGarrity turned a crank, and a section of the ceiling opened up, taking with it the roof and revealing the sky, which was gold tinged with magenta. The throwers began to flip the bodies upward, where they languished in space, hung for a moment above the Building, like weather vanes turning with the wind, and then quickly plummeted into the arms of the catchers, who strained and shuddered at the catch, the trapeze rope stretching, the sudden jar and jolt transmitted to post and beam and to the floor upon which Lowell stood. He could imagine the Building being wrenched apart by these acrobatics: beams pulled out of joists, brick walls cracking and separating, floors falling.

Lowell turned to mention this to McGarrity and saw McGarrity racing toward him, almost falling, his legs wrapped around a trapeze, hanging upside down, arms outstretched as if to welcome Lowell, smiling, and as he rushed by in his terribly swift arc, he grabbed Lowell, lifted him off his feet, carried him up on a continuation of his arc, and, just before he reached the opening in the ceiling, let go.

Lowell was launched into space, spread-eagle to the sky, and for an instant, at the apogee of his climb, he was able to review the city, to take in the gaudy tinges of purple and gold left on the horizon by the setting sun and to be reminded of the many desolate buildings in the city, buildings with fire-burned roofs, kicked-in doors, pipes burst and frozen in winter, and glaciers that crept down the stairs, all before the fear of falling and then his actual falling began.

35

NOT fat, but a rumplike appearance. Things in him settled toward the middle, even the stomach descended below the navel where it protrudes, providing ample company for the tremendous rump behind it. The musician spends much time sitting, composing, searching for three elusive notes. His bottom, his personal pot roast fattened by years of indolence, and his body, settle to the bench. He told Lowell, "I am very religious."

He is. Painfully so. He prays several hours a day, sleeps on a plank, wears a cilice, a device designed to inflict pain for the mortification and edification of the flesh. "But as to composing," he told Lowell, "I do not expect divine guidance. This composing business, that's on my own. God has more important things to do."

When the Pope came to Brooklyn, the musician was ecstatic. He learned about the itinerary beforehand. He planned to appear before the Holy Father and ask for his blessing. The Pope was a learned man who had himself some musical talent. He would appeal to that in the Pope.

He awoke early the day the Pope was scheduled to appear in Brooklyn. He put on a fresh black suit, first strapping his cilice into place, pulling the belt an extra notch so that the fork of the tongue slipped into a new belt hole (unexplored territory, the added dimension of pain and discomfort served to remind him of his own fallibility, his own wretchedness). Of course, a white shirt and a black tie, thin, something flimsy. While it would look good to dress up, it wouldn't look good to get too dressed up. He wore black shoes, spotted and wrinkled from a previous rain.

The train was late. Bodies uncomfortably packed in. He could barely push his way inside. The train stood on the track, doors shut, lights off, the conductor silent. *Didn't they realize the Pope was coming?* Finally some lights came on and the train crawled off. He was afraid he would miss the Pope. His cilice, pulled tighter because of the press of bodies and the awkward way he had to twist his body (and his great middle plumpness), dug into his flesh, twisted, reddened, pierced his skin. He wore a dark pad over it for just such occasions so his blood would not be visible. Someone kept pushing him from behind, twisting the cilice, plunging it deeper into his flesh. *Why do they keep pushing me?* He could feel sweat trickle down the deep crevice in his buttocks. The train kept starting, then stopping; the lights going off, coming on, going off.

The Pope is coming, the Pope is coming.

He kept repeating that to himself and thought of his three notes, the absolute limit he would allow to appear in any composition. The train kept jerking along, starting, stopping, whipping the passengers back and forth. His lower back was sweaty. Shifting back and forth on his feet, trying to hold on to a rung while someone else's hand kept pushing his off, he began to experience a sense of insubstantiality. He was draining away, melting into sweat; he would evaporate. The passengers on the train, the ads, the graffiti, the train itself—they would all soon be plunged in water. The subway was headed toward a deep underground pool, a turn-of-the-century cistern buried and forgotten in the bowels of Brooklyn.

His stop. He got off, with difficulty, feeling as if the passengers on the train had wanted to hold him back, keep him in. He shook himself.

His buttocks, his back, his stomach, under his arms—all soaked in sweat. He plodded up the stairs, shoes squeaking.

It was a bright, windy day, overcast, with scudding clouds that made it difficult to determine how the day would turn out. The cold whipped at his suit, drying up whatever reservoir of warmth the sweat had left. He shivered, felt chilly, freezing, thought he was going to die from the cold and also felt very substantial, very solid, as if at this very moment the cold had conferred on him a sort of "realness" that he lacked before.

His itinerary had the exact address of the church the Pope would appear at, and he reached back to extract it from his wallet, finding that his wallet was missing, having been picked in the crowded train. He tried to remember the address of the church and then saw mobs of people ahead, the sound of sirens, voices shouting. Pushing his way to the front, he was informed that the Pope had just left. Everyone was running to touch the ground he had walked on, touch the body of the little girl whose head he had brushed, hold on to the church railing he had used to guide himself up and down the steps.

Was this the church he had been scheduled to appear at?

No. This was a spontaneous stop. The other church, the official itemized stop, was several blocks away, he learned. He ran, panting, the cilice digging into his side, tie waving madly over his shoulder as if it were saying good-bye to someone behind him. Sweat began to appear in the pits and crevices of his sagging body, and his legs and heart, long accustomed to indolence, to the placid safety of his piano where he spent his time searching for three notes (for the combination of those notes, for the timing of that combination, for the codas, toccatas, and fugues of those three notes), asked politely that he stop, or at least slow down, perhaps rest for a minute. He sat on the curb, in a sort of a swoon. His body felt strange, as if it were marooned.

A large black car pulled up alongside him. The rear door opened. Sitting in the back was the Pope. He motioned the musician to enter the car. As soon as he did, a dark statue, dusky in hue, was thrust into his hands. Though the car was cold, almost as cold as outside, the statue itself was warm, if not hot. A piece of quilting, black and brown in color, was wrapped around the statue. He tried to ask the Pope about the statue and then attempted to kiss his ring, but the Pope silenced him with a finger to his lips and asked him to leave the car. With some difficulty he managed to crawl out of the back seat, the statue, wrapped in a quilt, quite heavy in his arms. He deposited himself on the curb and turned back to the car. The rear window, a heavy, blackened thing, rolled down. The Pope himself did the cranking, because the face of His Holiness was close to the opening. He started to speak, thought better of it, smiled, and slowly cranked the window shut.

The musician carried the statue home, unaccustomed to the weight and the strange warmth that emanated from it; shifting it from arm to arm on the subway, cradling it in both arms, he put it on his hip . . . nothing seemed to lighten the thing. It was only later, reading in the encyclopedia about Polish history, that he learned that it was the Madonna of Nie Zbyt Drogi Mieszkame, the Madonna of Heat and Hot Water.

He placed the madonna in a bookcase, on purple velvet, and draped orange velvet over and around her. The effect is hideous, but he is a musician, not a designer. He wonders: *Is she warm? Is she cold?* He puts a glass door in front of her to keep off the dust and then opens it so her compartment won't be airtight. He adores her, but he does not pray to her. "I venerate her," he told Lowell. "I respect her. I try to keep her as comfortable as I can, but I cannot pray to her. I do not yet feel it is proper. However, in her presence I tighten the cilice a notch or two, genuflect, and offer a Hail Mary and an Our Father. She is bound up in keeping the Building warm."

The musician is able to compose in her presence, and through the locked door Lowell can hear his three notes shimmering with an infectious cyclical urgency. "She likes what I play," he told Lowell. "How do you know that?" Lowell asked. The musician winked at him, his large, bulbous nose twitching. "She moves and glows," he said. "When I wake up in the morning, I can tell that she has moved."

At night she came to him in bed, a succubus, and yet also a madonna, a thing possessed of lust and piety, love and God, passion and purity. "She is all over me," he said to Lowell. "I am embarrassed. She is a madonna: pure, chaste, virginal. But she is all over me, breathing on me with that hot little breath, unfolding layers of skirt, peel after peel, and she wrestles me in bed, chases me in my dreams." There was more that he did not wish to reveal to Lowell. He felt he had to protect her, that perhaps he was talking about her too much, that what happened between them should remain between them. When he woke in the morning, the madonna seemed to have moved slightly, to be drooping, as if tired from her nightly labors.

Lowell asked him how she could keep the Building warm.

"That," the musician said, "is in her very nature. She is hot by temperament, a Sicilian saint, a close compatriot of the blessed Virgin Mother, yet she is also different. She is volatile, quick, easy to please and displease, quick to take offense and just as quick to take a liking. She does what she has to do—that is, she heats things up, and it is understood that certain attributes go along with that."

"How is she on boilers?" Lowell asked.

"That's her speciality."

Several days later he told Lowell that he had received correspondence from the Pope inquiring about the well-being of the madonna.

"What can I tell His Holiness?" he asked Lowell. "I watch her. What else is there to know?"

The Pope seemed to think there was something else and kept writing to the musician, who kept writing back, giving him assurance that the madonna was well treated, and then having second thoughts about how well one can treat a statue, other than leaving it alone and seeing that no harm comes to it . . . perhaps it wasn't just a statue, and perhaps the Pope had known that when he had handed it over to him in the back seat of his limousine (a lengthened Buick Electra 225, no Cadillac for this Roman Catholic). The musician thought he had noticed the Pope's wink, that famous gesture of his that says, "We both know this is just a joke," and that the Pope was writing him to confirm the diagnosis of that wink (Pope's Wink, a well-known phenomenon in Curia circles at the Vatican) and to establish the double nature of this statue, this inert and yet "ert" thing he had been given. He would not write about what happened at night. He was not exactly sure what happened at night, not even inexactly sure. He steamed the postage off the envelopes, adding it to his collection of Vatican stamps.

"I should have asked for his autograph," he told Lowell.

"But you have the letters," Lowell protested.

"I didn't see him sign them."

"For that matter, you hardly know it's the Pope who is writing to you."

That thought pursued him for several days, and Lowell noticed an almost plaintive, Oriental tone to his compositions. Then one day he told Lowell that he was dropping a note; he was only composing with two notes. "Three notes is a luxury, an extravagance, a symbol of softness and decay we have allowed to creep among us." He pulled his cilice tighter, played the piano, and bled copiously. But this did not last. The boredom of two notes made him suffer more than any cilice could. He added a note and unloosened his torture device.

"I think you made a wise choice," Lowell said, trying to calm several irate tenants who wanted to deposit the musician and his piano on the sidewalk.

There seemed to be some relationship between the boiler and the madonna, though what that relation was escaped Lowell. Some days the Building had heat; other days it didn't. There was a caprice to this rise in temperature, which occurred whether the Building needed it or not. Lowell began to have religious thoughts, or thoughts that centered around the time he was supposed to have religious thoughts. He thought of the days when he was an altar boy, how he had to hide the wine until Holy Communion because otherwise the priest, a gnarled old Irishman who was a missionary in China for twenty years and was well known for drinking up a month's supply of Holy Communion wine in a few days, would do the same here. The church had dried him out, put him through the wringer at some clinic in upstate New York, and the old Irishman had come back shaken, shriveled, silent, as if he had seen something in his sober moments that was denied the rest of us and the reality of that vision threatened to suffocate him. To breathe, he had to drink. In Lowell's mind religion was inextricably tied in with wine.

The musician invited Lowell into his apartment to sit and watch the madonna move. "You must be very quiet," he said. "She's very bashful. We must sit still." They did, like night air, sitting so still they hardly dared to breathe, and Lowell was conscious of nothing other than his breathing, the slow rise and fall of his chest and stomach, like delayed surf that gently filled and then was expunged from his lungs. He watched the madonna until his eyes grew heavy, his lids slowly sunk, and through a long narrow slit he saw a brown haze, guarded by his eyelashes. He imagined that the madonna moved, he tried to make her move, he dozed and thought he dreamed that she moved, but when he opened his eyes she remained in the same position, and he realized that she had not moved but that he had moved, and it was the *she* in him that moved and not the *she* in herself. "She moved," the musician told him, and Lowell neglected to nod, thinking that the musician's eyes, marble heavy, bobbing in a sea of rings, were unreliable things, the very instruments not to trust when dealing with a musician. "No she didn't," he said calmly. "She will never move. She is static." The musician looked at him as if he were lost, one of the damned. They watched her for another forty-five minutes. Lowell found that by squinting he could make her rise and then fall imperceptibly from the table. It happened as he breathed, was in fact timed to his breathing.

"You're right," the musician said simply.

He continued to search for his elusive fugue. He thought he could hear his notes in the moans of the Building and sat up night after night listening to the sounds the Building made, sounds as faint and as ethereal as those of the humpback whale. It was the wind, the hum in the electric wires, the creak of the beams; it was something else, bones screaming, a plaintive wail. It was the Building turning on its foundations, sagging. The notes chased one another, falling back on themselves, following themselves, inverting themselves, dancing around their counterparts according to strict formulas.

The musician thought, somewhere in the Building is the music of the spheres, the epicycles of Aristotle, the ellipses of Kepler, as if the Building itself were swinging around the heavens singing its own tune. He looked for the halo of himself and the sound that halo made, the singing, the tune, the pitch. If I am holy, he thought, if I am so holy as to be allowed to compose, if I torture myself to compose, then I will extract blood from my music (for my music), listen to the sound of penitence, the music of the holy scriptures, and having prayed for divine guidance see that it is wrong, that deaf heaven sets no store by my music, that heavenly choirs do not filter down, that the music I seek is of my own making, my own torture, my own burden.

The musician started to moan and pound the piano with his fist, taking in scores of notes at a stroke, pelting out his fury at a tune that lay buried in the piano. He was determined to extract it from that quarter-ton beast. He struck it with clenched fists, tiny, musicianlike fists, but fists nevertheless, demanding entrance into the world of three-note fugues. He shouted at his piano, wept over it, oblivious to the clamor of protests in the neighboring apartments.

What a horrible noise! A piddle of clanging, pots and pans falling down a metal staircase would have been more harmonious. Yet the musician banged on, believing the elusive notes were hiding, like cockroaches, in his piano and needed only to be extracted by force. There was a pounding on his ceiling. The plaster shook. A similar pounding took place at his door, rattling the frame. The musician, ossified by the tumult of composition, ignored these bangings, which sounded better than what he was expunging from the piano.

The piano, on rollers, jiggled across the room at his pounding. The musician followed it, beating the beast unmercifully, committed to sledgehammering his contrapuntal symphony, the sweat of, if not inspiration, at least perspiration cascading down his brow.

It is a tune beside myself, he thought, a tune within myself, a tune at the intersection, the juncture between piano and me.

By now the piano was leaping about the room, jumping, and the musician followed it, lifted up by the force of its inspiration, and the floor, wife to the husbanded coupling of the amorous piano, shuddered. The piano leaped, jumping several feet off the ground, followed always by the enthusiastic composer/musician, a smile on his sweaty face put there not so much from the genius of his composing but from the force of his playing and the vitality of the piano. See, he thought, if I beat him, pound the bejeebers out of him, he will release his secret, shower me with his talent. But the music, if music it could be called, only got worse, and the higher the piano leaped, as if ready to pounce on a waiting lover, the worse the music got. At some point it seemed to the musician that the tune could not become worse, that the very pit of awfulness had been plumbed; but he was soon shaken from this belief when the piano rose higher yet, clumped down harder, and the later tune made better what before had been bad. Why does this thing not break through the floor? the musician thought. Now the piano was almost flying, confined only by the room and the weight of the musician who managed to rise with it and keep his feet on its pedals, bumping against the ceiling, banging against the walls, shaking and shuddering the very bones of the Building. The piano careened around the room, the musician holding on, being dragged up, around, and down each time he struck the keys. He could not stop, any more than could the man on the blue guitar, playing a tune that, like us, is not what we are. The piano was a thing crazed, a wild beast recently caged (and yet in banging around the apartment nothing broke, no plaster fell). The heavy strokes of this wooden megalith shook the Building, bounced off walls and ceilings, dropping only occasionally to the floor.

As the piano flew through the air (short local hops, an uncommon carrier), the musician thought, I am St. John the Baptist parched in the desert, St. Augustine refuting the Manichaean dualism of light and dark, Noel Coward on a lark. The blues, a fugue, a polka, sonata, ragtime—all collapsed in a horrid parody. The flying piano, jumping, leaping, a winged instrument, a thing not of the earth but a creature of the air—ethereal tunes of the most awful sort, so bad that the pounding on the door and ceiling (floor) sounded better than this mephitic bit of dross—began to sound louder and louder. But even as the piano rose, the tune fell. The music plummeted to the floor with a crash; the notes buried themselves in the floorboards. "I had in mind a certain lightness," the musician said to absolutely no one, five feet in the air. "Not this weightiness that has descended on my music." He played with continued fervor, all fists, elbows, feet, and at times knees, banging, gouging, walloping his symphony from the skittish baby grand.

Lowell vaulted up the stairs. This had gone too far. The musician was ensconced in noise. He threatened to encapsulate the Building. He found a crowd outside the musician's door. They were taking turns pounding on the door.

"I must open the door," he shouted through the keyhole at the musician. "This noise must stop."

The musician, in midair, turned to the door. He played a waltz, a toccata, a fugue, the piano dipping and twisting with the music. "I am composing," the musician said. "I cannot be disturbed, even by well-wishers." He spoke with a certain assurance, with the composure of a man seated on a piano stool five feet in the air, the piano at his fingertips, trembling, meaning not to antagonize or to harshly criticize, but to state the rights of the artist. "The door must be opened," Lowell repeated, "and the noise must come to a halt." The musician snorted. "You cannot stop the music once it starts. You must let it run the course." And now with trills and arabesques and harmonic chords he exercised the piano fully. The piano turned and bowed in the air, a charming coquette, a pleasing if shy bit of fluff, lighter than air and lighter in air, a firefly. The musician scarcely realized that he, that they, were *up there*. This baby grand, once heavy, now lighter than could be imagined, sparkled, the musician thought, with sound. "The beauty of it," he said, "is more than enough to wrench your heart. Listen to the notes. They transport you, the melody comforts you. The harmony is to ecstasy what love is to lust; there is a judicious restraint to the harmonics, and the countermelody is nearly fatal and at the same time nearly exquisite."

The last speech merely inflamed the door bangers. Lowell produced a key, and the musician could hear it, miraculously, above the din and clamor. As the door opened, the music stopped, the piano dropped, and the madonna, secure on the table, leaped off her perch, poised briefly in the air, and then settled back, landing rock straight, without a quiver.

The musician looked up at the crowd around his door. He smiled, in silence, and cocked his head, as if he had forgotten to say something or was carefully listening for something he had forgotten to hear. The crowd at the door remained silent, and Lowell, who had a long speech prepared, a speech that he meant to deliver to the musician but that was meant to be heard by the tenants in the Building, said nothing. (The speech left him, took wings, settled in the air, out of reach, where the piano had been.)

36

THE commissioner was furious—not just because he had been mugged in front of Lowell's Building by three teenagers who took his four-hundred-dollar plum-colored pigskin briefcase and in knocking him to the ground tore his Oxxford suit (six hundred dollars) and scuffed his British Walkers (two hundred fifty dollars the pair, shoelaces extra but shoebag included). He was furious because he lost the papers in his briefcase, valuable papers, embarrassing papers, which floated tantalizingly beyond his grasp when he had been upended, flying up as he flew down, and though his Aquascutum raincoat (unlined, three hundred seventy-five dollars; lined, four hundred forty-five dollars) protected him from the vicissitudes of the sidewalk, it did not help the dapper commissioner reach these papers, which scattered in a sudden squall that descended on the block, a squall that pushed papers in different directions. By the time he decided which of the embarrassing papers to go after, they were gone. He was still cursing when a young man came out of the Building and helped him to his feet. The commissioner was surprised, almost shocked. In lieu of thanks, he spent the next three minutes agreeing with whatever it was the samaritan said.

Lowell had been in court trying to evict one of the tenants for nonpayment of rent. The judge not only evicted the tenant, he sentenced him to six months at Rikers Island because he didn't like the tone of the tenant's answers. The judge delivered his opinion standing on the magistrate's chair, waving his arms and screaming, yelling obscenities at the hapless tenant who was Haitian and didn't understand English. The judge later explained to Lowell, in a calm voice and measured tones of modesty, that he was being transferred from Housing Court to Family Court and consequently wanted to be prepared, mentally and physically, for the change.

"It's a jungle out there," he told Lowell. "You've got to stiff them before they stiff you."

He threw a short uppercut with his right arm, patting his biceps with the palm of his left hand.

"Look, if they come here, they're guilty," he told Lowell. "That's for starters. Bring your cases to me no matter where I am and I'll get you a conviction. They're all guilty. And if they don't answer to me, they can answer to the judge." He patted his calf, around which was strapped a snub-nosed thirty-eight.

"I leave the sob sisters for the other judges. Me, I get a conviction every time. What good is it being a judge if you can't find them guilty? What the hell is this country coming to if we can't throw them all in jail? Bunch of candy-ass liberals want to set them all free. You bring your tenants to me. I know how to deal with those candy asses."

Suddenly he bent down and whipped out the thirty-eight.

"Speed is what you need. If I can't get a conviction, I can always blow them away with this. Resisting arrest, insolence to duly constituted authority."

He lifted up his pants leg and put the gun back in its holster.

"Want to see my dogs? I keep them in my chambers. Pit bulldogs, all trained to kill. They go for the jugular. I'll show those candy-assed liberals who they're dealing with."

Lowell thanked him and left. The Haitian was being led away in handcuffs. A short pregnant woman who wore a kerchief around her head and had on a beige cotton dress and fluffy slippers was crying and speaking in patois, trying to hold on to the chained Haitian. The judge, hearing the commotion, withdrew his thirty-eight from its holster and tried to shoot her, but he was restrained by a court officer who told Lowell that the judge had gone over the edge about a year ago, when a dope dealer he had convicted appeared in court on the last day of his trial and spit lighter fluid on him, lighting a match to it as he did. The right half of the judge's face had been burned, and a jagged scar ran from his temple to his neck. While in flames, the judge had vaulted over the bench at the dope dealer and tore out his throat with his fingers. "They're going to remove him one of these days," the officer said. "But they're short of judges, and he does get convictions."

After watching the Haitian chained to seven other offenders being put in the rear of a Department of Corrections van, Lowell walked back to his office. He noticed the Criminal Court Building with its long, wide steps, where the New Africa Committee was holding a demonstration to demand that the United States turn over to them parts of seven southern states as reparations for their time of enslavement. Farther down, on the steps of City Hall, there was a confrontation between demonstrations. The followers of the Lubavitcher Reb, who were demonstrating against autopsies in Israel, insisted that their permit was from eleven-thirty until twelve-thirty, while the Armenians who were protesting the arrival of the Turkish president argued that their permit plainly said noon to one P.M. A small group of overweight Irish-Americans from Queens, clearly outnumbered by the two groups of demonstrators, looked for British faces they could throw bombs at. Lowell believed in all their causes, plus others not present: animal rights, reparations for Japanese-Americans interned in concentration camps during World War II, land and money for native American Indians, free the imprisoned Haitians, women's reproductive rights, save the whales (and the porpoises, dolphins, sea turtles), Kurdish rights in Iran and the U.S.S.R., freedom of speech for Russian dissidents . . . the envelopes poured into his mail slot daily, pleading, imploring ("Look at the pictures inside only if you have a strong stomach," a baby seal in the snow, white against white, battered senseless, a bubbling of red pouring from an eye), beseeching him to give ("even a dollar, a quarter, anything so that this crippled child . . ."), pleading with him to write ("Unless Congress hears otherwise, hundreds of wild mustangs in the canyons of Utah are doomed . . ."). He embraced them all, and more, but he would not give them a penny. Their outrage, the injustices perpetrated on them, showed the rest of us that evil still existed in the world, and Lowell wanted people to be reminded of evil, *he* wanted to be reminded of it so he could feel superior to it, so he could feel better, exalted, elevated, because he knew that *he* would never batter a seal senseless off Prince Edward Island or trap a wild mustang in Utah and sell it to the cannery for dog food or keep a Kurd from practicing his religion. And it was important to know that there were others who would do this, who in fact did this precisely because they knew that he would not, that he disapproved. Where, in fact, would justice be without injustice? Where would human rights be without a blatant disregard for them? Where would full stomachs be without empty? Where would hope be without despair? Love without hate?

He stepped into the elevator at 100 Gold Street positively bathed in warmth and suffused in well-being at the thought of all that suffering, all that injustice. Our jobs, he thought, depend upon it. If landlords didn't act so outrageously, if tenants weren't so vicious, there would be no need for his department—a perfect world had no justice or fairness because it had no injustice or unfairness. He smiled, walking down the halls, and it didn't bother him that as he walked heads popped out of offices to stare at him. He smiled back, dismissed their attention, and was determined to attack some paperwork that had piled up on his desk, to make short shrift of the undelivered cans of paint, Sheetrock, plumbing pipe, wiring, and steam risers.

When he walked into his office a crowd stood outside his door. He looked up at them and smiled. Someone giggled and pointed at his legs. He looked down at them. He still had the regulation number of legs and wondered what the object of their curiosity was. Then the crowd parted as Hector wheeled into his office. For a moment, Hector said nothing; he looked at Lowell with his chin in the palm of his hand and his elbow on the arm of the wheelchair. His hair was dyed orange, shot through with streaks of pink. Lowell had seen it once before. ("It's just a phase I'm going through," Hector told him.)

"Hey, English," he finally said, "didn't I tell you?"

Lowell looked up. Tell him what? What was he talking about?

"You thick or something? Didn't I tell you?"

"What."

"You are thick. I been teaching you and you still fuckin' up. When you gonna learn?"

"I know it all, Hector."

"You know shit."

"I know more than some crippled Puerto Rican."

An ashtray just missed him, a heavy glass ashtray with five corners, one of which stuck in the corroding Sheetrock behind him, holding the ashtray out from the wall.

"Your mother sucks syphilitic monkey dung, English. We seen the tapes. Everybody in the department seen the tapes, you cuntlicker."

The crowd outside the office pressed close to the glass. "Whip his ass, Hector," someone yelled.

"I'm sorry," Lowell said, "that was . . ."

He heard someone shouting. "Get back to work. Everybody get back to work."

Sanchez, in a yellow neck brace, stormed into his office, turning Hector and his wheelchair around and pushing him out. He slammed the door.

"Well, you did it this time," he said to Lowell. "I tried to protect you, but Hector is right, you are just too fucking stupid. The commissioner wants to see you. Now."

The commissioner had a corner office, surrounded by a warren of clerks. Outside his office, imprisoned along the wall, were hundreds of forms. There was a patina of seediness to the desks and chairs and filing cabinets, their edges worn down and their corners rounded off. The ceiling tiles were stained with water leaks; squares of linoleum were ripped, worn, peeling; chairs were missing casters, and desks, drawer handles; the plastic over the fluorescent lights was yellowed and gritty.

The commissioner's office was immaculate. It had a bright blue carpet on a floor half the size of a tennis court. A huge desk, composed of dark wood, inlaid with a leather top, surrounded by brass piping, was ensconced in one corner of the room, and behind it, on the wall, were nautical prints—clipper ships, barques, scows, early multiple-smoke-stacked steamships. The windows of the commissioner's office opened onto the river, at least the river could be seen from them, and one could imagine replicas of the boats in the prints sailing or steaming up the river. A brass lamp with two green glass shades stood on the desk, in front of a digital phone with seven lines. There was a leather sofa, a coffee table, three oak and leather chairs, five Charles Eames chairs, four padded card-table chairs folded up against the wall next to a long oiled oak table that gleamed in the dim light that came in through the partially pulled-back draperies.

The seal of the city, in gold, was emblazoned on the blue carpet, and Lowell was struck by its brightness, as if it were made of gold sprinkles. The blue carpet looked as if it had just been cleaned. The nap of the carpet lay in one direction; when chairs were pulled up to the desk, the legs pulled the nap in the other direction, leaving darker blue tracks in the carpet.

Lowell was directed toward one of the leather chairs. It was a chair designed for a huge bottom, with stiff springing in the seat, so stiff there hardly seemed to be any give. The commissioner was facing away from him, looking out the window, talking to someone on the phone.

"It's the mayor," Sanchez whispered to Lowell.

From the back the commissioner could have been forty to seventy, though his hair looked a little too thick for seventy; it was fluffed out, yet neat, each hair somehow belonging to the hair next to it. When he spun around in the chair, Lowell was shocked at how young he looked —maybe thirty-five. He was a young man with blow-dried hair, a dark pin-striped suit, and a black eye, a deep purple black that surrounded his eye like a hurricane.

"Is this the man in the tapes?" he asked Sanchez.

Sanchez nodded.

The commissioner looked at him and scratched his chin. Lowell was amazed at how, in such a short period of time, so many people had stared at him and scratched their chins, as if he carried a chin-scratching virus.

"What tapes?" Lowell asked.

"No one told him?"

"We assumed . . ." Sanchez began, letting the sentence trail off, feeling that what he didn't say was more accurate than anything he could say.

"What tapes?"

"I don't mind the tapes," the commissioner said, and turning to Lowell, "You should mind the tapes, but I don't."

"What tapes?"

"Do you want to see them?"

"No."

He knew what tapes. Just as he knew what pictures. But he couldn't figure out where the camera was and how he could have done what he had done with Kazima without knowing about a camera.

"You can rent these kinds of things," the commissioner said, "or buy them. I personally don't care one way or the other, but I wouldn't want the papers to get ahold of these tapes. They might want something from us to keep it out of the papers. We don't know. We got the tapes in the mail with no note."

The commissioner scratched his chin; Lowell's virus was in full flower, at the apogee of its season.

"It puts us in a compromising situation."

"Are you sure you don't want to see the tapes?"

"Am I recognizable?"

The commissioner laughed.

"By someone who knows you intimately . . . and by someone who doesn't."

He felt impaled, skewered. The pictures he didn't mind, but tapes, videotapes, pictures of him moving from one situation to another, walking, standing on his tiptoes, moving his hands; the look on his face as they coupled and uncoupled, a look that he imagined would somehow be unhappy, a stressful look, and yet he had thought the situation should have been, was, one of joy. Kazima had kept smiling the entire time, as if she had been expecting a knock on the door, a telegram, had just won the lottery. He would have to watch the tapes to see how he looked, to see what sort of character he exuded, whether he exhibited grace under pleasure, how he moved.

"We don't know what they want from us. They'll probably tell us shortly."

"We could fire Lowell here and make it retroactive. Then we'd be in the clear."

"Maybe we should wait to see what they propose."

"What if it's outrageous?"

"I'd like to ask a question," Lowell said. "How did everybody in the department get to see them?"

The commissioner shrugged his shoulders.

"It's hard to keep this kind of thing secret. I mean you lock it up —that doesn't mean much. There's no real security in the department . . . but don't worry, we're working on it."

"I'm not worried," Lowell said. "It's just that I didn't know you had this many lechers in the department."

Sanchez chuckled.

"People like a little laugh now and then. They're curious. It's good for morale. And I suppose if I were on that tape you would not watch?"

Lowell said nothing. He imagined Sanchez's penis, like his neck, in a cast.

"If I were you, I'd watch. It's natural to watch."

"If you're a pervert."

"I wouldn't exclude yourself."

The commissioner cleared his throat, and Lowell noticed his fingers searching for his chin, scratching the air.

"I don't mind the tapes," the commissioner said. "It's simply a question of what they want from us. We can deal with that. We know how to deal with those people."

"Revolutionaries," Sanchez hissed.

The commissioner ignored him.

"But the mugging bothers me."

"What mugging?"

"They took my case, my papers, right in front of the Building. Don't you have any security?"

"We don't have a budget for that."

"The attaché case they can have. But the papers inside, that could be a problem."

He found his chin.

"We would like to get those papers back, Lowell. We would like you to retrieve those papers. You can keep your job if you get those papers . . . uncopied."

"What if I don't want the job?"

"You have the job. That's your job."

"I can change jobs."

"Not in this city. We can get certain things in the paper that would make it difficult for you to get any job in this city. But then, perhaps you have a private source of income."

He smiled at Lowell, and Lowell noticed what a pleasant smile he had, how not just the corners of his mouth but his entire mouth slanted up, the crinkle lines at the corners of his eyes, like miniature smiles, and the way his nose wrinkled, just slightly.

"Are you threatening me?"

"Of course not. That's illegal. We're bound by law."

"I can look for the papers."

"Good."

"Can I have the tapes?"

"Sure. I'll even let you borrow a Sony Betamax."

"No thanks."

"They're quite good, really. You have nothing to be ashamed of. And that woman is, how shall I put it, engulfing. Yes, that's it. Positively engulfing. An amazing woman. An amazing performance."

Lowell stood up. No one else did. He looked around, expecting someone to hand him the tapes. No one did. He didn't know if he should ask for them again or just wait.

"Did you lose something?"

"No . . . not yet."

He walked toward the door.

"Please try," the commissioner said, "to keep to the construction schedule. It's very important to us to repair that Building."

"Things move slowly."

"Just mention my name. Have them call me if you don't think they're fast enough."

There was something else he wanted to say, but he said nothing, and Lowell stood rooted to the spot he had walked to, midway between the commissioner's desk and the door.

"You will find those papers."

"Yes."

"Good."

"What about the tapes?"

"Check with the property clerk."

"Property clerk?"

"Police department."

"Uh huh."

"But I don't think the police have seen it. Their Betamax is broken."

Lowell retrieved the tape from a blasé property clerk in a wire cage in the basement of the police department building. It looked like wide cassette tape. He turned on the garbage disposal when he got back to his apartment and, unwinding the spool slowly, fed the tape to the machine, listening to the high-pitched gurgle as it chewed and cut the tape to tiny specks, burped them up, and then flushed them down the drain while he turned on the water. He rolled the spool out, using his finger as an axis, until the disposal had consumed the entire electronic memory of his tryst, and then jammed the empty spool into it and heard a grinding complaint coming from the machine.

Too late, he now remembered he had promised himself he would watch the tapes, a small treat, to see if he exhibited grace under pleasure, to see how he moved from position to position, to test the smile, or smiles, or lack of, that greeted each situation. The bits of that electronic erotica were floating in the sewer, about to be washed out to sea to join the giant clump of sludge that floated somewhere off Atlantic City or the Grand Bank, a thick goo of human pleasure, rotting in the water. What he had left were the photographs of him and his wife, ex-wife, making love. She had left them behind in the frenzy of a past lust, and they told him nothing. He burned them in the ashtray and sat watching the tiny black molten bits of plastic in the heavy glass with the same fascination with which he would watch the dying embers in a fire. The record of that great broad woman, Kazima, whose body had held his penis, and had ransacked him of pleasure, was, as far as he knew, gone. So were his wife, his children, and the commissioner's papers, a concatenation whose significance eluded him. Substitute porpoises for the papers, and its meaning, as far as he knew, would remain the same.

37

A naked lady appeared on Eastern Parkway one morning heading toward Grand Army Plaza. Male-driven traffic, tantalized, slowed but didn't stop. It circled around the arch (a huge stone monolith featuring statues of Lincoln and Lee over whose heads rode the winged Goddess of Victory in her bronze chariot). Cars were backed up not just on Eastern Parkway but also on Flatbush (in both directions) and Union Street. She was a tall blond with long, hard legs and small, discrete breasts. She had a face that looked like a persimmon, too red for the body it stood on, with acne pits scattered across both cheeks. She walked with long, gliding steps, covering a lot of ground in a hurry, and yet she did not seem to be particularly rushed. In the crook of one arm she carried her clothes: boots, blue jeans, a western-style shirt, knitted vest, sheepskin coat, and knapsack. When she reached the fountain in the plaza, she stopped before a cavorting Poseidon as if she had remembered an errand, carefully laid her clothes at the edge of the pool, and stood before the larger-than-life god, immersed in some private ritual she chose to make public. Her hands joined palm to palm, raised to her face, she stood facing the tarnished statue, motionless, her slender legs touching at the calves and knees and upper thighs, the sun shining on her blond hair spotted with brown, as water tumbled over the statue's genitals and trident, over his metal beard and wickedly smiling face. The early morning light emphasized the crags in her face, the hills and valleys, the moonlike surface that surrounded her tight lips, small nose, and striking green eyes. Early drivers strained to get a look at her through the bushes that surrounded the fountain, and those behind them who knew nothing of a naked woman praying to the water god Poseidon honked and cursed at the sluggards in front who seemed inordinately fond of the fountain, the water, and the greenery around it. Poseidon, glaring down at her from his watery rock perch, seemed about to rush down and sweep her up in his great thighlike arms, tearing himself away from the rest of the statuary: several green-stained women joined back to back, in the same state of dress as the blond. Her homage, however, was not to these sisters but to the blustering foam-flecked god with the pointed beard and the three-pointed trident staff he plunged into the belly of a writhing sea monster at his feet. By the time the police came she was gone, or rather clothed, so that she was still tall and blond, but clothed, and instead of being astonishing, she was merely striking.

One morning she appeared in the entrance of the Building. Nobody had seen her come down the stairs; she had just appeared in the lobby, in her customary state of dishabille. The broken glass on the sidewalk did not seem to bother her, nor did the stares through the windows and on the street of the men and women who felt assaulted by her nakedness. Sometimes followed by hooting boys, catcalls, and cars reversing the wrong way on a one-way street, she would disappear as quickly as she appeared, finding hidden places to clothe herself and then resume her walk, and once clothed she did not only look different than when she was nude, she *was* different.

She appeared naked in front of the Building several times, sometimes at dusk, sometimes early in the morning, never at night. The urge to disrobe shook her at odd times: during a rainstorm, on a windy day, pelted by rain, her hair plastered about her shoulders and back, she made hurried strides around the neighborhood, walking with force and purpose, as if she were paid to do this. Dodging broken glass, dog shit, tin cans, and other objects too numerous and vicious to mention, she picked her way through garbage, almost dainty in her concern for her feet, a dispossessed queen tiptoeing back to her summer palace. Dogs quickly approached her and just as quickly backed off, having discovered in her a quality they did not wish to test. Men who tried to talk to her, who tried to grab her, found themselves holding on to nothing, somehow not being able to remember the interval between the time they first grabbed her, suddenly feeling an incredible chill, frostbite, and the time she slipped out of their grasp. But most men, especially those accustomed to having their way with women, were frightened of her. She flaunted what they were after, what they could have simply by opening their eyes, and yet by opening their eyes could never have. She disrupted block fairs, parades, weddings; her nudity was a knife that cut the event to the quick, that hastened its conclusion, shattered its premises. She came and went as the wind and knew just when to leave an event after the shock of her entrance wore off.

She disrupted work in the Building; Sheetrock wasn't taped, paintbrushes dropped; even the sniper, never a respecter of gender, gaped at this nubile blond as she wended her way around the garbage cans, nimbly stepping over oil spills and jagged tin cans.

Lowell was still being met with mixed reviews in the Building. The boiler worked; the hot water didn't. Then the hot water did, and the electric didn't. Then the electric did, and the roof leaked, and when that was fixed, when the boiler worked and the hot water came up in great scalding amounts (the temperature was turned down on the boiler to save energy) and the electric worked (Steckler having finished most of his arc welding) and the roof was dry, the Building settled into a holding pattern. Nothing was finished. The lobby was lit by bare bulbs dangling from extension cords. The Buick Roadmaster remained crumpled under the elevator, and the garbage in the courtyard was replaced by broken soda bottles. The naked woman was the least of his worries; but the tenants complained about her instead of the lousy paint job, the broken marble stairs (Lowell couldn't seem to get anyone to fix the marble; it was a lost art, this fixing of marble, nobody wanted to hear about stone, certainly not about cracks in stone), and the mysterious graffiti that suddenly appeared, like Egyptian hieroglyphics, in the lobby, halls, and stairwells. One warm spring night the smell of

Magic Markers wafted through the Building. The quiet squeak of felt tip on marble, plaster, and paint could be heard by everyone in the Building. Scrawls of words appeared in unknown languages, squashed words with their tops pressed down, words that turned into arrows and were promptly forgotten as words but became something else: spaghetti meanings, turf markings, snake language, dragon tongue. For Mama Jujubee it was the evil eye; for Abdul Karim a portent of Pakistani invasions; for Lowell it was gallons of ammonia, paint remover, alcohol, Zip-Strip. It grew, this scrawl, like fungus, a hydra-headed snake, until the walls and ceilings and stairwells were covered like a chain-link fence: thick, heavy black markings, some so thick that the markings dripped into lace, a tiny network of veins, a clogged delta. There were no curses, no names, no words he could make out. It reminded Lowell of some vines he had seen in the Okefenokee Swamp; there was nothing you could do to get rid of it. Having discovered its own strength, it was simply there. It existed to divide space, to hide naked walls. As fast as he had it cleaned, removed, painted over, it reappeared, sometimes as heavy, ponderous latticework; at other times it was light, frantic, and parts of words could almost be made out. Someone was peeing in the stairwells; the dank, acid scent wafted up the stairs. Then the hallway lights were stolen or broken. Garbage was placed in the hall and set on fire. The slowly burning grapefruit rinds, the burned coffee grounds, the latex condoms melting over empty boxes of Cap'n Crunch—it reminded Lowell of an archeological dig.

"Get ahold of the Building," Sanchez said. "You're losing it."

Sanchez was pasty white. His neck brace was strangling him.

"The commissioner almost loves you," he said. "But he wants that Building. He needs that Building."

Before Lowell could decide how to reverse the momentum in the Building, Hobson threatened to throw himself off the roof. "I'm coming down," he shouted to the tenants in the street, "airmail express. I'm coming down until you stop killing cockroaches." "Jump, you asshole, jump," someone shouted. Hobson looked bewildered. He had not expected to jump, he had not needed to jump, he only needed people to stop killing cockroaches, and now he was in a quandary. Should he sacrifice himself to these little beetles? Should he put his body in hostage to these nosy nesters? Before he could decide, the naked lady jumped on the parapet and, walking on her hands, went completely around the perimeter of the Building, her legs gracefully arched above her back, curved forward. Cheers rose from the street, and Hobson, forgetting about cockroaches and his oath to jump, forgetting everything about insects and their needs, saw only the upended legs of this magnificent creature as she circled around him, upside down, on the crumbling parapet. "That settles it," he shouted down to the crowd. "I no longer need to jump." "Jump, you asshole." But she disappeared, and Hobson was left with an empty roof and handprints in the tar from the gypsy children who had been nailed to the roof.

Lowell, while relieved, felt almost betrayed by his not jumping. It was as if Hobson had pledged himself to a public trust and then betrayed it. He still remembered the time the Scandinavian whore, the woman who would be Ingrid, had been launched off the roof just as he had come around the corner, and he had imagined her fall, gliderlike, onto the cement sidewalk. It had happened two years ago, and he was still filling out forms, and he knew that if Hobson should jump, taunted by the tenants who hated his cockroaches and held him responsible for every one of the evasive creatures they found in the Building, he would fill out forms for years, decades of forms.

Sanchez called him into his office.

"The commissioner wants to see you. He wants his forms."

"But I told you. I couldn't find them."

"You didn't tell me nothing. I didn't hear."

The commissioner was wearing a brown glen-plaid suit and a rust tie that flaunted a duck pattern. In his breast pocket was a blue silk handkerchief, and on his feet, brown wingtip loafers with tassels, which looked particularly good against the blue of the carpet. He was wearing the deepest-blue shirt Lowell had ever seen.

The commissioner was facing the window when Lowell walked in. He whirled around in his chair with such speed that Lowell thought he was going to continue spinning.

"My papers, my forms," he said.

Lowell shrugged his shoulders.

He thought he saw a clipper ship sailing down the East River.

"No forms? No papers? That's serious. That's too bad."

"I tried . . . used some contacts."

"Yes, yes, I'm sure."

The commissioner seemed distracted. He looked down at his suit and brushed off some imaginary lint. (Perhaps it was real lint put there for the sole purpose of being brushed off.)

"I hear you have a naked lady in your Building."

"Sometimes."

"We have four thousand buildings, and this is the first I ever heard about a naked lady."

"She's in the vicinity."

"What about the guy who loves cockroaches?"

"He doesn't really. He just wants the publicity."

"We don't want the publicity."

"He's harmless. He just wants attention."

"If he jumps, we'll get the attention, he'll get the burial."

The commissioner spun around in his chair, facing the window. He took out his handkerchief and tied it into a knot, twisting it around his finger. He spun around in the chair, gazing upward, a look of bewilderment on his face. Lowell felt he was looking for something on the ceiling.

"I'm just an old-shoe guy, Lowell," he said, "and you shouldn't look upon me as your boss, but as a friend who is always right. And right now you are in trouble."

Sanchez nudged him. Lowell wondered what that was supposed to mean. Sanchez had removed his neck brace, and his head flopped around as if it were about to fall off.

"We all like you, Lowell. Really, we do. Sure, you have some strange habits. But we're willing to overlook them. Right, Sanchez?"

Sanchez nodded, his head flopping.

"We don't want any gloomy, doomy types around here, do we, Sanchez."

Sanchez nodded again, and Lowell feared for his head.

"We're bureaucrats around here. Proud as punch about it, make no mistake. We don't apologize. We like what we do, Lowell, but we don't do what we like. Right, Sanchez?"

Sanchez nodded.

"We do what we have to. We don't set policy. We merely administer it. Right, Sanchez?"

Sanchez swallowed, unable to move his head. His eyes stared wildly at the ceiling and then dropped quickly down, so quickly it seemed they would fall over his cheeks.

"Your Building," he said, "is in danger of falling apart. That will not do."

He pronounced the last word as if he were a minister in a church. Lowell wondered what he was getting at. Sure the Building was going through some rough times, but it was a strange Building with strange tenants. Didn't they understand that? And what about the materials he had requested that never came, the security he asked for that never arrived, the endless delays in getting rehabilitation plans approved? None of that was his fault.

"You can't blame me . . ." Lowell started to say.

"Of course not. We don't blame you for anything. We don't blame anybody for anything anymore. We've all had sensitivity training here. I insist on it. It's done wonders for the department."

He smiled and thought about the training, thought about sensitivity and how sensitive he and everyone else was, and he felt this feeling fused the department into a glowing presence, as if there were no longer any department but in its place pure light, pure understanding.

"You see, Lowell, our job here is to wag our fingers. Yes, that's it. We wag our fingers. Sometimes we wag them yes, sometimes we wag them no. Yes or no. That's all we really have to do. That's all anyone asks of you. Very simple. All you have to do is look at a form and wag your finger at it . . . yes or no. That's not hard to understand, is it?"

Of course it was.

"No."

"I didn't think so. I knew you'd understand, even if we don't sometimes, because your understanding is predicated, a priori, on our understanding or not understanding. Do you understand?"

"I think it's almost clear."

"I knew you would."

Deliberately misanswering the question, Lowell thought.

"It's simply modern management theory. We have this incredibly sensitive network where we all respect each other's feelings. Right, Sanchez?"

Sanchez looked at him as if he had just swallowed a Coke bottle sideways.

"You mustn't look upon this as an inquisition. In the old days it might be that. Sort of a grand inquisition out of Dostoevski. But we don't blame, we don't indulge in recriminations. Because all that is an indulgence. We don't indulge. We facilitate. That's it, we facilitate, while wagging our fingers."

He seemed extremely satisfied with himself and smiled, not so much for Lowell's benefit as for the benefit of his own face, to ease the strain on his lips, to allow the cheeks room to flex, to stretch the eyebrows.

"And then, of course, we have this incredibly sensitive review board. If you feel slighted, if you feel wronged, they will take up your battle, they will push your cause. It's done wonders for the department, let me tell you. No more dictators here. Right, Sanchez?"

Sanchez had melted into his chair.

"About the Building," Lowell said.

"Forget T.I.L., forget the 235 Program, forget the H.I.P. Program. We're thinking artist housing in your Building. I just talked with the mayor this morning. He's got to do something for the borough presidents. Artist housing. Doesn't that have a nice ring to it? Everyone loves artists."

"What about the tenants in the Building?"

"They will have to leave."

"Where will they go?"

"We have other buildings."

"Who is going to tell them?"

"You, Lowell. You."

The commissioner sighed. By rights it was Lowell's sigh. He felt the commissioner had preempted him of his exhalation.

"But first," the commissioner said, "you have to get rid of the naked lady. The papers think it's a joke. We're not a joke, Lowell. It doesn't look good to be a joke. We want to be funny, human, sensitive as the next fellow or gal, but a joke, Lowell, is what we are not."

"She's hard to find."

"I trust you to do it."

"I'll try."

"Don't try. Do."

"It shouldn't be hard."

"Of course not. We like the can-do spirit here."

It sounded like he said "cat-doo" spirit.

The commissioner stood up. He was feeling expansive, majestic, overflowing with goodwill. He walked over to Lowell.

"Let me show you something," he said. "Let me show you how

many buildings we own, so you can grasp the magnitude of this problem, so you can understand some simple facts. One, there is a terrible housing shortage out there. Two, landlords are giving up on their buildings—they can't afford to keep up those rent-controlled buildings. I don't give a shit what the housing radicals say. Facts are facts. So we get the buildings. And we have to do something with them. Everybody is screaming at us to do something—politicians, radicals, tenants, landlords. Look at all those buildings out there."

He motioned toward the window, but as Lowell walked over, his eye was attracted to a traffic jam in front of 100 Gold Street and a growing circle of people who surrounded someone parading in front of their building. From where the commissioner and Lowell stood, they could make out the firm, shapely outline of a naked woman.

38

LOWELL got the writer an apartment in the Building.

"I want an apartment in the Building so I can write about it."

That piqued Lowell's imagination. He couldn't tell if the writer was a man or a woman, and didn't dare ask because it would be rude, and he was far from being rude, though perhaps not so far after all.

"A poet?" Lowell asked almost politely.

"Writer, prose," he/she said.

"Well, I hope you have fun writing."

"Writers don't have fun writing. They hate writing."

"Well, there's quite a story in this Building," said Lowell. "You should hear the stories people have to tell. It would amaze you."

"They all say that," the writer said. "They all say, 'You're a writer? Do I have a story for you.' It always turns out they don't have a story at all. What they have is something else. They have the dust from a story. They have a story that disappeared a long time ago. I have to find out where the story has gone. People don't realize that. People don't realize anything."

"I've got a great story for you," Lowell said.

"People always do that to writers. They never learn."

"Every day I could come and tell you a great story. A new story, a different story every day."

"Writers don't want to hear stories."

"If you like, I'll tell you the same story, but something new from the same story every day."

"I don't want to hear it."

"Things happen. You wouldn't believe the things that happen here. And then there's downtown. A mental ward. I have a commissioner who thinks he's going to be appointed mayor. He thinks the city is going to do away with elections to anoint him mayor. He's Catholic, Jewish Catholic, so he's got two voting blocs covered. On alternate days he can change the color of his skin and that covers the third. He's trying to learn how to eat chuchufritos. Did you ever eat chuchufritos?"

"No."

"You probably wonder why I'm telling you all this."

"No."

"Just like I thought. You're interested."

He/she yawned.

"Little signs tell me you're a caring person."

"I'm not."

"I don't care," Lowell said, "I'm dying to tell you this story. I'll burst if I don't tell it to you. It's about why I ran away from my wife, why she ran away from me. It's about the plumbing commune and the time I went mad and shouted into toilet bowls and swallowed a bottle of Demerol."

"I definitely don't want to hear that," he/she said.

"I'll tell you anyway. You should know. You'll need it for background material."

"There is no background material for this Building. Everything I want is on the surface."

"I'll tell you the story about the man in this Building who can change the color of his skin, almost at will."

"That I certainly don't want to hear. This is not a science-fiction story."

"This Building, the bricks came from Bulgaria. There is no water in Bulgaria so they hired gypsies to spit in the cement and make it stick. I'll tell you about the people buried in those bricks."

"I want to hear tax laws, records of violations."

"This is the human interest stuff I'm going to tell you."

"That will come from the statistics, from who stuck it to whom to get control of this Building. You can't manufacture warmth. Real warmth comes from the cold, from facts."

"I thought you said you didn't want warmth."

"I lied. Writers lie to suit their purpose. We can't be trusted."

"I thought writers told the truth."

"We do. We only lie on the little stuff. The important stuff, the stuff that explains how all this came about"—he/she waved his/her hand around the room—"that we tell the truth about. Trust us for explanations. Don't trust us for details. We use details to help with the explanations. We fudge a little to make the details clarify the explanations. Writers are logicians. We have no feelings. If we did, we would be in one of the artistic professions, something creative, like dancing. That's imagination. This is logic."

"How can I tell if you're telling the truth when you told me that you lie, and how do I know if you're not lying on this one?"

"You don't. If I was lying and told you I was lying whenever I told you something then you'd know that what you heard from me would be the truth. Now if I told the truth and told you I was lying, that would be a contradiction in terms. I couldn't be lying. So either way, you have to say, logically, that I'm telling you the truth."

"I have an old typewriter you can use."

"I have my own."

"Why not take it to please me?"

"We lost our manners a long time ago."

"Well, still, good luck."

"It's not luck. It's skill, talent, perseverance."

"Here it's luck."

Lowell left, wondering about his decision to rent to a writer. He had heard that they pay their rent late or else skip out on the rent, that they're paranoid, always imagining that everyone is against them. This one, anyway, had paid (his? her? its?) rent. He had two months' rent in his hand.

Lowell came back the next day.

"I feel I should explain something to you," he said.

"Don't bother."

"I have this urge to explain myself."

"Don't pay attention to urges."

"I have to talk. It doesn't make much difference what I say, but I've got to talk. Someone must listen. You could write down what I say and then send copies to everyone. You could teach me how to write."

"They all say that. That's what they all say to writers," she/he said.

Lowell walked out of the apartment. He kept thinking about "God's Grandeur" and the grandeur of shook foil in Hopkins's poem, and how the Building reflected God's grandeur because Hopkins talked about the "ooze of oil," and he could feel that "ooze" in the Building, the oil of people's lives being squeezed into kitchens and closets.

He came back the next day.

"The commissioner wants to take me off the Building, give it to someone else."

"Why should I care?"

"You see, he thinks I'm not handling it right. Wants me to be firmer. But he doesn't understand these people, don't you see?"

"So what."

"He doesn't understand their desperation!"

"So what."

"Why should they want to manage the Building when they can barely manage their lives? Something is missing here. He's got to understand that. I'm thinking of bombing his office."

"Don't do anything that would jeopardize my apartment."

"A small bomb. No one would get hurt. It would make a mess. He hates a mess more than anything."

He/she sighed. "You people," the writer said, "don't understand how it goes. Why are you always making it go in a way that it doesn't go? And then when we have to write about it, we have to write about it going in a way that doesn't go and that's the kind of writing that barely goes."

Lowell flexed his arm. He would talk with Tyrone. Tyrone wouldn't understand either, any more than the writer would, but Tyrone would not understand in a different way, and Lowell had need of that different way. Tyrone spoke to him in a way that showed that he cared and that he didn't care.

"I've never seen any of your writing."

"You probably won't. I'm a slow writer."

"How do I know you can write? Maybe I should throw you out of the apartment?"

"You can't now. I'd sue your ass off."

"I'd like to see some of your writing."

"You can't."

"I have to test it to see how good it is. Some big changes are going on in this Building. I want to see how well you can handle them. I've got to know that your writing shows openness to change; that it's flexible, innovative, creative."

"It's not, it won't, it can't."

"Tell me where you've published."

"Nowhere."

39

FORGETTING that he hadn't owned the Building in years, Haber returned. His mind took a time loop. The Building took a time loop. What was then, was now. "I am the forgotten owner," he told himself one morning. "I am the misplaced landlord." He was a completely religious man, Orthodox, who believed in the cabala and the transmigration of souls, and so it was only natural that he visit God, who was playing an out-of-tune electric organ on the Upper West Side in front of Zabar's. He wanted to have a talk with Her about his Building, and while She played "Nearer My God to Thee," in D minor (or what almost passed for D minor), and handed out Bible tracts wearing a pair of fingerless gloves that Tyrone had sold Her, Haber babbled on about his Building. She nodded at what he said, agreeing, mentioned God, which caused Haber to nod, and the conversation, which took place next to Tyrone's stand (gloves, hats, scarves—check it out—all colors, all sizes), was not so much a conversation in which bits of information or opinion were shared, or future sentences altered by previous sentences, but more a sort of battering ram of words, some of which were heard, but most of which were merely guessed at, read into, so that when Haber finished the conversation or thought he had finished the conversation, the esteemed Lady did an easy segue into "When the Blood of the Holy Virgin Lands on My Brow," leaving Haber confused.

He had presented his case quite succinctly. But if God didn't understand what he had to do with the Building, who would? If She could not incorporate into Her mental process the problems of cash flow, repairs, the cost of number six fuel oil, amortization, debt service, rent collections, and tenant deterioration, what then? Haber was Orthodox to the point of pain, could barely be criticized on this score, but clearly here was a situation that called for some outside religious help. Not religious conversion, but a little help, a nudge, assistance from one of the minor deities in one of the other religions that had more experience with this sort of thing, a somewhat more business-oriented religion than either Judaism or Christianity. Being in an expansive mood, eager to share his problem with another soul, Haber opened his heart to Tyrone. Tyrone suggested the Hindus, they had hundreds of available deities, you could always find the right one for this sort of work. Haber thanked him and vowed to return one day to buy a hat and some gloves.

He found a temple in Queens and consulted with the local priests. While not passing on to these holy men his specific plans for the Building, he nevertheless, in general terms, made it known that he was looking for a solution to a very local problem. The priests said it would take months to explain their religion; nevertheless, they did offer help. Hinduism had always been involved with, though not necessarily relied on, local deities—demons, ghouls, godlings, spirits, ghosts. Perhaps one of them, they said, would be suitable for this work. One that was peculiarly local to the borough of the Building. How, Haber asked, will I find such a thing? The priests shrugged their shoulders. That, they said, is up to you. But whatever you find you can be sure that it will be a woman. Men, they added, have little stomach for that sort of thing.

Affairs of the flesh prompted Haber to visit Forty-second Street, but he was depressed by the women he met. They all looked so used, even the young ones. There was something too sloppy, too insistent about them. He approached several of them: the young, the almost young, those with boyish bodies, those whose bodies looked as if they had undergone some rearrangement. The results were the same: inappetence. He felt that if he put his penis in one, he might never see it again. It was an organ he had some fondness for.

Haber went home and prayed. Then he stopped. He realized that this was the sort of thing that God did not want to know about. "I wash my hands of the whole affair," he could hear Jehovah saying. "Do what you have to do but don't tell me about it." Even the Bible had second thoughts, and that's what God had invented man for.

The apparition appeared through a double set of French doors at his home: a tall blond naked lady. He blinked his eyes. It was not an apparition. Tall, blond, still naked, she stood beyond his reach, tantalizing him through the glass. He was worried that his wife and the neighbors might see her. Then he realized she was standing outside, naked in the snow. Perhaps she had wandered over from Kings County Hospital; he was a good twenty-minute walk from the psychiatric ward. That was unlikely. Someone would have called the cops. Perhaps someone would have done the same here too, except that the bushes the lunatic had planted in his front yard early one morning before he shot himself with a pearl-handled revolver blocked a view of her from the street. Haber rushed to the French doors, threw them open, did the same to the second set, and stood on the edge of a field of snow, staring at the woman who was still naked. He invited her in, but she refused. They talked in the snow. Haber wanted to put his hands on her, but there was something muscular and chilling about her; she was taller than he was, and he had the feeling that if he tried she was well versed in the Oriental arts of twisting some sensitive part of his body.

When she appeared in the Building, there was a noticeable cooling of the boiler. While the temperature outside rose, slightly, indeed almost reached melting, the temperature inside dropped, slightly, as if a cold breath had been released from the walls and hovered over the tenants. Some called her the Queen of Ice, blaming her for the chill; others said it was Haber. Small parts were missing from the boiler, they ran out of fuel; Tontine had tried to repair some steel parts with wood, and then, cursing because he was unable to do so, set the boiler on fire, clogging the chimney with soot and fouling the burner. Singiat-Sing Dan Dinphuir denied it was the Ice Queen. "It is the demon ghost dragon come to take his revenge."

"It's a lot of shit, that's what it is," said Willy. "They're trying to drive us out of the Building by withholding heat. Let's drive them out by withholding rent."

Haber was finding it difficult to collect the rent, probably because he no longer owned the Building. He pleaded, threatened, promised heat as soon as he got a boiler part from a foundry in Pennsylvania. "No rent, you cut your own throats," he told a group of tenants. They stoned him, egged on by the Wilson Sister, who had just recently been released from the hospital after having been contorted into a knot that had taken weeks to get out of. "There's no Workers' Compensation on that either," she said.

The musician (the composer), an ace Roman Catholic, hummed himself into a trance, recalled his novenas, his retreats at a monastery in upstate New York where they made wine and bred police dogs, his Our Fathers and his Hail Marys, and summoned up the Madonna of Heat, sometimes known as the Madonna of Heat and Hot Water, or the Madonna of Nie Zbyt Drogi Mieszkame after the Polish saint whose reincarnation she was. Where the Queen of Ice was tall, she was short, where the queen was thin, she was fat, where the queen was naked, she was swaddled in rags. Where one glided, the other waddled, where one was silent, the other talked, and where one was distant, elusive, sterile, the other was always close by, somewhat bothersome, a prolific breeder.

The Queen of Ice glided through the hallways at night. She was unapproachable. The deaf-mute, inflamed with passion at the sight of her nakedness, had approached her on the stairway, pants at the ready, and as he was about to grab her was tossed down the stairs. His blood froze. The terror of her attack brought bubbles to his lips as he tried to talk, struggling with gasps of air. Some muggers, waiting in the lobby for the Wilson Sister and seeing this Nordic apparition, followed her. One of them had his wrists broken; the other had three fingers bent flat the wrong way against the back of his hand. All of the broken parts were frozen. She was strong and secure in her movements. But she was not quite naked. There were reports that she wore fluffy slippers. A cold woman, a virgin, impeccably undressed, with irreproachable manners, the Ice Queen bowed before no one. She had a sled, some said, pulled by a pack of stray dogs, who whisked her from apartment building to apartment building in the dead of night. All she needed to do was tap boilers with her hand, barely touch them, and these huge engines of heat would collapse, mortally wounded, the molecules slowed, caught, strangled, so that the heat was squeezed out of them. The colder the weather, the more she whipped her stray dogs to a frenzy, driving them from building to building, insanely jealous of basement warmth. She had a chilling effect on burners, caused ball bearings to fail, jets to clog, flames to go out. She could freeze water with a wave of her transparent hand, rupture fuel tanks, put clogs in steam pipes. When the borough was tilted away from the sun and the temperature dropped, she exulted. There were those who suggested she only had sex with her stray dogs, some of whom were better endowed than men.

Her sworn enemy is that fat tart who gorges on pizza, pasta, pepperoni sausage: the Madonna of Heat. She devours spaghetti, spumoni, scungilli, loves tortoni, can't get along without her afternoon helping of Sacher torte, is helpless before cannelloni, stuffs her mouth, face, fingers with marzipan, punctuates everything with linzer torte, smears on the grenache, dives into enchiladas, is simply ecstatic about éclairs, will kill for Bavarian creams, crullers, lusts after gugelhupf, stollen, and streusel, is partial to pastillage, likes puddings steamed, fried, boiled, baked (but never frozen), is mad for frangipane, could live on braunschweiger, wiener schnitzel, and weinschaum custard, crazy about spaetzle, sherbet, schnitzels, schnecken, schmierkase, and schaumtorten, and washes everything down with sidecars, toddies, Tom Collinses, or else spritzes it down with screwdrivers, silver fizzes, and stingers. Food is fuel. Food is warmth. Food is heat. The madonna burns it all in her own little furnace, metabolism cranked up, sausage-fat legs and bread-chunky arms pumping as she walks. Fat no longer applies to her. She is round, a thing to itself, built low to the ground, with a center of gravity that is untippable and a drive for heat that is unstoppable. This little Mediterranean fireball flounces her skirts and blouses, sweaters, scarves, pants, sashes, and stockings while she walks, uses all of her many chins when she talks. She grabs, pulls, pushes, tugs, cajoles, can be seen down on her knees, legs, back, in the muck, the dirt, the cellar damp nursing a cold boiler back to life, breathing the glow of heat into a dying furnace, striking fire in the clogged orifice of a burner, blowing out the congested contents of a stuck flue, wrapping her legs, thighs, belly, arms, breasts around a pipe—driving it insane for heat. This loud, raucous, smelly ball of sweat will open up the furnace deep between her legs and let the Bessemer of her lust revive a broken-down boiler. (Even a passionless burner picks up when her heat-filled moistness is near.) What is cold steel against this glow, this licking flame, this red-hot madonna? A bustling, brawling, bumbling lover of men . . . fecund, fertile, and yet, heavens! a bona fide madonna.

The Building is caught in this holy war, this Jihad of temperatures, this monstrous conniving of north and south, heat and cold, blue and red.

At times warm, a whisper of heat, a faint hiss of steam escapes into the apartments. At times cool, excessively so, a cold stillness comes over the engine of heat. It lies dormant. And at times a sort of neutral temperature, or a mixture, part heat, part cold, blended in equal amounts, escapes from the boiler and makes its way through the pipes. The pipes bang and crackle. A loud clanking can be heard from the engine room. The Ice Queen and the Madonna of Heat are wrestling.

In many ways it is a dream match, a match, as they say, "made in heaven."

The madonna, rushing with the fury of her shouting, bowls over the Ice Queen, who slides backward on her back of ice. She rises, all in a glide, and sends a terrific chopping kick to the midsection of that hot little hussy. The madonna keels over in pain, lets out a yowl, scrapes her knee on the boiler room floor, dirties her many skirts, curses and rises, huffing, in pain, bruised in some important part of her pudgy body. She rushes this freezing Norsk and clamps her teeth about the creature's ear, wraps her sweaty arms and legs around her body. She bites down hard, grinds. One gets a sense of flesh parting, of blood, if you want to call it that, coming. The Ice Queen, this regal lady, being held thus and bitten by this sweaty cockroach, this fire ant, suppresses a cry. To see the Ice Queen on the floor, her elegance encumbered, her long, beautifully kept blond hair enmeshed in grease and the sweaty armpits of this little hot-headed Sicilian, gives one pause. Why must the lovely suffer . . . even if they bear us no good? The Ice Queen, emotions barely in check, controls her nascent tears and, working her arms around, arches her body and with one heave tosses the fiery little greaseball to the other side of the basement. Suet collides with brick, producing a nasty thud, a bruising bump, a patch of blue and red, that dazes the madonna. Both rise. The battle, far from over, is far from won.

The madonna, sweating, an Italian wrestler in Lorenzo de' Medici's clothes, has the Ice Queen in a headlock and begins to apply pressure. The white queen, her Nordic eyeballs bulging (but still able to contain a sense of beauty), begins to sag under the relentless pressure of the hot little pepper from the south.

A trickle of steam escapes from the boiler. A faint fog of warmth, the passion of pipes and well-fed boilers seeps into the radiators and the acrid, drying smell of steam heat makes its way into a few apartments. Tyrone, spread out on two of his thirty-seven radiators, imagines that he is singing. Hobson does sing, a song with no words, a song that Abdul Karim believes is the sign for Pakistanis to take over the Building, as soon as the paraplegic stops sending out her mephitic smell. The Wilson Sister revels in the heat; Glasho is amused by it. The musician pays homage to the Pope at his portable shrine with the blinking electric lights, thirty-three candles, running water, and the verses of the Bible written, in a shaky hand, on thirty-three pushpins (with especially wide heads) placed directly over the candles. Tonton Tute, however, will have no truck with the Pope. He knows it is the work of voodoo, the work of Mama Jujubee.

But the queen is no knave to failure. She reaches up to grab the sweaty little tart's fat jowls and pulls her head around. The madonna screams, keeps the headlock, but feels she must give it up, then does, much quicker than expected. Oh blessed Mary Mother of God! She is tossed, with much force, against the boiler. Dazed, she lies in a heap, curled around the burner, an oil line running under a fat thigh. Now the Queen of Ice rolls her over on her back, preferring to apply a hold that will keep her at some distance from this dripping madonna. She swings the fat little arms about, twists them, along with the legs, and ties them in a knot at the wrists and ankles, a complicated arrangement but a rather effective one. Even the least amount of pressure extracts great pain from the sweaty Italian. And the Queen of Ice is not shy about applying pressure.

Oh Jesus! Oh God have Mercy! Oh Mother Mary and the Blessed Saints!

The pain is considerable, and this little heat pump feels it the length and width of her body, a pain that builds upon itself.

The flame goes out in the burner. The boiler stops. The water freezes. The steam turns to fog, to ice crystals. The pipes and radiators cool, turn cold, become bitter. An ice storm grips the Building; an Arctic hush silences conversation. Even Haber cannot speak.

The madonna is getting her ass whipped. No two ways about it. The little Mediterranean floozy with her flouncy skirts and her floozy makeup is all in a heap on the basement floor, her arms and legs twisted into a grotesque knot, a constant pressure being applied by the blue-white Nordic goddess, the Ice Queen. Searing tears of pain, not pity, appear on her face, and the aftertaste of her most recent meal, a lascivious gallimaufry of meats and sweets, is burped up between wrenching muscle spasms.

The Ice Queen places a finely turned ankle too close to the madonna, and the southern virgin imagines that it is a gaily festooned tower of shimmelkassen and takes a generous bite out of the frothy, sugary concoction. If the Queen of Ice had it in her to yell, she would, rending the air with one of her delicious icy screams, but this Nordic lady, this queen of control, holds it in, choosing instead to suffer, to melt.

A faint whisper of steam escapes into the heating system. The madonna bites down harder, reaching for muscle, tendon, bone. She chews her way through gristle, reaches calcium. The Queen of Ice twists the madonna's stubby little arms and legs as far off course as she can, willing to snap, break, crack, splinter, and split apart whatever it is that attaches the madonna's appendages to her body. But the increased pressure, yes, the pain of it, causes the fertile virgin to gnaw all the harder, like a rat testing its teeth on electric insulation.

More warmth, a subtle gift of heat, wafts into the fifty-eight apartments, a present from the Santa Claus of steam. The Building rises, shakes itself, feels its circulation.

Haber goes down in the basement to see what the problem is, or rather what the problem isn't. He finds the Titans of Temperature at a standoff. The Queen of Ice, her ankle a pulpy mess of flesh and blood being feasted upon by the madonna, holds the virgin tart's hands and legs in the same position, still trying to extract as much pain as she can from the situation. But the floozy, her epicurean lust inflamed, pays little attention to the pain and continues her gnawing. Heat, searing bolts of flame shoot up the Ice Queen's leg. It is an uncomfortable, unfamiliar feeling.

"What is this?" Haber asks. "What is going on?"

The women pause in their gnawing and bending and turn toward him.

"Heat, cold, heat/cold. What's going on? Make up your mind."

The women stare at him.

"I don't know what's going on," he says. "Nobody knows what's going on anymore."

Expected to talk, they say nothing.

"This is a free country, isn't it? I own this Building, don't I? I can do what I want to it, can't I?"

Haber didn't expect any answers. He never expected any answers. All he expected were questions, deep questions, the kind that remained with you for a long time, like beef gravy and hot potatoes.

"A decent profit. That's all I expect. How can I get it with the cockroaches I got living in the Building?"

He watches the battle between the two queens. He is silent, thinking of profit and loss, thinking of his property rights, which are considerable, rights that allow him a certain amount of freedom, an abundant latitude. He picks up a piece of wood and walks over to the struggling women. He looks down on the face of the madonna, a face that is full of passion and lust, a face whose mouth is full of the Ice Queen's ankle. It is a lively face, he thinks, a face that can quickly assume a position on any issue. He begins to beat that face with the piece of wood. He beats it tentatively, testing the flesh, unsure how well it will hold up. It is a soft piece of wood, or so he tells himself, and beating the face, bouncing the piece of wood off the cheeks and nose, simply serves to teach it a lesson. As he beats the face, he thinks of himself as a teacher, and the thought pleases him. He beats it harder, drawing bruises, bumps, blood to the surface, rearranging small bits of bone, rounding off sharp corners. To teach a lesson, he tells himself, one must be willing to apply force, one must be willing to push to the limits of bone, and beyond. The madonna lets go of the Ice Queen's ankle, and the latter deftly moves her swollen and mangled foot.

"Turn her over," Haber says. "It's my turn now. I want to fuck her."

40

HABER has no fine edge to his anger. It is a blunt thing, ragged at the corners, dulled and dented like the elephantine Plymouth station wagon he drives with the ripped upholstery, fan belt that sticks out of a hole in the rusty trunk, and the rippled, ball-peen-hammered fenders and cracked taillights (one covered with red plastic and taped at the edges). He has managed to bring cold into the Building, but he has not managed to drive tenants out. A few have left, but most have stayed. "A stubborn, intransigent, stupid collection of mottled psyches, the detritus of the nation's lax immigration policies," he says. He still thinks he owns the Building. He offers them money to leave. He wants to co-op the Building. He can make more than inflation, more than money market, more than convertible debentures . . . it is a way to charge his profits, boost them into the stratosphere. Empty, the Building with fifty units (or fifty-six, fifty-eight, he can't remember exactly) is worth more than full. People take away a building's worth, they defecate on his profit, the very breath of their presence puts a dent in his cash projections.

"I was a liberal when it paid to be a liberal. Now they mug, get more than their share, take over good Jewish neighborhoods."

He hired the Gorilla Management Company of the Bronx to manage the Building. He saw an ad in one of the landlord papers. "Difficult tenants our speciality," it said. That was all it said, along with the name, Gorilla Management, a phone number, and a post office box. The head of the company came to talk to him.

"Look, we ain't savages, we ain't animals," he told Haber.

"People get the wrong idea," he continued. "You might of seen us on television, interviewed by Gabe Pressman. They think we go in, threaten people, bust heads, rip out boilers, invite junkies and bums into the buildings, strong-arm tenants to get the rent. That's what they think we do."

Haber asked him what they did. "We do what we have to do," he said. The deal was simplicity itself. They got half the rent they collected and a substantial bonus when the Building was empty. A substantial bonus. He told Haber a figure that made him swallow twice, very fast. Haber said he would have to think it over. The man looked at his watch, then looked up. "Time's up," he said. Haber said he wasn't sure. The man walked closer to Haber, so close that Haber could see the tiny indentations in his nose, which looked as if they were made by barbed wire, and a thick, heavy beard submerged in his skin, which seemed on the verge of springing full blown from his face. He was so close Haber could hear him breathing, a rush of air through clotted nostrils that sounded like someone walking through tall grass. "I think you decided to hire us," he told Haber. "I think your problems are over, and that's because you decided to hire us, and I think you recognize that." He smiled at Haber, the smile of a man about to wipe something off his chin. "Don't worry," he told Haber, "we only use the most modern, scientific methods. We're not animals. Everybody thinks we're animals. Do I look like an animal?" He spoke this last sentence as if Haber had spotted him swinging from trees. "No," said Haber. "I'm glad we could come to an understanding. I'm sincerely glad." He looked slyly at Haber. "For your sake," he added.

Lowell was working on his anger, honing it to a fine, obsidian edge. He did not want to let it sputter about aimlessly, to dull it by banging against doors that would never open, walls that would never come down. He was mad at Haber for thinking he owned the Building, the city for thinking it could do whatever it wanted to with the Building, and the tenants for not giving a damn.

Lowell walked down to the cellar where he saw a short, hairy man hanging from one of the pipes, or rather hanging from a pipe wrench that was hanging from one of the pipes. Still hanging, the man turned his head around and shouted a cheery hello. "We're fixing the pipes," he said, still hanging but at the same time sawing the pipe. The sharp rasping noise of the hacksaw assaulted Lowell's ears. There was a growing pile of silver shavings directly under the saw cut. When the saw broke through the pipe, the man dropped the saw but still hung on to the pipe, which, slowly bending under his weight, gently lowered him to the ground. "That's a funny way to fix things," Lowell said, looking at the long bent pipe. The man looked up. "We're funny fixers," he said, smiling. He walked with one end of the pipe, the other still attached to its joint, so that it bent, spaghetti fashion, around another pipe. "It doesn't look like you're fixing anything," Lowell said. "It looks like you're ruining the pipes." The man looked up at him, smiling. "I have to take these pills," he said, "to keep smiling." He withdrew a small box of pills from his pocket. "Otherwise I get awfully angry. I get so angry I can't do my work." "Funny kind of work," said Lowell. "See," the man said, "I'm smiling. See how well the pills work?"

The following day someone came around to collect the rent. It was another small, squat, hairy man, swarthy of complexion like the ape in the cellar working on the steam pipes.

"Rent," he said.

"No heat, no rent," Tyrone said.

Tyrone slammed the door. He went back to his potatoes that were frying on the stove. Hearing a crash, wood splintering, he turned toward the door. A fist was poking through the door. Slowly the fingers uncurled, making an open palm. "Rent," the voice on the other side of the door said. "Sure," Tyrone said. He walked over to the door, frying pan in hand, and placed it on the palm of the outstretched hand. He heard a scream. The hand was withdrawn from the hole it had made in the door. Tyrone began to think about how he could repair the door. Wooden doors, old wooden doors like his, were not easy to find.

The next day Lowell heard someone chopping. Where the hell was it coming from? What was there to chop? He walked out to the sidewalk in front of the Building. The sound came from above. A man, a small, swarthy man, was on the roof. Lowell ran up six flights of stairs to the roof, panting, and banged open the door to the roof. The man, as hairy as the others, was chopping a hole in the roof.

"Hey," Lowell said, "what the hell you think you're doing?"

The man looked up, between chops.

"Chopping a hole in the roof."

"Why?"

"So the gas can escape."

"What gas?"

"The gas line I chopped through."

"What?!"

"See," he said, "I could have set it on fire, but then I would have gotten burned."

"Why . . ."

"See, the gas line was a mistake. I was chopping through the water line, or what I thought was the water line. Turns out to be the gas line. Ain't that a scream?"

He looked up at Lowell, imploring him to laugh.

"Now," he said, "I got to go back down and chop through the water line. They didn't even pay me to do all this chopping. All this chopping is, in a manner of speaking, on the house."

Lowell grabbed the ax from him and pitched it off the roof. It twirled fiercely in the air, the lighter end spinning ferociously around the heavier, and fell, burying itself head first on the roof of a car, a Lincoln Continental Mark VII, whose driver was so stunned to see an ax head appear through his ceiling that, thinking it was some kind of omen, he tried to drive the Lincoln into the trunk of a parked Chevy Vega, failing miserably in the attempt.

Lowell rarely saw Haber in the Building. There was competition to collect the rent between Lowell and Gorilla Management, with the latter employing more forcible methods. The water was disconnected, reconnected, disconnected, and reconnected again. Several bathtubs were ripped out of apartments and carried to the roof and piled next to the José chimney. Steckler caught a Gorilla manager trying to rip out the fuse box and, in uncharacteristic fashion, patiently explained to him why the fuse box was needed. The explanation did not take, however, and a brief scuffle ensued. At the termination of the scuffle, Steckler welded the unfortunate to one of the steam pipes, threatening to start the boiler. Fortunately for the employee but unfortunately for the tenants, the boiler was quite bruised, having been bludgeoned beforehand with a sledgehammer. The burner, though still attached to four legs and set in cement before the boiler, looked like two huge misshapen hands, the fingers gnarled, bent and twisted into some primeval shape, clasped together for refuge.

During the night, Tyrone heard shots in the Building. Several came through his patched-up door, passed through several walls, and one spent itself in the gut of one of the Wilson cats while another buried itself in a lead water pipe, flattening slightly in the process so that it looked like some kind of official water department seal. A few tenants moved; their apartments remained empty. When Tyrone complained to Lowell about the garbage left outside, a garbage dump was made in one of the empty apartments by Gorilla Management and set on fire. The fumes, low and oily, sick smoke, slithered through the Building, depositing a layer of dirty grease on all horizontal and many vertical objects.

Lowell thought he could hear the Building moan: a sweet, soft sound, timbers bending in the wind, bricks cracking under the weight of brick, the ground shifting, tilting the Building.

The cold came again, with strong winds, forcing the Arctic air through the tiniest cracks and holes in the bricks, mortar, plaster, window frames, putty (now dried, cracked, peeling off in huge sections, leaving the glass to rattle against the rotting wood frames), and gaps in the doors. Two of Mother Ozmoz's children froze to death, turning to ice in their dresser-drawer coffins, which had been placed too close to the windows. TV newsmen came and did a brief story, but Mother Ozmoz never appeared on the news; she was not contrite enough. They couldn't get her to cry on camera, so Mary Smith cried for her, on camera, and it was implied, though never explicitly stated, that she was the mother of the children, despite the fact that many children were almost white, a sort of light green, while Mary Smith was black.

The tenants huddled around gas ovens and kerosene heaters and used electric heaters when Steckler wasn't welding.

Several small fires were set, put out, set again, put out. The tenants formed a fire watch. Armed with two-by-fours they sat on card table chairs in the lobby drinking instant coffee out of Styrofoam cups with water they had boiled using a hot plate that was wired to a nearby street lamp.

An electrical storm swept the Building. Small yellow balls of revolving electricity hovered over the electric outlets, keeping the tenants from plugging anything in. There was an electrical fire in front of the Building in the sewer. Lowell watched the eerie light the flames cast on the acrid puffball clouds that billowed out of the manhole and heard the rapid-fire explosions, somewhat muted, that reminded him of firecrackers. He walked down to the street and peered into the sewer hole. The frequency and intensity of explosions increased, bathing him in an orange-yellow glow. It looked, he thought, like a scene out of hell.

The gas was turned off for a day when the gas company had to come out and repair the lines damaged by the electrical fire. Ovens and gas heaters died down and then stopped, but the cold persisted. Several tenants had frostbitten fingers and earlobes. These were mailed to Haber by those tenants who thought he owned the Building. They were packed in ice—melted, of course, by the time he opened the package that contained the mauve tips of fingers and toes. Enraged, Haber had them spiked to the bricks over the lobby door, where they remained, turning deeper and more opulent in color, devoured by small creatures, until only the spiked bones, tips of bones, remained, or in the case of the earlobes, almost nothing.

Lowell stood in front of the Building. He thought he could see Haber's face scratched in the brick. The longer he looked, the more he could make out the features. The following day the face had changed; the lines were deeper. The next day all the lines had disappeared, save one, which was deeper yet—a diagonal crack that ran from the top corner of the Building to the bottom. It was a large crack, large enough to threaten one corner of the Building—a fault zone that might whip out its underpinnings. The crack widened. Heavy trucks bouncing over potholes caused the nearest corner of brick to shudder and undulate in a very un-stonelike manner. Bits of mortar and cracked brick fell to the sidewalk. Snow and ice collected in the crack. It got warmer, rained, and then the temperature plummeted to zero. A frozen river appeared in the crack, with boulder-size cresting waves that were stone hard, bulging over the edge of the Building as if fists of ice had engulfed the brick. As the temperature crept up, the river melted, and as it dropped, the river froze, leaving daggers of ice pointed at the sidewalk. He noticed a fine network of plaster cracks on the wall behind the crack. It seemed as if the network of cracks was expanding. He thought he could see them inching their way along the plaster, like a river overflowing its boundaries. He could hear the wind whistling through the crack, and with his hand over the plaster feel the rush of outside air.

He looked up on the roof and saw Haber with a jackhammer trying to separate the corner from the rest of the Building. Several bricks fell. But the jackhammer, like a huge heart beating madly, flew out of Haber's hands, and tumbling quickly in the air, fell to the sidewalk.

"The Building," he shouted down to Lowell, "the Building must come down."

41

"It is the little-wee-wee people who have done this," said the African Dictator (who lived in apartment 6D along with his most exalted pillow bearer and the human alarm clock, the cockcrower, who cackled the approach of every hour for the time-conscious African Dictator) when he learned that Haber had tried to take the corner off the Building. He strode about his apartment in a huff, followed conscientiously by his most exalted pillow bearer, being the only one of nine pillow bearers that had escaped with the mighty ruler when he fled his sun-drenched African country after his government was overthrown by Methodists, sometimes referred to by the king as the small-penis people. The pillow bearer's job was to insert the royal pillow under the most exalted dictator just before he deposited himself on a chair, or anywhere else he chose to sit. In Africa, the mighty ruler chose to sit in a variety of places, at a variety of times, and because of his ever-changing moods, it took nine pillow bearers just to keep up with him. Eight pillow bearers were left behind and retrained under the auspices of the People's Liberation Army, run by the ruling party, the Methodist Marxists. They studied the precepts of the head Methodist and avowed Marxist, Dr. Yrneh Regnissik, and learned how to weave hemp rope. Still, they were luckier than some of the king's other staff. Of the nine exalted food tasters, one succumbed to food poisoning, one to crocodiles, while the other seven performed hygienic rituals for the present ruling council too embarrassing to relate. The dictator's three chauffeurs drove the country's entire fleet of tanks, while the Royal Gatherer of His Most Exalted Fingernail Clippings, a privileged post, was now the country's only podiatrist.

The African Dictator believed that the same people who had driven him out of his country ran the Building. He believed this because Lowell took exception to his keeping cows in his sixth-floor apartment, and would not allow him extra rooms for his goats and chickens. The dictator vowed to invade the Building. He kept his invasion money around the corner in the Chemical Bank on Flatbush, a rather ample fund that was periodically added to by the United States Government in hopes that the ruler would rid his country of Marxists and restore it, Biathawnaland, to its rightful place as a dutiful supplier of cocoa beans.

And so, one morning, a day that dawned clear and cold, "a cold as silent and sweet as the breath of ice-filled moths," as the king put it, parachutes appeared in the sky over the Building. Attached to each parachute was an unemployed teenager from Bedford Stuyvesant, attracted by the large sums of money the dictator promised them as soon as they had liberated the Building from the tiny-pee-pee people. The king was ecstatic because the parachutes appeared in the sky just as his most exalted cockcrower had cackled out the early-morning hour, and the honorable dictator believed that this was a good omen.

The king had practiced his breathing exercises on the roof before the invasion and then waved peacock feathers in the early-morning sunlight to guide the nine paratroopers, resplendent in orange-and-purple-silk combat jackets, linen Brooks Brothers boating pants, seventy-five-dollar leather Pumas (untied), and bandoliers strapped across their chests holding thirty-caliber machine-gun bullets for which they, unfortunately, had no machine guns. Instead they carried twenty-two caliber marksmen's pistols with blued barrels and pearl handles in hand-tooled leather holsters.

It was a most propitious landing. A few of the parachutists actually landed on the roof (two, to be exact: one on the José chimney; the other, almost on the roof, had his parachute entangled on a fire escape and hung precariously from the sixth-floor landing until the honorable dictator arrived and cut him loose). The remainder landed on adjacent roofs or in adjoining backyards. The pilot, one of the defected dictator's crack aces, a disbarred crop duster from Kenya, had done well, and the king would assign him the lead plane on their triumphal invasion of Biathawnaland.

Quickly the king assembled his troops and had them surround the Building. He waved his peacock feathers and shook his impala-horn headdress, stamped his foot three times on the ground, drew a circle with his staff, and swallowed a pinch of rhinoceros-horn powder to prepare himself for the grueling sexual adventures ahead. "Gentlemens," he said (while his sense of command was impeccable, his knowledge of English was not), "gentlemens . . . " (The king was in the habit of repeating himself. He entertained a doubt about human communication, believing that at bottom it was impossible, hopeless, at best a vain goal.) ". . . We are now in a position of power and will proceed to secure our territory. We will proceed with a search-and-destroy mission through the Building and reconvene here in front of the lobby."

Of course, no one listened to what he said. The Building looked secure to them. Who would steal it? Nevertheless, they went through the entire Building, pistols drawn, knocked on doors, and asked tenants if everything was all right. That was, of course, a mistake. Nothing was "all right." The tenants proceeded to list their grievances to the armed teenagers, beginning with the lack of heat and hot water and often ending with the pack of wild dogs the landlord and the city let roam through the Building in the hope of chasing them out.

The parachutists reported back to the king through their leader—MasterCharge. He announced to the honorable dictator that they had the Building under control. Where, the king wanted to know, was his woman, his women? MasterCharge shrugged his shoulders. What woman? Women? The king patiently explained that in any military operation of this sort, women were the spoils of war. "There is no victory without the conquest of many women," he said. But the parachutists were unmoved by the king's plea. They demanded their money. And MasterCharge confided to the king that he had better pay up shortly, otherwise things would get "ugly." The king summoned his most exalted pillow bearer to explain the situation, but MasterCharge waved the brown man aside. "Hey, listen," he said, "we ain't no fucking natives. That kind of motherfucking shit might go down in Africa, but you here in America. We ain't no fucking slaves. A day's work, a day's pay. We done the work. You pay. Otherwise . . . " The king repeated his demand for a woman, and MasterCharge offered to grease a cat's ass for him. The king looked puzzled. Something, he thought, must have been lost in the translation. Either that, or the respect for royalty, so apparent when he had first landed in this country at Andrews Air Force Base, greeted not just by the vice president but the chief of the C.I.A., the chairman of the Joint Chiefs of Staff, along with the chairman of the board of the company that sold infant formula in his country, was not what he had been led to believe. Nevertheless, his original epistemological question about the validity of real human communication was confirmed. He paid.

Seen in another light, the military operation was a success. It confirmed the dictator's habit of command. It was a testimony to his tactical and logistic genius. It was a successful dry run for his invasion of Biathawnaland. And temporarily, at least, it had driven Gorilla Management and Haber from the Building . . . who had run, screaming, down the stairs and out the front door when they saw nine armed teenagers roaming through the Building. "Now," the king said, "the Building is the first foothold of Africa in the New World, the international headquarters of the Yoruba tribe."

Tonton Tute, however, had his doubts. He had known about the invasion because the African Dictator wished to receive his blessing and to gain any special favors the Haitian computer designer could waft his way as a high voodoo priest. But favors were in short supply. "There are not enough chickens in all of the city to ensure that the Building would be turned over for the benefit of the people," Tute said, "and even if there were, the amount of bloodletting that would be necessary, the number of chickens with broken necks that would clog up the parks, the general pandemonium that would ensue when the parks were invaded by rats to feast off the voodoo-killed chickens would kill any chance for the success of such a blessing." When the African dictator inquired about the despoiling of virgins, the number required to be despoiled, and offered his services as a leader of the "despoillemente," as he put it, willing to lead the first charge into the vale, so to speak, Tonton Tute advised against such measures. "Not suitable for this occasion," he said.

To bring the Building back to life required not just voodoo, but Brooklyn voodoo. It was not enough to hold a goat-slitting ceremony, or to drink the blood of a dove, or to bury comatose bodies. The goat had to be cut in the back seat of a stolen Buick Riviera. No longer would blood from a dove do, but from an old cigarette-stained pigeon from Flatbush Avenue. And even that wasn't enough. Tonton Tute, though he had a hand in the design of one of the world's first 32-bit microcomputers, had still to learn the convoluted ways of Brooklyn voodoo. There was a god that used to dwell in Brooklyn that one must pay homage to. It was a god that was very powerful, that touched all aspects of Brooklyn life. The sacred ground of this god, the most sacred ground in all of Brooklyn, was now a housing complex. The god was called the Brooklyndodger god; the sacred ground was called Ebbets Field Housing. The official bible of this powerful Brooklyn god was also dead. It was called the *Brooklyn Eagle.* Odd, Tonton Tute thought, how all the most powerful gods of this country called Brooklyn are dead. He thought there must be a curse on the borough, that other nearby gods, the gods of Manhattan and the gods of Staten Island, were jealous of the power of the Brooklyndodger god and conspired to throw him out. It was rumored that they threw him so far he landed in another country far to the west. Lasangles was another god who hated the Brooklyn-dodger god and had no doubt conspired with the Manhattan god and the Staten Island god to bring about the downfall of the Brooklyn-dodger god. None of them were strong enough to do it alone. It must have been a very powerful god, Tonton Tute thought. Very powerful. He wondered how he could harness the power of this dead god. He found who were the high priests of this dead god. The highest was Jackie Robinson, also dead. Another was Gil Hodges, dead like the first. Brooklyn, Tonton Tute thought, the god of death, the god of disappearance, the god of being thrown away. He found another, one called Carl Furillo, and one called Duke Snider. He traveled to Pennsylvania to talk to one, who had no idea what he was talking about. The other he could not find. It was strange, Tonton Tute thought. Not only had the great god Brooklyndodger been killed, thrown away, but his high priests had either been killed or else had no memory of the rites of the religion, except for some foolishness that one had told him about a stick and a small ball. Surely the great Brooklyndodger god had more to do than that. Despondent, close to despair, Tonton Tute then discovered a picture of the great god in a Brooklyn bank. He could hardly believe his good fortune! There it was. The Brooklyndodger god with row after row of his priests. It said BROOKLYN DODGERS: WORLD CHAMPIONS 1955. When no one was looking he tore the poster off the bank wall and ran home with it. He put it up on his wall, lit several candles, which he placed in small bowls of water, and set them in front of the picture. The light from the flickering candles made the faces flinch, the folded arms on the picture twitch. He studied the faces, each one of them, looking for a clue to the power of this god. He thought he saw some of them blink, but it was the candles shifting their flame. He stood as the men in the picture did: feet apart, arms folded. Then he sat as the men in the front row did: back straight, palms on the knees. He waited. Nothing happened. Sacrifices performed in front of the picture achieved nothing. The great god had lost its power. There was a curse on the borough. The Building was doomed. Tonton Tute would continue to perform his voodoo ceremonies, but deep in his heart he knew it was an expatriate's religion, a spiritual force that could not compare to the god that had once dwelt in the borough. That god was dead. It had no power beyond the grave. Brooklyn had been abandoned.

42

STILL dreaming he owns the Building, Haber hires a Yogi plumber,
an ersatz holy man, an extra-pious connector of pipes who medi-
tates in the basement, sitting on the lake of ice (which contains the
iceberg Tubbo Rivera) with his legs crossed and his hands on the inside
of his knees, index fingers to thumbs, oblivious to the blue glow that
emanates from the frozen Tubbo, meditating on the tantric pipes that
circulate water in the Building and connect not only the pipes with one
another but with the meridians that run through his body, the energy
channels, loops, that circulate Pranha, his interior plumbing. He hums,
hums in a way that no one can hear. He breathes slowly, deeply, five
breaths a minute, four breaths a minute, then one breath a minute, his
metabolism slows down, takes a nap; he burns but dozens of calories
an hour, "Ommmming," humming. Though there is no heat in the
Building there is water, and Haber, unable to disconnect the pipes,
afraid to saw them, fearful of bombing them, has hired this tantric
plumber, this pipe Buddhist, to burn them, to melt them, to dissolve
their connectedness. He has paid this defrocked holy man in loincloth
and staff to meditate in the basement and do the job on the pipes that
Gorilla Management failed to do. But this charlatan, this bogus Siddha,
is no Buddhist, though Haber believes him to be, is barely a Yogi, is
in fact a Hindu plumber. He is a Hindu from an obscure sect in north-
eastern India who learned to plumb on bamboo pipes. After persecu-
tion by Moslems he fled to this country and to remain a plumber had
to learn the intricacies of joining metal with metal, a process that
required a flow of energy, a flow he believed had to stem from the
internal organs of the plumber himself, an energy that had to be generated from the very kidneys, liver, spleen, and pancreas of the plumber.
It was a process that required meditation, building up the energy
needed to fuse pipes, the energy to make water run, to urge it to keep
running. But the idea of stopping water from running upset him. He
was good at opening valves, poor at closing them. He believed in
unblocking energy passages. A blocked passage, a valve turned off, was
an assault on the sacred doctrine of meridians.

His business suffered. He offered unbroken loops of plumbing, continuous running water when his customers wanted the water shut off. Haber met this unsuccessful businessman in Queens, the home of Hindus, and invited him to Brooklyn. The Hindu plumber tried to explain his philosophy of plumbing, of the unbroken river of water that runs through pipes, a river that is a stranger to valves that try to dam the flow, block it up, shut it off. The gentle trickle of running water, he patiently explained, is one of delight, and running water invigorates the body. Just a trickle, he explained, so that hardly any more water is needed than one would normally use. But Haber saw only his topknot and the finely woven braid of hair that was piled on his head; the words the plumber wove, his philosophy of plumbing, he scarcely heard. Here, Haber reasoned, was a holy man. Anyone who came from India and wore a topknot must be a holy man. He must have powers from beyond. Waterfalls sprang to mind. Haber had visions of lakes, of rushing rivers, of spring torrents inundating the Building, flushing all the tenants out the way one might spray cockroaches down a sink drain.

He hired him. Though each spoke English, they barely understood each other. Haber thought the plumber wanted money to set up a Hindu temple in Queens and was willing to sit in the basement for weeks until the pipes melted, the water stopped, and the tenants left. The plumber thought Haber hired him to complete some vast plumbing job, the details of which were rather complicated and somewhat vague, but which involved all the pipes in this huge Building in Brooklyn. He thought perhaps the Building and Haber were willing to try his new plumbing philosophy, a modality based on the philosophy of the river. The river always flows, he told Haber, and Haber, reading metaphors that had nothing to do with plumbing, thought he was mentioning some exquisite philosophy of life. In fact, the Hindu was talking about plumbing.

Lowell walked into the lobby. There was still a steel-enameled sign nailed to the wall: THIS BUILDING MANAGED BY GORILLA MANAGEMENT. It showed a gorilla holding a hunter by the neck, his feet madly scrambling for support in the air. He ripped the sign off the wall. Just let the bastards try to come back.

He walked down the steps to the cellar. Tubbo, sitting in a wooden chair, his feet and lower body under ice, tied to the chair with clothesline, his upper body stiff, blue, arms tied behind the chair with window drapes, looked as if he had spotted something on the wall across from where he was enthroned and was determined that his gaze would never waver from that spot. Little chance of that, Lowell thought, noticing the blue glow that emanated from his body. When spring comes, he thought, and the ice goes soft, we ought to dig him out and get his father, who runs a Chiba shop on the corner, to bury him someplace where they have names on the headstones, where they cut the grass, where people put plastic flowers on the graves.

And then he noticed the little man in the corner sitting cross-legged. The man winked at him, and Lowell walked over, carefully, on the ice.

"What are you doing here?" he asked.

The guru of pipes looked up and smiled ever so sweetly.

"I have come to fix," he said. "The owner he asked me to fix, and so I have come."

He smiled before he spoke, after he spoke, and while he spoke, so that each word was punctuated with a smile, the entire effect being that of a man who tape-recorded his conversation beforehand and then smiled while he played it.

"There is no owner," Lowell said. "Not anymore."

"Pardon?"

"The city owns it. The owner no longer owns it."

This Pather Panchali of pipes smiled once again. "Thank you," he said. "Thank you, again."

"For what?"

"Thank you."

He put his palms together and bowed his head.

"Did you hear what I said?"

The Dalai Lama of plumbers nodded. "Oh yes, indeed I did."

"Then why are you here?"

He smiled and bowed his head.

"What the hell is that supposed to mean?"

"One doesn't just interrupt things."

"What things?"

"Any things."

"What the hell are you down here for anyway?"

The little man stood up, stiffly.

"My it's cold down here."

He brushed off the back of his pants, which were wet . . . and impervious to brushing.

"I'm asking you, nicely so far, why you come down here?"

"Thank you. I am sure you did ask me that."

He smiled and bowed again. Lowell waited. He wasn't sure if the man answered any English that came to mind, really didn't understand, or else did understand but wanted to pretend he didn't.

"I was caring for the pipes. Gathering my energy to heal them."

"Who hired you to fix the pipes?"

"The owner."

"Haber?"

"His very words, if I repeat correctly, were to mend the various joints where liquids were wont to leave their proper path."

"That's not Haber. He's not a liquid man."

"What about the new owner? Would there be a wish to have the pipes repaired?"

"Where are your tools?"

"When the time is auspicious, I will get them."

"I bet," said Lowell.

"I don't," said the plumber.

"You don't what? Who the hell are you?"

"Perhaps you would show me the pipes in the Building, yes? Then I could begin my diagrams."

"We need a boiler man, not some flower plumber."

But the plumber, his baggy pants billowing in his wake, began climbing the steps, and Lowell walked after him, puzzled at how meekly he followed the little man.

43

WHEN the sniper ran out of ammunition he threw bathtubs, refrigerators, sofas, easy chairs, bricks, tires, bales of hay, trash cans, and baby carriages off the roof, but when supplied with ammunition he lay supine on the roof parapet and fired at people and other living creatures in the street. He had more luck hitting dogs than anything else. Large, furry, fashionable dogs littered the street, their owners fleeing after the first shot to the safety of their brownstones where they could watch their expensive watchdog being used for target practice.

The tenants knew who the sniper was. They paid him little mind, but made sure he had plenty of ammunition so they wouldn't find themselves underneath a refrigerator or stove hurled from the roof.

The sniper usually appeared the same day Lowell did for a tenants' meeting. Though the city had owned the Building for years, it treated the structure with mixed attention. Perhaps three winters had passed, perhaps four winters and seven springs. It had gotten cold and then warmer, and water was running in places where it had no right to run. The pipes had burst, or someone had stolen the plumbing, or someone had stolen the boiler, which caused the pipes to burst, or someone had stolen neither the pipes nor the boiler but had forgotten to order oil and the Building, icebox cold, had succumbed to a spring thaw, having burst what could be burst and then melted what could be melted.

He could see more women flying off the roof, being launched like gliders, apartments jammed with whirling dervishes until the Building began to shake, or stuffed with fireflies until it began to glow. It was a Persian minaret, each room exhibiting a new sexual perversion or intricate torture. It was a medieval memory palace, where the entire body of Western philosophy, from St. Augustine to Wittgenstein, was given an architectonic presence and resident philosophers vividly battled, with guns, memos, and cockroaches, their opposing intellectual concepts.

Lowell was by turns listless, confused, and eager. He was sure of himself and yet out of place, a white face in a sea of color, out of place even among the other white faces in the Building, as if they, by being among blacks and browns and yellows, had taken on a deeper shade of white. He came away from the tenants' meetings wondering if the city would do what it said it would do.

For a while it did nothing. Free of Haber, the tenants unleashed their own animosities. No longer able to take it out on Haber, who was not around, they took it out on each other. The African Dictator led three cows up the steps to his sixth-floor apartment. Cows and their refuse, he felt, were sacred, and while the smells in his apartment did not seem objectionable to the kingly ruler, his esteemed cockcrower, or his royal pillow bearer, they were to the other tenants. He was forced to lead a cow out of the Building. "It is the Methodists who have done this," he said, "and I will see to it that their runty wee-wees are made even smaller." Unfortunately, the cow was clipped by the sniper and collapsed on the front steps. The dictator tried to coax her up, but the great milky beast was content to chew her cud under the warming winter sun. Her knee had been blown away, making walking, never easy for a cow, that much more difficult. She lay there for days and then died of a collapsed udder, bloating up in the process. Stern blamed Hobson, thinking that he had set cockroaches upon the cow who simply ate her to death, and he nailed Hobson's door shut. Abdul Karim was sure that the paraplegic was breeding moths in the belly of the cow, and every morning he threw down his personal refuse on the bloated, expanding, bovine body. He pounded on the paraplegic's door, demanding that she remove the offending cow with her crutches. Lowell had to quiet him, a process that did not please the Kurd. The African Dictator asked Lowell if he could keep two more cows in his apartment despite the fact that sexually jealous Methodists who lived in the Building had taken offense at the celebration of the dictator's religious beliefs, a concept, he had thought, that was sacred in this great land of capitalism and the McDonald's hamburger. Lowell politely demurred. Mary Smith sent Dorah, Willy, and Shanker to cut some steaks from the carcass of the dead creature, and they were joined by Tontine, Tontine's blindingly blond wife, and their six straw children. It reminded Lowell of a pygmy-killed elephant in which the whole village gnaws its way through the belly of the beast. The African king was incensed at this violation of his religion and set his cockcrower down among the tenants to jabber at them in his unpleasantly high, tinny voice with its babbling falsetto. Even Steckler, phantom Steckler, came out of his apartment to view the carnage and sent Visa down, on a rope, to cut off some steaks.

The ribs, skull, entrails, brains, hooves, tail, and leftover organic parts of the deceased cow attracted other forms of animal life, including dogs, cats, squirrels, pigeons, chipmunks, rats, mice, raccoons, maggots, and, of course, cockroaches. They poured out of the Building to feast on the remains and then poured back into the Building to follow the steaks. The bones of the creature were kicked aside to join the garbage at the front and sides of the Building, and the tenants got up a petition to slaughter the other two cows.

Then the city began making repairs in the Building, but this only served to incense the tenants. Those who had paid their rent to

Haber, always on time, and had been rewarded for their efforts by abuse, a broken boiler, a leaky roof, now withheld their rent from the city, which was putting up new Sheetrock, cleaning the garbage out of the interior courtyard, repairing the broken marble in the lobby, and making plans to install a new boiler in the basement. Lowell explained to them that the Building was in grave danger if they did not pay their rent; but the tenants, having some attention paid to them, thought the Building was theirs by rights and that paying rent was the final indignity.

Boilers came and went, sucked out of the basement like snow in spring. The tenants cheered for heat, but warm weather was approaching, and their cheers became less fervent, almost lackadaisical. Now that he was melting, they wanted Tubbo chipped out of the basement. They wanted the roof fixed again, the floors straightened, they wanted new doors, new windows, fresh plaster and paint; they wanted lower rent, they wanted nonexistent rent. Hobson appointed himself tenant leader and announced to Lowell that officers in the tenants' association would not have to pay rent because of their duties in the association. The African king felt that he should be the tenants' association president, indeed that he should be the entire tenants' association, but his nominating speech was interrupted by so many catcalls that he was driven from the tenants' meeting, leaving only his cockcrower to heckle the tenants with metallic tintinnabulations.

There was another tenants' meeting. Lowell pleaded for rent, announced more repairs for the Building, a temporary boiler to replace the one that had been stolen, and, forgetting what the commissioner said about artist housing, said that the Building was going into one of the city's avant-garde management programs, either the T.I.L. Program (Tenant Interim Lease), the Community Management Program (having a few problems with the community organization that was supposed to manage the Building; its director, a brother of a state senator, was under investigation for mismanagement of funds, having used money for a day-care center to finance a pool hall—economic development was his defense—and money for a mental-health program to open a chain of variety stores that dealt in controlled substances, but Lowell and the city were confident that the director would come through the investigation squeaky clean, since the director's brother was the chairman of a state committee that oversaw state funds that were dispensed to the city) or the 421(a) or 421(b) Program (the details of which dealt with tax abatement, as did all the programs, except those that didn't, which usually dealt with direct subsidy, or if not, something else). It was, Lowell explained, quite simple, except in those cases where it was rather complicated.

Lowell promised that the Building would be a showcase, that the city was going to publicize the Building, show how it could be fixed up and run by tenants. He finished this last sentence expecting cheers but got none. The tenants sat through his speech . . . nodding off, drowsing. Tontine announced that he was the new tenants' association president and that Lowell could deal directly with him on all tenant matters, bypassing the tenants. He also said that he wanted the Building to adopt an official religion. "A building without a religion is like a foundation without spirit," he said. Wood worship, he said, would be the foundation of the Building's official religion. Abdul Karim leaped up and called him a stinking pig eater, a defiler of dogs, and said that Kurds would never bow to such foreign religions. He suggested that a mosque be built in the lobby.

Tontine was voted out of office but no replacement could be agreed upon. In his place was a standing revolving committee that was permanent, yet changed, whose number was constant, yet varied according to the dictates of the season, and whose members, while appointed and confirmed, varied from floor to floor according to some unexplained need. A vote on Lowell's proposal was postponed for some future, unspecified, meeting. Hobson suggested that the Building needed an official mascot, to revive flagging spirits, and suggested the cockroach. This proposal was voted down, as were the next three, which involved commissioning an official biography of all the famous people who had lived in the Building (none), giving the Building a name ("It should sound like a car, flamboyant, and yet solid, practical and yet mystical, powerful but . . .") and commissioning a national anthem for the Building ("It should sound like a nation, flamboyant and yet solid, practical and yet mystical, mythical but . . . "). The eight-hundred-year-old man suggested that he be named the Father of the Building, but it was pointed out that in fact he was not eight hundred years old but only two hundred, and that the babies he was alleged to have fathered were not babies but some other indiscernible creatures. While they talked, Mother Ozmoz gave birth to her twenty-fourth or twenty-fifth baby, an event for which the eight-hundred-year-old man claimed credit but was denied on the grounds that the old man and the baby had different skin colors. The baby was christened with a bottle of warm Pepsi and Wing Dings were passed around. To celebrate the event the Wilson Sister tied herself into a knot and rolled around the floor. Stern promised he would paint the boiler room as soon as the ice cube that was Tubbo was hacked out. Singiat-Sing Dan Dinphuir said that Tubbo could never be removed, that he was in the clutches of the water demon, now the ice demon, and that the only thing to do was to hack out all the ice as one piece, including Tubbo, wrap it in sawdust and newspaper and ship the entire thing to Bangkok. Someone suggested that Puff the Magic Dragon, the German shepherd who lived in the electrical supply room, not be fed for a week and then let out to eat Tubbo out of the ice ("Hey man, Tubbo was one tough dude," someone said. "He'd never let that happen. I once saw him tear this dude's finger off, then pull down the dude's pants and stuff it up his asshole").

The last comment sobered up most of the revelers, who stood quietly by making faces at Mother Ozmoz's latest, a tiny thing whose body still glistened. Lowell suggested they toast a farewell to the woman who was pushed off the roof. There was a moment of silence as everyone raised paper cups to the ceiling. It seemed to him as if she were in the room, watching, but not approving.

Is it spring?

Is it winter?

Heat from the boiler comes and goes, as does the boiler. Hot water, a gift from the city, springs from the faucet in steamy ejaculations. Sheetrock goes up, is taped but not painted; small strange people somewhere between midgets and children (dwarfs? tiny gypsies? elves?) do something to the roof, perhaps fix it, or put a new one down, or put parts of a new one down, patch up the gaping holes left by the fires and the time the muggers cut through to the apartment below where the diamond dealer lived.

The tenants are not grateful. The attention puzzles them. They find fault with the heat, the hot water, the freshly painted hallways. "There was something comforting about the garbage in the courtyard," said one of the tenants. With the courtyard clean, the lunatic planted a garden, growing huge, strangely shaped and grotesquely colored vegetables that frightened the tenants. Vines grew up the interior walls and from the vines came flowerlike fingers that seemed to suck the cement out of the mortar.

Lowell's relations with the tenants grew worse. The African Dictator, originally attracted to him, had become distant, aloof. He blamed Lowell for the cow problem, as he called it, feeling that Lowell had a special dispensation to allow the dictator to have his bovine friends in his apartment but that it was mere malice on Lowell's part that he did not help him. Each day he went off to the United Nations, dressed in rich ceremonial robes, to give a speech on American imperialism and then collect from the American embassy his latest installment of invasion funds, and when he passed Lowell's office he instructed his pillow bearer to leave a liquid memento of their passing, a practice that would have continued had not Lowell caught the offending pisser in the act of relieving himself and inflicted a disability on the surprised, wizened little black man.

Tontine hissed at him in the hallways. He blamed Lowell for wresting the Building away from Haber and turning it over to the city, possibly depriving Tontine of his job as super. It was unclear whether the city intended to keep Tontine in the role. They were unsure of his "supering" abilities, and Tontine prayed nightly to the huge wood logs he kept in his apartment and instructed his children to leave sawdust offerings scattered about the Building. His wife decided she should become pregnant, and mounting the little Norwegian extracted the sperm necessary to fertilize one of her many eggs.

Abdul Karim thought that Lowell was a Pakistani agent. The graffiti that appeared in the Building was the work of Lowell, or at least orchestrated under his direction, and during the latest installment of "Sunrise Semester," Abdul Karim had noticed that the man in the glass tube (who was able to move back and forth very swiftly on the tiny wires that connected the TV set to the wall and so appear in millions of sets) mentioned "Plato," surely an oblique reference to Lowell, and Abdul thought that this was a signal for Lowell to commence his operations: the breeding and release of tiny, furry insects in the cellar.

But Mary Smith still loved Lowell. Malice was as foreign to her as tofu, and she kept in her heart, a huge hamlike affair that squeezed blood through thousands of extra miles of capillaries, a warm spot for him. She fed him when he was sick and introduced him to the Cadillac Dream Lady, a meter maid who drove a Chevette, who refused to answer Lowell's questions about the commissioner's papers and who argued with him so fervently while they were driving she almost ran down a man who was taking his pet turkey out for a walk.

The city, though charged with redeeming the Building and providing the tenants with better housing, now felt in some vague, unarticulated way that the tenants were a nuisance, a bother—they broke things, they wore them out—and that it would be better if they could fix up the Building without the tenants, leaving the Building pristine and tenantless, providing heat and hot water for a vanished populace.

Someone keeps stealing the boiler. It is one of the tenants; they all know who it is, but they don't know how he does it. He is a magician, in a manner of speaking. He has removed large objects—boats, tanks, locomotives—from buildings that were built around them. Some say he uses voodoo. Others say he uses Aruba, Santario, or perhaps just large cranes. He is a mechanic, a painter, a real estate dealer, a contractor. He sells used boilers. (But no one has actually seen him remove the boiler, so perhaps it is someone, something else.)

To repair the wiring in the Building, the city hires electricians who steal the plumbing. It hires someone to prevent theft; he steals the electrical wire. Dwarf gypsies repair the roof. They leave their children nailed to it. This is a lesson. The world of adults is fraught with peril.

44

THE apartment next to the pigeon apartment starts to bleed. Drops of blood appear on the walls. Is there a leak behind the walls? Is the water rusty? This is not the red of rust. This is a brighter, thicker red, not a red from veins but a red from arteries. The walls sweat blood. A Chinese refugee from Hong Kong, a pants presser, lived in the apartment until he noticed the blood on the walls and fled. He left his suitcase (small, black), shirts (three, white, short-sleeved), underwear (boxer shorts, too big for him), a dozen cans of Hershey's chocolate syrup, and some men's magazines with pudgy naked women. The blood appeared in small drops, irregularly spaced on the walls. It left a brown stain, which the Chinese refugee never noticed since he fled before the red turned to brown. The drops seemed to travel about the wall. Tontine scrubbed them off, but the following day new blood appeared; they were tiny drops, something that would come out of a pinprick, bubbling out of the wallpaper. The drops could be wiped off with a sponge while wet; but when dry, powerful solvents had to be used, and then to slight effect.

Before the pants presser lived in the apartment, the fireflies almost did. The holes in the roof that would have allowed the creatures entrance had been made by thieves intent on relieving the inventory from a gold and diamond dealer who lived there (obscurity is the best form of security, he once said). But who lived there before he did? Were there corpses in the walls? Are they still there? Was blood used to set the plaster?

Was it animal blood? Human blood? Did it come from adults? Was it from the children who were nailed to the roof?

Did the walls have stigmata?

The apartment is not spacious. Three rooms, French doors between the dining room and the living room. The door to the hallway, once sturdy beyond imagination, has been replaced with something that has been broken down many times. There is a small, vinyl-topped kitchen table, some chrome tubular kitchen chairs, rusting where the metal bends to form a right angle. Inside the kitchen cabinet, taped to the door, is a copy of the Lord's Prayer, and the plates over the wall switches are white plastic, with a scene of the Virgin Mother and two children. This has been painted over many times, in light pastels, so that the details of the figures have been lost and the only things that remain are the three finger-long bumps that represent these figures.

Was there a murder in the apartment? A double murder? A suicide pact?

The apartment is next to the stairs that go up to the roof. The same stairs that the woman who would be Ingrid was dragged up so she could be thrown from the roof, stairs that both Ramon, his friend, and Glasho used to get to the roof and watch her being launched. It is the stairs the sniper used to reach the roof and take potshots at people in the streets, the stairs the chicken man used to reach the roof and perform his necrophilia with birds, the stairs that Hobson climbed when he walked on the parapet, and the ascent used by the artist who adorned the José chimney.

The door to the apartment remains unlocked, and the tenants come up and look in. The meaning of this object lesson is not clear, the leaving of the door unlocked, and though Lowell asked Tontine to keep it locked, and he did, somehow it manages to remain unlocked. One of those who wishes to see the blood is the paraplegic. She cannot escape from her wheelchair, her braces, her metal encumbrances, and the elevator has long since given up, so she persuades Hobson to drag her up the stairs, which he does with a considerable amount of effort, pulling her surprising bulk up the steps, one at a time, until the paraplegic and her wheelchair arrive at the top floor. Staring at the blood on the walls she has visions of disasters: horrible butcherings, multiple stabbings involving berserk families with meat cleavers and kitchen knives; sickbeds with the occupants coughing up blood in unison; a gangland killing, a sort of St. Valentine's Day massacre in Brooklyn. The wonder and mystery of it captivates her, and Hobson, soothing her, thinking she is terrified, suggests that they leave. He does not understand that terror is part of her understanding, that the violence and destruction already done to her body has charged her imagination, taken hold of it, a dybbuk that possesses her and gives meaning to what otherwise would be a senseless world. This is all that is left in the world, she thinks; violence, destruction, havoc. Hobson thinks there is order, rationality, and that even his beloved cockroaches can be made a part of this, can be taught to think, to communicate. She, on the other hand, likes nothing better than to watch them curl up in flames, watch the black liquid that comes out of their bodies in fire and the acrid fumes that rise in the smoke.

The deaf-mute comes up to hear the blood. He can hear the sound of it coming through the walls, late at night, when everyone else is asleep. He can hear nothing else; the sound of blood makes a soft "hushing" sound, not quite a moan, but a sound like velvet being dragged across thick linen paper. When he hears that sound he climbs out of bed and goes up to the apartment, and if the moon is out can watch the blood being pushed through the walls, hear it moan, if you wish to call it moaning, and watch the tiny beads forming on the walls. He does not know why he can hear this, but he can, and he does not know the meaning of his hearing this. It could remind him of Puerto

Rico, of the sea birds and the silver fish in the ocean, and his small village in the provinces . . . but it does not. It propels his mind forward, beyond what he is hearing, and his mind sees things he does not understand and therefore does not see. His mind knows, but he does not; he recoils from knowing. He knows and he does not know what will happen in and to the Building. He does not like the sound of blood coming through the walls, but when he hears it he must go up and watch the tiny beads forming. His mind will let him do nothing else.

The city, it seems, is frantic about the Building. Lowell calls for more tenants' meetings and announces new programs, new ways to get money and supplies for the Building, and new ways that the tenants can manage it: through direct ownership, through a neighborhood organization, through a nonprofit corporation. There is a frenzy that attaches to the city's work. Workmen hurriedly come and go. A great banquet is held to celebrate the Building, to which none of the tenants are invited. Lowell catches flak for that. He apologizes. Perhaps it is not his doing. Forces beyond him are at work; he is a minion in their hands.

New problems arise. A vast flooding runs through the Building. Some call it a river. The city cannot seem to repair it. Electrical storms sweep through the Building, shorting out wiring. The tenants blame Steckler, who is indifferent to their concern. The city, Lowell, is in a rush to correct these damages and yet is never able to correct them. Lowell harangues the tenants about their lack of involvement, their lack of care for the Building. "This is your home, you should care. Sweep its hallways, put its garbage in cans," he admonishes, like a petulant father. The tenants complain about the city's repairs: "You didn't fix the water leak. My apartment is still flooded, and the roof still leaks."

Lowell watches the apartment sweat blood. It seems to him that there is a great amount of work involved in this, as if the apartment, or the Building, were engaged in a struggle, some vast effort to accomplish something. He had no idea what it could be. The blood suggests neither violence nor its lack. Blood itself is neutral on this matter. He puts his ear to the wall, thinking he can hear something, not knowing what it could be, but hears nothing other than the scurrying of rats up and down the studs inside the walls. He can also hear water rushing through the pipes and the crackle of electricity in the wires. He wants to get at the essence of the Building, to go into its bowels, to crawl through its intestines.

The wall that Haber built in the cellar to block off the furnace has been dismantled. The Yogi Hindu plumber has fled long ago and retired to an ashram in Manhattan run by a black Jewish guru from Nepal. Reality has vanished, died. There is another year of summers, a year of winters. The parade of seasons becomes not so much the passage of time as the remembrance of time, the awareness of time, the compression of what could happen into the bulge of what did happen. Like cookie dough squeezed from a baker's cone, events in the Building merge into one another so that their mixture becomes more substantial than the isolated event. Lowell can sense a fine, dry spray of unreality in the Building, but an unreality so intense, so unfragmented, that the imagined event becomes more real than the real event. I can do anything I want, he thinks, precisely because what I want to do I have already done. (The contemplation is the act; the will, the achievement; the desire, the object.)

Politicians tour the Building—the mayor, congressmen, City Council members—and papers are filled out for the Emergency Loan Program, the 7A Leasing Program, the 8A Loan Program, a Participation Loan at 1 percent, Construction Financing at 1 percent, and Section 8 under the city's Division of Alternate Management Programs. Sweat-equity loans are offered provided there are no middle-class people in the Building that can afford them and pay back the loan. "We're looking for rich poor people," said the administrator of the program. "Poor people cannot afford the payback, and the middle class is disqualified because of income limits. The only people who are right for the program are rich poor people." The politicians and the officials see most of the apartments but not the apartment that sweats blood. Lowell, the newly appointed 7A administrator for the Building, is also H.P.D.'s interim administrator for the Building, interim because the city wishes to get the Building off its back, hopes to have it purchased by either the tenants or some other group or individual mentally unbalanced enough to own it.

There is a pause; the Building holds its breath. The tenants watch the city, which watches the tenants. The city is jittery. It isn't sure what will work but it wants something that works, is nervous about new programs, and is willing to try them provided they aren't too new, wants the tenants or someone else to take over the Building because they can't afford to subsidize housing for the poor. The tenants are uneasy. They want someone to take care of them, they want cheap rent, they want everything fixed, heat during the winter, they think they might get a better deal from the city but they're not sure, the city makes them nervous because it keeps changing its mind, the city will commit itself to nothing, the tenants must sign all the pledges and releases when work is done in the Building with no guarantees for what they sign. Some tenants would like a warm-hearted Haber, an understanding Haber, a Haber who has their interests at heart. In short, a crazy Haber.

Lowell held more tenants' meetings. He pleaded, cajoled, threatened, and the tenants in turn were angry, receptive, confused, frightened. They were searching for an enemy as much as they were searching for friends, and at times the city and its concerns filled both bills of particulars. Lowell wanted more involvement by the tenants. He wanted to know who was stealing the boiler, why Buick Electras kept appearing and disappearing mysteriously in the basement, where the dead chickens on the roof came from (the chicken man, everyone knew that, not the voodoo man who left his headless chickens in the park), and he wanted the tenants to be ready to take over the running of the Building. When he had rented the bleeding apartment to the five revolutionaries, they subtly argued against him, doing it not by direct confrontation but by gathering small groups of tenants and trying to persuade them to demand the city do more, not less, for them. But the tenants were wary of anyone trying to persuade them to do anything. They viewed the Five Bleeders, which is how they came to be known, and Lowell, with varying degrees of hostility, warmth, and skepticism. While they harbored no hostility toward the Bleeders, neither did they harbor any warmth. Toward Lowell they harbored hostility and warmth. He, they understood, was just trying to do his job. They could sympathize with that. But his job was made more difficult because they, the tenants, were being unreasonable. Lowell saw to it that holes in walls were fixed, that a temporary boiler was hooked up in the street, that broken water pipes were fixed, that electrical lines were repaired. But for this he extracted a price: a demand that the tenants get involved, pay their rent (a curious sort of involvement), help him collect it, check on the workmen doing the repairs, and keep the rent records. The tenants withdrew. They wanted the services. They didn't want the responsibility. The Bleeding Five supported them in these demands, but the tenants mistrusted the Bleeders because they knew their own demands were unreasonable, and they mistrusted people who supported unreasonable demands. Lowell was right, the tenants thought. It is only us, the tenants, who are messing things up. Perhaps we should go.

When one of the tenants let slip to the Bleeding Five that the tenants called them the Bleeding Five, they became huffy, almost hostile. But the Five, who referred to themselves as the July Fifth Committee (the Second American Revolution), believed that they could not afford to get angry with the proletariat, that to do so would be traitorous to the working class (despite the fact that most of the tenants did not work), and simply smiled stiffly, unpleasantly pricked at the double meaning of the epithet. A small wrench had been thrown into their ideological machine, but it would get ground in with the gears, like all the other objects that had been tossed in. Indeed, there was something admirable about their position. Though they longed to be members of the proletariat, they also abhorred the thought, and it was this conflict that kept them from belonging to either the ruled or the ruling class. They were couriers who shuffled from one class to another.

Feeling uneasy in this, they softly argued with the tenants, politely demanding that the tenants take a more militant position with Lowell and the city. The tenants, however, found that the Bleeding Five wanted as much involvement as Lowell did. The Bleeding Five chose a new direction. They became a brooding, silent presence at tenants' meetings. Lowell thought they had been won over. But it was a silence of dissent, not a silence of assent.

They asked Lowell if they could move to a new apartment. They had never asked for anything before, but, they explained, the walls were bleeding too heavily and no longer confined this activity to the night. Lowell gave them another apartment, vacated by a Vietnam veteran in a wheelchair whose single goal in life was to shoot the president of the United States.

45

MONTHS passed, perhaps it was years, or just weeks. The Building got better and worse. The electrical service improved (Steckler rejoiced), but quantities of water, of varying shades, temperatures, and amounts appeared in unusual places. New Sheetrock walls went up, but they were rarely taped. A minute leak seemed to have been installed along with the new roof. Apartments were painted, and then the paint fell off in huge snowlike flakes, which gathered in mounds at the foot of the walls. Random doors were punched into the exterior walls of apartments. Signs appeared over the doors, warning tenants not to open them.

Lowell hardly knew what was going on. Orders for other buildings were inflicted on the Building so that all manner of tubings, conduits, stairways that ended nowhere, pipes, lighting fixtures hidden inside boxes, and steps dug into holes materialized. A huge tunnel was dug under the Building, mistakenly, for the Second Avenue subway in Manhattan, a disappearing subway that existed only briefly, like Arctic wildflowers, just long enough to undermine the foundations of scores of buildings. The tunnel was filled in with traprock brought down from Albany on barges and unloaded in the East River. A parquet floor was installed in the lobby ceiling. Outdoor lights were put in upside down, casting their glow several stories up. When it fogged, misted, or rained, a neon cloud settled around the perimeter of the Building, like an electric belt, that buzzed and sizzled in the wet.

The city was *not* neglecting the Building; thousands, hundreds of thousands of dollars had been poured into it . . . and yet it seemed as if every other dollar was put in to thwart the purpose of the dollar next to it. Elaborate plans for the Building were drawn, but before they were finished those who drew them came down with dyslexia. An entire department of draftsmen was fired. They were replaced with computer graphics. There was a flaw in the software program; unbeknownst to the programmers, it began to develop architectural drawings for urinals in the hallways and a rooftop parking lot.

The Bleeding Five, now the Revolutionary Five, purchased some cheap handguns from an East Harlem gunrunner who had stolen them from the private collection of a Klansman, who was a general in the New Jersey National Guard and planned to liberate the oil fields around Union City within the year and deny gasoline to those with less than white faces. One of the Five, a thin man with a wispy beard who wore overalls (all three of the men were thin, with wispy beards, and wore overalls), accidentally fired a pistol in the hallway, surprising the gunrunner who didn't think any of the guns he sold them would fire, and the shot set off a guerrilla war. Though somewhat taken aback at the swift tumble of events, the Five thought it was important to "ride the tide of history once the beast had been unleashed" and made on-the-spot plans to liberate the Building. Twelve-year-old Iranians tied together and led into battle singing songs could be parachuted in immediately to blunt the first attack.

The war began when an off-duty Pathmark guard was walking up the block and, thinking he had been fired upon, returned the fire with a snub-nosed thirty-eight, which he carried strapped to his ankle. He fired blindly at the Building, expecting perhaps that it would keel over, but the steel-jacketed bullets merely dug themselves into the brick. The shots surprised an off-duty Riteway Drugstore guard, who lived on the first floor of the Building and kept a sawed-off shotgun under his mattress. Whipping out the shotgun, he punched out a window frame with the barrel of the shotgun and let fly at the Pathmark guard, who by this time had crept behind an Oldsmobile Cutlass. The pellets, number six shot, shattered glass in the Cutlass and in a Toyota Corolla that was parked behind it. Hearing that blast, an on-duty private security guard for Kentucky Fried Chicken panicked and began to fire his gun, a thirty-oh-six Winchester, at random. He pinned down the Pathmark guard under the Oldsmobile Cutlass but took it in the wrist and shoulder from the second blast of the Riteway guard.

The Revolutionary Five changed into battle fatigues and brought out their flag, a red-and-black affair with crosses and crescents. The flag was blackened and frayed, stained and slashed by police truncheons. The Five quickly tied white ribbons around their foreheads and put on "revolutionary dog tags."

The immediate problem they faced was who to shoot. Shooting Lowell was out of the question. Lowell should be tried by a court, a people's court, in a fair trial, found guilty, and then dealt with accordingly. They couldn't shoot the tenants—this was the proletariat. There were no police around; the police rarely came around anyway; and the

Five had taken themselves through a series of self-criticisms to determine just who the enemy was. Preliminary investigation had shown them that the enemy was anyone making over $30,000 a year, blacks excepted. Some wanted to shoot those making $40,000 and up; others wanted to shoot anyone making more than $12,000 a year. Fortunately, cooler heads prevailed, and the cutoff point was put at $30,000. For the Five, whose collective income was about that, $30,000 represented an easy number to shoot at.

Breaking the windows in their apartment, they began to shoot at anyone walking down the street wearing a suit. This proved boring, since few people walking down the street wore suits and, moreover, the few who did were black. A collective decision was made to shoot at expensive objects—luxury cars, brownstones across the street, white men who carried attaché cases. Of the few white men fired upon, one, unfortunately, was a new dope dealer scouting out the neighborhood. He had a folding Israeli machine gun in his attaché case, which he whipped out, spraying the Building with machine gun fire, hitting one of the Five, one of the men, in the shoulder. He jumped into a two-tone lime-colored Lincoln Mark VII with an ax in the roof and sped off. The Revolutionary Five were now the Revolutionary Four and a Half. Their fallen comrade, wounded in the upper half of his body, lay bleeding profusely on the floor. The time for heroics had passed. He did not want to look at his blood, neither did anyone else, and he did not want to know that he was bleeding. He was not in shock but was afraid that he might soon lapse into shock. He was fully conscious. He expected the worst. The color of his blood was unfamiliar, and he thought that it seemed to dribble out of his body like gently lapping waves.

When he first heard the shots, the African Dictator was caught in the lobby, and he decided that those who had fired the shots were Methodists, those who had taken over his country, now planning to do the same here. He climbed the fire escape in his ceremonial robes to reach his apartment so he would not be caught in the hallway by these vengeful cross-bearers. Once up in his apartment, he would secure his wife and cows and then unleash his bush commandos. For months now they had been training in the Florida Everglades, holding their bivouacs in the swamps, making forced marches through spongy forests thick with creeper vines and deadly coral snakes, wading through alligator-infested streams, fending off cottonmouth snakes whose deadly puffball bites could cause a man to swell up and burst. Using a phone booth on the corner, he would call Miguel's Bodega in West Palm Beach and one of the shoeshine boys who hung outside spit-shining the high-heeled pumps favored by the Cuban coke dealers would get on his bicycle, a three-speed Schwinn with a telescopic fork, and ride out to the sergeant who lived in the abandoned Airstream trailer on the edge of the swamp. By nightfall of the following night, the Defense Department would have airlifted his bush commandos to Brooklyn in C–39 Bell Attack Helicopters.

The thin Revolutionary woman with the small breasts began tearing strips of cloth and bound the wounds of her fallen comrade, but the strips of cloth seemed only to slow the bleeding, not stop it. The red seeped through the cloth and then slowly dripped on the floor, on his arm, on her arm, on whatever was underneath the wound, and she tried to tighten the strips, remembering that she might cause gangrene, but tightened the strips anyway to stop the bleeding. The blood still came, the body turning pale, as if bleeding were its manifest destiny, and she began to cry. What was he dying for? Who was the enemy? Why had he been shot? She had made love many times before with him (as she had with the other two men; sexual liberation was their communal motto) and in doing so had hidden, even in the throes of passion, the immensity of her feelings toward him. She had hoped that she would get pregnant by him. She hoped that even now she might be carrying his baby (the Revolutionary Five having decided, collectively, that the time was not ripe for pregnancy) but doubted it. Why couldn't she stop his bleeding? It just kept coming. She embraced him, tightly, wrapping her legs and arms around his chilling body, trying to stop the blood, trying to redirect it back into his body, back through his veins and arteries. She knew nothing about the man she embraced. That was one of the rules they had adopted. They were all ignorant of each other. It was better that way; the group could act more effectively if they weren't burdened by personal considerations. She felt that made sense. Still, she wanted to know something about this young boy who was dying in her arms. She unbuttoned her shirt and pants, her body warmth would help him. He turned his head toward her. His eyes were pale, gray. She remembered that he had never been particularly strong or even very adept physically. He had to be shown how to do things over and over. Not a natural leader. The other men occupied that function. He had felt, he had told her, that he was always on trial, that the others seemed to be born revolutionaries but he had to work hard at it. He found it difficult to make friends. Wherever they went, he always hung back, somewhat shy, but more often afraid of his abilities. He took a lot of criticism from the group. At times, under verbal lashing, she had wanted to come to his support but had not done so. It was not considered proper. Group decisions had to be enforced; individual decisions did not matter. But there was something about him that she liked. His clumsiness. His eyes. The way he miscombed his hair, silly things. Still . . . his eyes. Gray. And always sparkling, even under criticism. He tried to hide his enthusiasm for things, small things, was too easily diverted into tiny joys, like the time they all went to the beach and he found the minuscule crabs that lived inside abandoned shells, crabs that were as cautious as he was about making their way into the world. He would never, she knew, be a success in anything he did. He would always be able to make a living, but he would have to be protected. She held him tighter. He was dying. The other two men had tried to make a dash for the phone booth on the corner to call for an ambulance, but each time they appeared at the lobby door the Pathmark guard and the Riteway guard fired, forcing them back. The two private guards, having never fired their guns on duty and feeling wronged, had decided to take their anger out on the Building and its tenants.

They were joined by an off-duty Key Food guard who carried a .357 Magnum. He emptied the chamber of his small cannon into the Building, the bullets tearing through several layers of brick, angrily popping out plaster walls, screaming through rooms, passing through several other layers of brick before they had exhausted their explosive power. The food guards, the drugstore guard, and the fried chicken guard quickly gave up firing at each other and picked out the Building as their enemy. Their blasts were returned only by sporadic firing; they gave ten times what they got. The Riteway guard was joined by a guard from a mom and pop liquor store with a CB who called for backup force. He was a member of a Nazi militia in south Brooklyn and saw this as a chance to test out some weapons their group had stolen from a Connecticut armory—a National Guard unit that had recently gotten some sniper rifles, flame throwers, and grenade launchers, enjoying them for only two weeks until the National Nazi Party, Brooklyn Chapter, had stolen them, storing them in the boiler room of a local Catholic church, Our Lady of Perpetual Bleeding.

She held him tighter. She tried to squeeze the blood in, tried to hold it with her fingers, her arms, her body. He had no right to die. He was too young. He hadn't had a chance to do anything, not even a chance to make a real fool of himself, not even a chance to fail. He needed more time.

The Revolutionary Five were down to two. They knocked on doors and announced that the Building was liberated. "Liberated from what, honey?" one of the tenants shouted from behind a locked and bolted door. They asked if they could use a phone, one of their comrades was dying . . . he needed an ambulance. They would be lucky if they found anyone in the Building with a phone, a tenant told them.

The Key Food guard tossed a hand grenade into the front hall, a prelude to storming the lobby and claiming the Building for that giant food chain. Several bathtubs came flying off the roof, scattering the armed food guards. Since it was known that God worked his wonders in mysterious ways, the sniper had his ear to the asshole of his Doberman pinscher, listening to His word.

The hand grenade had blown three playing children against the wall. Anyone who tried to help them was fired on by the Key Food guard. The children were lying limp against the wall; one of them had blood over his face and an eye missing. The Pathmark guard was broadcasting over a battery-powered megaphone: *Attention, tenants, throw down your weapons and come out with your hands up. This is your only warning.*

"Fuck you, you assholes!"

The suggestion came from one of the upper floors, and the guards directed their fire in the direction of the voice, which was heard from again, though this time from a different window.

"Stick it up your ass!"

A grenade was lobbed into an apartment. A tremendous explosion, almost muffled, the shattering of glass, and bits of furniture were blown out the window. This was followed by a headless cat, which described a parabolic arc as it fell to the sidewalk.

"Motherfucking faggots!"

Two more bathtubs flew off the roof. Smoke billowed out of the grenade-shattered apartment.

"Search and destroy," shouted the Key Food guard to the other guards, and they ran for the lobby door, as did the Kentucky Fried Chicken guard, who limped from his wound, and as a result got hit by the tire from a Toyota Celica thrown from the roof by the sniper, sending him sprawling backward into a six-foot mound of empty TV dinner trays. The tinfoil crackled as he landed in it, smearing the rancid leftovers on a blue guard uniform already stained red. Wounded, dazed, the guard lay in the trash, surveying the containers that pressed in on him from every side: Swanson's Hungry Man, Weight Watcher's Flounder, Enchiladas, Tamales, Veal Parmigiana, Stuffed Clams, Chicken. He removed his Kentucky Fried Chicken cap and tried to figure out what it all meant. Perhaps in the next world, the world of slow food, he would find out.

A strange quiet settled into the Building, the silence after death, the silence of an ambulance that no longer needed to run its siren but stood parked outside the Building with its red-and-white lights revolving while the two medics inside the apartment of the Revolutionary (Two? Three? Four?) were busy trying to pull off the thin woman whose arms and legs were wrapped tightly around the dead man. She was not hysterical but sobbing softly, and a terrible strength seemed to have settled into her body. She would not let go of the body of the dead man that she embraced, and the medics spent a full twenty minutes trying to pry her loose from him, until, failing that, they simply placed both of them on the stretcher, dead man and live sobbing woman, and carried them down the stairs (the elevators still did not work) and out into the ambulance. And then it was as if she had been released from some duty, seeing the inside of the ambulance, and she loosened her grip on the dead man and for the first time looked at the blood on her arms and legs, and knowing that it was his, stopped crying, and started to pray that she was pregnant, prayed that she would deliver his baby and that she had finally been able to stop the bleeding.

The Building seemed to keel over like a huge elephant. The hiss of escaping steam could be heard for weeks. Then it was gone, and cold invaded the Building, flowing under every door, even the most tightly sealed, finding its way into every room and closet. Lowell went down to check on the boiler and found that someone had again cement-blocked up the entrance to the boiler room. Ovens were turned on, along with electric heaters, which were frequently "browned out" by Steckler's arc welder.

My Building, Lowell thought, is dying.

46

"Iт's all part of our policy of planned shrinkage," said the commissioner, short, thin, ever so sensitive to his employee's feelings as he explains to Lowell why he is firing him.

"We solve the housing problem and the employment problem by concentrating the poor in low-maintenance housing and at the same time promote economic development by giving tax breaks to rich real estate developers to co-op slum apartments for upper-income people." The city plans to move the tenants to other city-owned slum buildings and sell the Building to the highest bidder at auction. Lowell is stunned before he can become furious.

He tried to organize the tenants. He pleaded with Mary Smith, who was worried because Shanker had been busted for what was probably the last time; he tried to cajole Mother Ozmoz, who was expecting her twenty-sixth, or twenty-seventh; he held his nose and tried to convince Glasho, the excrement artist, to stay (an unpopular move in the view of most of the tenants); he talked to the remaining Wilson Sister, who was somewhat hard of hearing as a result of the latest knot she had tied herself into, a knot involving her elbows, ankles, and ears; he made an earnest appeal to the paraplegic, who, absorbed in the details of a family drug killing in East New York, paid him little attention; he made his case before Hobson, who, miffed at the reception his cockroaches were getting, was thinking of importing a hive of killer bees from Brazil to store in his closet.

He tried to blot out of his mind the graffiti on the walls of the Building, pencil thin to paintbrush wide, the horizontal strokes having dripped down the walls and onto the floor; and he tried to blot out the smell of the remaining Wilson Sister's thirty-seven cats and the cockroaches that an erratic Hobson was cooking for his supper, and the sound of Abdul Karim as he nailed egg cartons to his walls and ceilings and the dreary radio disasters of the paraplegic, and to forget the stories of the Celtic monks who lived in the cellar on cheese and beer, huddled underneath the leather boats they sailed on from Ireland and the Coptic signs they scrawled on the cellar walls, stories that Tontine the super had told him, embellished by the super's wife, who every year presented the super with another straw-haired Norwegian; and having blotted all this out, or not having blotted this out but simply pushed it down, as one would a child's inner tube under water, expecting it to burst through the surface and spurt into the air, Lowell began to think about the Building. He wanted to follow the labyrinth of its foundations, find out the why of it, who built it, find out when it was built and how, trace the owners, examine the assessment, see if any architectural drawings were filed with the Buildings Department. The Building was shelter to many families, a mute thing that was far from mute, and he remembered when he asked Haber why he wanted to burn the Building, and the landlord at first had told him that he wanted to burn it so he could fix it. But this subterfuge was too transparent, and the landlord began berating him for managing such a "hellhole." Lowell listened to him as one might listen to a jackhammer, annoyed at its sound and yet amazed at its persistence. When he discovered that he was being listened to, Haber stopped, jaw slack, as if he had just discovered an ache in his tooth, and began to rub his gums with his finger. "The Building stinks of humanity," he said. "Parts of it work; parts don't. I can't separate them." He continued to rub his gums as if he were massaging a thought. "It stinks of people who flush Kotex down the toilet, who jump on sinks and break the plumbing, who won't pay their rent and it takes half a year to legally kick them out. I can't subsidize these creeps. It's my God-given right to make some money on my investment. I could empty it, co-op it, make a little money. Where's the crime? Who said I don't have the right? Show me the person who said that!" He cried the last phrase, weeping on his teeth, and Lowell felt that he should hold him and pat his balding head. He did none of these things.

Tenants began to leave. The remaining tenants were frustrated because they didn't know who to be angry at and angry because of their frustration. There was a garbage riot. Organic and inorganic sailed out of windows, forming a huge mound and then a series of mounds, a garbage mountain range. Traffic was blocked by grapefruit rinds, Pamper boxes, broccoli, and TV dinner trays. The evening news came. Cameramen were pelted with lettuce and rotten apples. The commissioner of sanitation was blamed and was subjected to an on-camera tongue-lashing by the mayor, who was running for reelection on the clean-government slate and was also promoting sales of his autobiography, a solipsistic account of his rise through Brooklyn College, New

York Law School, the mire and mulch of back-room Democratic politics, and the front pages of the city's three conservative newspapers.

It took a day to clean up the garbage. More tenants left. Water flooded the basement, submerging Tubbo. Someone said they saw bubbles coming from his lips, that he was still alive after all these months, or years. The water subsided, electrical service was restored and then cut off by Con Ed.

An official notice was clipped to the front door of the Building (or what was left of the front door after the machine-gun fire and shrapnel from several hand grenades). It had the official seal of the City of New York, plus several other seals, including the seal of Brooklyn (a garbage can turned upside down), and said, in so many words, that the Building was being consolidated in terms of efficiency and listed the legal tenants in the Building and nearby city buildings that would take them. Those listed as legal tenants were people who hadn't lived there in years, including the Balaban and Katz doorman with the stubble head who left for Germany in the late thirties, Eschopf's Turkish cousin who sold him a breed of dog that would only shit on *New York Times* editorials, the last Orthodox Jew (who had died from a stroke after struggling with the Mormon missionary over a frayed Old Testament), both Wilson Sisters, the lunatic, and other assorted prewar whites.

Resistance, Lowell said. We must resist. We must not let them drive us from the Building. He opened the vacant apartments to the homeless (including one individual of whom it could be said the only difference between him and a gorilla was that a gorilla had less hair).

But even the homeless were less than enthusiastic about the Building, being accustomed to heat, hot water, and electricity when they found shelter. Without such services, they reasoned, why stay in a building? The very reason for a building was denied. "Get out," a bag lady told Lowell. "This place ain't gonna die no natural death. This place put a hurtin' on you the longer you stay." But Lowell tried to reason with her about the Building and explained that it was more than just a building, it was a home for people who had no home. The bag lady, a wizened, toothless troll of indeterminate color, looked up at him and stuck her lower lip out. "Home," she said, "is on yo' back. Ain't no other home. Other is temporary."

A small man with a dark, precise beard and a navy pea jacket who smoked a short pipe, a Mr. Kurtz, moved into one of the apartments. Lowell apologized for the condition, but Mr. Kurtz did not seem to mind. He paid his rent, which Lowell intended to use to have the boiler fixed. Mr. Kurtz had a small sea chest filled with papers that he was concerned about; otherwise, no luggage—nor would it seem any other concerns. Later, in a visit to his apartment, Lowell noticed African statuary sitting on platforms nailed to the wall. On numerous occasions Lowell found him down in the cellar. He paid no attention to the electric lines, the water pipes, the furnace. He seemed to be terribly intent on digging or moving objects around, and late at night, with tenants complaining about noises coming from the cellar, Lowell investigated and found that it was Kurtz, at first embarrassed at being found, engaged in some mysterious practice whose function Lowell could not discern. Later, unconcerned about being discovered, Kurtz continued with his digging and moving objects around.

"That man," MasterCharge told Lowell, "he's crazy, down there rolling in the dirt and dancing with natives."

"What natives?"

"He calls them natives."

"Who are they? What are they doing down there?"

"I don't know. I didn't see 'em."

Lowell swore. He didn't like anything he didn't understand, and not only did he not understand what this Kurtz was doing but he disliked the man's quiet arrogance, an arrogance bred not so much from anything he said or did or any posture he adopted, but an arrogance that seemed to emanate from his being.

"They make an idol out of Tubbo."

"What?"

"Yeah! They prayin' to Tubbo and everything. They got him all decked out in flowers and beads and ribbons. They got something soft and sweet that looks yellow in plates set before him. And they doin' things to him."

"Who is 'they'?"

"I don't know."

"What are they doing?"

"Something strange. Looks funny. Something weird."

"Is it just Kurtz?"

"I don't see no one else."

"Why do you say 'they'?"

"I don't know."

Lowell went to see for himself, but Kurtz was gone. He saw only

Tubbo in the dark, glowing his ghastly blue; it was too dark to see much else. He had a feeling that MasterCharge was making it all up. But then at night he heard the noise, as did everyone else in the Building, and he thought otherwise. He ran down to investigate, but Kurtz, and whoever or whatever was with him, was gone. There was the faint, acrid smell of smoke or incense.

With several apartments empty, windows smashed, wooden mullions broken, scraps of curtains fluttering through the empty holes like surrender flags, the Building did a curtsy and sagged in the middle, the prominent crack in the exterior widening. A glitter of bottle caps, glistening like dragonfly wings, appeared in the mucky tar of the street. The sniper launched a three-hundred-pound barber chair onto the shining roof of a black Cadillac Brougham, depositing the missile nearly into the lap of a real estate broker who considered buying the Building from the city for speculation. Gypsy cabs with Caribbean stickers pulled up in front of the Building, and large black women squiggled out of the back seat onto the garbage-laden sidewalk, their hair wrapped in colorful kerchiefs, fabrics of many hues wrapped around their bodies, and made their way up to the apartment of Tonton Tute. The men in the cabs—husbands, relatives, lovers, brothers, sons —sat mute and sullen, refusing to go along. They kept the engines of their Dodges and Plymouths running in case of an attack by customs officers. Strippers came in from New Jersey and began making off with the brass plumbing, until the sniper caught one with a Coldspot refrigerator. Junkies showed up, looking for vacant apartments.

"Hey," MasterCharge said, "it's the wild time, the beginning of the end. Like an old whore on her last legs, everyone coming by to get a free piece, last licks. You take what you can, you pick, you pluck, you scrape up what ain't nailed down and what is you pry up and sell. Dudes coming from all over the borough to this Building. They heard 'bout it. Young bloods from the ghettos be coming here with the blasters to snort and riff. Those Jersey and Bay Ridge whites putting their move on the Building; they can sniff money with their big dog noses." "What about the basement? What's happening in the basement?" Lowell asked. "I'm coming to that. They got the voodoo priest and all them fat black mamas down there, hardly room to turn around with all the bodies they got down there, dead and alive. They got Tubbo . . . you should see Tubbo . . . they got Tubbo, the part of him that can move . . . you know, where he ain't frozen . . . they got ribbons and bells on his head and arms, and the arms, get this, Lowell, the arms move, they got some special way of moving the arms, so that with all the singing and chanting and everybody moaning and dancing and swaying this way and that, they got Tubbo waving his arms, and they painted something on his face, and they sacrifice to him. Ya, they put stuff in front of him, they kill things, small things, and they do lots of sex in front of him, and they got him moving around while they doing it, waving his arms and moving his lips—wonder how they do that?—and this Kurtz, you should see what he does, they got blood and this sex stuff all over, and dead bodies coming out of the ground, wrapped in white, a funny smell, like something you fix a tire with—you know, that glue? —and then when they come to the real interesting part, you know what they do? They block off the door. A damn shame. Now how the hell you supposed to know what those motherfuckers are doing when they got the doors blocked off? You can't see a damn thing! Ain't that a bitch. But I know they doin' more because the noise that comes from there, it gets louder and louder, someone screaming, I think, a woman maybe. I think something ugly is going on, but I don't know exactly what. But if you want, I'll find out for you, consider it an honor too."

But honor lay in other things. Bricks disappeared from the Building. Someone tried to steal the sidewalk. Lowell was able to save the sidewalk; but as he did, he thought there must be bounds to rape, there must be limits to the sacrileges that can be committed, and thinking this and setting those limits, then saw them broken, saw someone going beyond what he thought it was impossible to go beyond, and felt that if there were no God in heaven, then one would have to be invented simply to punish those who found new sacrileges to commit.

And, as if sensing the wounding of the Building, churches sprang up in the neighborhood.

"What mind can conceive, man can achieve," said a sign in a Christian Science bookstore down the block. Around the corner dozens of storefront churches popped up: The Church of the Irreversible Redeemer, Brotherhood of God, The Church of the Wash 'n' Wear Christ, The Total Immersion Baptist Church. You could tell when a neighborhood was going down, Lowell thought, by the number of new churches that opened up. Windows that once displayed meat or flowers, shoes, surgical devices, or baked goods were now bricked up and painted, a steel security door put in, the name of the church painted in gaudy colors on a metal sign as wide as the walls, and, hand lettered down in the corner (as if author of the production), the name of the pastor, the whole affair hoisted over the doorway and nailed to the brick. On Sunday, in richly starched white dresses that the women wore and stiff, black, mothball-smelling suits the men preferred, the parishioners stepped over the drunks still passed out from the night before, and clutching Bibles entered the storefronts. The clamor of their singing woke those trying to sleep off the previous night's debauch, or else joined in with the cacophony from an all-night party. Sometimes fledgling ministers with electric-powered bullhorns stepped out onto the street corners and exhorted slugabeds, delivering their sermons to an unreceptive, hostile audience. New denominations sprang up: The Holy Dollar Church (a member of the Lean Green and Mean Religious Coalition); the Virgin Mothers for Christ; the Rampant Evangelical Brotherhood. Most of the churches kept to themselves, would take no part in any social program, and, indeed, seemed to delight in the misery and decay they found around them. Being holy was not enough. One had to be a sinner first, the bigger sinner the better, and many of the pastors brought new meaning to the phrase "a wicked past, which so delights the Lord when it can be turned around."

And then it rained for a month, almost every day. Gutters, sewers, were swollen. The ground, spongy underneath, like a small, cardboard blotter meant to catch the overflow of a leaking faucet, became water-logged, was no longer able to absorb the rainfall. It was the Brooklyn monsoon, and it struck with the fury of love spurned. Awash in water, backyards flooded, cars submerged in low-lying streets, and basements turned into cisterns. Underground rivers flowed through Brooklyn with a vengeance, while the subway tunnels leaked and dripped so that gondolas would have been appropriate. The residents of this maimed place began to turn inward, cringing at the wet. They experienced a mild anomie. What had they done wrong?

When it stopped, a wave of green spread over Brooklyn, as if some set designer had personally taken over interior decoration for the borough. Buds and blooms burst forth from cement-hard dirt in vacant lots that had lain fallow for years. Tiny sprigs of grass pushed their way through sidewalks, buckling them. Tree leaves turned blindingly green. Vines encircled inorganic objects and threatened to squeeze the life into them. Flowers of a hue, a dazzle, a variety never before seen sprang up all over the borough, with a hardiness that astounded. Flatbush Avenue sported azaleas in cracks that no number of car tires seemed able to push down. Maple trees grew on the roofs of vacant buildings. The grass was a tough leathery substance that could not be worn down and, when cut, gave off an odor so divine grown men wept and children refused to go to school.

Spring came in on the sea air. Gentle zephyrs, an air of velvet, fell on the borough and produced a shameless ecstasy. Commingled with the odor of cut grass was a subtle mixture of flower fragrances that produced a narcotic, one not addictive only because the source was capricious and whimsical, but one whose effect was longer lasting and more powerful. A sleepy, balmy mien descended on the inhabitants, a strange malady attacked the borough, a softening, blurring hard edges, quieting loud noises. Garlands of flowers were woven around the steel cables on the Brooklyn Bridge. Flowers were strewn in the paths of out-of-state trucks.

A great pacific air had swept over Breuklan, leaving ". . . a feeling so wonderous soft, the very soile so fertile it must be blest, the aire of a qualiti (sic) that the natives do fall downe and pray before it, and the entire spectacle would lead one to believe that heaven, if such a thinge exist, is here in this new world."

47

T HE fire: a slow burner. Inside the walls, consorting with pipes and wiring, between the lathing and the plaster, it licks its way up. A lazy ignition. Time to burn. Room to expand. Feeds on thin strips of wood, piece by piece, crawls up and across floors. A glowing presence. The wood hardly burns—it melts, produces orange ingots, throbbing yellow, tiny flames puckered about the ends, darting cautiously toward the next piece. The old plaster walls feel warm, almost hot to the touch. It is winter, it is spring, it is somewhere between the two, the gap between seasons, that terrible leap of faith the earth makes when it begins to tilt on its axis. Languid oxidation, a swift, slow burning. Inside the walls all the pipes are hot and the cold water is hot, even the hot water is hot. The temperature outside goes berserk, bounces decades of degrees, sixty, fifty, then a quick tumble to thirty, then a boost to forty, and back up again, and down, and . . . smoke, barely seen, flows up the inside walls, finds holes in the roof, exits in the haze of the afternoon. It mixes with carbon monoxide, carbon dioxide, and other organic and inorganic gases the city produces; it is the first almost-warm, almost-cold day, and everybody has decided to drive to work and drive home again, and the product of this mobility is a thick dish of purple-gray gas that hovers about the city. The Building is steamy, a slight smoky presence. Not quite nature made, this little fire. Started because Haber thinks he can redeem his lost Building for back taxes; he hires Solly and Mobutu to torch it, drive the tenants out, he repaints, and co-ops. But Lowell is suspicious. So Solly and Mobutu, Fric and Frac, the Gold Dust Twins, don't have time for a big slam-bang, gasoline-dousing, pile-of-furniture bonfire. Lowell keeps watching them. They try the vacant apartments, which are locked, except for the bloody apartment on the top floor, which they refuse to enter and which doesn't make much sense to torch since you want to set the bottom floor and burn everything above. Dashing through the halls, Lowell in pursuit, they pause for a minute on a landing, inhabited by one wing of the recently returned endless Chinese family (Northern Shaolin, Crane Style), and finding a small hole in the wall, set fire to a piece of lathing. Lowell rounds the corner and Fric and Frac are off, a pair of Jack the Rippers, up the stairs, plowing through more endless Chinese family: old, stooped Chinese women elbowing them angrily as they bound up the stairs, upset at being forced aside, are forced aside twice when Lowell comes after them, shouting to each other in high-pitched squawks, showing their anger in smiles. The pyromaniacal pair reach the roof and pause before the place where, screaming, shouting, biting, clawing, they threw the pregnant Scandinavian whore, the woman who would be Ingrid, into space. They can see the marks her heels made across the roof and the place down below on the sidewalk, the bloody place, where she landed. But they are not sentimentalists, these two, and they climb down the fire escape and into the bloody apartment just as Lowell reaches the roof, and as he walks out onto the roof they escape through the open door of the bloody apartment, stepping on the brittle hands of old Chinese women as they race down the landing, old, arthritic elbows punching them in the calves, endless Chinese shouting by the endless Chinese family (Southern Shaolin, Flower Form), and Lowell runs back to the José chimney and slowly walks down the stairs, waiting for the myriad Chinese to part and make room. The fire is doing its business, thriving inside the walls. [Perhaps this is all a figment, a fantasy, a painting. Here is the real story. That fat little floozy, that religious object, that mother of the sacred shrine of veneration, the Madonna of Heat and Hot Water, had never been vanquished by the Ice Queen but only temporarily subdued, locked up in the basement, huffing and puffing, flouncing her hot-blooded Mediterranean temper, anxious to torch up the boiler, put a glow in the Building. But how to do this thing? She raced around, flamboyant in her intentions, looking for burnables. Finding only cold things, soot things, steel and stone things that would scarcely support combustion, she screams, a tiny yet piercing wail, her earlobes sweating, water collecting on her upper lip, under her mustache, crying for the men who left her, found her too hot, too sweaty, too forceful (*she* made love to them, forced them to come on their backs, held their arms down, pinned them with her breath, left bruises on their legs, made them cry, tortured them for love). She cries, a sound rising in register, a tone so pure and complete it begins to glow, and glowing turns toward the hot end of the spectrum, the sound of the hottest colors, the sound of heat, a high-pitched whine that has an overlay of a low-pitched hum, the deep roar of molecules at work, battling entropy, marching about their business of light and motion under pressure, becoming excited. She cries, she glows, she is a red-, a white-hot thing, she belts out heat, a crooner of temperature, a singer of warmth. She runs, trailing sparks, the air can hardly contain her, she is excited, the sounds she makes and the noise they make excite her, and a halo of heat, an aura of hotness, fills the space around her, lights the surface of her body; her boundaries erupt, her skin is lava, her extremities are molten, they warm what they touch, melt what they come in contact with, burn what they bump. She is all heat, all screaming, all passion, a siren of lust, and her burning lights the Building, her fire pours through brick and stone and ignites the studs in the walls, her glow melts the ice that Tubbo half sits in, her glowing fires a river that lives in the upper extremes of the Fahrenheits, swiftly oxidizing wood. The walls of the Building burn. At last she has given heat to this cold thing.] And now flames appear. There is a cry, an outcry. Smoke begins to collect, the fire breaks through a wall and though there is no one around to notice this breakthrough it pierces the wall like a scientific discovery and licks at the plaster on the other side. Now the tenants smell smoke. There is reasonable panic, a subdued hysteria. Lowell phones for the fire department. They will come, in their time. Before they do, Steckler's time has come. He has worked on the supercharged Chevy Nova for years, waiting to launch it from his fifth-floor window. The ramp is in place. He has chained Visa to the driver's seat. Visa's driver's license has expired, but no matter, where he is headed there is little need for that sort of paraphernalia. The Nova has a big bore block V–8, 454 C.I., with an Edelbrock manifold, four-barrel Holley carburetor, highlift camshaft, a supercharger that runs at 100,000 R.P.M., a stainless-steel belly-pan, railroad springs and dump-truck tires for the five-story fall. Visa at first looks nervous, agitated. Then he is yelling and screaming from his chained seat, but Steckler, counselor to his machine, explains to Visa that he will be taking an automotive vehicle where no one else has ventured before, that he is, in the true sense of the word, a pioneer, about to enter a new frontier. (Visa, wetting his pants, has no wish to be on any motherfucker's frontier, and he tells, pleads, begs this of Steckler, who is unmoved, a true believer of machinery.) The Nova has been washed and Simonized, polished to blazing, a glimmering piece of metal set to hurtle through space. He tells Visa to start the engine. Visa has no wish to do so. Little matter, Steckler says. He chains Visa's hands to the steering wheel. (You can steer it all you want when you're in the air, he says.) He starts the engine. The big V–8 rumbles with a roar that promises to deplete oil wells. Minute by minute it sucks in pints of gasoline, a greedy bear for fuel. The engine has its own rhythm, running with the stress on every fourth beat. Steckler checks the timing, adjusts the fuel-air mixture. Everything must be perfect, everything must be beyond perfection. The Nova will live for only a few seconds, but while it does it must run better than any engine has ever run, better than any engine has a right to run. It must blaze, glow, incandesce. Launched across the wooden floor of Steckler's apartment, huge tires grabbing madly for the floor, spinning, both rubber and wood burning at the point of contact, until the melting of the tires, each three feet wide, grabs the floor and the huge engine gets down to business and, with a mighty heave, pushes, launches the ton-and-a-half Chevy Nova across the wood and up the ramp, barely touching the windowsill, and just before the Nova is launched Steckler will experience those few seconds that justify years of existence. The engine screaming, a banshee wail in his ears that punctures the eardrums, the car is poised on the edge of greatness, wider than the window so that its bumper scatters brick and wood. This fan-shaped spray heralds the car's trajectory, occupying the vicinity in the air where the car will appear. And then it does appear in the air, an apparition, a miracle of metal. The firemen look up and see the car overhead. It hangs for a moment, wheels spinning as the engine goes crazy in the air, and then falls. The fire is slowly, deliciously consuming the Building. Flames are inside apartments, devastating the first floor, crawling out of windows, tenants screaming, smoke clogging the stairwells. A thing of horror is about to begin. The fire has burned for too long, people were not given enough warning. Solly and Mobutu thought about warning the tenants (such boundless humanity!) but got into an argument as to who should do it, and Mobutu, being bigger and meaner (the first by a lot, the second by very little), throws Solly out a window and then runs down the stairs to see his crumpled body on the sidewalk, and Solly, looking up, a smile of blood on his face, a wily, screwed-on, never-can-you-trust-it smile, twitches, flips his hands around, his clawlike hands, motions for a cigarette, and Mobutu, big and mean, leans down to give him a cigarette, an uncharacteristically generous act from a man who likes to hurt living things to a man who likes to watch living things suffer and die, and Solly, still looking up, a smile on a built-in dirty face, the dirt a part of his skin, having the cigarette in his wet lips, the cigarette damp from the spittle and blood in his mouth, asks for a match, and Mobutu, having once done his hurt is now ready to grant this request, strikes a match, brings it close to the potholed face of Solly, aligns the flame with the cigarette, is about to light it, when Solly, hands flipping back and forth, dying bird claws scratching the air, has in his hand a small thin knife, barely a blade, which he rakes across the throat of Mobutu, who is still trying to light the cigarette for him, even after the blade cuts his throat, is drawn across, slicing the jugular, the blood coming, even then is intent on lighting Solly's cigarette, forgets or ignores the cut and the bleeding and his dying until he can attend to the lighting of the cigarette, finish the lighting of it, and then, with his throat cut, bleeding on the dying Solly, the dying Mobutu stands up, bleeding on himself, down the front of his tremendous chest, down his powerful legs, and with his huge arms and hands scratches his neck, as if to flick off an errant fly, and then looks at his hand and the color of his blood, his bright-red rusty blood. The fire has climbed floors erratically, some apartments feature flames at the window, others merely smoke or serve as a conduit for the air that feeds the conflagration. The basement, barely burnable, is an oven. Eschopf, the old owner who built the

Building and sold it to Haber many years ago, so many years ago that people thought he must be dead by now and was believed to be so by everyone but the lunatic who said he saw the old Turkish Grandmaster in the basement with his chess set, still eager for a game, not sad that he had sold the Building but sad that he had not removed the heads carved in stone and set in brick at the top of the Building of all the famous Turkish Grandmasters—Yakub Chelebi, Yilderim Bayezid, and, of course, Murad, designer of the famed Sicilian and Bulgarian Defense—Eschopf, coughing, his hand over his yellowing handlebar mustache, his other hand holding his chess set, led by Puff the Magic Dragon, the cat-eating German shepherd who lived in the basement, is seen scrambling up the side steps from the basement and into a narrow corridor that separates the Building from the building next to it, a look on his face that suggests he has not ventured aboveground for many years. The basement, now pizza-oven hot, revives a frozen Tubbo whose lower half has been frozen for months, years, in a cake of ice and whose upper half had been hacked away at by rival drug dealers; scarred Tubbo, his iceberg melted, no longer a frozen TV dinner, but sitting in a pool of water, warm water, feeling the soothing liquid temperatures on legs that had been stiff and solid for eons, stirs, twitches long-immobile calf muscles, wiggles old gangrene toes, and rises, Lazarus-like, stiffly, the muscles and tendons protesting their mobility, the scarred saw marks still on his knees from the time they tried to saw his legs off, the healed-up bullet holes in his fat, puffy body barely visible, disappointing those who were going to go down and hack him out of the ice when it was spring and put him in a coffin, packed in dry ice, so he could have a proper Colombian burial with his father who ran the Chiba shop around the corner in attendance and his sweet long-suffering mother who supported Tubbo in each of his many endeavors—a kinder, braver mother a boy never had—disappointed them all, because like Eschopf he had been revived and stood, on wobbly legs, in the warming thigh-high water, wondering which way the stairs were, beginning then to splash his way through the pool as if he were a duck hunter, hardly the worse for wear except for the aforementioned scars and a strange blue glow that emanated from his body. He wondered about the bells and beads and flowers attached to his body from the time Mr. Kurtz and Tonton Tute made him an object of worship and sacrificed creatures and virgins before his frozen form. He wondered about his apartment and his record collection, all burning now, and as he sloshed through the therapeutic pool, the Brooklyn hot springs, his legs still stiff and torturous to move after all these years, found the same steps Eschopf had and slowly climbed them, legs dripping water, and finally appeared in the same narrow corridor that Eschopf had found, except that where Eschopf had been dry Tubbo was dripping, and now, his entire body radiated a bright blue, a sort of ionic halo that would have delighted De Forest and other early pioneers of the radio-vacuum tube if they had been around to see this walking cathode ray. The burning is not slow now. Trees of flames appear in the apartments, whooshing out their terrible branches with a suddenness that deprives the air of oxygen. The Building heats up, pillows of smoke burp from the holes in the roof, black, turgid, foul-smelling smoke. Mother Ozmoz is busy launching her twenty-seven or twenty-eight babies, children, out the window, certain that out of view there is someone on the ground who is fielding them with great regularity, and so she does not look where she throws them, does not want to look, but merely chucks them one at a time through the broken window. A flock of fire trucks is on the street, extruding a huge spaghetti of hoses that intertwine with each other and connect with several fire hydrants, all of which are blocked by parked cars, forcing the firemen to chop their way through car doors and run the hoses through the cars. The smoke—at first, puffballs of stratocumulus, then black billowing mushrooms of altocumulus, and finally blue-black acres of cirrocumulus—threatens to blanket the borough, and from Manhattan, that ancient haggard city, it looks as if the very core of Brooklyn is oxidizing. Flames cut through the smoke and burn out timbers that hold floors, which collapse to the floor below, simultaneously sucking in and pushing out acres of air, spraying showers of sparks, burning pieces of wood, red-hot pieces of mortar and glowing iron reinforcing bar. With each floor that collapses, a wall of hot air rushes out, sizzling anything organic dozens of feet from the Building. Tontine, his straw Norwegian wife, and his straw children crawl down the fire escape, followed by the glistening light-brown bodies of Singiat-Sing Dan Dinphuir, his wife, and their monkey children. Stern the painter, raging at the flames, launches his paintings into the air, and they glide, swoop, flip, tumble, and fall to the street below, and then he tosses out the end of his endless painting, painted toilet-roll fashion, *The Madonna of Heat and Hot Water, The Madonna of Betrayal, The Madonna of Ruined Dreams,*

The Madonna of Sex and Bitterness, The Madonna of Broken Plaster, The Madonna of Subways and Pocket Change, The Madonna of Lost Causes and Failed Love, The Madonna of Spent Passion and Small Intentions, and the madonnas, respectively, of *Whispers, Hair, Toilet Thoughts, Midnight Wanderings, Icebox Sufferings,* and finally the all-knowing, all-hip *Mahatma Madonna,* who knows everything there is to know plus much there isn't. Miles long, it takes days for this endless painting to reach the ground, and as it tumbles out the window, Stern, the borough's and the city's greatest painter, finds refuge in the arms of one of his many madonnas, who cradles him softly and carries him safely to the ground, where he can stand and watch the rest of his madonnas, a multitude of madonnas, as many madonnas as there are souls in heaven, flee the apartment and find safety on the ground, a canvas-painted freight train of blessed women, of which there is never any end. Through the dense smoke Hobson searches for the paraplegic, forgetting about his cockroaches, and finding her lying in the hallway, rights her wheelchair and drags her into it, wheeling, bumping the contraption down the one set of stairs that has not yet collapsed. Two tremendous explosions shake the Building, not from gas lines but from exploding cows, the intense heat having swelled the anaerobic digestion in these ruminants so that the cows explode belly first, and the African Dictator, who keeps the cows in his bedroom, while planning his escape through the front door of his apartment, is greeted by a shrapnel of intestines, stomachs, gall-bladders, spleens, livers, and other organs that precede him out the door, or arrange themselves in a thick goo the length and width of his body so that the king, by the time of the second explosion, sports entrails on his ceremonial robes. Exploding cows are a signal to the Multi-Gravitational Aerodrome Company. These failed aviators, these bankrupt Canadian inventors-turned-acrobats, crank open their roof and send all seven, all six and a half, of their troupe flying through the air, landing with a nonchalance on the adjoining roof, hopping from one leotarded foot to another, eager for another flight. With the heat burning through the floor of his apartment, Tyrone watches his thirty-seven radiators drop, one by one, into the blazing inferno below, and when three radiators are left, he makes good his exit by the fire escape, bumping into a six-foot chicken, Willy, who just home from work has not had time to take off his chicken suit. Mary Smith has led Dorah, James, Shanker, and Leroy, sometimes known as Goodchild, out of their apartment and down the hall, only to find that the only stairway that will carry them to the ground has collapsed. Heavy gray smoke swirls around their heads; she hustles them back into the apartment. Shanker, coming off his fix, is sweaty, jumpy, his nose runs, and he seems more concerned about the itching on the balls of his feet and palms of his hand than the fire. Goodchild cries, wets his pants. Mary Smith goes to the window and throws it open. A ladder can reach her window, and her children are safely carried down, but there is no way the ladder, or a fireman, can support Mary Smith's weight, which hovers close to a quarter ton. She remains in the apartment, now starting to burn, as does Glasho, the excrement artist, who has decided that his final project will be immolation. Head shaven, wearing tan robes and saffron-colored sandals, the flames burn his eyebrows off before they attack his skin. His robes, miraculously, do not burn. The Wilson Sister, Ester or Beth, sits crying in her room. The hall is filled with smoke. She gathers her photos about her, photos of her and her sister in Catskills and New Jersey nightclubs, photos of them twisted into astounding knots, a record of her crinkum-crankum life, their act, her only mementos of the time when her sister was alive and she had someone to fight with and hate. The fire knocks at her door, a soft knock, a brushing of flames against the door, and the last Wilson Sister, Ester or Beth, remembers the dancing bear her father kept in Brooklyn Heights and the scarred leather medicine ball it danced on and the Sunday afternoons when she and her sister were banished to the backyard so her father and mother could make love in the bedroom, in the huge cherrywood bed with the silk canopy that sat next to the maple dresser where her father kept his cannon balls which he used to drop on the bear when the surly beast angered him, but all these memories were quickly receding, had to go, she knew, because soon she would be burned up, a frazzle, nothing but a crisp bit of bacon. Now with a roar the fire explodes, attacking the writer's apartment, flowers of flame squirming under the door, consuming the floor, and the writer crumples up the thousand-page manuscript and throws it at the flame page by page in the hope that the weight of literature, the power of words, will shame the fire into extinguishing itself or, at the very least, will cause a parting in the fire, like that in the Red Sea, so the writer can make his/her escape. Lowell, across the street, hears the explosion as the entire Building fills with smoke and fire, walls collapse, ceilings drop, and fire hoses spray water that turns into steam mixed with smoke. The city is denied its final desperate humiliation of the tenants. Whoever and whatever is left in the Building, all things organic and inorganic, all sofas and chairs, refrigerators, stoves, pawn tickets, books, Bibles, plastic Virgin Marys and rosaries, beds, lamps, cockroaches, photos, postcards, all fears, all dreams, all hopes, burn, melt, explode, and the Building, as if in a dance, turns slowly, almost pirouettes, and falls.

A NOTE ON THE TYPE

The text of this book was set in a digitized version of Baskerville. The face is a facsimile reproduction of types cast from molds made for John Baskerville (1706–75) from his designs. John Baskerville's original face was one of the forerunners of the type style known as "modern face" to printers—a "modern" of the period A.D. 1800.

Composed, printed, and bound by
The Haddon Craftsmen, Inc.,
Scranton, Pennsylvania

Designed by Virginia Tan